The Week The World Ended
-by-
Thomas A Farmer

ISBN-13: 978-0692613276

ISBN-10: 0692613277

The following is a work of fiction. All persons and events depicted in this novel are wholly the product of the author's imagination and not intended to represent anyone or anything that has happened in the real world.

For my Wife, Stephanie.

Chapter 1

It was Summer when the Ancients returned.

Owen Madoc stepped through the door of his modest-sized apartment. From his shoulder hung a large, triangular bag that banged into the doorframe with a hollow thunk and a rattle of metal-on-metal from inside. He hung his keys on the rack beside the door and dropped the big bag from his shoulder, catching the handle with one hand and carrying it the rest of the way into the apartment like that.

Samantha Bennett—"Sam" to anyone who wanted to stay on her good side— followed a step behind. She had no such bag, and watched with a wry smile as Owen maneuvered the awkward burden through the tiny foyer of his apartment. She smoothed her fire-red hair from where the humidity fuzzed it up.

Somewhere in the distance, thunder rolled. It had rained earlier, just long enough to drive the humidity through the roof and wet everything down. Aside from thick, lingering clouds, the sky was clear now. Now, the sky had turned fairly dark, dark enough for some of the light-sensitive streetlights to come on anyway. That was no real surprise; East Tennessee weather, as Sam's father used to say, "had a one-hundred percent chance of 'maybe.'"

Owen dropped the bag next to the couch and asked, "hungry?"

"A little, yeah," Sam replied, shedding her motorcycle jacket. She hung it on a the coat rack that stood in a nearby corner, then lowered herself onto the couch. She curled her feet under her hips and reached for the TV remote. After a moment, she added, "I'm not starving, though, so go ahead and get all the rain off your gear first."

Sam turned the TV on and pulled up the channel guide, scrolling through it to find something to watch.

Owen crouched next to the bag and unzipped the oversized metal zipper that ran from end to end. It contained a couple of blunted swords, his padded fencing jacket, a mix of modern and pseudo-historic armor, and a well-worn fencing mask. All of it had seen years of use, taking him through endless practices and tournaments with his friends.

Every Sunday, the lot of them liked to practice outdoors. The location always varied from park to park depending on who wanted to drive less that day, and Knoxville had won out this week.

His jacket and gear would have been soaked enough from sweat on a normal day, but the sky had seen fit to rain on their practice more than once. It never stormed or even rained enough to warrant canceling their weekly meeting, instead being just hard enough to drive the three of them to a nearby gazebo to wait out each downpour.

He himself was dry, at least. After practice, he had planned on meeting at Sam at the Botanical Gardens between Knoxville and Oak Ridge. Spending the afternoon wandering among the trees and whatever wildflowers remained this time of year always served to put him in a good mood, especially spending that time with his best friend. That feeling went double for the days he had outdoor practice. The rain was done with their area by then, and the two of them stayed out until Owen—and his clothes—dried.

The same could not be said of his gear. The rain had soaked everything. The leather and fabric pieces would dry on their own in due time. The important things, like his swords, were still susceptible to the ancient bane of swordsmen everywhere: rust.

He hung the jacket and other cloth pieces up on the coat rack that most days only serviced his gear and Sam's leather motorcycle jacket. Silently, he went to the bedroom to fetch a small towel to dry the metal items off. He had towels and things in his gear, but like the bag, they were still soaked with rain.

When he came back, Sam had settled on a channel: the news. Owen saw, and was unable to suppress a small laugh.

"What?" Sam asked, grinning. "Some of us like to stay informed, you know."

Owen laughed again and made a dismissive wave with the towel. "It's not that," he said, "it's just that that was your first choice."

"It wasn't my first choice," she countered. "You'd know that if you were paying attention."

"Yes, well," he replied, and laughed again.

"There was nothing else good on."

"What do you expect at six on a Sunday?"

"Something besides ESPN, for starters."

"Good luck with that one." He sat down on the floor in front of his bag. "Anything new?"

Sam shrugged. "Not really. There was another earthquake in the Atlantic, but that's about it."

"Another one?" Owen asked, surprised. "That's, what, the fourth one this month?"

"Fifth," Sam corrected. "Same place, too."

"Weird. Any cause yet?"

Sam shook her head. "Not that they'll tell us, but I just caught the last few minutes, so I don't know if they had anything new to say earlier."

He nodded, then turned his attention back to his gear. Drying everything off was going to be a time-consuming process. Normally, he simply wiped the blades down and called it done, but as wet as it all was, he would have to disassemble his weapons to dry and clean the insides.

He looked over his saber as he took it out of the bag. The replica blade had blunted edges and a springy rubber tip, but that never stopped him from pretending he was a nineteenth-century soldier strutting around the practice field whenever he held it.

Sam shifted abruptly on the couch. However, it was her, "what the hell?" that broke Owen's concentration.

Her attention was raptly focused on the screen as a calmly professional news anchor said, "...more developments about the attack on Washington D.C. earlier today."

"What...?"

Sam shushed him, and Owen set the half-disassembled saber back down and joined his friend on the couch.

The screen showed Washington D.C., the Capitol Building specifically, or it would have on a day not suddenly made of nightmares. The rotunda of the capitol had been smashed in and a pillar of thick, oily black smoke poured out of the ruined facade. Other nearby buildings were in a similar state, though the camera was focused on the burning dome.

"Once again, you are seeing footage from the National Mall at approximately four o'clock this afternoon," the offscreen reporter said. There was a faint quaver in the male voice, but every word was tightly controlled and came out the very image of professionalism. "We've gotten unconfirmed reports that the devastation you're seeing is the result of a sudden and unprovoked attack by a large group with advanced weaponry.

"We're going to go now to Kayce Fletcher, our who normally runs our Life Sciences program on Monday afternoon. Kayce was at the Museum of Natural History covering a new exhibit when the attack started this morning.

"Kayce?"

The image never changed, remaining fixated on the black cloud billowing out of the shattered dome of the capitol building. The rest of the scene was unnaturally eerie. Normally, people and birds moved around everywhere in the capital, but nothing moved right then except the roiling black smoke. The camera was, thankfully, aimed a little above ground level, giving no indication of how many bodies might be laying stiff just out of view.

Perhaps more disturbing than the image of the burning capitol building was what else the screen showed. Inset into the bottom of the video were similar views from around the world: the Kremlin, the Reichstag, and several others. Each little window showed another world capital, and each one had been demolished just like Washington.

"Thank you, " a female voice replied. A few seconds delay sat between her responses and the words from the TV station proper. However they were communicating, there was significant lag between the sides.

"What can you tell us about what happened?"

"Not much," she confessed. "I was in the back room of the museum when I heard commotion from the front. Doctor Bright and I came out to see what was going on when it didn't stop after a few minutes, but the army had already passed our windows, and..."

"Hold on, you said 'army?'"

"That's right," she agreed.

"But not the US Army?"

"No, whoever did this was certainly not United States Army. In fact, I couldn't figure out what people were so excited about, I thought, you know, it was come sort of parade, until the gunfire started."

"And where are you now?"

"With Doctor Bright and most of the museum staff in the vault of the Natural History Museum. The destruction has stopped outside as far as we can tell, but the air's still dry and full of smoke."

"Where are the museum's visitors?"

"Some of them," she replied, and a hitch crept into her throat, threatening to break her veneer of professional calm, "went outside to see what the commotion was about. Most of those who went outside haven't come back. The others are in the lower levels of the museum. I don't know anything about the other buildings."

"How long has it been?"

"Over an hour since we last heard anything. Even the alert sirens have stopped now, but no one wants to go out and check."

"I can understand that. Stay safe and keep us updated," the TV-station voice said. A few moments passed before he spoke again. "Before she could call us directly, Kayce was able to upload footage taken by the security cameras at the museum."

Another off screen voice added, "the cell towers were all jammed with people trying to call in and out, but the Smithsonian has a hardline connection and they were able to send out this video from earlier today.

"As a warning, the images you're about to see are graphic."

The screen went blank for a moment before the high-resolution destruction was replaced by footage from two other vantage points. The screen split vertically down the middle. One half pointed toward the Washington Monument in the distance and the other toward the capitol building. Both views combined showed the entire green space in front of the capitol through the distorted fisheye view common to security cameras.

The weather in Washington that afternoon had been idyllic. The storms that had been plaguing East Tennessee were nowhere to be seen five hundred miles to the northeast. For a minute, everything was normal, then came a rumbling thunder the likes of which no one unfortunate enough to be present had heard outside of movies. Some people fled at the sound, but most stayed nearby out of curiosity.

From outside the camera's field of view came a column of horsemen preceded by a steadily-growing throng of panicked men and women fleeing in front of them. Those who had initially stayed, wondering what the noise was, now ran as well. They joined with, or were swept up by, the onrushing tide of people.

The army glittered with steel in the bright summer sun as they marched down the National Mall in perfect lockstep. The horde passed the camera's viewpoint with no sign of ending or stopping. In the camera's poor-quality imagery, little else was visible other than the fact that the passing army did not seem, in any way, to be modern. The audio pickup only heard the overwhelming roar of uncountable hooves.

If he had not heard the descriptions of what this army—because that was all it could be—had done to his nation's capital, Owen would have thought this was a publicity stunt or perhaps the first shot of a movie trailer. The way the original camera had fixed on the wreck of the capitol's dome, though, removed all doubts or suspicion that this was anything but reality.

The army marched far past the security camera, parted to go around the Ulysses S. Grant Memorial, and then was gone. Nothing happened for several long minutes before a bright flash, like a flare going off in a cave, lit up the area. When the camera's overloaded circuits reset, whatever happened was already over; the capitol dome crumbled, burning.

Owen's stomach went cold. To see the wreckage streaming smoke was one thing, but to actually watch the flash, see the debris falling, was another level of horror all its own. Unbidden, comparisons between this and the footage he saw in school of the World Trade Center collapsing in New York came to his mind.

His brain tried, and failed, to convince itself that what he was watching was not actually real. As the view on screen switched back to the feed showing the capitol burning and the news anchor spoke without Owen hearing it, cold reality remained.

"Sam," he said, quietly.

Wordlessly, she shifted around on the couch and settled one arm around his shoulders. He looked over at her. Tears stained her cheeks, but the grip of her hand on his shoulder was firm. Few other people would have gotten even that brief glimpse into her soul. Frightened though she was, "vulnerable" never came close to describing her emotional state. For Owen, the sight of his best friend, a woman who was normally so in control of things, on the edge of a breakdown hit him harder than the horrific sequence playing out on the news.

He leaned against her, glad at that moment for simple human contact.

Sam raised her free hand to point at the TV. "Owen, look."

"...ootage from one of our sister stations based near the capitol that was able to scramble a crew on site."

"Warning," another voice said, "the footage you are about to see is likely going to be extremely graphic."

The screen blanked again, this time coming back with a view from the roof of a nearby building. The army from the Smithsonian video had already split to go around the Ulysses S. Grant Memorial.

A voice boomed from the capitol. "Stand still and identify yourself!" Unlike the Smithsonian's cameras, the news crew on site had high-quality microphones trained on both the army and the steps of the capitol, which picked up everything.

The army rounded the memorial and was past it in moments. They reformed into ranks in the western yard directly opposite the steps leading to the capitol. For a moment, they took even with the new crew's perch.

If anyone leading the army understood the command, none of them wavered. The faces in the horde were all a dusky gray color that, with only small variations, was uniform as far as the camera could see. Their faces were only visible for a few moments before the pace of their march carried them out of view.

Those faces held something inhuman. The proportions of the jawline were wrong, as were their cheeks. Yet the most unsettling feature was the furious intelligence that lurked behind their deep eyes.

"This is your last warning," the voice boomed again as the horde marched across the lawn. "Stop your march and identify yourselves. We will open fire if you refuse to comply."

The army continued forward, spreading out to fill up the area between the Ulysses S. Grant Memorial and the capitol. By this point, armed National Guard troops had taken up positions on the capitol's steps. The roar of helicopters and other aircraft filled the air as the horsemen drew closer to what should have been their deaths.

Having already seen the aftermath of what this army did, Owen felt sick as the Guard assembled to stop them.

One of the defending squads must have ordered a volley of warning shots, because a dozen bullets pocked the ground in front of the horses. Grass and dirt, dislodged by the small volley of antipersonnel rounds, flew into the air and spattered against the armor of the horses in the front of the line. None of them stopped.

The view briefly panned skyward to show a wing of heavily armed attack helicopters coming into range. The camera panned again and zoomed, showing tanks and other armored vehicles being prepped at the National Guard Armory on the opposite side of the Capitol Building, far from the horsemen.

"The hell is going on?" one of the camera crew asked. The camera's microphone, aimed at the ground, barely picked up his voice.

"No idea," a female voice, also out of frame, replied. She must have had a headset tied into the video feed, because her voice came across clear. "Drill, maybe? Looks like a promotional stunt or something."

"One moment," a third voice on headset, added. This voice, also female, carried considerably more seriousness than the other two. "Ma'am, we're getting reports that similar things are happening across the globe."

"What the devil..." the woman on headset asked, then, quickly, "Jay, turn the camera back down there!"

The camera obeyed, centering on the mounted army. It had finally stopped its advance. It was not clear whether it had simply reached the end of its march, or if the threat of modern weaponry finally sank in—at least, not for a few seconds more.

A figure advanced from the center of the horde, arms out to his sides and hands held high. Seen under any other circumstances, Owen would have wondered why the leader would march as far as he did, get as close to the capitol as he had, only to surrender. Now, having seen the wreckage these people left behind, he could only see the threat that that man, if "man" was even the right word, posed.

"Identify yourself!" demanded a uniformed man standing on the Capitol steps. He shouted through a megaphone. Dozens, if not hundreds, of weapons were trained on the apparent leader of the mounted army.

"My name is Hereg Solsinis!" boomed a rich baritone completely devoid of any human regional accents. He enunciated every syllable equally, but drug out the last of each sentence, lending his voice a strange, strident quality. "I am the King-by-Blood of the Korovega!"

"Who or what are the Korovega?" the man in the combat-suit asked.

Rather than reply, Hereg simply indicated the army at his heels. The horde, however, responded with a thunderous roar, snarling and yelling a thousand threats at once.

"What is your purpose here?"

Hereg Solsinis turned his attention back to the capitol and laid his hands on the reins of his horse. The camera zoomed in on his face. His yellow eyes glinted in the sun like a hungry snake. "We have slumbered for a long time, haven't we, brothers and sisters?"

Again, the horde hooted and yelled.

Hereg continued. "Now, we are awake! Now, we will take back what is ours."

"And what is 'yours?'"

He waved, indicating the landscape. "All of it! The land, sea, and air belong to us!"

"What are your terms?"

"Terms?" Hereg laughed derisively, stepping his horse forward slightly as he spoke. "We have no terms, ashman! We are here to exterminate you and your kind from this world and reclaim it as our own."

"Stop right there!"

"No," Hereg replied, taking another step.

"If you come any closer, we will be forced to open fire."

Hereg took one more step, holding his left hand in front of his body, palm facing the Capitol and its guards. A light glowed in his palm. The guards, true to their commander's word, opened fire. Most of them were aiming at Hereg or his horse, but enough of them shot at the army itself that the horde was forced to react, defensively at first.

The bullets popped and cracked against some sort of barrier in front of Hereg's horse. Light like miniature fireworks spangled the space in front of the alleged king. Several tense seconds passed as the guards emptied their magazines first into Hereg, then into the rest of the horde.

Much like they had done against the king, the rounds simply stopped as they impacted a scintillating shield made of thousands of similar, overlapping, energy barriers protecting the army proper. The army of Korovega now shone an iridescent blue from the light of their massed shields.

The bullets from the guards were joined by heavier weaponry from the attack helicopters, but nothing seemed to be getting through whatever barrier the Korovega were using. Instead of dealing out death for the Korovega, the thousands of bullets dropped harmlessly to the ground with a clatter of falling metal.

"You have ruled this planet long enough," Hereg pronounced amid the clatter of reloading weapons. He raised his right hand high above his head and held it there for a second, before chopping it quickly forward in a gesture that even the human guards could not mistake.

As one, the mounted army of the Korovega drew their swords and surged into forward motion. Beams of light in every direction sprang from the horde, scorching and destroying everything they touched. Within a minute, everything on the ground that was human and within sight of the hellish army was dead, dying, or simply gone.

One of the beams lanced by the building where the ground crew had set up. An explosion off to the right side rocked the camera itself. It recovered and panned that way in time to see half of an attack helicopter billowing greasy black smoke for a second before exploding. Burning debris spiraled to the ground.

Another beam streaked by the camera. This one went underfoot and, for a tense moment, seemed like it had missed the people operating the camera, no matter what had happened to the building underneath them. That moment passed as the floor buckled and collapsed. The crew screamed as their perch all but vanished out from under them and the camera toppled over the edge.

The feed mercifully cut out after a few seconds of vertigo-inducing spinning as the camera plummeted to the ground.

The TV switched back to the same newsroom. "We can now confirm that this sight has been replicated all over the planet," he paused and a hollow look invaded his eyes for a moment. It never made it to his voice, which he kept under fierce control. "We cannot confirm the whereabouts or condition of the President at this time.

The anchor paused, choked down a fresh wave of panic, then continued, "we will survive, America, but as yet, we cannot offer any speculation..."

"Turn it off," Sam muttered. "I don't want to see it again."

Owen almost changed the channel, rather than powering the set off completely, but reasoned that the same broadcast would likely have been picked up by every channel in the world by then. The TV went blank with a click.

"Sam?" Owen asked, still staring at their reflections in the glossy black surface.

"Yeah?"

"What the hell are we going to do?"

"We're not going to die, that's for sure," she replied, forcing herself to uncurl her arms and legs from where she had been sitting with her knees tucked under her chin. The muscles in her arms had tightened into cords like steel cables that slowly smoothed out as she forced herself to relax.

"How, exactly?" Owen asked, feeling more despair than anything. The whole thing was too unbelievable, too horrific, too terrifying to get worked up over. He felt like he should be raging against Hereg and the Korovega, promising their defeat, but instead he felt nothing but cold.

He asked himself how he could fight against something that just slaughtered so many heavily armed soldiers, and came up with no answer.

Sam shook her head. "I don't know, Owen. I really don't, but we'll think of something, right?"

For a second, he acted like he had not heard her.

"Right?" she repeated, stronger.

"Right," he admitted finally, still staring at the blank TV screen. "You don't think they'll attack Oak Ridge, do you?"

Sam was silent. She turned her eyes away from Owen and stared at his floor for a minute or more. "I don't know. Maybe? Does this Hereg bastard know what nuclear power is? Would he know what a coal-fired plant looks like?" She chuckled bitterly. "I suppose, that is, if he does know...

"We have to do something," she finished, voice firm.

"We?" Owen asked with a bitter laugh. He weakly gestured toward the blank TV screen with one hand. "What can 'we' do?"

"You didn't think I was going to stop that horde on my own, did you?" she asked. The question was so utterly ridiculous that part of her smile was genuine that time.

Owen gave a laughing sigh. "No," he answered, "no, I suppose not."

"Call the others," she said, as though the idea were a sudden, if simple, revelation. Her voice picked up energy as she went. "If you can, anyway. God only knows how bad cell service is going to be. Text people, email them, get in touch with as many of our friends as we can trust."

"'The others?'" Owen asked, skeptical. "Are we the Avengers now?"

She laughed, shaking her head. Her fear had given over to disconnected giddiness. "No. Not yet, anyway. But the lot of us could come up with a way to stay alive a lot better than we could on our own, don't you think?"

Owen nodded. She had a point, and he was glad to have something to focus his mind on. He had no idea where her confidence came from, but it was something he could piggyback on and use to fuel his own willpower. He already felt stronger simply from having the beginnings of a plan. "Alright. Do we want to meet here?"

Sam surveyed the apartment with a sweep of her head. "I think so. Be sure to have everyone bring supplies, food..."

"...weapons," Owen supplied.

Sam sighed. "Yes, weapons. There's no way of telling how much time we have until the Korovega show up at our doorstep."

"My apartment isn't exactly a fortress."

"It's out of the way," Sam said. "I live near Bull Run. If they attack, my place would be a hundred times worse than yours."

"We can't stay here," he said, almost pleading. He had no idea where to go, and so hoped she would, or could, come up with something. Then, a thought struck him, "maybe Ben's?"

"For right now, everyone knows where 'here' is. Let's figure out step one before we tackle step two."

"And what is step one?" Owen asked. "Because 'bring everyone here' sounds a lot like step two to me."

Sam closed her eyes, sighed, and looked back at the floor. Worry and fear crept back into her voice as she spoke. "I need to go back to my apartment. I didn't bring anything with me but my bike."

Owen nodded. Some part of his mind focused on her motorcycle. He had always liked riding on it, and if the world was about to end under the heels of some ancient army with magic powers, there were worse vehicles to have around.

Aloud, he asked, "what for?"

"Like I said, supplies," Sam replied. "We'll fill up my car and bring it back here."

Owen had known Sam for most of his life, and he could already see where her train of thought was going. "You're not thinking of just bringing some food and guns, are you?"

She looked at him for a moment, then shook her head. "No," she admitted. "I suppose not."

Owen nodded. After discussing the possibility of the Korovega attacking power plants, the idea of her going back to Oak Ridge alone was frightening. "We'll both go," he said, "we can take my car."

Sam regarded him with a single raised eyebrow for a moment.

"That way we can fill up both cars up," Owen added, thinking up the reason as he said it.

Sam smiled. This one almost looked not forced. Like Owen, she was glad to have something to focus her mind on instead of replaying the sight of the Korovega's massacre over and over in her head.

"We'll survive."

* * *

Leaving immediately turned out to be the best decision the two of them could have made. Traffic into the city was already bad, and rapidly growing worse. Leaving any later would have put them on the wrong side of hours of traffic jams.

Oak Ridge itself was a madhouse of foot and vehicle traffic. Armed security forces, ranging from regular-duty police officers to SWAT troops in riot gear stood on nearly every street corner that Owen's car passed. Police cars and black SUVs belonging to Plant Security and the DOE were everywhere.

Tension filled the air. Everyone, civilian and police alike, were terrified or in shock at what they had seen on the news. Neither side, a distinction that Owen was reluctant to use but could already see forming, wanted there to be any trouble. Ironically, he thought as they passed the high school and the police station a block later, the police presence seemed to reinforce an air of normalcy in the city. Oak Ridge had been "high security" off and on for decades, and most of the city's residents were used to seeing black government vehicles driving around.

The civilian traffic, on the other hand, was worse than he had ever seen it. Rush hour jams around the Plant were nothing compared to the sheer numbers clogging the major streets as people fled in both directions. A comparable number were headed back toward Oak Ridge and the DOE's presumed heavy security forces.

Owen could see the lure. He even thought about suggesting they they move all of his things to Sam's apartment instead, but ignored the urge. They already had made their calls; everyone was to meet at Owen's for the time being. Plus, he thought with a twinge of anxiety, Sam had been right before. As many people as were already flooding into Oak Ridge, the city would be packed to the gills within the week.

Oak Ridge was home to more than its share of sensitive and Top Secret material, and the police and security forces were conducting regular stops of cars as they tried to get from one end of the city to the other. The slowed traffic down considerably, but Owen wondered if it, in some way, actually helped. By keeping things slow, and regulating where people went, he supposed the police had traded disaster for inconvenience. Those on their way out were being diverted to the main roads, while local traffic was being ushered through the twisted, but completely interconnected, backroads around the city.

The only good part about the regular searches was that, when the police got to his car, Owen had his badge ready. The little piece of plastic marked him as an employee of ORNL—Oak Ridge National Labs—and as someone who held a "Q" clearance. For all practical purposes right then, it functioned as a "get in free" card, and the police let them move freely.

Fortunately, Sam's apartment was relatively far from downtown Oak Ridge and near the access for the highway. Unfortunately, she lived off of Edgemoor, which meant that her normally convenient access to the highway turned into a nightmare around rush hour. Edgemoor was not only one of the largest roads for people entering and leaving that end of Oak Ridge, but also the main road to the Bull Run Steam Plant, which rose high into the sky behind them. What should have been a short drive quickly turned into an hour's trip for the two of them.

"Maybe this wasn't such a great idea right now," Sam muttered, glaring at the backed up traffic. The rain had, in true East Tennessee fashion, given way to bright evening sunlight from a cloudless sky. The humidity, however, had not gone anywhere. The roads themselves had gotten so bad that some of the drivers were getting out of their cars to stretch their legs, but she had no intention of leaving the air conditioning unless she had to.

Owen eyed with suspicion a large group of people standing in the middle of the road a hundred meters ahead. Whatever they were talking about, no one in that little gathering seemed pleased with anyone else.

"No," he replied after a moment, "it's only going to get worse as time goes on."

Sam sighed, leaning her head against the frame of her open window. She watched the birds for a moment, before turning her attention back to Owen. "How's the heat?"

Owen looked down at the dashboard. "We're fine," he replied. With a nod of his head to the left, he added, "I'd rather be stuck next to the river if we've got to be stuck anywhere. The breeze and the shade is keeping us cooler that we'd be on the Turnpike."

"A bit," she grumbled.

"We could leave town on the Turnpike if you like," he offered with a wry grin.

Sam bit back a sharp reply. Heat and traffic jams were two of her least favorite parts of Summer. Instead, she smiled, or tried to anyway. "No thanks."

Half an hour passed and Owen's car moved a mile down the road. The brewing fight he had been watching dissipated as more people, cooler heads presumably, had joined the gathering and sent everyone back to their cars. The turnoff to the road Sam lived on was just ahead.

"Too bad this isn't a movie," he muttered.

"Hmm?" Sam asked groggily, coming out of the light sleep the warm evening sun had lulled her into.

Owen repeated his statement.

"Owen, dear," she said with a heavy dose of sarcasm, "if this were a movie, we'd be in the crowd that gets blown up in the opening shot."

He managed a smile. "Hey, our luck's not that bad. Besides, if this were a movie, maybe the Korovega have a weakness some protagonist in some major city somewhere can exploit."

"Sure. They're just misunderstood."

"Maybe they don't understand this human emotion of love," he said.

Sam laughed. "God," she paused. "Listen to us. The world's probably going to hell as we speak and we're making jokes."

"Can you think of a better way to pass the time?"

Sam stared out the window at the river. "No, not really. I'd like to be reminded I'm still alive, thanks, and laughter's the second best way to do that."

"What's the first?" he asked.

"Pain," Sam replied.

Owen opened his mouth to reply, but realized halfway though the motion that he really had nothing to say. Instead, he pointed ahead, saying, "we're almost there."

"Finally."

"Think we can fit everything we need into both cars?"

Sam thought for a long minute. She grew visibly more despondent as the car inched forward. "No," she said finally, "but we'll fit what we can. I don't think we'll get a second trip."

"I'm not going to let your place get looted, Sam."

This time her laugh was a bitter one. "I don't think we'll have a choice once things get worse. We'll stuff everything we possibly can into your car and mine and then figure out our next plan from there."

"With everyone else," he added.

"With everyone else," she agreed.

Another half an hour passed, during which the sun finished setting. Twilight offered a welcome reprieve from the oppressive heat and humidity, but the idea of moving in the dark sat poorly with Owen. It felt like running away, he thought, and despite having no better plan, he was not exactly keen on the idea.

They pulled onto Sam's street and the traffic dropped almost to nothing. Plenty of cars and other vehicles were leaving the subdivision, but they were one of a small few headed back into it.

"Just park in the grass," she instructed. "I don't think the Cops are going to be in a position to complain."

Owen did, pulling as close to her apartment door as he could.

"Food first," she said, unbuckling and opening her door simultaneously. "Start piling everything non-perishable by the door."

"What are you going to be doing?" he asked. As soon as the words left his mouth, he realized that they were a touch more accusatory than he meant for them to be.

Sam glared for a fraction of a second, but then her face softened. She was still on edge, and had no reason to take things out on Owen. "I'm going to bring my car to the door too, and then help you load."

Owen laughed awkwardly. "Yeah," he replied. "Good plan. Keys?"

Sam reached into her pocket and fished out her key ring. "Car key's on here, too, so let me open the door for you first."

Owen nodded.

Door unlocked, Sam laid a hand on Owen's shoulder. "You alright?" she asked. He sighed. "Honestly? No."

She squeezed Owen's shoulder before letting her hand drop. "Then we better work fast." Forcefully, trying to snap Owen out of his dark thoughts and keep her own at bay, she added, "inside. Start stacking."

He grinned, snapped a sloppy mock salute, and said, "yes'm."

He went inside, looking over her apartment. He had spent a lot of time here, and wanted a few moments to remember it as it was before they tore everything apart in the grand name of survival.

Owen sighed, and forced himself to think practically. "Let's see..." He talked himself through everything he was doing and ticking things off on his fingers. "Non-perishable stuff first. Cans, flour, rice, pasta, eggs. Do eggs go bad? I always eat them too fast..."

By the time Sam came inside, he had a sizable pile of food by the door. None of it was in boxes other than whatever it came packaged in, but that was a minor concern at the moment.

"I'll start in the bedroom and bathroom," she said, walking past where Owen was working.

"Bathroom?" he asked, surprised.

"We're going to need soap, pain meds, sunscreen, and whatever else I can fit into a box once things get bad. Hell," she replied, "I've got some water purification tablets in here from when that water main burst a few months ago."

They ran out of boxes, bags, cases, totes, and even purses long before they ran out of things to pack or room in their cars. Sam insisted on a few nick-nacks and heirlooms, but most of her nonessential possessions and all of her furniture short of a few folding chairs were piled in the bedroom and locked up.

In addition to food and general safety items, their cars were loaded down with cooking utensils, clothes and spare fabric, and books.

"Jewelry?" Owen asked, watching Sam shove a small wooden box into the trunk of her car.

"There's some sentimental stuff in there," she replied, only slightly defensive.

Owen left it at that. He suspected there was more to it, but he had no reason to press further. They had the room for the time being, so he had no objection.

"Help me get my computer, and I think that'll be it."

"What for?"

"We've got electricity right now," Sam replied. "So long as Bull Run's still standing, even your end of the county should have power for a long while yet."

They disassembled the various parts of her desktop quickly, spreading it between whatever free space was available in their cars. Sam's car got the monitor and other peripherals, while Owen took the tower itself and her laptop.

The last thing was the rack for her motorcycle. It weighed well over a hundred pounds, but had wheels on one end. Attaching it to her car was easy enough, and they used the extra space it provided—expecting to be able to put those boxes and pieces of furniture in someone else's vehicle later—to pack still more things.

They finished close to midnight, and stood panting and sweating in the parking lot, drinking directly from a bottle of soda.

Sam pressed a small pistol, holster, and box of ammunition into Owen's hands. "Here."

"You know I can't shoot worth crap," he protested. "You keep it."

Sam lifted up the bottom of her shirt to reveal a much larger revolver in a holster clipped to her belt. It was obvious, now that he looked for it. It was amazing, he thought, how easy it was to miss things like that. "I've got this one. Keep the .380."

Owen nodded reluctantly. The simple act of hanging a gun, even Sam's old pocket pistol, from his belt only cemented in his mind exactly how bad things already were.

"Let's get back to your place," Sam said. "We've still got a lot of work to do."

Owen nodded, trying to think of something to say. After a moment, he, in his best attempt at an inspirational tone, said, "alright. Let's go. Just," he sighed, "this is only the beginning."

"I know," she replied, shutting her car door.

Back in his own driver's seat, Own fervently wished that the last few hours were only a dream. Even a nightmare would be preferable to knowing that, in all likelihood, he would be dead before the end of the year.

Chapter 2

Owen shuffled out of the bedroom, wearing a pair of blue pajama pants with stripes. Sam never could decide if they were supposed to look like tuxedo pants for some reason, or look like something that was supposed to be making fun of tuxedo pants. Either way, he did not look ready to be alive, let alone awake. His short, dark brown hair stuck out in tufts here and there—stopping at the bathroom to brush it had obviously not been on his to-do list right after waking up.

Sam had been awake for a while. She used that time to unpack and start to sort through some of the things they had brought the night before. The smell of coffee filled the air, unaccustomed and strange. Like so much else, the pot and the beans had been taken from Sam's apartment; Owen never really developed a taste for the stuff, preferring tea instead. Sam's presence, and that of the stacked boxes of her things, hammered home once again that the events of the previous day had been real.

Between the time it took to pack everything and the congested traffic on the roads between her home and Owen's, it was well past midnight when they made it back to his apartment. Both of them were ready to collapse as soon as they got to his place.

"Good news," Sam announced upon seeing Owen. "First, there's water heating on the stove so you can make some tea."

"Thanks," he muttered.

"You know," Sam teased, "if you liked coffee, it's already ready."

Owen laughed. "I know," he replied with a smile. "I almost thought I'd woken up at your place somehow. Doesn't smell right in here."

"You look like you could use some, though," she offered. "Coffee, that is."

Owen shook his head. "What I need is food. We didn't eat dinner last night." Then, "that bad, huh?"

Sam took a sip of her coffee. "You look like a fratboy the morning after finals."

"I slept like crap," he said, rubbing his shoulders with alternating hands.

"Yeah," she admitted. "Me too. At least your couch is comfy. My body's rested, for all the good that does for my brain."

Owen grinned. "I've watched enough zombie movies to know how important taking care of your body is."

Despite everything, she laughed. "If only shotguns were as effective against the Korovega."

Owen grimaced at the mention of the name. "Yeah, them. Let's put that off for a bit while we eat breakfast."

"Speaking of," Sam said. "What's for breakfast?"

"Me? You're the one who's been awake."

"Yeah, but you're the cook. I burn water," she quipped. "I had a grocery store muffin when I got up, but that's it."

"You made coffee."

"Coffee isn't cooking," she retorted, "it's art."

Owen grinned, shook his head, and plodded into the kitchen. "Can't argue with that."

For the time being, yesterday's trouble was forgotten as he dug around in the kitchen, first making tea and then fixing breakfast for the both of them. His constantly growling stomach saw fit remind him that the last thing he ate had been before practice yesterday and it was not happy with that decision.

"What about work?" Sam asked. The kitchen and the living room were separated by a half wall over the sink, which made it easy enough to talk back and forth.

"I got an email," Owen replied. "They said not to come in. The labs are shut down right now. Managing the database apparently isn't a 'critical' position. Not that I'm complaining. You?"

"I had today off anyway," she replied, "but I called last night on the way back here and said I would be out, 'for the foreseeable future.'"

Owen had nothing to say to that and, twenty minutes later, he set several plates on his small dinner table. They both had a pair of eggs, a waffle, and several thick slices of bacon sitting between them and the rest of the day's work.

"Earlier," Owen said, slicing his waffle into pieces, "you said you had good news, then you said, 'first.' I'm guessing there's a 'second' too?"

His question caught her in the middle of chewing a mouthful of eggs. She finished quickly, muttered an, "oh, right," then said, "I called Ben earlier. The signal was crap, but I managed to get through."

"Is he alright?"

She smiled. Talking to Ben that morning, simply hearing his voice in fact, had started her day off well. She had not known him for as long as Owen had, but considered him a good friend nonetheless. Knowing he was safe did a lot for her outlook. "Better. He's on his way."

Owen laughed. "Good, good. I couldn't get through to him yesterday; not that cell signal is worth anything at his place anyway. I'm glad he's coming."

"Yeah," Sam nodded, "me too."

They ate for some time in silence. Sam watched Owen's face as he ate. His expression shifted around through a broad spectrum of emotions, most of which were negative. She thought about her own reaction to things yesterday and wondered where the idea, and the drive, to bring everything here had come from. More importantly, she tried to figure out where they were going to put it all, especially with Ben bringing even more.

Charts and floorplans spun around in her head as she tried to account for the logistics of it all.

"Sam?" Owen asked. She looked up. His plate was empty, while half of her breakfast remained, forgotten as she thought and planned. "You alright?"

She forced a smile. "Yeah," she replied. "Just thinking."

"About yesterday?"

"Tomorrow, actually. How we're going to deal with all of," she waved at the stacks of boxes they brought in from the cars. It accounted for less than a third of what they had packed. "This."

"Whatever we do, we need to do it quickly," Owen said. "I checked online before getting out of bed. There's more footage from another camera from yesterday."

"How bad?"

His voice wavered. "They stormed the Capitol. Burned it all the way to the ground. Nothing's left."

"Christ," Sam muttered, slumping backward in her chair.

"Yeah. Then they made a big show of demolishing the Washington Monument. Then," he trailed off for a moment, made an evaporating gesture with his hands, "poof, they dispersed."

"We know D.C. wasn't the only place they hit," Sam said, forcing her voice to stay level.

"Agreed. And if they come after Knoxville, I don't know what we're going to do."

"What about your plans yesterday?"

He never answered. A moment passed before he said, "you know, if they killed any Korovega during the fighting, you'd think that it'd be all over the news."

Sam, taken aback by the apparent non non sequitur, blinked. "Yes, and?"

"We have no idea if they can be killed at all."

"Anything can be killed," she said. Sam pushed the idea of hurting them out of her head; dwelling on it would help no one. The what and the why were easy—she just needed to figure out the how. She folded her hands on the table. "So what do we know about them?"

"What do you mean?"

"I mean anything," she replied. "We know they want us dead. All of us. Why?"

"They're evil? They want control of the planet? It's Monday? All I know is what we heard from their king."

"Hereg." Sam interjected. "You know everything I do about them at this point." She ticked things off on her fingers, growing more frustrated with each sentence. "We know they attacked. We know they've got a king. We know they want us dead. We know they're riding horses and carrying swords. We know that bullets don't work on them."

Owen started to ask, "then why..."

"Did I tell you to keep that .380 on you from now on?" she finished. The tone of her voice had changed completely. She spoke slowly, enunciating everything with a firm tone. Inside, she felt a chunk of ice in her stomach, and was unsure whether she wanted to chip away at it or not. "There's going to be more to worry about than mystical armies. People can be pretty terrible to each other, Owen, there's no two ways about it."

"I'd hope people would band together against them."

"You'd hope," Sam growled. Her voice held a hint of derisiveness. There was something in her eyes; something that was not quite anger and not quite disaffection smoldered behind their warm amber color. Her tone was not directed at Owen as much at it was to the world at large. "And maybe eventually everyone will do just that, but first people are going to be killing each other."

"That's..."

"Reality," she said, cutting him short before he could argue. "Think about every major disaster in the last century, in the last two centuries. There's going to be rioting and looting once people realize that food is going to start running out."

Owen sighed. "What do you propose we do about it, though? If the Korovega really are coming for us, and I've got every reason to expect them any day now, then we can't exactly stay holed up here of all places."

Sam shook her head. "No, you're right. We're going to have to go somewhere." She emphasized the "some." Then, realizing that he had not heard a thing she just said, "Owen?"

"You said they carried swords," he said.

"And?"

"They obviously knew enough about modern technology to prepare for bullets, right?"

"I can't say for certain, but it seemed that way, yes."

"Which means that, if they had a use for guns, they'd carry them, right?"

"But they don't carry guns," Sam countered. His logic dawned on her slowly. "They still carry swords. What is it you always say when you and Ben get to talking fencing? 'Every defense has a weakness?'"

"That's it," he replied. "Maybe we can kill them if they ever show up here."
Sam said, "when."

"When?"

"Not 'if,'" Sam corrected. "'When.' They're going to show up here sooner or later. We just need to be prepared for them when they arrive."

"Speaking of arrival, were you able to get in touch with anyone other than Ben?"

She shook her head. "No, at least not directly. I left a bunch of voicemails, but even that was iffy. Emails, texts too, but who knows how reliable they're going to be if the cell towers are already overloaded."

"Same," Owen replied. "Still, I'd rather know all of my friends are safe."

"I'm sure they will be," Sam said. It felt like a lie, and they both knew it, but neither wanted to own up to it, and suddenly neither of them wanted to continue that particular conversation, either.

* * *

After breakfast, Sam offered to clean up. It was the least she could do, she argued, since Owen had actually made the food for them.

Before Sam could do much more than fill the sink with water, however, the front door of the apartment boomed and thundered as though someone with a sledgehammer were trying to break it down.

"Swear to God, Owen, if you're already dead," shouted a loud voice with a thick Southern drawl on the other side of his thin apartment door.

"Ben's here," Owen called over his shoulder.

"I heard," Sam replied, suppressing a laugh.

Owen unbolted the door and, before he could reach the knob, it flew open towards him. His reflexes saved him from a broken nose, but the unexpectedly-moving doorknob smacked him hard in the back of the hand.

"Son of a bitch," he swore through gritted teeth. "I'm not dead, Ben, but I might be if you hit me with the door again."

"Aw, I didn't open it that hard," Ben chided. A grin flashed across his ebony face. "'Sides, ain't nothin' a doorknob can do to your hand that my sword can't."

"I've got to give you that one," Owen admitted, then gestured Ben inside.

"I'll add it to your tab," Ben said, stepping through the doorway. He wore a white tshirt under a dark blue button-down shirt and jeans with a backpack hanging off broad shoulders that nearly filled the doorway. As always, Owen expected to see him bang his bald head on the top of the frame, but he came in without incident. Despite living up to the nickname their sparring group had given him on his first day, "Big Ben" was not quite tall enough to embarrass himself like that.

He looked past Owen, finally seeing Sam where she stood behind the sink, partially obscured by the half-wall.

"Samantha!" Ben called across the small apartment in a voice pitched to carry across an open field.

"Benjamin," Sam replied, significantly more quietly.

"You know I hate m'full name," he said. His attempt to look pissed off would have been convincing to anyone who had not known him for as long as Owen and Sam. They could easily see the laughter struggling to come to the surface, despite his every effort to the contrary. For a moment, pretend anger covered his dark face. The moment was brief, however, and his mouth split into a wide grin within seconds.

"And I don't like 'Samantha' either, so there." She stuck her tongue out at him.

"Touche, touche," Ben laughed, closing the door behind him. "I smell breakfast."

"I'm not cooking!" Sam said automatically.

"Then whyfore is you in the kitchen, woman?" Ben asked, laying his already thick accent on thicker.

"Owen made breakfast, for your information. I'm being nice and cleaning up."

"Owen made breakfast," Ben said looking from Sam to Owen and back. With a raised eyebrow, he added, "for both of you?"

"It wasn't like that," Owen protested. They had had that particular conversation more than once. Ben always insisted that he and Sam ought to hook up, but it never had. He knew it never would, too, but it had long since become a running joke between the three of them.

"Sure," Ben countered.

"It wasn't," Sam said. Her joviality from moments before was gone, replaced again by the grim, flat tone her voice took on when she thought of the Korovega's massacre. "We were here when the news broke yesterday." Her emphasis on "the news" removed all doubt about which news she was referring. "I didn't feel like going home afterward."

"Heard that," Ben said quietly. He stared at one of the few blank spots on Owen's living room wall for a moment. Then, just as quietly, he added, "hell. Now you guys've gotten me thinkin' all dark and dreary. Shit."

The next few minutes passed in silence. Owen sat down heavily on one end of his couch, and a minute later Sam wordlessly joined him at the other end, leaning on the opposite arm of the couch. They exchanged a long look, each of them searching for something to say that would alleviate the dark mood that had settled over the room.

Behind her eyes, Owen could watch the wheels of Sam's mind turn. He wanted to play the hero, but if they were going to survive when the Korovega came for Oak Ridge, she was the one to figure out how to do it. Maybe he could deal with the people themselves, get them to work together, but Sam would be the one with the logistics all mapped out.

Before Owen could sort out his thoughts, Ben dropped down between them, draping both of his arms across the back of the couch. His muscular form was larger than either of them by far, perhaps even larger than them both put together, and took up much of the spare room on the couch.

"So, what's the plan?" Ben asked.

"Plan?" Owen asked, almost scoffing.

"That's why you're here. Owen and I, we could survive for a while," Sam replied calmly. "This is going to be bigger than the few of us, you know. With more of us on hand, we stand a better chance of surviving."

"What about hiding? Kinda hard to hide a whole mess a'people. Harder than hiding two, anyhow."

"Did you see the news?" Owen asked. When Ben said he had, Owen continued. "I don't think stealth is going to be any good against those," he searched for the right word, "people. Those things."

"Besides," Sam added, "there's still stuff Owen and I don't know how to do. At least not well. Canned food won't last forever."

Ben managed a grin, white teeth bright against his dark skin. "Redneck to the rescue!" He laughed. "That it?"

"Something like that," Owen said, feeling Ben's insatiable good cheer infecting him. He laughed.

"What?" Ben asked.

"Just thinking," he replied. "If we do get killed..."

"We won't," Sam interjected.

"If we do," Owen continued, "I know I can count on you to make me laugh right before I keel over. And, so long as we're still alive, someone once said that laughter was the second best way to remind you of that fact."

Sam grinned. "Can't imagine who that 'someone' was."

Ben laughed. "But seriously," he said, "what's a'plan?"

"Right now?" Sam asked.

"Right now."

"Get as many people together as would be willing to go with us, take as much canned food, hygiene supplies, weapons, and ammo as we can transport, and head for the hills."

"I thought y'all weren't interested in hiding."

"Not hiding," Owen argued, "biding time. They're going to come for us eventually, there's no doubt about that, and..."

"Now," Ben interrupted. "Just so we're clear. How exactly do you know those Korovega are going to hunt us down personally?"

"Their king used the word 'exterminate,'" Sam said. "That seems pretty clear to me."

"So why move now?" Ben asked.

"They're coming," Owen said firmly, "but we don't know when."

Sam added, "could be in a month, or ten years from now, or they could be right down the road right now."

"That's just it," Owen continued. "We don't know when they're going to attack. So we move now. Take everything we can, and hole up somewhere."

"I hate to break it to you, but your apartment ain't exactly a castle," Ben said.

Owen scoffed, then sighed. "Yeah, I know. That's why, 'somewhere' isn't here. That's part of what we need to figure out."

After a moment, Ben asked, "my place?"

"I don't know," Sam replied. "Something about being that close to open water makes me nervous, thinking about the Korovega. I know we couldn't see it, but I swear they had to have marched straight out of the Potomac."

"So we really will be heading for the hills," Ben said wistfully, then grinned. "Always wanted to run away from it all, you know? I just never figured hell would be on my tail when I did."

"What do you think we should do?" Owen asked.

"Right now?" Ben asked, echoing Sam's question from moments before. He rubbed the back of his head in thought. "Sam, you said you wanted to gather up food, supplies, and ammo, right?"

She nodded.

"I got plenty of each at my place. Want me to go get it?"

Owen turned, moving the curtain aside to look out the window. For the time being, the apartment complex's yard was relatively empty. A few people moved around nervously, walking like they were resisting the urge to look over their shoulder with every pace.

"No," Owen said finally. "Not until we decide where we're going to go. Sam's things are here because we know we're not going back to her place."

"My place is pretty big," Ben pointed out. "It's pretty far away from the cities too, up in the mountains, and..."

Sam interrupted, "we'll keep it in mind. I just want all the options on the table first. Before we go anywhere, we need to know what kind of supplies we've got."

"Now, before we go stockpiling bullets, I gotta ask. The army couldn't stop them Korovega. What are a few hunting rifles and pistols going to do?" Ben asked.

"They're not for the Korovega," Sam said quietly.

"Do what now?"

"They're not for the Korovega," Sam repeated, louder. "We've got to look at this rationally."

"Ain't no kind of 'rationally' that involves helping those things kill people off," Ben snapped, momentarily letting his real temper through.

"Relax, Ben," Sam said, doing her best to put on a soothing tone. "We're not going to be hunting down human beings or anything."

"Then what...?" he demanded.

Owen interrupted, saying, "they're for defense. Just because we won't be shooting people over food and shelter doesn't mean other people won't try to shoot us over the same."

"I don't like it any more than you do," Sam said, lightly placing a hand on Ben's arm. "But that's the reality of it. We need to be prepared for anything."

Ben took several deep breaths, closed his eyes, and sighed. Finally, his calm restored, he said, "alright, let's deal."

Sam nodded. "Ok, what we need in terms of a plan is where we're going to go, what we're going to do for food, and who's coming with us."

"How many more are supposed to be here?" Ben asked.

"No idea," Owen replied. "Between Sam and me, we tried to get the word out to three or four dozen people easy."

"They're not all going to come, of course," Sam added. "Other people are probably thinking along the same basic lines that we are right now."

"Gather up and hole up," Ben agreed. "There's some mountains south of here, little to the east of Clinton. Think those'll do?"

"Over by the interstate?" Sam asked.

"Yeah," Ben replied, "but there's a bunch of land the highway don't touch. I reckon we could set up camp there. You wanted options. Owen, you got a map?"

"On the computer."

Ben shot him a sarcastic look that said, "really?" Out loud, he said, "no, I mean a real map. Road map or an atlas'll do."

"Somewhere, why?"

"'Cause I'm running on memory here, and I want to make sure I know what the hell I'm talking about," Ben said, as though the point was obvious and ought to have gone unsaid.

"Yeah," Owen grunted, levering himself up and off of the couch. "There should be one in the bedroom. Let me go look."

After he left the room, Ben shifted in place to better face where Sam sat. "Tell me straight," he said slowly. "We're gonna die, ain't we?"

A bitter grin tugged at one corner of her mouth. The straightforwardness of his question, despite its morbidity, almost made her laugh. It probably would have if the outcome he was asking about was not highly probable. After a moment where she tried to figure out how best to phrase her thoughts, she said simply, "yeah." Then, with a slightly wider grin, she added, "eventually. Old age will get all three of us eventually."

Despite himself, Ben laughed as well. "Yeah, but what're the odds of some ancient bastard doing us in before then?"

Sam sighed, sinking into the couch slightly. "Pretty good," she admitted. "Owen's right, though."

Ben raised his eyebrows. "What's that?"

"I'd rather die with friends around me, maybe even die actually fighting back against the Korovega, than sit idly by and wait for the end."

"Sam," Ben said.

"Yeah?"

"You said your guns were for," he paused. His mouth has suddenly gone dry. He had been a hunter for years, but the prospect of taking another human life disturbed him deeply. "They're for defense, yeah?"

She nodded. Her echo of, "yeah," was almost inaudible.

"You think you could do it?"

"'It?'" she asked.

"Shoot someone."

Sam was quiet for several long moments. Finally, she said, "I... think so. If I had to. I got a license for a reason. If they were a threat to my life, or Owen's life, or your life."

"My life?" Ben asked, real surprise showing through on his face.

"You're a friend, too."

"Yeah, but I'm just a rowdy, drunken..."

"Ex-drunken," Sam corrected, holding up a hand in protest as though the distinction was the most important part of their conversation.

He laughed softly. "Ok, ex-drunken mess. I'm not worth that much. Much less you all getting hurt on my behalf."

"You're our angry, loud mess though," Owen announced, returning to the living room with a folded up road map of the area. It looked as though he had picked it up at a rest area, opened it once, and never looked at it again.

"Keep that talk up and I might think you people like having me around," Ben said with a laugh.

"Alright boy scout." Owen lightly tossed the folded map in Ben's lap, then sat back down in his spot on the couch.

Ben unfolded the sheet with as little difficulty as was possible with gas station maps. He ended up only having to rotate it twice as he spread the map across their three laps. He quickly located Clinton on the map and folded the unneeded margins of the large sheet underneath the front face.

"Here we go. We're here," Ben said, tapping one finger over the rough area of Owen's apartment. He traced a line from that spot to a series of mountains about eight miles to the east. He put his finger down in the middle of the small cluster of hills. "What about here?"

"There?" Owen asked, not following Ben's unspoken logic. "Why?"

"Here," Ben said, tracing another line with his finger, one that followed the lines of the roads marked out on the map. "No roads, leastaways no paved roads, go up here. Trust me, I've been up there to hunt." At a crosswise look from Sam, he added, "not that I'd hunt in Anderson County outta season, mind you. That's illegal." He grinned.

"I don't know if I like how close it is to the river," Sam added.

Ben shook his head. "'S about three miles, but it's all hills and trees. Besides, we need to be near water, too, if we're going to be thinking 'super disaster' here. If we've gotta run to the hills," he explained, "then city water probably ain't gonna be working no more."

"But rain..." Sam began.

"Rain barrels are heavy," Ben said, matter-of-factly. "If the world's going to hell in a handbasket around me, I ain't luggin' a bunch'a rain barrels up the side of a mountain."

"But..." she protested again.

"We go up that far," he continued, talking over her comments, "I'll knock a tree down and make me some damn rain barrels."

"Ben knows this area better than both of us combined when it comes to going places off of the beaten path," Owen interjected. "I trust his plan."

"First stop has to be my place," Ben said. "I got the big truck there, and a couple of trailers. We load up everything we can and try our best to ride out Ragnarok."

Sam laughed, amused. An image struck her of the three of them calmly working on her motorcycle while riots and killing erupted all around them. She smiled. "There is that, I suppose," she said. Then, forcing herself back to seriousness, added, "alright. We leave the day after tomorrow for Ben's, then make for the hills the day after. Sound good?"

Ben shook his head. "Not to me. You talking about rioting and theft has got me not too keen on wanting to leave my place, my stuff really, un-looked-out-for for too long. I was actually thinking we'd be heading that way tonight.

"More to the point, I still say my place's better'n the woods. I've got, you know, walls an' a roof."

Sam nodded once. "He's right, Owen. I was thinking of going for the woods when it was there, my place, or here. With Ben's help..."

"With Ben's help," Ben added, "y'already got a house t'live in. So, when we leavin'?"

"Not tonight," Owen said. "I want to leave early in the morning, whatever we do. Let's wait at least a day to see if anyone else is going to show up."

"That's fair," Ben said. "Why don't we head out tomorrow morning, then? First light. Shit ain't hit the fan yet, least not as far as riots are concerned, so one night should be fine. Two nights makes me nervous, though."

Owen smiled, despite the pit in his stomach. "Don't worry, we'll see that cabin of yours by noon tomorrow, because I call dibs on the loft."

Ben laughed. "As usual."

* * *

The atmosphere in the apartment had slowly improved as the hours crept by. Ben, protesting that Owen had not made breakfast for him too, fixed them all lunch, while the three of them passed the time playing, of all things, poker.

"Straight," Sam said, laying her cards down.

"Ga' dang it," Ben exclaimed, tossing his losing hand onto the table.

Owen laughed, but immediately stopped when a knock came at the apartment door. He checked the time on his phone—three o'clock. It also showed no signal, which was no surprise at that point.

Ben, closest to the door, stood and crossed the room. He bent and peered through the little peephole as a tense silence fell across that part of the apartment.

There was a slight hiss near the door, like a spurt of gas escaping a barely-open valve. Owen, recognizing the sound as Ben biting back the urge to say something unpleasant, had a sudden sinking feeling. Of all the people he called, there were a few who were simply perfunctory calls—people that his moral compass would not let him ignore by virtue of their being human beings.

He also had not expected any of them to show up at his door, especially not one of a short list of people whose presence Ben would find objectionable. He looked up in time to see Ben rounding the small wall that separated the apartment's entryway from the rest of the living room area.

"Owen. What is he doing here?" Ben demanded, speaking very deliberately, clearly, and softly. He placed extra emphasis on "he," as though the pronoun itself were a curse.

"Who's at the door?" Owen asked, keeping his voice as low as Ben's.

"You invited that slimy bastard along to help save the world?" Ben snarled.

"Ben..."

"Damnit, Owen," he hissed. "Don't you 'Ben' me."

"Ben," Owen repeated. "Who's at the door?"

Ben opened his mouth, closed it, then opened it again. Owen had seen the motion before as he tried to decide whether to actually answer or simply swear profusely. Finally, he clenched his jaw tightly for a moment, then with considerable forced calm, said, "George Sinon."

"Piss," Owen muttered.

"Piss?" Ben demanded. Then, slightly louder, "piss? You called him here and now you're upset about it?"

"Ben, I didn't want to leave anyone to die."

"Even him?" he demanded.

Owen nodded. "Even him."

"I'm not gonna let him in."

"Hear me out."

"No."

"Look...."

"No!"

"Damnit Ben," Owen snapped. That, coming from Owen who so rarely raised his voice, got the other man's attention. "Listen."

"Alright." Ben folded his arms across his chest. "Talk fast."

"He's a smart guy," Owen explained. "Good with chemistry, decent with machines. With all your experience hunting, have you ever gone out there with nothing but a pack of equipment and chemicals, just to see if you could?"

"Well," Ben said, thought for a second. He supposed "a bag of water purifiers and a knife" was not exactly what Owen had in mind. After a moment, he added, "no. I haven't."

Owen jerked a thumb at the door. "He has. I know you and he have some bad blood, but he can do a lot for us."

"Some 'bad blood,'" Ben scoffed. "Yeah."

As Ben walked toward the door again, as slowly as he could possibly manage without literally dragging his feet, Sam caught Owen's eye from across the room. She cocked one eyebrow, and tilted her head at Ben's back. Owen closed his eyes and shook his head slightly, then mouthed the words, "long story." The look on her face at that was less than amused and told Owen that he was going to have to explain himself the next chance they had to talk alone.

Ben opened the door—"flung open" would have been the most appropriate description based on how he "accidentally" banged the door against the wall—and said in a surprisingly polite tone, "George. You got Owen's call, I see."

"Ben," came the tense reply, and then, "Yeah. Email, actually. Spent the whole evening packing the van."

Ben's eyebrows rose. "'Packing the van?'" he asked.

"Yeah," he replied. Owen could not see either of them around the dividing wall, but he suspected Ben was doing his best to be intimidating. George quickly added, "you know. Food, gear, clothes. That sort of stuff. Important things."

"Uh-huh," Ben said with a slow nod.

"You going to let me inside?"

Slowly he drawled, "I'm thinkin' about it."

"Ben..." George began.

"Can it," Ben said. "Owen called you here 'cause he thinks you can help us save goddamned civilization. That's good enough for me."

"Who's this?" Ben asked.

"Michael," George replied. "Michael, this is Ben Stuart."

They introduced themselves to each other, with Ben acting as though he had met Michael alone and without George's initial introduction.

"Inside," he said. "Both of you."

Sam looked up from her notebook momentarily as the two newcomers stepped into the apartment. She made eye contact with Michael, who offered her a friendly smile before going to introduce himself to Owen, and then with George. The latter smiled as well, but he had a too-friendly gleam in his eye that she found off-putting, like a used-car salesman. She suddenly wished she had more on than a tanktop—at least something under it, at any rate. She watched Michael and Owen for a moment before turning her attention back to her notebook.

Both men were close to Ben's age, probably not quite ten years older than Sam and Owen. Michael was the taller of the two, and probably would have been considered gangly fifty pounds ago. He carried a backpack. George was stocky, with the sort of build that said he could do manual labor, but preferred not to, or at least preferred to hit the doughnuts afterward.

George had taken three steps toward her table when Ben noticed where he was going, changed directions in mid stride, and made for the table as well.

"Hello, beautiful," George said, sliding into the chair across from where Sam sat. He rested one elbow on the small table and tried his best to put a charming smile on his face. The apocalypse, it seemed, had not dampened his mood.

Sam replied with a disinterested wave and kept her attention on her writing. She projected a careful air of business rather than coming across as deliberately ignoring him, however. George looked down and, as his eyes finally made it to her notebook, tried to make sense of what she was working on. Reading upside-down was difficult enough, but the fact that the page he was looking at seemed to be a hodge-podge of notes, questions, lists, and diagrams in at least two different languages made the task impossible.

"What's your name?" he asked as Ben sat down next to them.

"Sam Bennett," she replied, not taking her eyes off of the paper.

"I'm George."

"I heard."

"What're you working on?"

"Probably a plan to keep all our asses alive for the next few weeks," Ben said, laughing.

"Longer than that if I have anything to say about it," she replied, finally looking up from her work. It was clear that Ben was not leaving until George did, and he would not be leaving her alone until she engaged him in conversation.

She eyed George for a moment, trying to figure him out. She knew of him, from Owen, but had never met him before. He was smart, she knew that much, and from the confidence spilling out from his end of the table, he knew it as well. That was not necessarily a bad thing in her book, but it gave her reason to keep an eye on him. Sitting next to Ben, he seemed soft around the edges, like he had been someone tough once but had led a overly comfortable life in the years since.

George smiled. "Personally, I'd just as soon plan to die of old age."

Ben looked as though he were on the edge of a biting retort. Instead, he quietly said, "yeah, same here. I doubt we'll get there, but what the hell."

"Why's that?" George asked, leaning toward Ben slightly.

The big man laughed. There was humor in it but also a fair amount of derision, as though he could not imagine that someone relatively intelligent could have given voice to such a thought. He drawled, "'tween you, me, and the fencepost, I don't know how much chance humanity stands against some army of beady-eyed devils what come crawling up out the past to kill us all."

"Ever the pessimist," George accused. Before Ben could say anything in reply, he continued in a slightly more cordial tone, "me? I think we can take them on. They may have struck first, but we're American. Hell, we're human, and if a century of sci-fi movies have taught me anything, it's that humanity will find a way to survive."

"If I admire anything about you, Georgey, it's your optimism," Ben muttered.

"At least I still have one redeeming quality," he replied with a touch of bitterness. In a flash, all traces of anger were gone as he turned slightly and asked, "so what's the plan, Sam?"

"Right now? There isn't much of one. We were going to head for Ben's house and try to turn it into a fortress."

George nodded. "I," he eyed Ben, "can get behind that. What are you basing your plans on?"

"How much supply we have," Sam answered. "Food, water, tools, weapons, vehicles. Anything that could help us, really, and..."

"Earlier," Ben said, butting in. Sam was familiar enough with him, and expected him to have something useful to add, that she let him talk. He continued, "you said something about your van? You're still driving the creeper van?"

"I've still got the red Chevy, if that's what you mean," George replied with a small, but obvious, roll of his eyes. "I only drive it when I have to haul a lot of stuff—like today. Michael's got an Outback stuffed full as well. I did actually come here to help, you know."

Ben's eyes narrowed slightly. "I know," he said. "We wouldn't've contacted you if we thought you wouldn't help."

George nodded, but said nothing. The self-satisfied look on his face was enough communication for the moment. To Sam, he said, "anyway, if you're making plans based on what we've got on hand, you'll probably want to see what we brought."

"Good idea."

"Want me to start bringing stuff in?" George asked. With a wave at the boxes from Sam's apartment, he added, "looks like you've already got a lot here."

"Everything from my apartment," she said.

"We inventory, then we haul ass to my place," Ben said. Trying to be civil with George Sinon was surprisingly easier than he expected. Perhaps enough time had passed since the last time they had seen one another, he thought. Aloud, he said, "you ain't gotta unload anything here. You make a list of what you brought?"

George shook his head. "Started to, but after I got the important stuff, I just threw everything I could think of into the van and forgot the list. I made a few of my own calls to people, then headed over here. Michael was the only one who answered, so I picked him up on the way. That's why we're late." He stood up. "Let's go take a look at the van. I can give you a general rundown of what's in the boxes if I can see them. We can go through your stuff after we do mine, Michael," George added.

"Sounds good," Michael said, standing to follow the others. They made their way out of the apartment in a short line.

"So what do you bring to this little party?" Ben asked, slowing his stride to walk beside Michael. He was about Owen's height with black hair and a beard that did not quite, yet, merit the badge of "bushy."

"Not much, I'm afraid," he admitted. "I can play the drum and a few other instruments and sing a little. I never really was the outdoorsy type beyond going hiking here and there in the Smokies."

"You a quick learner?"

"I think so? I mean, I've never really had to pick up a life-or-death skill. I've got rhythm, for whatever that's worth. Drumline."

Ben laughed. "I played snare in drumline way the hell back when."

"My sympathies."

Ben laughed again.

"Here we are," George called from the front of their small group. They stood next to an old, beat-up, burgundy panel van. Rust dotted one corner where it had been backed into something more durable than it's bumper. The paint was at least a third primer and the windows were clouded over with a grimy mixture of pollen and dirt. In addition to the dirt, it sat low on its wheels, like the suspension had been broken and poorly repaired.

"You drove that?" Sam exclaimed.

"Yep," George replied. "I've had this ugly thing for, damn, sixteen years now. Bought it for eight hundred dollars right out of high school and kept it running for the last ten years to haul things around."

"What for?" Sam asked, still obviously surprised that something so ungainly and in such poor repair could still be road worthy.

"What do you mean 'what for?'" George asked, fighting to get his key to turn in the van's back door lock.

"I mean what could you need something this size for?"

"'Abducting people' comes to mind," Ben muttered, out of George's hearing.

"I used to work in construction," George said in answer to Sam's question. "So I had to haul around a bunch of tools and materials." After another few moments worth of struggle, his key turned and he opened the first door. He stopped, shrugged, and continued, "afterward, I kept it running in case I ever needed to haul anything big. You know, help people move, go pick up things from the hardware store, prep for the apocalypse, that sort of thing."

Even before he unlatched the other door, Owen could see that George had been telling the truth about how much he had packed. Unless they were all shoved against the back of the van for dramatic effect, the run-down vehicle had been literally packed full.

Behind him, Ben whistled. "Impressive," he said. His voice had the tone of grudging admiration Ben would get when confronted with something the existence of which he did not particularly want to admit, despite it being right in front of his face. "You still don't do nothin' half way."

"Nope," George agreed. "Still want to try and inventory things out here?"

"How secure are the locks?" Sam asked absently, stepping closer to try and peer between the stacks of boxes and get a feel for how much might be packed in there.

George laughed. "It's hard enough sometimes to get the actual key to turn."

Sam hummed thoughtfully, then tapped on the body of the van with her knuckles. She was answered with a dull, metallic thud. Old though it might be, it was obviously still sturdy, she thought to herself. "Open the side door?"

"Yeah, sure," George said, threading his way around the crowd at the rear of the van.

The side door's lock turned easier than the one on the back door had, but he still had to wiggle the key back and forth several times before getting the lock to disengage. He opened the door, revealing another sea of boxes and plastic totes. Behind the driver's seat was even a metal desk that looked like it had been salvaged from a Navy warship. Even the passenger seat was piled high with things, mostly soft-sided bags and backpacks.

Sam ran one hand across the inside of the side door's window like a potter checking for damage. "Windows ever been broken?"

"Five or six years ago, why?"

Sam thought for a minute, folding her arms across her chest. Having everything inside meant that they could keep a collective eye on it and she would have an exact idea of their resources. On the other hand, unloading—more importantly, reloading in the morning—that many boxes would be a royal pain.

"Lock it up tight," she ordered. "Give me a rough rundown of what you brought once we're back inside, but we don't need to go through it until we get to Ben's house tomorrow."

"Done and done," George slammed the heavy, metal side door and locked it. Moving to the rear of the van again, he said over his shoulder, "Michael, go ahead and unlock your beastie."

The group, momentarily without George, walked a few yards to where the other car, a station wagon only slightly newer than George's van but in better shape, was parked. Like the van, it was packed tight with boxes and bags.

"I'll go ahead and tell you guys," Michael confessed, unlocking the tailgate, "the locks on this thing aren't near as strong as the ones on George's van, and," he tapped on one of the wagon's fenders, producing a hollow rattle, "it's definitely not as sturdy."

"Makes me think we should bring this stuff inside," Ben said. He addressed the comment more toward Sam than anyone.

She reached out and opened the wagon's rear window, feeling around for the latch. She found it, frowned, wiggled the window on its hinges, and frowned deeper. "We'll unload this one," she said finally taking a step away from the wagon. Over her shoulder, she added for Michael's benefit, "no offense intended."

"None taken," he replied. "The van's a tank compared to this thing. I'll help you move the boxes inside."

"Let's do it!" Ben shouted, pleased to have a task to focus on.

Chapter 3

The hour was late when they finally finished unloading Michael's car. Between the boxes and things inside and the things strapped to the roof rack, he probably had as much packed away as George had, but none of it was as secure. Owen and Ben made dinner while George and Sam worked on their logistics.

After dinner, they broke up into small groups to relax. Michael fetched a small Celtic drum from his luggage and played a soft beat that did a lot to ease their frayed nerves.

When they, by mutual assent, agreed it was time to sleep, Ben claimed couch first. George and Michael inflated a pair of air mattresses in the living room floor, and Owen and Sam retired to his room.

For his part, Owen did not sleep well.

In his dreams that night, Owen rode at the head of a great army. His horse was black as night, black as the jacket he wore. The sky overhead was black as well, and storm clouds boiled amid thunder and lightning, billowing in great stacks like the smoke from the capitol. The air was clear for the moment, but the smell of ozone hung thick around him, a leftover reminder of the storm that had turned the hard ground into mud. No matter how many massed behind him, they were still outnumbered by the horde ahead.

Some miles away, another army stood ready. Across the impossibly flat plain, Owen could make them out as a blur on the horizon, stretching from one edge of his peripheral vision to the other. They moved, writhing and twisting around each other like piranha ready for the kill. Their dark silhouettes merged seamlessly with the storm clouds overhead. The rain must still be over them, he thought, because no human army had such an indistinct outline. No light of any kind burned in their midst.

Unlike the battlefields of his daydreams, he was not dressed like a soldier in some grand nineteenth-century army. He wore his black fencing jacket and gloves. The mesh of his mask sat comfortably close around his face, letting the breeze from the edge of the storm cool the sweat beading on his forehead. A sword hung at his side, not the blade he was used to sparring with, but a real saber with a razor-sharp edge.

Ben rode to his right in his charcoal-gray gambeson, another anachronism. His big frame was borne up by an ever bigger horse, one which dwarfed Owen's own mount. Neither of them had ever ridden together like this before, but that fact seemed of little importance at the moment. He held a huge basket-hilted sword in his hand.

To Owen's left was a much smaller figure. Obscured by a fencing mask, but definitely female, he had no idea who she might be until he saw the red hair dangling below the leather pad on the back of the mask. A saber, like his, hung off of her waist.

Sam on one side, he thought, and Ben on the other. Suddenly, the dark horde marching toward him seemed less of a threat. With the two of them by his side, and the army at his back, they could take on anyone, no matter how numerous.

"Every defense has a weakness," he muttered, then repeated it louder as a crash of thunder drowned out Ben's reply. He heard it in Sam's voice, too, but never was sure if she said it or if it was just in his head.

"They're coming!" Sam's sharp call cut through the noise of a second thunder clap, a roaring rumble that turned into the sound of a million charging hooves.

Owen blinked.

The dark horde that had been menacing from the edge of sight was suddenly in his face. Up close, they were indescribably terrifying. Gold eyes peered out above needle-lined mouths in faces the color of ash.

In another eyeblink, they were within striking distance. They came together, clashed, and Owen blinked again.

* * *

He opened his eyes with a start and came upright in his bed, ready to do battle with the enemy charging him. Instead, he saw the dark of his bedroom. His heart, soaked with adrenaline, jackhammered in his chest. His breath came in ragged gasps and the sweaty sheets around him felt clammy. Slowly, he forced himself to be calm, to unclench his fists and release the wads of sheet they had grabbed.

Beside him, Sam stirred. She was normally a heavy sleeper, but he had awoken so violently that it woke her up as well.

"Owen?" she asked sleepily, rolling over to face him. "Is everything alright?"

"Yeah," he replied. His breathing took a second longer to get under control, then he continued, "just a dream."

"What about?"

He sighed. "The Korovega. You and Ben were there."

She smiled, sliding up into a sitting position. "Did we win?"

"I," he paused, "I don't know. I woke up just as they attacked. It didn't look good, though. It's fading now, like any other dream. Just images, terror."

Sam was silent for a long time, searching for the right thing to say. She wanted to be reassuring, to tell him that his fear was only the uncertainty he felt every time he sparred with a new opponent. But she had seen the footage of the Korovega attacking the capital, watched them slaughter trained soldiers with modern weapons. She had to believe that their chances were better though, because the alternative would be devastating.

In lieu of anything to say, she reached out a hand and placed it gently on his shoulder. They had slept in the same bed plenty of times and even the relatively intimate touch was nothing new, but it did what she wanted it to do. Some of the tension melted away from the muscle under her hand and they sat there for a minute in silence before she finally spoke.

"What's on your mind?"

"I wish I knew how to fight them. I almost wish they would march on Knoxville or Oak Ridge so that I could stand in their way and make them pay for what they've done." He spoke quietly; his apartment was terrible for sound bleeding from one room to another. He wanted to let everyone else sleep—if they could.

"Just you?"

"If I have to."

Her hand on his shoulder, almost forgotten, tightened momentarily. "Don't forget your dream. If anything, you've got me and Ben to stand with you."

"Yeah," he said. Then, "what time is it?"

She turned, picked her phone up off of the nightstand. "Four in the morning. Try and get some more sleep, ok?"

He nodded, slowly sinking back down into the sheets. Sam followed a moment later. He needed to sleep, but at that moment, all he could think about was the Korovega. Images kept flashing in his mind, haunting him. His mind raced, filled with thoughts, theories, plans of how to fight them that all depended on knowledge he just did not have.

He tossed and turned, eluded by sleep for another hour, until finally Sam rolled toward him and laid an arm lightly across his chest. That was all he needed just then—human contact—and he drifted off to sleep shortly afterward.

* * *

In the morning, Owen felt anything but rested. The Korovega nightmare never returned, but he still slept poorly afterward. He stayed there, alternately staring at the ceiling and the morning light streaming in through the east-facing window, for nearly fifteen minutes. Something tugged at the back of his brain. Eventually, he gave up trying to pin down what was worrying him, instead attributing it—with little concern at that particular moment—to nothing more than the end of the world.

That thought amused him. Not that civilization was on the brink of destruction at the hands of some ancient evil, rather that he was so nonchalant about it after the nightmare that had interrupted his sleep.

Was it really that unimportant? He asked himself. Or was it just, as Sam was fond of reminding him, that laughter proved he was still alive?

Either way, he and his friends had things to do before the next sunset. He had every intention of making it to Ben's house long before then, though. If—no, he corrected himself, when—the Korovega showed up in the area, he wanted to be as far from concentrated civilization as possible. He hated to think that way, to think about throwing an entire city under the proverbial bus so that he and his friends could survive, but the logical place for an invading army to strike would be the larger cities.

He decided to discontinue that line of thought.

Sam was already awake and elsewhere in the apartment. That was nothing new—while he had always prided himself on being a morning person, her idea of "sleeping late" was "missing the sunrise" most mornings. He heard low voices, Sam's and someone else speaking too quiet to be identified just then. He smelled coffee brewing, which told him that Sam had not been up for long.

The fact that there was still coffee to be had told him Ben was still asleep.

Owen crept into the living room, looking around to see who else, if anyone, was still asleep. George lay sprawled out on the air mattress he had inflated against the wall behind the dinner table; the other one was empty. Sam and George's friend Michael, who had taken the other air mattress, were standing in the kitchen talking and drinking coffee when he came in.

"...called me yesterday afternoon and told me he had a plan to stay alive," Michael was saying as Owen caught their eyes.

Sam smiled. "You're awake. I assumed you'd stay in bed a little longer after how bad you slept."

He shook his head. "Couldn't sleep any more."

"More dreams?" Sam asked.

Owen shook his head again. "No, just couldn't sleep any more," he replied. "It was either get up and come see what you all were doing or stay in bed and drown in some pretty black thoughts."

Michael smiled, trying his best to look positive. "Sam's been filling me in on your plan. I like what I'm hearing."

Wordlessly, Sam turned and poured a third cup of coffee and handed it to Owen. He took it automatically. Sam enjoyed fancy sorts of coffee and had mixed cream, sugar, and a small pinch of spices into the mug first. He had to admit; it might not have been tea, but the beverage in his hands was rather nice.

"Anything to add, now that you've slept on it?" Sam asked, picking up her own mug.

To Owen's surprise, Michael looked slightly embarrassed. He made an odd face, then said, "no, sorry. I'm really only here because George called me and told me about you guys."A moment passed and, as if he realized how negatively his statement could be taken, he quickly added, "not that I'm not glad to be here! I just... I don't know. 'Surviving the end of the world' was never on my to do list."

Owen laughed quietly. "Yeah, me neither. But we play the hand we're dealt, yeah?"

Michael smiled in return. He seemed to be feeding off of the confidence Owen exuded, even if Owen himself felt very little of it.

"Yeah, but I don't have any skills that are any good at keeping people alive."

Owen shrugged. "You play a right smart drum, that's for sure."

"Thanks," he replied.

"And so what if you don't have any skills now," Owen added.

"What do you mean?"

Owen shrugged. "I've never gone hunting, never had to worry about purifying my own water. I've built a few things over the years, but never more than a wall or two of something that I actually had to live in." He sighed. "I suspect there's going to be a lot of learning going on."

"But you've got your sword, and Ben's got his sword at his house, and Sam and Ben have their guns. I have... a drum."

Owen clapped Michael on the shoulder. "Morale's important, even if you never learn to fight. If you can keep the rest of us in good spirits, then we might just walk out of hell alive."

"And Sam's the brains, yeah?" Michael asked, grinning.

"One of us has to be," she replied, grinning. She poked Owen in the ribs.

"Are you you..." Michael asked, pointing at Sam and Owen in turn.

"Are we?" Sam asked, not quite sure where he was going with his question, even though she realized a moment later that his implication was obvious.

"You know," he said. "Together."

Neither Owen nor Sam was sure who started laughing first, but both of them dissolved relatively quickly into laughter that was just quiet enough not to wake George where he was sleeping nearby.

"That would be a 'no,'" Owen said after catching his breath.

"Really?" Michael asked. "But you two slept together last night, and..."

"Slept in the same bed," Sam corrected. "We don't exactly have a lot of sleeping room here."

"She slept on the couch the night before last," Owen added.

"You two seem very compatible, though," Michael said.

Owen and Sam eyed each other again but managed to avoid another fit of laughter.

"We are," Owen admitted after a moment. "We've known each other for years, and..."

"We can practically finish each other's sentences?" Sam asked. Her mouth quirked into a wry grin.

"Yes," Owen said. "That. Truth is, we grew up together and never saw one another that way."

"Cool," Michael said with a smile. "I just, I don't know, thought you two would be good together."

"We are," Sam replied. "But not like that."

"Were a team!" Owen held his fist out dramatically.

Sam rolled her eyed and fist bumped him, but then, with sincerity, said, "in essence, yeah."

"Are we all..." Michael began, then stopped.

"All what?" Owen asked.

"Are we all a team?"

"Hell," Sam muttered. "Right now all of humanity ought to be a team. But, yeah, the five of us are a team."

"And anyone else we come across," Owen added.

"Anyone else we can trust," Sam corrected.

"Do you trust me?" Michael asked. The tone of his voice suggested that he would be surprised at an answer that began with anything other than, "no."

Owen eyed him for a moment, suddenly wondering if he did, in fact, trust him. After all, he had never met the man before yesterday and George Sinon was not exactly known for keeping the best of company at times. Real trust, the, "hand them a gun a close your eyes," sort of trust, would come much later if it ever came, but he had no real reason to actively distrust Michael either.

"You didn't kill me in my sleep last night and take off with all of my canned food," Owen said, putting what he hoped was a light tone in his voice, "so I guess I trust you."

Michael smiled. "Alright, Captain. What's the plan for today?"

"'Captain?'" Owen asked with a cock of one eyebrow.

Michael shrugged. "It seemed appropriate. If you don't like it..."

"I don't mind it."

Behind him, Sam rolled her eyes again. "Another thing to inflate your ego," she said, poking at his shoulder. "Anyway, the plan is to pack everything we can fit into the vehicles we have and head for Ben's house as soon as possible."

"Doesn't that require someone to wake him and George up?"

"You want to do the honors?" Sam asked, and Michael nodded. "Owen, can you get Ben up?"

"Can do," Owen replied. He turned, finally looking directly at the couch where Ben was sleeping. Not only was it shorter than he was, forcing the big man into almost a fetal position, but the blanket he had been sleeping under was really more of a lap blanket than a sleeping blanket and barely covered his muscular torso.

"He looks like a cartoon," Owen muttered, laughing to himself and shaking his head.

* * *

After breakfast, and after cleaning up the kitchen as a group, George suggested turning the news on again, because none of them had yet checked it that morning. They all gathered around the couch. The area in front of Owen's TV was never intended to hold more than three people at a time and no one had very much room, but they managed to fit all five of them. Michael sat in the floor, Ben sat on one end of the couch, then Owen, then George. Sam perched on the arm and used Ben's shoulder at a back rest.

Thus far, the news had not been good. They repeated the images of the capitol burning, interspersed with shots of Hereg Solsinis, the Korovega's king. In still shots, many provided by cell phones, but some of high quality, he looked even less human. He had all the right features, but Owen's initial impression of them being slightly off was reinforced each time the TV showed another shot of his face.

Sam stood up, stretched, and went back to the table. She said she would check the news later; she had work to do. Owen followed. On the couch, Michael considered sitting between Ben and George, but, despite their almost tolerant attitudes toward one another, the electric tension directly between them was too much even for Michael to take and he stayed on the floor.

The national news started to loop, they changed the channel. Ben decided on a local station instead.

"...as you can see from this orbital imagery of Washington DC," the haggard-looking reporter said. She was backed not by the standard screens and animated pleasantries of the newsroom but by the blank concrete walls of a bunker. In front of her, she held a large tablet with a dim, brown image on its small screen.

"Whatever it is the Korovega have done," she continued, "the capital has, for all intents and purposes, been completely destroyed."

Ben had to admire her resolve. Despite the wide-eyed look on her face, the reporter's voice barely wavered. The display of professionalism, even though he was sure she was nothing like that when the cameras were off, was grounding for him.

She held up the tablet which quickly filled the TV screen as the camera zoomed. The image it showed was of the entire area surrounding Washington. At its center was the brown-gray smudge that the national news had called a "blight." Whatever was causing it, the reporters had been clear that it was simply dry and dusty dirt, not ash or any kind of pseudo-magical destruction.

The image zoomed in, manipulated from a mirrored screen on the back face of the tablet, until it showed the area around the capitol building and the National Mall. The grass had turned brown-gray and lifeless, and the reflecting pool's water had been drained, leaving a tepid puddle of brackish sludge in the bottom.

Worse than the grass were the buildings. What little remained of The Washington Monument listed to one side. Rubble from the once-proud obelisk had been strewn at its base, left there when then Korovega blasted the tower to pieces one floor at a time. Other buildings in the area showed a similar state of damage as the image panned around. Broken glass, crushed bricks and stone, and a fine brown-gray powder covered everything.

The image was just that, a single image. Nothing moved of course, but Ben got the distinct feeling that even if the satellite had somehow captured video, that nothing would be moving anyway. There would be no birds, no animals, no breeze to stir the blight dust, no life at all left in the land.

The image blanked out momentarily, then was replaced with another similar scene. From behind the tablet, the reporter continued speaking. "We have similar images from across the world. The Korovega have blighted Pyongyang," the image shifted again, "Canberra," another series of fast shifts during which the anchor's voice nearly broke into sobbing more than once, "Moscow, Berlin, Khartoum, London, Johannesburg, Tel Aviv, Bagdad, and scores of others."

The camera zoomed back out to show the reporter as she set the tablet face down on her desk. "Communications with several imaging satellites were severed shortly after the Korovega began spreading the blight across Washington D.C.. We believe nothing has happened to the satellites themselves, but the groundside links to many of them have been destroyed. Workers at NASA are trying to reestablish contact with them right now.

"Current conditions there are unknown," she continued, "and will likely remain unknown until we are either able to reestablish communications, another agency that still has satellite imaging capability makes contact, or we are able to safely regain control over the blighted area.

"As yet," she went on, managing to maintain composure despite the grim subject matter it was her job to report, "we have no information on the blight, other than the complete dehydration of the area. Also unknown is the exact size of the blighted area and whether or not it is expanding."

The image shifted slightly. The same reporter was on the screen still, but her clothes looked slightly more rumpled. The dark circles under her eyes were darker, the worry lines on her face deeper. Sweat stained her now-unbuttoned collar. Much of the composure she showed before had been lost as the imagery changed from something prerecorded to a live feed.

"Since we recorded that segment last night, teams working around Washington D.C. have managed to enter the area. They broadcast live at seven AM this morning, and then distributed the footage online.

"What follows is all we know. Warning," she said, then choked down a lump in her throat, "the footage you are about to see is graphic. Viewer... viewer discretion is advised."

The screen blanked for a moment, then showed a scene of Washington D.C.. Like the image the anchor had been showing, everything was the brown-gray of dry, dead vegetation. No animals moved on the ground, but some sort of bird whose silhouette failed to match any vulture or bird of prey any of them had seen before circled overhead.

"We're here on the ground," a lone man announced. He wore a sweat-soaked tshirt, likely the only remnant of whatever professional suit he had put on that morning, and was sweating liberally from his face and head. Already, his skin was covered in brown dust. A keffiyeh-style scarf covered his face. "As you can see behind me, everything here in DC is dry. From pictures," a few of which flashed up onto the screen, "we know when the Korovega left the area they left some sort of device here that seems to be the source of the dryness."

He walked on. "Eyewitnesses at the time talked about suddenly feeling thirsty and scratchy. One described it to me like being in a sauna, but not hot. I can attest to that personally. I don't think I've ever felt quite so thirsty as I do right now."

He fished a water bottle out of a pocket and drank heavily from it. After taking it away from his lips, moisture seemed to steam out of the opening of the bottle. He capped it tightly and replaced his scarf.

"A few moments after the initial feeling of dryness, a thunderstorm rolled in. It dissipated in minutes, and doesn't seem to have left any water on or in the ground. That tells me we've got a massive pressure differential here.

"Anyway, I'm going to try and get close to it to see what, if anything I can figure out."

From off camera, a voice asked, "are you sure that's a good idea?"

He laughed and shook his head, sending beads of sweat flying. "Not really, but once I realized what this thing was doing," he paused, laughed again, "well, someone had to check it out."

They walked on a moment, moving with the sluggish pace of roofers after a long day in the sun, before he turned back to the camera. "On a serious note, someone needs to figure out how bad this thing is. All of the water it's pulling out of the air and the ground has to go somewhere, and if it's not going back into the water cycle, it's going to be a lot worse than a few dry areas."

He stopped, now close to the rubble of the Ulysses S. Grant Memorial. An object stood in the grass twenty or thirty feet away. It was crystalline, with six sides and a wider base than top. The top narrowed dramatically to a point, but was otherwise featureless.

As far away from it as they were, it seemed nothing so much as a chunk of blackened quartz. Without anything near it in the shot, guessing its size was hard. If this was the obelisk they had been mentioning, it seemed a small thing to be doing the amount of damage it had done to the area.

"It's definitely drier here," the man said. He worked his mouth for a moment, as though trying to work up some saliva with which to talk, but failed. His voice had grown hoarse. "I suspect that if I got much closer, I would start to see even more negative side-effects."

He looked straight at the camera, took a long swig of water and, in a voice that was now just barely hoarse, said, "if this thing is doing what it feels like it's doing, and it doesn't stop, we could be looking at it emptying the water tables here. Right now, I have," another swig of water, "I've got no idea how wide an area it's really affecting, or how much it's going to affect.

"If it doesn't stop, if it keeps sucking up water and not depositing it anywhere, we could be looking at a complete disruption of the planet's water cycle, wrecking the biosphere in the process, and..."

"Matt!" the offscreen voice shrieked.

He and the camera both looked up. The bird-things were circling them now, and they had dropped much lower than they had been when the two weathermen first arrived. One of them specifically, was even lower than the rest.

The cameraman took a slow step away.

The bird that had descended from the circling crowd resembled a monstrous eagle. Vivid black and white coloring on its broad wings stood in stark contrast to the sky above. Long, thick legs trailed from its body, already extended to strike and grab. The heavy, hooked beak backed by fiery red eyes was locked on the weatherman.

The big eagle flared its wings, dumping speed, and reached its legs out even further as the doomed meteorologist put his hands in front of his eyes. The bird latched onto his arms with its claws and flapped twice, regaining momentum and sending the man tumbling backward.

Flat on his back, he flailed ineffectually at the bird as it struck and tore at his arms and face with its claws.

The camera panned away and shook as the reporter holding it fled as fast as his dehydrated muscles would carry him. Behind him, screams of anger pain turned into screams of fear and pain, and then into crushing silence.

A shadow crossed the ground in front of the fleeing cameraman and the screen blanked. A moment later, the feed resumed, showing the same bunker-like room and the same hollow-eyed anchor.

"The time is now 9:47 AM, Eastern Standard. We do not yet have confirmation about the status of the President or Vice President. More that four hundred members of Congress are also unaccounted for. May God have mercy on us all."

"Turn it off," Ben said, gazing intently at the cup of coffee cradled in his hands.

"Shit's getting real," George muttered, pointing the remote at the TV and hitting the power button.

"Shit's been real," Ben growled, looking away and watching Sam and Owen for a moment.

They had commandeered the small dining table, covering it with paper and electronics as they made their plans. Over the course of the forty-five minute broadcast, the two of them had raised their voices a dozen times or more as they attacked the problem of survival from as many avenues as possible, taking their frustrations out on one another for lack of anywhere else for the tension to go.

It was like watching two halves of the same person arguing, Ben thought. One would start a thought, then the other would run with it or discard it, and the cycle would begin again. He thought he heard less than a dozen complete sentences as they went back and forth. Instead, they bounced concepts off of one another, each seeming to have its own conversation attached to it, but no one outside of the two of them could ever hear it.

"We are so screwed," Michael muttered.

"No," Ben snapped, harsher than he had intended, "we ain't."

"Yeah, we pretty much are," Michael argued, though his voice had little strength.

"No," Ben repeated, firmer. "We ain't."

"Yesterday, didn't you say..." Michael started, but Ben interrupted him.

"Yesterday was yesterday. I've slept since then. World looks a whole lot better after a decent night's sleep," he said. Slightly louder he added, "even on Owen's shitty couch!"

Owen either ignored the remark or was so buried in whatever it was he and Sam were working on at that moment that he missed it completely. Ben made a dismissive wave and turned back to George and Michael. "Listen," he said, "I do my best thinking before I fall asleep, and I think we can beat this."

"So that's your secret," George muttered.

"Shut it, Sinon," Ben barked. "Anyway. I was thinking, if there's enough of these Korovega to kill us all at once, they'd do it. Instead, they hit our capitals. Big cities are probably next, right?"

George nodded. As much as he wanted to argue solely because it was Ben's idea, he had to admit the man's logic was clear so far.

Ben continued. "That means there ain't all that many of them, right?"

"I suppose so," Michael admitted.

"I figure we got a pretty decent chance of surviving if we all put our heads together," Ben said. Louder, he added, "Course, that means we gotta get our asses in gear!"

"Working on it," Sam replied around pen a clenched almost stereotypically in her teeth, never looking up from her laptop. She had another tucked into her ponytail, leaving Ben to wonder what she needed with two of them at once, and when she would tuck a third one behind her ear.

"I hate to say it," George said, turning to face Michael, and consequently putting his back to Ben, "but the big guy's right this time."

Ben snorted. "'This time?'"

"I'm agreeing with you. Shut up and take the compliment," George quipped over his shoulder. To Michael, he added, "We've got enough skills between the five of us that we ought to be able to live a pretty long time. I've got enough chemicals and equipment to outfit a hell of a lot more people than this with clean water and maybe even power if the Korovega don't decide to blot out the sun next."

"Don't give them ideas," Michael said.

"Then we will fight in the shade," Ben said, quoting one of his favorite movies.

"Pretty much." George found himself agreeing almost pleasantly. "The brain trust over there," he pointed at the table where Owen and Sam looked to be wrapping up their planning session, "could probably out maneuver George Patton at a game of RISK. And Ben can..."

"Ben can what?" Ben asked when George failed to finish his sentence.

"He'll keep us fed," George said. "Clean water won't do us any good if all we have to eat is blighted grass. Better make a bunch of jerky and stock up on dried beans and rice while we can."

"That's the plan," Owen said, sliding his chair away from the table. "Alright, we've gone over everything we have here. Between my stuff, Sam's stuff, the stuff we brought in from Michael's station wagon, and George's packing list, the best answer we can come up with is that when we get to Ben's house we..."

Sam interrupted. "The short version is that we strip this place bare of everything we can pack into the vehicles. Right now, anything that has any utility is needed."

"What about furniture?" George asked.

"We'll take what we can," Sam replied, "but small items come first."

Chapter 4

Packing the vehicles went smoothly for a while, but hit a bump when Owen and George began to argue over what was needed and what they ought to leave behind. George objected to anything that did not have immediate utility, but Owen argued, with Sam's support, that it was necessary to bring some keepsakes, "to remember what they were fighting for." George backed off, but not without reminding Owen that useful things still came first.

Later, when George admitted that not all of his boxes and things were packed as tightly as they possibly could be, the five of them hurriedly unloaded the large van and repacked as much as possible. In the end, they were able to fit a few extra paper boxes worth of supplies. That left more than enough room for the rest of the things they deemed "essential" in the other cars.

That left only one problem.

"We're still running out of space," George grumbled. He leaned lightly against the iridescent blue motorcycle strapped to a rack attached to the rear of Sam's car. He turned to Owen. "If we take this thing, we can't use the trailer to haul things we need."

"'This thing,'" Sam growled. She had quickly grown tired of George's constant desire to be her center of attention. "Is mine, and it's going to be a lot more useful in the long run than my little sedan will."

George threw up his hands. Even he, who had spent most of the morning putting on a pleasant face, was nearing the limit of tension he could shrug off. "Right, right. Sorry. Your motorcycle; not a thing. Right. Point is, how important is it really? We've got one more vehicle than we have people."

Sam shrugged. He had a point, much as it galled her to admit it. George himself was not the problem, it was his idea. That motorcycle had been the first, and only, vehicle she bought new off the lot. The car it was attached to—the car whose shocks might not even make it to Ben's house—was barely nicer than a junker. She kept it around because there were times where a motorcycle was, surprisingly, not convenient.

However, it went a lot farther on less gasoline than her car, and did so faster. Once they were done hauling things around, she expected—no, she knew—that Big Blue would be worth a lot more than her sedan.

She articulated those thoughts, and George admitted that, maybe, bringing the motorcycle was a good idea.

"What're you two carrying on about?" Ben demanded, shouldering his way into the conversation. He grinned, but like the others, he found that particular facade to be growing more difficult to maintain the longer they labored in the sun.

Sam explained the situation. When George tried to talk over her, she spoke louder and faster. A gesture from Ben hushed him the rest of the way.

Once she was finished, he turned to George and asked, "you wanted to add something?"

It took him a moment to respond. His face said that he already made up his mind that Ben was not going to let him speak, and the surprise took a moment to overcome. Finally, he said, slowly, "not really," then, "I mean, Sam covered everything I was going to say. We could take a lot more if we didn't take her motorcycle."

Ben nodded. "He's right, you know."

Sam nodded once, reluctantly. "I know."

"But?"

"But, first, we've already gotten everything we need from the apartment. Second," she gestured to her car, which sat low to the ground, then to George's van, which struggled under its own load. Nearby, Ben's surplus police interceptor seemed to be the least burdened. "I don't know how useful my car is going to be in a few weeks or even a few days. Big Blue, however, will be useful until and unless we run out of gas."

Ben turned to George, looming. It was clear whose side he was on, though Sam looked askance at him because of it. She wondered how much of his position was coming down on her side of things and how much was coming down against George.

"Got anything to add?" he asked.

"Not really," George admitted.

"We're keeping it," Sam said. She crossed her arms in front of her chest. Coming from someone her height, the image might have been petulant, she had certainly gotten that response before, but the muscles that stood out on her shoulders around the straps of her tank top told another story.

"It's." George closed his eyes, grit his teeth, and sighed. He opened them again a moment later. "It's your call."

Ben turned to look at Sam. "Come on," he said, gesturing back toward the apartment. "Let's go see if there's anything else we need from inside."

Sam looked at him funny for a moment before he winked conspiratorially and nodded once.

"Yeah, alright," she said.

"Owen!" Ben called to where the latter was helping Michael cram one last box into his station wagon. "You sure we scoured the place? Don't want you mad at me tomorrow 'cause some fancy nick-nack got left behind."

"I checked over everything," he replied, "but it can't hurt to check again."

"Good idea," Ben said, drawing the words out and laying the sarcasm on thick. He motioned for Sam to follow him. After they were a few meters away, he added quietly, "and it'll let me get away from George."

"Seriously," Sam said. "What's with you two? I mean, he strikes me as a little annoying, and he's definitely paying me more attention than you or Owen, if you catch my drift, but he doesn't really seem like a bad guy."

"We got history," was all Ben would say.

"I can see that. Are you going to tell me what that history is?" When Ben refused to answer, Sam continued pressing. "What? Did he kick your dog? Steal your car? Was there a woman?"

Ben's dark face flushed ever-so-slightly darker but he stubbornly refused to speak. Instead, he turned and stepped between Sam and the door to Owen's apartment. The moment he needed to open the door allowed the warmth in his face to fade back to normal.

Sam stepped around him as he shut the door. "You know," she said, putting a hurt look on her face that she knew Ben could see right through. "Most men would jump at the chance to spill their guts about this kind of thing to a pretty redhead."

Ben snorted, grinned, then busted out laughing. "Ain't that the truth."

"So why won't you?"

"Ain't important no more."

Sam laughed. "'Ain't important,' he says. Obviously it is, otherwise you wouldn't be so hostile around him."

Ben shrugged. "Maybe. Maybe I got over her, but not over what he did."

"This is when when you tell me the 'old Ben' would say that it's a four beer kind of story, right?"

"The old Ben would'a called this one a six or seven beer story," he replied. The blank look on his face told Sam that his comment was not as sarcastic as she first thought.

"Damn," she muttered.

"Eventually," he promised.

"Eventually?" Sam asked. She laughed, making a noise that might charitably have been called a giggle if it was a little less dark. "Right before the Korovega gut us all?"

Ben laughed. "Something like that. Whose bright idea was it to leave the two of us alone in here, anyway? We keep this up and there's gonna be serious all over the place when Owen and the other guys come back inside."

"And we can't have that."

* * *

The parking lot was a buzz of activity. Other people were loading cars, some in even larger groups than Owen and Sam had organized. There were however less people present than lived in the complex; that much was obvious simply by comparing the crowd to the number of cars in the parking lot. Some of them would invariably stay; that was human nature, after all, and people always tried to ride out disasters in the comfort of their own living rooms, confident that it would never reach them. Others, either smarter or more afraid, were on their way out.

Most of the cars driving around were leaving, which actually proved the easiest part of the ordeal. No one wanted to stop anyone from getting out and once the evacuees were loaded and in their cars, they wanted nothing more than to be on their way as fast as possible.

A dark green Jeep pulled into the parking lot, one of the few vehicles on its way in rather than out. Whenever that happened, everyone took notice for a moment, then went back to packing. The people scattered around watched it with an air of excitement, and perhaps apprehension, as it circled the area, finally coming to a stop near Ben's Charger.

"Excuse me," the driver, a tan-skinned brunette called. "Do any of you know Ben Stuart?"

Owen jerked upright. "He's inside," he replied, dusting his hands off on his pants and approaching the jeep. "Can I help you?"

The woman looked around at the commotion, apparently decided that there was enough room in the steadily emptying parking lot for cars to drive around her, and killed the engine. She unbuckled and slid out of the doorless vehicle by the time Owen made it around to the driver's side.

"He said to meet him here," she replied.

Owen nodded, putting the logical pieces together. He was glad Ben, at least, was able to get in touch with more people. He held out a hand. "Owen Madoc."

She took his hand and shook it once. Her grip was strong and reminded him of shaking Ben's hand, only on a smaller scale. "Jessica Santiago," she replied. "Call me Jessie."

Owen clapped his hands together once, then immediately regretted the motion because it made him feel like a salesman, and smiled anyway. "Like I said, Ben stepped inside. Want me to introduce you to everyone?"

"Sure."

Owen turned and waved Jessie ahead.

"If you didn't hear," she started, "my name's Jessie. Ben called me."

George and then Michael introduced themselves.

"Looks like I barely made it in time," Jessie observed.

"I was going to leave instructions," Owen replied.

Jessie raised an eyebrow. "Instructions to find you don't make evac any easier."

Owen laughed. "True, but if I write, 'meet at Ben's house,' anyone we've tried to get in touch with will know where to go."

"Point," Jessie said. "Is there much else to load?"

Owen shook his head. "Not really. That's why Ben went inside. He and Sam are doing a once-over of the place before we lock up."

"If you've got an inventory going, do you want a copy of my packing list?"

Owen smiled, pleasantly surprised, and more than a little amused, by the offer. "That would be great. The best we've got is a general idea of what's where."

"You seem to be doing well enough," she observed.

"We've got a lot of smart people," Michael said.

Jessie laughed. "I hope I fit in, then."

Michael flushed, "that's not..."

Jessie's laugh grew louder. "Kidding, kidding. Friends with Ben and you're not used to a little ribbing?"

Michael grinned sheepishly. "Actually I just met Ben yesterday."

Jessie stopped laughing at that. "Oh, well," she paused, still stifling a bit of laughter, "in that case, I apologize."

"It's alright."

"What did you bring, anyway?" George asked, gesturing toward the back end of the Jeep.

Jessie gave a brief rundown while rummaging around in a bag in the passenger seat for the promised packing list. Her inventory consisted of food, clothes, weapons, the same sort of things they had spent three days now packing into their own vehicles.

The conversation drifted to the specifics of some of the machine parts and tools she packed—a subject in which George actually seemed more interested than he was in Jessie herself, Owen noted—when Michael announced that Ben was back.

One end of a tall stack of wide boards was tucked under Ben's arm. The other end, about six feet behind him, was balanced on Sam's shoulder. The two of them walked in step, carrying the heavy load balanced between them.

Owen, knowing Sam for most of his life and having seen the sort of things she was capable of, made no move to interrupt their progress. George, on the other hand, stopped what he was going and quickly sprinted towards Sam.

"Why didn't you come get one of the guys?" he asked. "Here, let me take that."

"I've got this, don't worry," Sam said. She would have rolled her eyes if all of her attention had not been on balancing the stack of shelving.

"Seriously, let me carry it for you," he insisted.

"I will drop this on your foot," Sam grunted. "All I need is for you to not stand in my way. We're almost to the parking lot."

"G'won," Ben said. "Outta the way."

George looked back to Sam for a moment, but the only response he got from her was a sideways nod in the direction of his van. Once he was out of earshot, Sam muttered, "you know, I appreciate the sentiment. I really do. I'm tiny for god's sake, but I'm also obviously not about to drop my end."

"Plus," Ben said in equally low tones, "you ever tried to hand off one end of a two-hundred pound stack of boards without settin' 'em down before?"

"Can't say I have."

"Don't. It's a bad idea."

"I assumed."

"Hold up," Ben said. When Sam stopped and he kept going, he quickly added, "no, no. Not really 'hold up.' I meant hold up, figuratively-like."

Sam caught up with a quick double step. "What is it?"

"No way! Hot damn, she actually made it! Jessie!"

"There you are!" she said. She grinned, gesturing toward Sam, "Making women pick up your slack again?"

Ben grinned. "Not five minutes and you're already on my case."

"That's not why you called me?"

"That's only part of why I called you," Ben replied with a mock haughty tone.

"Whatever the reason, I hurried here as quickly as I could. Apparently the Korovega haven't knocked out Google Maps yet."

He laughed, softly so as to avoid shaking the pile of shelves. "Small miracles, huh?"

"Something like that. Do you need a hand?"

He shook his head. "Naw. We're almost there. Just gonna drop these in the parking lot and Figure out where the crap I'm going to put them."

"You going to introduce me to your girlfriend, Ben?" Sam interjected.

"Hey now," Ben said as the three of them reached the parking lot and threaded between George's van and Owen's car. "She's not... hold on. Set your end down first."

"She's," Sam said, then grunted as she set the heavy shelves on the ground. A moment later, as the exertion caught up with her, she panted, "she's not what?"

"We're not dating," Jessie supplied. She folded her arms across her chest. Like Ben, the muscles on her forearms stood out like ropes under her tan skin. Sam wondered if she was a fighter like he had been when he was younger.

"Not for lack of trying," Ben said after setting his end of the shelves down on the pavement.

"I feel like there's a story there," Owen said, stepping around the shelves.

Jessie shrugged. "Ben asked me out a long time ago. I told him no, but he asked again a week later. So we went out for drinks, nothing happened, and..."

Ben interrupted with, "the short version," then, "is that we ended up sparring partners for a few years. She even helped me get sober."

"Then I moved away."

"Yeah!" Ben said, in a mock accusatory tone. "Then you moved away. I still ain't forgiven you for that."

"Yeah, well. Life called, and now life called me back here."

"By the by," Sam said, holding out one hand. She poked Ben in the ribs with the other one, saying, "I'm Sam Bennett, since Ben here decided not to introduce me."

Jessie took her hand and shook it vigorously. "Nice to meet you, Sam."

"You too," she replied automatically. "I'm guessing you've met everyone else already?"

Jessie nodded. "Yeah. Owen, is his name?"

Sam nodded. "Yeah."

Jessie continued. "He introduced me."

Ben turned to George who stood leaning against his van a little ways away. "Thanks for telling me Jessie was here, by the way."

"I assumed you could see her," he replied.

"To be fair, I was hiding," Jessie added with a smirk.

"Anyway," George said, "I dug these out of the van after Sam sent me back up here." He handed Ben a fistful of ratcheting tiedown straps. "Thought I'd be helpful."

"Thanks," he said. "This'll actually help."

"Anyone else hear that?" George asked. His voice dripped with sarcasm. "Ben just thanked me!"

"It happens," Owen said, jumping ahead of whatever hot retort was on the tip of Ben's tongue.

"You mind letting me use your roof rack?" Ben asked, ignoring George's jibe, or trying to, at any rate.

"For that?" George asked, gesturing to the stack of ex-bookshelves. "Sure."

"Then that's the last of it," Ben said. "I turned that place upside down. All that's left is furniture we can't use and stuff we don't need."

Owen nodded, satisfied. "Then I'll lock up and we'll be off."

* * *

"We're going about twenty miles to the North, on the other side of Andersonville," Owen said, addressing the small gathering. They had formed a circle around him in the apartment complex's parking lot, listening to him recite the plan he and Sam devised. He was unsure how he ended up in the center of the circle, or why it was him they were listening to in the first place, but those thoughts came only after he was halfway through his explanation. He had simply started talking and one by one they all gathered around—it struck him as almost eerie.

"Anyone else coming?" Jessie asked. She scanned their small group, looking for signs that others might have gone on ahead. "We can't be the only people you called."

Owen sighed. Contemplating what could happen to the people he was with was bad enough, but the thought of absent friends, some of whom he cared for almost as much as he cared for Sam or Ben, was painful.

"They know to call," Sam said. She turned slightly on one heel, angling her shoulders an inch or so. Owen did the opposite—a pair of gestures that was lost to everyone else in the circle, but between the two of them signaled a passing of the conversational torch. "If the Korovega..."

"When the Korovega," Ben interrupted. "Don't know what you're about to say, but chances are it's a 'when' not an 'if.'"

Sam resisted the urge to roll her eyes at Ben's pedantry. He was right and she knew it, but that changed nothing. Arguing about meaningless distinctions would get them nowhere.

"When the Korovega take out cell communications," she said, pointedly eyeing Ben, "if the apartment building is somehow still standing at that point, we left notes inside for people to follow. No addresses, because..."

"Because we don't know what sort of trash might follow us," George muttered.

Sam shot him a look that would have melted the armor on a tank. He tried to look defiant for a moment, then withered under her glare. A further moment under her sharp eyes and he found something else to pay attention to for the time being.

She snapped at him. "No one, no human being left alive in this blighted, damned world is trash. Understood?"

"Yes," he muttered.

"That goes for anyone we come across," she continued. "The moment the Korovega struck, everything else became meaningless. Everyone we save is another person to fight back against them."

"Sam," Jessie said tentatively. "What if... What if someone's beyond saving?"

Sam closed her eyes. Her sigh was short, tense. Finally, she answered. "We take care of our own, if that happens."

The atmosphere grew heavy for a minute before Ben spoke up. "Before we go, I want to say something. Sam's right. We're all in this together, so this is your last chance to high-tail it out of here if you don't care for our company."

He said the last line with a pointed look across the ring at George, who, after visibly mulling over his options for potential replies, said simply, "don't look at me. I'm not going anywhere until the Korovega are dead."

Ben nodded, thoughts racing. There was no way he would ever forgive George, too much bitterness remained between them, but perhaps they could work together for some greater good. Ben had never considered himself vengeful, but he had also never thought it was worth his time to even consider extending any sort of forgiveness to one George Sinon.

"Forgive and forget," was how the advice always went, Ben thought. But that would never work for him. He might be able to manage the "forgive" part, but the "forget" part was just bad advice as far as he was concerned. "Tolerate" was about as good as he thought he was going to get.

Aloud, he continued, "there ain't many of us right now, but if we can do this, more people're gonna come. And they'll keep coming as long as we're alive, so I've got just one order for the lot of you.

"Don't. Fuckin'. Die."

A grin spread around the circle at that, followed by a shared laugh so quiet that no one outside their ring could have heard it. Owen extended his hand into the middle of the circle, palm down.

"Come on. It's cheesy, but let's do it," he said. "It'll make me feel better."

George laughed, but stuck his hand on top of Owen's. "So we're Musketeers now. I can roll with that. All for one and one for all, and all that."

Michael's hand came down next, followed by Ben's, Jessie's, and Sam's.

"Lead the way, Cap'n," Michael said, clapping Owen on the shoulder after they broke hands.

"You have got to stop calling him that," George muttered.

"Follow Ben," Owen ordered.

"What if we get separated?" Michael asked. "I don't know where we're going."

"George does," Ben grunted. "He should still remember anyway. Used to know real well how to get there."

"I do," George admitted. "Even thought about stopping by a time or two on my way to the campsites up there."

Ben narrowed his eyes. "What the hell for?"

"I just," he started, but pulled himself up short. "Do we really want to do this in the middle of the parking lot? The sooner we get to your place, the sooner I can unpack my things and set us up some clean water. Alright?"

Ben continued glaring.

"Alright?" he asked again.

Finally, Ben relented. "Alright," he said.

"Why don't we go in pairs?" Michael suggested, he shifted slightly in place, interjecting himself between Ben and George. The little action managed to wordlessly diffuse a small part of the tension between them even as his suggestion put the group back on track for leaving.

"I think that's a good idea," Jessie said. "I can pick Ben's car out of traffic easily, so I'll go with him, if that's all the same to you."

Sam smiled and patted Ben's broad back. "That's fine by me. I'll follow Owen. Michael, you follow George."

Ben nodded. "I've got the house keys, so I'll go first. If you lose your partner, just look for Sam's big-ass blue bike."

Sam chuckled, shook her head, but said nothing.

"Godspeed," George called as they dispersed, heading to their vehicles. The drive to Ben's house was not a short one, but he had no real idea why he had said that. It seemed appropriate, somehow.

"Ben," Jessie said after the two of them had broken away from the group. She had parked her Jeep behind Ben's Charger, in the middle of the aisle instead of a parking spot.

"Yeah?"

"That was 'that' George, wasn't it?"

His only reply was a terse, "yep."

She sighed. "This is all real, isn't it?"

"Yeah. I wish it weren't. I ain't got no idea what we did to deserve the Korovega, but they're as real as we are."

"Be safe."

"You too, Jess."

She climbed into the driver's seat of her overstuffed Jeep, shoving aside a bag that had fallen across from the passenger side, and turned the engine on. Another moment to adjust some of the things packed around the vehicle, and she moved backward to allow Ben to back out of his spot.

Never in her worst nightmares or the darkest periods in her life had she conceived of something like the apocalypse that was happening around her. Aliens would have been one thing, and she, like so many others had a "zombie apocalypse plan" all set up in case the dead ever rose from their graves. Even global nuclear war would have been normal in comparison, an Armageddon that had a human source and a human failure to blame. The Korovega had nothing human, nothing to blame or curse. They simply were, and because of that they were infinitely worse than any human-started doomsday could have been.

To distract herself, she turned on the radio. Her stomach sank into a cold pit when the station that she always listened to returned nothing but static. Her mind immediately ran to the worst possible explanation: the Korovega had taken Knoxville, where the station was located. That meant that they were only a few dozen miles to the South, and probably on their way here at that moment.

She changed the station. Another Knoxville channel came in just fine and she breathed a huge sigh of relief. Whatever had happened to the first station was bad, but the existence of the second meant that Knoxville still stood.

"...local authorities have instituted a curfew of sundown for the greater Knoxville metropolitan area. Oak Ridge and Anderson County police will be enforcing this curfew in the Anderson County and Oak Ridge areas, but are urging everyone to say in their homes while the movement of the main Korovega body is being tracked."

"Wonderful," she muttered, and changed the channel again. The next station was more talk. She almost turned it off because being alone with her thoughts was preferable to continued dissatisfaction with the options the radio was giving her. The words they were saying caught her attention first.

"...Korovega seem to be using bodies of water to move around. If you live near a river or lake, pay special attention to the water. They will give little warning before emerging from the water, so always be on alert. Right now, it seems the main horde that attacked Washington has broken up into several smaller groups. Expect to see groups of between two and twenty.

"Do not engage them in any way. If you see them, flee or try to hide. There have been no confirmed instances of humans killing Korovega.

"May God be with us all."

"Christ," Jessie muttered. "And we're headed to Norris Lake."

Chapter 5

A short distance outside of Clinton, the traffic going north thinned considerably. The lanes going south—most of which was probably headed past Clinton and into Oak Ridge—remained packed with cars for miles. Ben wondered what, exactly, the local police were going to do when the legal curfew hit at sundown and hundreds, if not thousands, of people were still stuck in traffic.

Of course, he reasoned with a bitter laugh, the jails were made of steel and concrete. Until the Korovega got inside where they could massacre everyone with ease, behind the gates of a prison was probably one of the safest places to be at the moment. Not that he had any intention of going there. If he was going to lock himself in a tiny concrete room, he would head to Oak Ridge High School, not jail.

Back when everyone was afraid of a nuclear apocalypse after the end of World War Two, Oak Ridge, home of the Manhattan Project, built bomb shelters all across the city. Some had been filled in or torn down, but the deep pits under the high school were still there. They had been used for storage for decades, but they were built to withstand the worst apocalypse mankind could create. He could think of no reason for them not to be up to the task of weathering the current one.

Yeah, he thought. And when the Korovega burn the school down, then what?

Then, he realized, he would either be buried alive under a thousand tons of rubble, or killed by Korovega and then buried dead under a thousand tons of rubble. Neither option appealed to him.

In fact, what he really wanted was a drink. He had had no alcohol for years now but the craving never quite went away. It was not an addiction, he told himself, not like smoking would have been. No, he just understood all too well the power that alcohol had to make his problems vanish. But the problems that he drank away would always be there in the morning, along with a splitting headache.

He took a long drink from the bottle of apple juice resting in his car's console instead. It at least slaked his thirst for the moment. Rather than fall into alcohol, he would put his back into the work of unloading their convoy and building what fortifications he could onto his house. Then he and Owen would spend the rest of the evening beating on one another with their swords. Given the fervor with which he had originally embraced the idea of fencing, Ben suspected that Owen knew that he had used swordplay as the final lock to seal away his alcoholism for good, effectively trading one addiction for another.

But there was nothing he could do until they got to his house. Until then, he tried to enjoy the drive. The Korovega had yet to blight the area, and the further away from the city they got, the prettier the land became. A friend had once told him, and claimed that he got the saying from his grandfather, that, "if heaven don't look like Cades Cove, I ain't going." Norris Lake was on the opposite end of East Tennessee, but as far as Ben was concerned, the saying was true about his home as well.

He turned his attention back to the nearly-empty road in time to spot a hitchhiker ahead. He was headed north and loaded down with a huge pack. Two other, more important, things caught Ben's eye as well. First, and most obvious, the man had no car. Assuming he even made it to anywhere with his huge backpack without collapsing, it would get dark long before he would find a place to stay. Second, the other cars were passing this man without so much as a second glance. The backpack he was carrying was not the emergency kit of a homeless man; where ever he was coming from, even without a car, he was coming prepared. That was enough for Ben to make a snap decision.

He signaled a lane change and pulled off onto the shoulder. Jessie's jeep was right behind him as he slowed to a stop a few hundred yards from the would-be hitchhiker. The man had already turned around and was now headed for Ben's car. As he drew closer, it became obvious that what was on the man's back was actually not a giant backpack, but a normal sized backpack, two duffel bags, and a satchel.

Ben unbuckled and opened the car door, stepping out just far enough to clear the cabin of the car but not enough to put him in the path of any traffic that might decide the that right side of the lane was the best place to be.

"Where you going?" Ben called, his deep voice booming.

"Does it," the stranger panted. "Does it matter?"

"'S long as you don't stab me over my car, it don't," he replied, adding a laugh that he hoped would ease whatever fears the man might have.

"I never stabbed nobody in my life," he called back. "I don't plan to start now."

"Good to hear," Ben said. He checked the road. Owen and Sam had just passed them and were about to pull off the road as well when Ben stepped fully out of his car and shut the door. He approached the stranger at a fast walk. He assumed that a run would startle him, given his size, and so he walked quickly and with his hands spread and in plain sight.

"Let me take some of that," Ben offered when the two men were closer.

The stranger eyed him distrustfully and kept walking. Under all of the bags, he was surprisingly thin and rather lanky. Between black hair dripping sweat from the hot summer sun and the two-day stubble on his face, the man looked anything but threatening. If Ben could have put a word to the man's expression right then, besides "tired," he would have called it "suspicious," or even "afraid."

Ben kept pace with him. "Look, if I wanted to kill you and take your stuff, would I do it now, when you can't fight back, or after you give me a few things, when I'll be moving about as well as you are?"

The stranger eyed him again, laughed, then shrugged one duffel and the satchel off of his shoulders and handed them across.

"Better?" Ben asked.

"Better," he agreed.

"Ben Stuart," he said, extending one of his large hands.

"Kenneth," the man replied. "Kenneth Cooper. Friends called me Ken."

"Called?" Ben asked, picking up on the hesitation in his word choice as they turned and headed back for Ben's car.

"Yeah," Ken said angrily. His accent was even thicker than Ben's was most days. He spoke quickly, and his words ran together. "Called. Bastards are out right now, probably beating up old women or something. Said I was stupid for not coming with them. I said I wasn't gonna live off of stealin' an' killin'. Don't matter what's on TV, what them Koro-whatsits done. I'm a human-goddamn-being, I told them. But off they went.

"Damn," he laughed. "Listen to me going on and on and you didn't even ask."

"Don't worry about it," Ben said in what he assumed was a soothing tone. He thought he sounded like Owen, except with more swearing. "Bad shit's happening right now. It's going to bring out the worst in some people. But it's also going to bring out the best in others."

"Sounds kinda, whatchacallit, morally inflexible like," Ken observed.

Ben eyed him for a moment, then shrugged. "I s'pose," he replied. The man's accent, thinker than his, was starting to wear off on him. He added, "but ain't no way I'd let someone who could do some good for humanity get dragged down by a bunch'a fuckin' barbarians."

Ken laughed. "I don't know as that applies to me."

Ben shrugged again. "If it don't, then it don't. Right now, you look like you need a hand and you're not trying t'stab me. I call that a win."

Ken managed a smile. "I guess you're right," he paused, adjusting one of the bags on his shoulder. "Where you headed anyway?"

"North," Ben replied, gesturing over his shoulder. "Past Andersonville. I live near the lake. We're gonna try and arm up and figure out how to beat the Korovega."

Ken laughed. "Gotta beat human nature first," he said. "I guaran-goddamn-tee you my 'buddies' ain't the only ones decided to live like there ain't no tomorrow."

"Well," Ben said with a small laugh of his own. He still thought he sounded like Owen, but it seemed to be doing the trick. "The lot of us like to do a fair amount of thinking and planning. Trust me when I tell you that we plan on living not just today but tomorrow and all the days after that."

"Listening to you talk makes me think we just might. Tell you the truth, I'm more afraid of my 'fellow man' right 'bout now than I am of the Koro... Koro..."

"Korovega," Ben supplied.

"Them."

Ben pointed toward where Jessie had just parked. "We'll load your stuff into the jeep there. Then you'll ride with me. Sound good?"

"You'll trust me that easily?"

Ben studied him for several steps before replying. "For now. If you say you're a good person, I'll believe you unless you prove you ain't. Got it?"

"Got it."

"Plus," Ben said with a grin. "I got a gun in the car."

"Point taken."

* * *

Owen and Sam made it to where they were loading Ken's things into Jessie's jeep about the time George and Michael, held back by the former's van and its low top speed, passed them. The two of them stopped still further up the road, but stayed with their vehicles.

Ben had just finished introducing Ken to everyone when the buzzing roar of twin-cylinder engines backed by a chugging growl cut through the air. Two off-road motorcycles and a Harley, riding in frighteningly tight quarters with a big truck, sped past them. The group got about a quarter mile down the road as the motorcycles pulled away from the truck, then executed a surprisingly coordinated set of u-turns across the grass median.

The group passed them by again, executed a similar set of u-turns, and headed directly for Ben's car. The bikers dismounted as the big truck slid into the space between Ben's car and Ben himself.

The truck's door opened and a big, pot-bellied man dropped out of the tall cabin. He wore mud-streaked jeans, a white sleeveless t-shirt, and a leather jacket that looked like it came straight out of a 1980s action flick. Ben dropped the two bags he had been carrying.

"Well, Kenny," he drawled, "looks like you didn't get too far after all."

"These your ex-friends?" Ben asked quietly.

Ken said nothing, instead turning ghostly pale.

"Ex-friends?" the big man asked, feigning hurt feelings. "Well, I guess that means we don't owe you a thing, Kenny."

"Seriously?" Sam demanded. "We've got Korovega marching across the country headed God-knows-where, and this is how you spend your time? Highway robbery went out of style a long time ago."

"Oh, look," the biker sneered. "The bitch thinks she can talk down to us."

A woman had gotten out of the passenger side as two more men jumped out of the bed of the truck. She glared, apparently unable to decide if she wanted to direct more hatred at Ken or at Ben, then joined the five men as they congregated around their apparent leader.

The truck driver spat on the ground, leaving a greasy tobacco spot. "Knock 'em cold and take their shit. Kill them if you gotta, but don't take too much time. Leave the pretty redhead to me."

In the moment before the gang rushed them, Ben looked Sam up and down. He had never seen her so completely furious. Hell, he thought, he had never seen anyone that angry, ever. It was almost enough to make him feel sorry for the object of her rage.

Almost.

Another person would have screamed profanities until they were red in the face. Another person would have launched herself at the object of her rage to tear him apart with her bare hands. But not Samantha Jean Bennett. The moment Ken's ex-friends went into motion, Sam's fury coalesced into a white-hot flare of rage.

Her pistol hung at her belt from a snap-close holster. Her right hand shot downward, riding on adrenaline-fueled instincts. Her hand moved before her brain even registered the threat. She undid the snap with the same motion that wrapped her fingers around the rubber grip of the gun. In less time than it took for her attacker to register her movement, the gun was drawn and in her hand.

Yet with her attention focused on the pack leader, she almost failed to notice the other, closer, threat closing in on her.

It was over in a heartbeat of light and thunder. She started to turn as her attacker lunged, but the fool reached for her gun with his right hand. If he had reached with his left, his momentum would have pushed her arm out of the way, and the shot would have gone wide. Instead, he pushed her the other way, pushed the gun on more target. It was the last mistake he would ever make as the .357 slammed into his chest with the force of a freight train.

Deathly silence fell in the wake of the gunshot as two of the bikers and the woman from the truck ran for the two dirtbikes. The first got away, but the other two both went for the same bike. Panicked, they fought each other instead of cooperating and managed to do nothing more than knock the bike to the ground. The woman kicked him in the crotch, then threw him roughly to the pavement. She turned and sprinted for the Harley. She nearly knocked it over in her haste, but got it moving and sped down the highway.

Four were left. One was barely able to come to his elbows and knees. His face streamed blood from where he had been thrown to the pavement by his erstwhile "friend" and his eyes had trouble focusing. The second was white-faced and clung to the back of the leader's jacket for a moment before stumbling away, towards the last of their group. The leader was the only one who seemed in control of most of his faculties, though his face was a shade paler and his knees looked uncooperative.

"You bitch! You fucking whore! You..." he ranted as Sam's knees gave out and she dropped hard to the pavement. The gun clattered out of her hand, away from anyone else. Still ranting, he took one shaky step toward Sam, then another.

To his left, Ben heard Owen break into a run. Ordinarily, the two of them would have had a good natured argument about who got the honor of finishing the fight. Of course, their normal fight was a fencing match with blunted weapons. Ben wished he had a real sword, or even a club or pipe, right then. Instead of arguing, Ben took three long strides toward the gang leader.

The leader turned as he saw Owen coming, or he tried to. He pivoted halfway away from Owen, trying to run. Owen was on him before he was able to take more than a single step, spearing him with his shoulder and the full force of his sprint.

He went down, but Owen was no trained wrestler. Instead of landing squarely on top of him for a pin, Owen continued forward and somersaulted painfully, hitting the pavement with first with one shoulder before tumbling into an awkward sitting position.

Ben took a fourth step, one that coincidentally ended with the toe of his shoe in the other man's ribs. He yelled with pain and surprise, which mutated into nothing but pain as Ben's other foot came down squarely on his knee.

The big man squatted down next to the gang leader. He gripped the man's jacket by the lapels with both hands and lifted, hauling him to his feet. "Get outta here. I ever see you again, you're gonna regret it. I ain't as nice as Sam is," Ben growled

The erstwhile gang leader nodded once shakily and Ben dropped him to the pavement. His knees failed to hold him up and he hit the road hard.

The gang leader looked around at what was left of his gang. The Harley was gone, as was one of the dirtbikes. The man who had been clinging to his back was a hundred yards down the road, and the last was grappling with a woman by the jeep he had planned on stealing.

He came to his feet, refused to look at Ben or Owen, and limped toward his truck. Ben felt a small stab of satisfaction knowing how much it would hurt trying to shift that stiff manual transmission with a broken knee.

* * *

The gunshot still rang in his ears. One of his friends—well, not his friends. That was giving him far more credit than he deserved—was dead. Another lay on the ground in pain and the others were in the process of fleeing.

Logically, he should have fled as well. He told the others that stopping here was a bad idea. They needed to let Ken go, he was no danger to them, but Boss had insisted that he needed to pay for embarrassing them, and so here they were. Every intelligent part of his brain was telling him to run; nothing good would come of his staying and trying to fight.

What, exactly, did he think he could accomplish by taking them on? The big black man and his friend could wipe the pavement with him, probably literally, and if the redheaded woman got her nerve back, she would probably just shoot him.

He also knew that as soon as Boss was back in his truck, he was going to hunt down the ones who ran. The poor bastard who was literally running would probably end up under the truck's wheels. He had no idea what would happen to the others, though there was no way it would be anything good.

If he stood there and did nothing, his fate would be marginally better, but not much. He had to do something, and he was more afraid of Boss than he was of these people. They might leave him alone if he ran, but Boss would hunt him down like he did Ken.

Then he saw Jessie.

She had been standing with Ben and Owen when they took off, but had remained close to her jeep to make sure none of the gang got around the others. She was not a small person, objectively—she had for years been able to go toe-to-toe with Big Ben in the boxing ring—but she was dressed in relatively baggy clothing that de-emphasized her muscular figure, and all the last of the gang saw was a woman standing alone, an easy target to keep him in Boss's good graces.

He made his decision in moments, leaping into motion toward Jessie. He had no idea what he was going to do once he came within hitting range, but it was going to hurt.

Jessie, unfortunately, was focused on watching Owen and Ben beating the hell out of Boss himself. The man's wild haymaker took her in the jaw, staggering her backward a step. He kept coming, throwing another wild punch that hit her square in the chest. That second punch knocked her backward and into the guard rail.

She slumped against the sun-warmed metal rail, momentarily grateful for its presence. She felt like it was the only thing that kept her on her feet just then. Her jaw hurt. Her chest hurt worse, and she knew she would be feeling both of them for days to come. Her embarrassment at having missed his attacks burned worse. He had been reckless, though, throwing his full force behind blows to two of the hardest parts of the human body, and Jessie knew just then that he was hurting just as bad as she was, if not worse.

"I know it's not polite to hit a lady, but," he began, rubbing his hands. He did a good job of not wincing when he touched the fingers of his left hand. He tried to make a show of it, looking like he was cracking his knuckles for a fight, but she knew better.

Jessie interrupted him, not with words but with laughter. She had been in enough fights, both real and in the ring, to know how much he had just hurt himself. Plus, the look on his face, half confused and half enraged, was almost worth the pain in her jaw and sternum. His momentary hesitation also gave her the second she needed to regain her balance and get her feet back underneath her.

Rather than reply, she lunged forward, covering the two yards between them in a pair of loping strides. Anything she might have said would never have registered anyway, because the bottom of her fist hammered his ear, probably hard enough to burst his eardrum.

He howled in pain and recoiled away, but tried to strike again a moment later.

In the second and a half he was out of balance, Jessie planted her left foot and grounded her weight. As he punched, she blocked with one elbow and stepped around, planting her right foot in front of her body. The rest of her momentum was transferred into a heel kick aimed at his temple. It connected, but he was able to throw both hands in the way first. The blow still knocked his head sideways, but his hands soaked up most of the force from the kick.

Jessie would not have been surprised if one or both of his hands were broken now. If they were, that particular pain failed to register. He shook his head and somehow managed to block Jessie's followup strike to his solar plexus. He tried to grab her wrist, but failed with a wince that told her that her initial suspicions of a broken hand were probably right.

He threw a punch with even less finesse than he had shown before. Jessie pivoted under and around the sloppy attack and grabbed for his wrist with her right hand. He grunted, then screamed as she clamped down on it, pulled, then drove her right heel into his gut with a brutally fast snap kick.

Her final movement, just to make sure he had absolutely no intention or ability to continue fighting, was to pull his right arm forward and drive the heel of her left hand into the back of his elbow. It made a sound like a green twig snapping and bent the wrong way. She dropped his wrist as he fell to the ground, wide-eyed, hyperventilating, and clawing at his broken elbow.

When she turned her attention back to the others, the gang's leader had gotten back in his truck and was already headed down the road. The other one, the man who had been knocked to the ground by his friend in their scramble for the two dirtbikes, had managed to struggle to his feet and limped away down the road.

"You!" Ben snapped, pointing a finger at Ken where he stood, dumbfounded at the carnage that had erupted around him. "You plan this? You bring those shits here? Get us to lower our guard while they rob us?"

"No! No, I swear to God," he stammered. His blue-gray eyes were wide, panicked. His gaze darted around the group like a cornered animal trying to figure out which predator was going to eat it first.

"You start talking and you start talking right the hell now," Ben growled. He grabbed Ken by the shirt, balling the front of it into his fist.

He rambled. "I told you everything, I swear! God, I never thought. I mean... We did, but I never thought..."

"You did what?" Ben demanded, taking a step closer.

"I, we, that is..."

"Spit it out!"

"I used to ride with them, alright? We... we did some stuff that wasn't too nice. I tried to get out before, but they drug me back in," he said. Then with a bitter laugh and a rub of his wrists that left no doubt about what he meant, he added, "literally drug me back."

"Go on," Ben said, arms folded across his chest.

"When the Korovega, when they showed up in D.C., I..."

"You what?"

"Just, let me finish, ok? Please," Ken protested. When Ben kept quiet, he continued his explanation. His accent, Ben noticed, was gone. "I snuck out in the middle of the night the day before yesterday. The night after the news first broke. I thought I was far enough away by now that they'd not find me. Guess I was wrong."

"Damn right you were," Ben growled. "I'm gonna be keeping en eye on you, you hear?"

"You're not leaving me here?" Ken asked with genuine surprise.

"No. Ain't right to leave a man in your situation, if you're telling the truth. And if you're lying to us, then you'll end up like the rest of these losers." Ben indicated the dead biker and his crippled friend with a sweep of his hand.

"You're still going to trust me?" Ken asked.

Ben jabbed a finger in the air between them. "Not on your life, but right now, there ain't much option. Korovega could be here any day now. This isn't the time to be fighting each other. So you're coming with us if you still want. Safety in numbers and all that. Just don't forget that we're gonna be watching you, understand?"

Quietly, Ken replied, "I understand. You've got to believe me that I didn't know that they were on their way."

"And that act earlier?" Ben demanded.

"It wasn't..." the other man said, prepared to argue. After a moment, he admitted, "I drove a long way up from Chattanooga then ditched my bike outside of Knoxville and walked the rest of the way. I camped out at a truck stop last night. I figured Boss would find my bike and turn around, but it seems like he had other plans."

"Yeah," Ben said with a short laugh. "'Had' is right."

"I didn't mean you play you, promise. I just wanted to hide out somewhere where they'd not be able to find me, and I thought trying to talk like a local would help."

"Don't matter now," Ben pointed to the toppled dirt bike. "Put that thing upright again and get ready to ride."

"You'll trust me on my own like that?"

"For the last time," Ben growled, "and if we have to have this discussion again it'll be cause you screwed up and we're about to turn you into goddamn origami. It ain't about trust right now. It's about you being human and us being human, and we've got to work together against the Korovega. Got it?"

"Got it."

"Besides," Ben said, allowing a smirk to creep onto his face for the first time since the biker gang drove up, "we've got all your stuff, so if you drive off, you're gonna do it without any of your bags."

"Well let's go then," Ken said, forcing a good-natured tone into his voice despite his reservations and, more importantly, his fear.

* * *

While Ben spoke with the newest member of their caravan, Owen rushed to Sam's side. She was still sitting on the ground, staring at her revolver when he approached.

"Sam," he said, reaching out to lay a hand on her shoulder.

She swatted it away.

Without saying anything else, Owen sat down next to her. They sat like that for a long moment until Sam leaned stiffly against Owen's shoulder. He sat still for a second longer, then draped his arm around her.

"Sam," he repeated, quieter this time.

"I didn't mean to," she muttered.

"Mean to what?"

"Shoot him."

"Sam," Owen said a third time. "I... Yes, you did."

"I didn't want to!"

"I know. But there's a difference in wanting to and being forced to. They attacked us. Hell, that guy threatened to do a lot more to you than robbery. You defended yourself from him; that's all."

"I know," she said, then fought down a sob. "I know. I think. Is this really what humanity is reduced to?" She scoffed quietly. It was a soft, defeated noise. "As soon a disaster strikes, we're no better than... this."

"There's no way these guys got this organized since the Korovega attack. They're probably been doing this for a long time. The Korovega didn't turn them into animals; they were animals already." Owen laughed, despite himself. "Rabid animals too, from their attitudes. All you did was put one down."

Sam pulled away, a look of horror on her face. Owen blinked, confused for a moment, before she forcibly shoved him away and stood up. Her pulse hammered again, but this time with a totally different sort of anger.

"Owen, I killed someone! I killed a flesh-and-blood human being! You can't," she groped for words for a moment, "he was a fucking person! It doesn't matter what he did or had done, he's a person."

Owen jerked back. He felt like she had physically struck him. "Sam, I..."

"The moment, the second, you dehumanize someone like that is the moment you start down the same road. Understand?"

"I," he repeated, at a loss.

"Do you understand me?" she growled.

Owen's shoulders sagged. "Yeah."

Sam glared for a moment, feeling each and every breath and heartbeat before reaching out with one trembling hand. She grabbed his shoulder, holding a firm grip but not actually squeezing.

"I killed someone, that's," she said. Then, "I don't even know how to describe it."

"Not ok?" he offered.

She nodded slowly. "Yeah. That's about the size of it. Just," she grabbed his other shoulder and pulled him into an embrace. "Don't be like them, alright?"

"I can do that," he said, returning the hug. They stepped apart after a moment, but Sam left a hand on his shoulder. "Can you drive?" he asked, suppressing a wince.

Sam's eyes went wide as as she remembered the fall he had taken. She pulled back, looking at the blood on her hand in confused horror, then turned that expression on Owen.

"You're bleeding!" she observed aloud, realizing how useless the statement was only after saying it.

He grinned. "Noticed that, did you? I hit the pavement a little hard when I tackled that jackass in the leather coat. It's nothing."

"Nothing?" she demanded. Part of Owen's brain, the part that was busy with things other than the stinging pain in his shoulder, was glad to see the dazed expression clearing from her face. The fact that it was being replaced with panicked worry for his own well-being bothered him a little, but anything was better than seeing her shut down.

"Yeah," he said, still grinning. "It's nothing. Just a little road rash. I've gotten worse on my knees from tripping and falling on the sidewalk. There's nothing we can do about it here, anyway."

"You're going to clean it and bandage it as soon as we get to Ben's," Sam ordered.

Owen's grin turned into a genuine smile, then widened a bit more as he heard Ben talking to Ken. The old saying was "the more the merrier," but Owen suspected in the days to come it would become, "the more, the more likely to survive."

Sam inhaled deeply, forcing some calm back into her muscles, and her knees stopped trembling. She stayed there for a moment, simply breathing, before wiping Owen's blood off on her jeans. Out of the corner of her eye, Sam watched Ken set one of the fallen motorcycles upright.

She had killed a man, a fact which would not leave her mind. When she closed her eyes, she saw the flash again, the spurt of crimson, and watched him go down. He had been coming for her, he and the others. Sam knew she had acted in self-defense, and in defense of her friends, but that was cold comfort when she opened her eyes again and saw the corpse leaking blood so dark it looked black against the pavement.

She looked at Owen. She looked at the damage he had taken from his fight, examining it with the clinical detachment of a fading adrenaline rush. His shoulder was scraped badly, like a child's knee after falling off of a bicycle. There was a lot of blood, but the wound was shallow, and shallow wounds bled a lot. Aside from the pain, nothing about it would harm him long term. It might not even leave a scar.

She looked over at Jessie. The other woman seemed fine, aside from wincing if she moved her torso the wrong way and an unwillingness to open her mouth very far when she spoke to Ben. Sam had seen the two hits that had almost taken Jessie down, though, and made a mental note to check on her in a day or so to make sure nothing was broken. She had watched her fight, if the encounter could even be called a "fight," and had been ready to intervene and help. Jessie had taken down her attacker before Sam could have gotten to her feet, let alone crossed the distance between them to offer any help.

"Don't forget this," Owen said. He scooped her gun up off the ground and offered it, handle first to Sam.

She stared at it, heart thundering with a new surge of adrenaline. That had enabled her to kill a man in an instant. How, she asked herself, could Owen think that handing it back to her right then was a good idea?

He had no idea, she realized. Nothing in his expression or posture suggested that he thought she would have any objection to taking her gun back.

Objectively, she knew he was right. She had had no choice, she reminded herself again. More than that, she was afraid she would need that gun again in the future. The worst thing she could do would be to cultivate a fear of it. Fear of taking life certainly had its place, but fear of the tool that had saved her own life was foolish.

She forced a smile, extending one hand and taking the pistol. Reflexively, she opened the cylinder and looked at the six cartridges in it. In the middle of the street, the action felt strange, but the familiarity of it put her at ease. Five of the rounds inside looked normal; the sixth had a tiny dent in the primer cap. She removed that casing, turning it over and over in her free hand like a piece of jewelry.

Such a tiny thing, she thought, to have so much power.

She held it out to Owen. "Here."

Owen could see that the tips of her fingers still trembled. He knew that Sam knew he could see it as well; it was a small measure of trust whose importance was not lost on him. "What about it?"

"Keep it," she said, "as a reminder of how frail we really are."

"That's not exactly very comforting. Ben can reload it, and..."

"No." Sam took the casing back and slipped it into a pocket. "Not this one. I don't mean 'frail' like we're all going to die. I mean," she stopped, searching for the right word, "it's a reminder that, because each day could be our last, we need to live each day to the fullest, no matter what happens."

Owen smiled. That was the Sam he knew. Not emotional, exactly, but with a clarity of vision that he had envied on more than one occasion.

Sam holstered her pistol, watching Owen out of the corner of her eye as she did so. He seemed entirely too cavalier about the violence they had just seen. She wondered if the last ten minutes had really not bothered him or, if they had, how he managed to avoid showing any indication of it.

"Alright people," Ben shouted, breaking both of them out of their thoughts. "We need to get the hell gone. We've been standing around a dead body for long enough that people are starting to slow down and look."

"And if the cops show up?" George asked.

"If they do, I'll talk to them," Sam said.

"Me too," Ken added. "I can provide," he hesitated, "character witness for these thugs, and maybe a story or two. I don't think we'll have any trouble."

"Good enough," Ben agreed.

"Same order?" Owen asked.

"Same order," Ben agreed.

Ken raised his hand in a gesture that was almost comical. "Where do I fit in?"

"Pull in between Owen and Sam," Ben replied after a moment.

"So more of you can keep an eye on me?"

Ben laughed. "Pretty much."

Ken eyed the dead man on the ground. With a sigh, he said, "I can't blame you for that, really."

As the group was dispersing, George approached Sam and Owen. "Hey," he said. There was a look of genuine concern on his face. "Are you guys alright? We saw what happened, but we were way too far away."

"We're alright," Owen said.

"Really," Sam added. "Don't worry about us."

"I mean," George continued. His face was a mix of admiration and adrenaline as he spoke. "They came out of nowhere, and Jessie decked that asshole, and you killed one of them, and, and you look so in control..."

"I'm fine," Sam grated. "Alright?"

"Ok, ok," he said. "No need to get upset."

Owen interrupted Sam's retort. As stressed as she still was, dealing with George's sometimes-abrasive personality was the last thing she needed. "Cool it, alright?" he said in his best placating tone.

George nodded once, slowly. "Yeah. Sorry."

Sam forced a smile. "It's alright. Adrenaline's running high all around, though, so you'll have to understand if the rest of us aren't quite as excited as you are."

"Sorry," he said again. "I didn't mean anything."

"I know," Sam replied. "But go ahead and head back to your van. We don't want to be standing here any longer than we have to.

"If you need anything, you'll know where to find me for quite a while, I'm sure," George replied, already turning back toward his van. He gestured for Michael, who was behind him and seemed reluctant to approach the scene of carnage, to do the same.

Sam laid a hand on Owen's unhurt shoulder. "Come on. Ben's right; we need to get going."

"Are you alright to drive?" Owen asked. "Seriously."

Sam smiled. "I'll be fine, at least for the drive to Ben's. We can deal with afterward afterward."

Back in her car, Sam shut the door and buckled her seatbelt. She sat staring out through the windshield for a moment, waiting for Owen's car to move.

"How many more times is this going to have to happen before people learn?" Sam asked quietly.

Her only answer was silence.

Chapter 6

Ben's house was built into the side of a hill, which meant it had two "ground floors" depending on which side someone was standing on. The first floor had the larger parking area, including a sheltered space large enough for two cars to park side-by-side. The second floor had little more than a driveway, despite being the "main floor" as far as the house plan was concerned. Owen, George, and Michael parked at the upper level; everyone else parked near the bottom floor.

The house also sat "in the middle of nowhere" several miles on the far side of the city of Andersonville, roughly halfway, geographically speaking, between it and Anderson County park. A few generations before, the house had been a weekend retreat for his great-grandparents. Each subsequent generation had done small improvements to it, but kept it as only a part-time residence. Ben was the first to live there permanently, trading a long commute to work for the convenience of living mere miles away from three different state parks and the peaceful isolation of faux-countryside living.

Now, it seemed like that isolation would be their best hope for safety. Unfortunately, as far as peace was concerned, the convoy that had just arrived at Ben's house brought their own particular brand of chaos with them. Several heated arguments had broken out before they were done unloading the first of the vehicles.

"...and that's bull," George grumbled as Owen approached his half-unloaded van with an empty hand truck.

"What is?" Owen asked.

In lieu of answering verbally, George gestured angrily at Ben's house while loading boxes onto the cart.

"He's mad about the sleeping arrangements," Michael supplied. He had been the recipient of George's tirade.

"What about it?"

"Ben and Jessie are sharing a room, you and Sam are sharing a room, and I'm stuck with Michael and that guy we picked up on the side of the road!"

Owen raised an eyebrow. "Seriously?"

"What?"

"You're pissed because you're rooming with two guys?"

"That's not it!" George snapped.

In the periphery of Owen's vision, Michael gave a quick nod and mouthed, "yes it is."

"Then what?"

"Why do I have to be the one stuck on the only floor with three people?"

And no women, Owen added mentally. Aloud, he said, "you three are on the main floor. You've got the largest bedroom and, if you're unwilling to share the bed, you've got a couch to sleep on."

"And the alcoholic is going to sleep on the floor with the bar," George grumbled.

"The empty bar," Owen corrected. "You know better than that, and that's been his room for years."

"He's still got someone to sleep with."

At that, Owen laughed. "You think those two are going to sleep together?" he asked, stifling another laugh. "No, Ben's probably trying to convince her to let him sleep on the couch while she takes the bedroom down there."

George eyed Owen as if he were trying to figure out exactly why someone would want to go out of his way to avoid sleeping with a beautiful woman. "Bull," he finally grunted, unable to convince himself.

"Ask her yourself." Owen's tone said that he was less than keen on hearing any more about George' problems with the sleeping arrangements.

Not taking the hint, he continued, "and you and your girlfriend get..."

"She's not his girlfriend, dude," Michael said. Owen had walked inside and, if he heard George's quip at all, chose to ignore it.

"They slept together last night," George accused.

"And?"

"And nothing," George said defensively.

Michael smiled and clapped him on the shoulder. "I wouldn't let it get to you, man. I mean, just think, we've got the only bathroom where we won't have to worry about the toilet seat!"

Despite his frustration, George laughed. "Yeah, alright. You've got a point there. Besides, if Owen wants to hold a torch for her, that's not my business."

Michael rolled his eyes, expecting some comment about "the friend zone," but it never came. There were certain conceits that even George would not sink to.

As Owen returned, George quipped, "still don't like it, though."

Michael, caught between rolling his eyes once more and laughing, suspected now that George was simply poking at Owen because he could. It would do no good in the long run, but he supposed it was harmless enough.

"You've seen the inside," Owen said, oblivious to Michael's thought process.

"So?" George demanded.

"So you know that there's three doors on this floor. We need more people to keep watch here than we do in the basement."

"That," George replied grudgingly, "makes sense. How are we going to fit all of this," he indicated his still mostly full van and Michael's untouched station wagon with a sweep of his arm, "in there?"

Owen looked down at the dolly, then to the packed interior of George's van. Right then, getting everything inside was most important. Sorting out what went were and carrying things up and down stairs could wait until the vehicles were unloaded. Despite his grumbling, Owen had to admit that George still seemed to have a strong back and was doing more than a fair share of carrying. "We'll figure it out."

"If you stack that box," Michael said, pointing to a medium-sized plastic tote. "On the dolly, I think that's all we can fit. George can take the one next to it, and the one it's sitting on if he can. I'll get that one," he pointed again, "and you can show us around?"

"Once we get everything unloaded, sure."

George hefted a stack of three boxes. "Lead on."

Owen suspected he had taken Michael's suggestion to carry a second box as a challenge and decided to one-up him by carrying a third. If he could keep it up until they got the van unloaded, then so much the better. On the other hand, if he tired himself out halfway through the task, Owen was going to be unamused.

Owen brought the cart up two small steps, around an empty hot tub, and to a glass door. The door opened into a single huge room. The ceiling was easily twenty or so feet up and the room itself spanned the width of the entire house. To one side were stairs leading up to the pseudo-bedroom loft that Owen and Sam had claimed years before. Under the loft were the master bedroom, storage closet, bathroom, and another set of stairs leading down. Immediately in front of the door was the dining table and, opposite it, the kitchen. The living room area—which had two couches, a large chair, a TV, and fireplace—was on the far side, including another door directly opposite the one they just came in through.

Despite its years of occupancy, this floor still felt more like a vacation house or hunting lodge than a real place to live. Stuffed bears and antler accents on the lights that Ben never got rid of came together with the wood paneling on the walls to create a feeling that was simultaneously homey and campy.

Michael whistled. "Nice. If there's three of us on this floor, how are we doing watches?"

"Watches?" Owen glanced at his wrist, immediately thinking of timepieces instead of guards for the doors.

"Yeah," he continued. "You know, 'keep watch through the night,' and... stuff."

"We'll have to figure that out," Owen admitted, shuffling boxes off of the cart. "Adding Ken to our roster, if we can call it that, has changed how we had planned to do some things."

"I think we should sleep in shifts," Michael suggested.

Owen agreed. "Not a bad idea."

"Aren't you jumping the gun a bit?" George asked.

"I wouldn't say so," Owen replied, grabbing the handle of the dolly and wheeling it back through the open door. With one hand, he made a "follow" motion as he guided the cart. Over a shoulder, he said, "to be perfectly honest, this is the time for paranoia. We know the Korovega are out there somewhere and if we're going to survive, we need to take every precaution and make every preparation we can."

George made a noise that was almost a word, but stopped somewhere short of actual articulation. He hummed, then went silent again.

Owen looked over his shoulder. George had walked the opposite direction, toward the face of the house on the lower side of the slope. Less than a hundred yards away from the house on the downhill side the river's tributary branched into a small stream. It looked maybe waist deep at the most. More importantly, though, at least from where George was standing, was that the stream was moving relatively quickly.

"Something on your mind?" Owen asked.

"I brought a couple of generators," he replied. "Trying to figure out if the stream down there is moving fast enough to use them. See if I can keep us from getting killed."

"We'll be fine," Owen insisted.

George stared for a moment, trying to determine if Owen was being genuine or not. Finally, he decided that Owen was about as capable of lying, especially to him, as he was of flight and he shook his head. "No, we won't."

"Why not?"

"Don't you get it?" George demanded.

"Get what?" Owen insisted. "Go ahead and speak your mind."

"Nuh-uh. I'm not getting into it with you."

"George," Michael started.

Owen interrupted, "no, let him talk."

He eyed Owen. "Alright," he said. "You and Ben? Your talk about saving everyone? Bullshit. Bull. Shit. The world is screwed, whether you want to believe it or not. Your delusions of heroism are all well and good, but someone's got to do the grunt work of keeping us all alive, capisce?"

Owen nodded. George's sudden shift in tone surprised him, but he promised to let him have his say and he would be true to his own word. "What are you getting at?"

George shook his head and turned back to look over the balcony rail. "I don't doubt that your heart's in the right place, but you start thinking too big and that could get dangerous. Survival comes first, and I will survive this."

"If you can use the water, could you power the whole house?" Michael asked. He pitched his voice a little higher, trying to sound upbeat.

George pinched the bridge of his nose, sighed, and forced himself to calm down. "It's a question of timing, really. Given a couple of months and enough manpower and material, I could set up a generator with enough power to keep the lights on for a dozen houses like this."

"And short term?"

He shrugged. "Probably. I'd have to test it first."

"Later," Owen said, his voice not quite a growl. George might be able to reign himself in that quickly, but Owen had no such talent.

"Come on," Michael said, gently taking George by the shoulder and turning him back toward the van. "We've still got work to do."

"Yeah," Owen agreed absently, deep in thought, "we do."

* * *

"The hell is in this?" Ben grunted, hefting a black-with-silver-fittings steamer trunk onto one broad shoulder.

"Clothes, mostly," Jessie replied, dragging out a duffel bag and classic-styled leather suitcase. She followed Ben into the house through the basement level's main door. It opened into a large room that had, at one time, done double duty as a bar and cozy den-type area for when the summer-only occupants of the house grew tired of the spaciousness of the main floor with its lofted ceiling and bright windows. The basement was paneled in dark wood, with dark carpet, and dim lights. After sobering up for good, Ben removed everything that had made the bar a "bar," and replaced it with accoutrements to rival the main kitchen upstairs, the one he rarely ever used when he lived by himself.

The basement's furniture was plush leather that, like the level of light, contrasted sharply with the deliberate roughness and fabric finishes of the furniture a floor above it. It also looked significantly more worn and the carpet had more than its share of dirt ground into the fibers. Ben went straight for the workshop behind the staircase to deposit the steamer trunk.

Because the house was set into the side of a hill, the workshop was actually underground. It had a cement floor, cinder block walls, and only the tiniest of windows just higher than head level that let in whatever paltry amount of light filtered through the boards of the deck above. The room was also a cool relief from the hot summer sun outside.

In actuality, it was a converted storage room that Ben had filled with a variety of power tools and material for the various projects and hobbies he had dabbled in other the years. Woodworking tools sat here and there, interspersed with machine-shop equipment and even a surprisingly well ventilated forge and anvil in one corner.

Jessie had at one point several years before joked that, in the event of Armageddon, Ben would have enough esoteric skills to ride out anything the Four Horsemen could throw at him. Now that the apocalypse was here, and there turned out to not be four, but millions, the comment came back to her unbidden and she laughed.

"Hm?" Ben asked, quirking an eyebrow.

"Just thinking," she said. "I always wondered if this collection of yours was enough to survive the end of the world. Guess we'll see now."

Ben smiled. "Yeah," he said, looking over the room full of tools as though seeing it for the first time. "We just might. Got a lot of skills to brush up on, though. World won't save itself, you know."

She laughed. "Of course not. Someone's got to watch your back."

"Hey now," he said with mock seriousness. "I reckon it's gonna be me who's saving you when the shit hits the fan."

Jessie smirked, putting her fists on her hips. "Keep dreaming. 'Sides, you'll be too tired from sleeping on that couch to do any saving."

"That's a pretty comfy couch."

"Then why don't you let me take it?"

"It ain't all that comfy, besides, the couch is for whoever's got watch down here. Th' other one, don't matter who it is, sleeps in the bedroom."

"We're gonna need to expand the workroom," Jessie observed after a few moments of shared silence.

Ben nodded agreement. "Or build another one."

"You're not thinking of digging a sub basement, are you?"

He laughed. "Crossed my mind, but no. Leastaways not just yet. We just might end up doing that at some point, but I don't want to break up this slab if I can avoid it. Know what I mean?"

"Yeah." She nodded. Breaking up the foot-thick concrete foundation would be a huge labor challenge and could result in some serious complications with the foundation. Digging back into the hillside, on the other hand, was entirely different. She said as much to Ben, describing her plan to expand the ground floor even further by tunneling sideways.

"Could," he agreed once she was finished. "That's part two, though."

"Part two?"

"I'm thinkin' the next thing we need to do is load up the trucks with cinder blocks and make us a whole 'nother building. Dig it out and make it two, maybe three, floors. Move most of the workshop stuff into it; keep food an' the like in here."

"Tomorrow," Jessie said with a laugh.

"Yeah," he agreed. "Tomorrow. Good to have plans."

Just then, from the main room, they heard Sam shout, "are you two done flirting in there or do I have to move all this stuff myself?"

"Hold your horses, woman!" Ben shouted back. He grinned. "We're planning."

"Less planning, more hauling," she said, coming to lean on the door frame of the workshop. "Chop chop and such."

Jessie laughed. "She always this bossy?"

Ben's voice was grave, but his bright smile betrayed what he actually felt. "You don't know the half of it." Cheerfully, he added, "come on, before Sam strains herself."

"I heard that," she said, and stuck her tongue out.

Ben grinned again. "I expected you to. How much more is there?"

Sam laughed. "Most of it."

"Wait a minute." Jessie stopped suddenly in the middle of the den. "Did you leave that Ken dude out there by himself?"

"Yeah, why?" Sam shrugged.

"Because we don't trust him yet?" Jessie asked, as though that consideration should have been the most obvious thing in the world. "Do we?"

"No," Sam replied. "But..."

"Hell no," Ben interjected.

"But," Sam continued, "what's he going to do?"

"He could hop on that bike, or your bike, and high-tail it out of here with whatever he could stuff in his backpack."

"He could," Sam agreed, "but these walls aren't all that thick. We'd hear the engine before he got ten feet away."

"Have to agree with her there," Ben said. "I stuffed a bunch of insulation in the walls a few years back, but they're still pretty thin and the door's open," he sighed and ran a hand over his bald head, wiping sweat away. "That's another thing to add to the list of crap we gotta do."

"Hmm?"

"Fortify the walls," he said. "Thicken 'em up a bit. Anyway, Sam' right. We'd hear it if he took any kinda vehicle."

"And if he walked?" Jessie demanded.

"He might get to the end of the first switchback if he ran and he was fast." Ben shrugged. "I'd just drop a rock or something on him from up here."

"All right, all right," Jessie said. She held her hands out in defeat, but smiled. She found herself unable to resist the humor inherent at "Big Ben" playing the part of a mountain troll lobbing rocks downhill.

Sam smiled back. "He's been nothing but polite, too, if a little timid around me. I think the fact that we didn't leave him for dead when his 'buddies' showed up helped us gain a little loyalty. And shooting the first one..."

Sam had only paused for half a breath, but Ben saw the color drain from her face. Loudly, forcefully, and with all of the charisma he could muster, he said, "alright! Let's get this done! Sooner we unload, sooner we can eat!"

If Jessie caught the unspoken exchange of tension between Sam and Ben, nothing betrayed that fact outwardly. Instead, she simply announced, "sounds good. I don't know about you guys, but I'm getting hungry. Let's wrap this up."

* * *

Dinner went quickly. Ben volunteered to grill a large batch of hamburgers out on the deck, claiming it was his, "duty to make sure his guests had a good first evening." Conversation drifted around to different subjects, always coming back around to survival—what they could eat, how they could get water, where electricity would come from, and so on.

George shared his ideas about using the river for power, which was met with nearly universal approval. Ben took exception to the lack of specificity in his design, tasking him to put together a materials-needed sheet for their expedition the next day.

During dinner, George had watched how the others acted toward Michael. George had his own skillset. At the absolute minimum, he would provide the infrastructure that would keep the rest of them alive when they were at home. Michael, on the other hand, did not exactly have a plethora of practical talents.

He could keep morale up with music, but there was only so far that could go if things turned truly bad, George thought. Yet, morale was important, and if Michael could keep everyone happy, George's life would be easier. After dinner, he did exactly that, playing some improvised music on an electric keyboard he brought with him.

After handling the cleanup as a group, everyone slowly dispersed. Ben and Jessie went downstairs. Owen, Michael, and Ken made themselves comfortable in front of the television. That left Sam and George to occupy the dinner table, which quickly became a sea of paperwork and small, glowing screens.

The two of them had been working in silence broken only by cursing the lack of cell signal for some time when Michael stood, stretched, and said, "I'm going to go make some coffee, does anyone want anything?"

Owen raised his eyebrows. "It's almost eleven."

"I know. But if I'm going to take the first watch tonight, I'm going to need a little extra energy. Anyone else want anything while I'm over here?"

"I'm alright," replied Owen.

"Is there any iced tea left?" Ken asked.

Michael checked the fridge. Inside, among enough tightly-packed food to fill three refrigerators of equal size, was a gallon-and-a-half jug of iced tea. It had been full when it was put in earlier, but the sweet drink had been their refreshment of choice for most of the evening and it was running low. Carefully, he extracted it from the meticulously packed foodstuffs, trying not to cause an avalanche.

He was glad that they were planning on getting a second fridge along with their other supplies in the morning. He had been known to pack his fridge a little tightly, or tightly as he had understood the word to mean before he had seen Ben stuffing container after container into the seemingly endless space inside the stainless steel appliance, but that had been nothing that compared to this.

Michael finally extracted the jug of tea and held it over his head. "'s about half full. Anyone else want some?"

"I would," Sam replied, looking up from her paperwork. From Michael's perspective, she looked tired, but something told him she would be one of the last ones asleep once they started turning out lights.

"Might as well, while you've got it out," George added with a friendly smile. Knowing him as long as Michael had, he could tell that the smile was forced. Not that George was upset with him, personally, but he was frustrated by something and trying not to take it out on the people around him. Most likely, Michael theorized, he had hit a wall with his designs. Perhaps, given what he was working on, it was a literal wall.

Michael poured three glasses, thought for a moment, and poured himself a fourth one. He held up the jug, which only had a small amount left in the bottom. "Owen?" he asked, swishing the tea around.

"Sure," Owen replied, and Michael took a fifth glass out of the cabinet and filled it, emptying the jug. He started to toss the empty container in a nearby trash can, but Sam spoke up before he could.

"Keep the jug," she instructed. "Set it in the sink."

"What for?"

"It's useful," Sam replied. "We can rinse it out and reuse it. I think there's some tea concentrate somewhere in my stuff. If anything, we can fill it full of fresh water if something happens to our water lines."

Michael shrugged, setting the jug in the sink. "Makes sense." He looked at the glasses, of which there were five, and then at his hands, of which there were only two. "George," he called, "come help me carry these?"

George looked up from his own stack of papers. His expression plainly said that any distraction, however momentary, would be welcome. Michael normally saw him eager to throw his brain against a problem, but he suspected that he was running out of things to plan. Either that or, more likely, he found himself trying to plan for every contingency and outcome of his initial set of plans. Michael gave an inward shrug and, aloud, said, "maybe you ought to take a break for a bit anyway. Get some fresh air."

George shook his head, looked back at Sam, then to Michael. "No, I've got to keep working on this. Need to be ready for anything, you know."

Michael nodded. "Right," he agreed, "but there's such a thing as being too prepared. You can't plan for everything."

George shot him a disbelieving look and tilted his chair back. "Can't I?"

"Can you?"

"What's that supposed to mean?" However Michael had intended the comment, George took it as a veiled condemnation of his abilities.

"Nothing, don't worry about it."

"No," George said, forcefully. "What did you mean?"

Michael shrugged, trying to be placating. "Just that there's a lot we still don't know."

"So?"

"So." Michael sighed. "Look. What were you just working on?"

"Plans for a water wheel, why?"

"What size?"

George gave him a brief description of what he had been drafting. "...and it'll produce enough energy to power four houses this size."

"Right," Michael said. He shook his head, then quickly regretted the gesture as George's expression told him that he had taken it personally. "And all you'll have to do is reroute a chunk of the Tennessee River to do it."

"So?"

Michael sighed, and this time he could not have cared less if George took it personally. "So we don't have four houses this size and we don't have the manpower to do something like that anyway."

"Doesn't mean we don't need to have a contingency plan in place. You heard Sam, we want to eventually have enough people here to have our very own freaking commune. We'll have the manpower then!"

"And we can worry about that sort of thing when we start getting more people here. But right now, we need to focus on the immediate future. Food and water for tomorrow first."

George glared for a moment, but Michael crossed his arms with an exasperated look and refused to back down. After a moment of their staring match, George sighed. "You're right."

Michael smiled. That admission was more than most people would have gotten out of George Sinon's stubborn mouth.

"Anyway," George said. "Wasn't there something you needed?"

Michael nodded. "Yeah. Help me carry these glasses. I can only manage two. Not all of us used to work in a restaurant."

George rolled his eyes. "God. Don't remind me," he muttered, but crossed to the kitchen and deftly picked up two glasses with one hand and the last one with his other.

Michael took his glass and one other across the room. He handed the spare to Owen, then reclaimed his seat on the couch next to Ken.

George handed Ken a glass, then shuffled the remaining two cups in his hands around so that he was carrying one in each hand. He crossed the room, heading back to the table where he and Sam had been working. He set his glass on his end of the table, and placed Sam's beside her stack of paperwork.

"Thanks," she said absently, then looked up and smiled. "Michael's right, though, I think it's getting close to time for a break. I'm starting to see double."

George chuckled. That was a familiar feeling, and one of the things he hated about paperwork. At least when it came to building things, he usually did not have to stare at endless lines of small printed text. He picked up his tea again and headed for the nearby glass door. "Care to join me outside?"

"Sure." At the moment, anything other than writing would be welcome. Maybe a break would allow her hand to uncramp. She had been writing for some time now and her hand hurt worse than it had since her comprehensive exams in college.

* * *

Despite preceding her out the door, George was nowhere to be seen when Sam came outside. Her first assumption was the hot tub, but the cover was still on. The tub itself was tempting, especially after a day's worth of carrying, loading, and unloading boxes.

Things would only get worse in the coming days, she thought, best to take advantage of opportunities to relax while they exist. On the other hand, the idea of sharing a hot tub with George, especially with him only, was not on her top ten list of desires.

"Where'd you go?" she asked, turning away from the hot tub.

"Over here," he replied from the far side of the deck, around the corner of the house.

She went around the corner and found him leaning on the railing, glass in hand. His back was to the large windows that took up the majority of the house's wall on that side. The chimney made a large stone median in the windows, but otherwise anyone inside had a view of the valley almost as dramatic as the one from the porch itself.

Sam leaned against the railing a couple of yards away from George, resting her elbows on the top and holding her glass over the edge. He looked over and she was keenly aware of his eyes on her hips, so she adjusted her posture, leaning forward to make herself seem a little taller and de-emphasize her curves. Being appreciated physically was one thing; she just wished that George would lay off once in a while.

Not that she was afraid of confronting him about it. "Eyes up here," she said sternly.

"Sorry," he replied automatically. His body language said he was anything but sorry. He turned in place, leaning against the rail with one arm and facing her fully now. "Believe it or not, I didn't ask you to come out here so that I could check you out."

Sam snorted, but grinned nonetheless. "So you say."

"It's true."

"And?"

"And what?"

She turned completely around, facing the window. On the other side was the dining table, piled high with paper. She was aware of him watching her, but for the moment did not care. Her mind was elsewhere, thinking again of the sorts of things that had been going into her paperwork. Food and how they would get and preserve it occupied most of her thinking.

"And nothing, I suppose," she said bitterly, taking a long drink of the tea in her glass.

"There's something."

"Why does there have to be something?"

"There's always something," he said.

"I thought you were a chemist, not a psychologist."

"Engineer, actually," he said, as though the distinction mattered little to him. "But no, I just know people."

"How's your work going?" she asked after a pause.

George gave a small shrug. "It's going," he replied, "but I'd kill to have gotten that desk out of my van today."

"I just want a filing cabinet," Sam added.

"Another one, yeah."

She turned toward him, "another one?"

"I brought a small one, three drawers," he said. "It got put in the bedroom."

"Having them out in the main room would be good." Sam paused, thinking. "At least until we get a decent workroom built."

Somehow, he managed to not be upset that that line failed to work. He even thought he might have been disappointed if it had worked, because it would mean she was not as smart as she seemed, and easily swayed by small accomplishments. He shook his head. There would be time for that later.

"That's next on my list," George said. "Picky as Ben gets, I'm going to draw up three or four different options for him."

"Probably wise," she said, and turned back to look over the darkening yard.

A minute passed before George asked, "what's on your mind?"

Sam laughed quietly; it was a dark sound and she turned away from George to hide the hard look that passed across her face. Her inner thoughts were far more tumultuous than she let on and her voice was surprisingly—even to her—free of any wavers as she went on. "Earlier."

"Earlier?" he echoed.

"On the road."

"Ah," George said. He sensed that there was more to it than that but did not want to pry. His desire to know more warred with his desire not to push her away. Eventually, one won out and he asked, "what started all that?"

"Ken. Sort of," she answered. "Well, no. That's not exactly fair. He didn't do anything," she added, then summarized what Ken told them about how the gang used to be just a "social thing" until the news about the Korovega broke.

"People are shit," George said, free from his usual bravado.

"Sometimes," she agreed. "Everyone's fundamentally good, but..."

"Ah, blue hell," he growled. "Not you too."

"What?"

"Owen," he replied and shrugged. At Sam's, "go on," gesture, he added, "just all his hero talk rubs me the wrong way. He won't sit down and look at things the way they really are. Everyone has a limit, a price. They'll always turn on you in the end if it means saving their own skin."

"Trust me," she said, ignoring the cold, slimy feeling his words gave her, "I don't have rose-colored glasses on. But people are fundamentally good. That's why it bothers me so much—the thought that those assholes aren't the only ones who are going to hit on that same train of thought, and..."

She felt a pit open in her stomach and a lump welling up in her throat. She fought it down forcefully; she could not cry in front of someone like George. He would take it as an invitation to "comfort" her, which was exactly the last thing she wanted right then. If she was honest with herself, what she really wanted was to find and kill the rest of that gang and anyone who thought like them, but she also knew, intellectually, that that would solve nothing.

"Let's not talk about this anymore," she said after a moment.

"You sure? We can..."

"I'm sure," she snapped, cutting him off. "In fact, let's just not talk for a while, alright?"

"Alright," George said slowly. "Are you ok?"

Sam shook her head. That was as much as she would let him see. She leaned back against the rail, looking up at the sky. "No," she said. Her voice was quiet. "But I don't want to talk about it. Not right now. Right now, I just want to enjoy the starlight and the feeling that I'm not alone in the world."

George started to come closer, to reach out to her, but a quick stern glance told him that it was a bad idea. He backed away a step and turned back to the landscape, watching the clouds drift across the moon.

* * *

Crickets and bullfrogs buzzed outside, the loudest noises amid the nighttime cacophony that was summer in the South. A waxing gibbous moon hung overhead, blazing with enough cold, white light to cast black shadows and let even Michael with his professed terrible night vision see easily.

He had taken the first watch on his floor, nursing a cup of coffee to stay awake. George went to bed first, refusing to talk to anyone about what he and Sam had discussed. That left Ken to sleep on the couch. Whenever his confidence wavered, he reminded himself Ben was downstairs keeping an eye on the basement door. That thought reassured him.

On their floor, Sam and Owen were both still awake. An unusual, tense silence hung between them. Owen stood at the edge of the loft, leaning on the rail that overlooked the main floor. Ken adjusted his position on the couch, eliciting a startlingly loud creak of leather, but otherwise no sound or movement came from the floor below. Michael merely stood at the window, occasionally taking a sip from his steaming coffee, with one hand behind his back as though he fancied himself a solider at his post.

Sam sat on the edge of the bed with her back to the house. Moonlight from the loft's windows bathed her face, giving her features a ghostly paleness. Whatever was going through Owen's head, nothing went through hers. Not just a lack of active thought; she would have found that relaxing. Instead it was a complete absence of conscious processing that would have been zen perfection had it originated from a place of stillness instead of the cold abyss that yawned inside her spirit.

She wanted to scream, but nothing in her being could make a sound right then.

She wanted to run, to fight, to throw or break something, but her body had forgotten how to move. She simply stared at the landscape outside the window, looking without seeing any of it. Something moved in the trees outside, a deer probably. She saw it in her peripheral vision, her eyes might even have tracked it for the brief moment that it strayed near the house, but no conception of "deer" registered in her brain.

Her hands were cold, tight. Somewhere, some neuron that was still alive realized that her hands were clenched in white-knuckled fists and that she needed to relax them before her nails cut her palms open. Somehow, she relaxed her fists, but they remained curled and clawlike in her lap. They were heavy, especially the right one which was weighed down with the mental echo of a gun.

She had killed someone. She, Samantha Jean Bennett, had ended the life of another human being. She knew it had been the right thing. She had protected herself and her friends, but that did little to erase the memory.

First there had been fear, the danger had frozen her muscles for a moment too long. Then, righteous indignation replaced fear; "this bastard is trying to kill me!" she had thought. Then the gun went off, and she could remember every heartbeat of the next few seconds like crystal. The bullet ripped its way though blood and gore that had been a man's stomach mere milliseconds before. It did little damage going in, only blowing a small amount of blood back out, but the exit wound on his back would have been huge, gaping, and ragged. The biker's leather jacket prevented blood from fountaining, but a fair amount had still sprayed out. Even more pooled under his body as he lay on the pavement.

Dimly, she was aware of movement behind and then beside her.

"Sam?"

She knew the voice. The voice belonged to someone she cared about, someone she had killed a man to protect. But nothing in her conscious mind reacted.

"Sam?" the voice repeated. "Are you alright?"

Owen. That was the name that belonged to the voice.

"You're frightening me," Owen said. He was whispering.

Finally, Sam reacted. Her eyes moved, followed by a slow turn of her head. She moved with glacial stillness. She locked eyes with Owen in the darkness. "Owen," she rasped, even quieter than he had been. Her throat was dry.

He placed a hand on her arm. His hand was warm, but the touch that should have been comforting was alien. She recoiled as if stung, and in the same movement seized his wrist with her other hand.

Her grip was like iron, and she twisted it sharply.

"Sam," Owen said, afraid to fight back, lest her reflexes put him in a more painful position. "My wrist?"

Her eyes went wide and she released his arm. Suddenly, like a dam collapsing, everything came rushing back to her. Instead of cold emptiness, a chaotic storm of emotions and feelings swirled inside her mind. "Are you ok?"

He managed a smile. "It's fine." Then, "are you alright?"

"I'm," she started to say that she was fine, that everything was fine, but she knew it was a lie even before the words came out of her mouth. "I'm," she repeated. She closed her eyes and tears welled up. She sighed. The sound rattled in her throat. "No, I'm not alright."

She leaned heavily against Owen, limp at first, then wrapped her arms around his shoulders like a drowning swimmer clinging to a buoy and sobbed into his shirt. He managed to work an arm free after a moment and put his hands around her waist, trying to offer what comfort he could. If he was honest with himself, he had no idea what to say or do, so he just sat there and held her.

In the face of her anguish and the knowledge that he was well and truly in so far over his head that the sun had gone out overhead, he realized that he was holding her even tighter than she held him. He rested one cheek on the top her her head and sighed. There was a lump in his throat to match the hole in his gut and his breath caught. He felt like tears were just behind his eyes, but they never came out. His eyes burned all the same, though. Instead, he felt hollow, impotent rage at the world, at the Korovega, and most of all at the depravity of mankind.

Neither of them knew how long they sat there like that, but they finally disentangled. Wordlessly, Sam changed clothes and slipped between the bedsheets.

Owen joined her moments later, leaving a foot of space between them. That space remained for perhaps a minute until they both silently moved to fill it.

"Owen?"

"Yeah?"

"This." She sighed. "This is only the beginning, isn't it? This really is the end of the whole damn world."

"Yeah," he said. It was weak, and not very useful of a reply, but it was all he had right then.

"And?"

"And," he muttered. Like Sam, his voice carried a tone of helplessness that he would never have revealed in front of anyone else. "And I don't really know. Things are only going to get worse from here."

Sam took a deep, shuddering breath, willing her tears to stay buried. She failed. "Christ..."

Chapter 7

The old house creaked and settled in the cool night air. It reminded George, for a few brief moments in the dark, where no one else could see, of the handful of pleasant memories he had of his friendship with Ben before things went sour between them.

He had taken the third watch and with it the job of waking everyone up in the morning. He made a fresh pot of coffee, mixed up a batch of pancake batter, and set a dozen breakfast sausages cooking before making his rounds. The early morning had been still, devoid of the night noises which had kept the others company.

"Can one of you watch these for me?" he asked, addressing the occupants of the living room. He gestured vaguely to the various breakfast items cooking on the stove.

"You know me," Michael replied. "I burn everything but coffee."

"I can. I need another cup of coffee, anyway," Ken replied, standing and snagging his empty mug on the way to the kitchen. "Sleeping for a few hours, being up for a couple more, then napping again is not my idea of a restful night."

George nodded and went up the stairs to the loft to wake Owen and Sam. He felt a pang of jealousy as he saw them tangled up together under the sheets. They were both still dressed as far as he could tell, not that that bit of knowledge did anything to alleviate his feelings. His ignorance of what passed between them the night before only meant that his imagination was free to run wild and settle on whatever thought he felt most appropriate. In fact, he felt even more jealousy at the thought that there might be nothing physical happening between the two of them.

It would be just like Owen, he thought ruefully, to waste a perfectly good opportunity.

He kicked the foot of the bed lightly. When neither stirred, he kicked the bedpost again. That failed. George sighed, and moved to the nearer side of the bed, where Owen slept.

"Hey," he said, tapping Owen on the shoulder. "Rise and shine, Englishman."

"Rwy'n Gymro, dwp," Owen muttered.

George prodded his shoulder again and Owen opened his eyes slowly. His eyes were red and had big enough bags underneath to pack for a weekend trip. Whatever had happened the night before, George realized, Owen had not slept well—if he slept much at all. Suddenly his feelings of jealousy were gone, replaced by something approximating pity.

"Crazy gibberish," George quipped, grinning.

"Mornin' to you too."

"Sleep alright?"

Owen shook his head, slowly levering himself up into a sitting position. The wound on his shoulder had scabbed over already, but he left a dark, not-quite-blood stain on the sheet where his shoulder had been. A moment later, he replied, "no."

"Breakfast's almost ready downstairs. Wake your girlfriend and come eat."

Owen rolled his eyes, but said, "will do."

"Hey," George added from the edge of the loft, "I'll put some tea on for you."

"Thanks."

He spared a look toward the kitchen on his way down the stairs. Ken had taken the sausages off of the griddle and set them on a paper town to cool and drain. He had enlisted Michael's help as well, and the latter was busying himself setting the table. George watched as Michael set the last glass on the table just in time to hurry back to the kitchen to take another pancake from Ken's skillet and add it to the stack waiting on the counter.

George nodded, pleased. He had ended his first night watch by making everyone breakfast. Not only that, but he had gotten several of the others involved. If they could cooperate over matters like cooking, he had no doubts he would be able to get them to cooperate when more important things came along, like shelter or actually going and hunting for food once things that came from a grocery store ran out.

This, George thought, was good. With Michael's assistance, he could hope to manage these people. If they could be managed, they could be protected. If they were protected, they would survive. He would survive.

While George was upstairs, Ben came up from the basement, seated himself on the couch, and turned the TV on. He spent a few minutes flipping through channels, somewhat amused to find an even mix between cartoons and entertainment, and talk-show news.

He was still barely awake, as the coffee cup perched precariously on his pajama'd knee attested, and he settled on the first thing that looked like it might convey some useful information.

On screen, three men, all wearing expensive suits, sat around a kidney-shaped table having a heated argument, complete with grand gestures.

"It clearly states in verse thirty-one that Christ shall gather his elect after the tribulation is over. And I'm telling you, brethren, it's just beginning! Not to mention..."

The second man on TV, who appeared to be more a kindly grandfather than anything, interrupted forcefully, saying, "the book of Revelation says..."

The first man gave a dramatic sigh as George descended the stairs and wordlessly took a seat on the couch next to Ben.

On the TV, the man said, "Revelations is a metaphor! In chapter nine, verse two, it says that 'there arose a smoke out of the pit, as the smoke of a great furnace; and the sun and the air were darkened.' When the Korovega put Washington to the torch, don't you think that qualifies as smoke of a great furnace?"

"What's more," the third man said. He was younger and with nut-brown skin that contrasted with the snowy whiteness of the other two. His authoritative tones overrode any possible objection from the man sitting between them. He said, "didn't the Korovega come out of the water? I mean, the Potomac is hardly a bottomless pit, but as long as we're talking metaphor here..."

The first man made a grand wave with his hand. "Thank you!"

"Now hold on," the man in the middle interjected. "The things that come out of the abyss are locusts, and the Korvega are hardly locusts. Demons of Satan, certainly, but it's a bit of a stretch to call them locusts! Plus, those locusts are specifically not given power to destroy the land, and the Korovega are done just that with their Blight."

The three of them dissolved into inarticulate shouts for a moment as each one tried to override the others. Finally, the one in the middle made a sweeping gesture with both hands that got the attention of his two comrades. He continued. "If this really is the End Times, where are the horsemen? Where is the rider going forth conquering?"

"If it's a metaphor..."

"If it's a metaphor! If!" The second preacher interrupted. "I thought you were sure it was. I'm telling you I won't accept that this is Armageddon until I see some signs that fulfill prophecy!"

"What did the Korovega king say when he took down the capitol?" the third preacher asked, growing exasperated, but trying hard not to show it. Without waiting for an answer to the clearly rhetorical question, he continued, "he said he was here to take the planet away from mankind. That says 'riding forth to conquer' to me."

Without missing a beat, as though it had been planned that way, the first preacher took up the line of thought. "And we're already seeing the work of the second horseman. We're seeing the work of the second horseman in our streets right now. People are already fighting over food, killing each other in the streets. That sounds like someone has taken peace away from the Earth to me."

"Exactly!" the third preacher agreed. "And, you're a student of history, aren't you?"

The second preacher, caught between two arguments going faster than he could follow right then, reluctantly agreed. "I am."

"Then you know what comes next after war and rioting. Not talking about Revelations here, not talking about the End Times. Talking about war. Real, historic war. What comes after war?"

"Famine," the second preacher said. "Then plagues."

"Thank you!"

"But all that is predicated on the assumption that this is, in fact, and you'll have to agree with me here, that this is the start of the tribulation."

"And you say it isn't?"

"I say it isn't. The gospels give some pretty clear signs, too, you know. Wars like we've not seen in thousands of years. 'Nation against nation' and whatnot."

"But he goes on to say," the first preacher added, "that that's not the only sign. People 'shall betray one another, and shall hate one another,' and in verse fifteen, he mentions the desolation of Daniel."

"Desolation of Daniel?" the second preacher echoed.

"'And arms shall stand on his part, and they shall pollute the sanctuary of strength, and shall take away the daily sacrifice, and they shall place the abomination that maketh desolate,'" recited the first preacher.

"They're talking about an idol," argued the third preacher. "Siqqus misomem."

"We know that obelisk is causing the blight and..."

"So Revelation is a metaphor, but the book of Daniel takes things literally?" the second preacher scoffed. "Even if you take it literally, especially if you take it literally, he's talking about the invasion of Alexander the Great leading to spiritual desolation."

"So it's a real event, but metaphoric desolation?" the first preacher asked with a grin. "Now who's picking and choosing his interpretations?"

The expression on the face of the third preacher clearly communicated that was an area he had no desire to approach. Aloud, he said, "let's get back on track here. Do you, or do you not believe that this is the End Times written about in the book of Revelation?"

The first preacher replied, "yes."

At the same time, the second man replied, "no."

"You don't think this is God's judgment?"

"Oh I never said that," the second preacher protested. "I think this is divine punishment of the highest order. God is visiting the Korovega on us to make us pay for our sins."

"But it's not the apocalypse?"

"No. It is most certainly not the apocalypse."

"If this isn't the start of the Tribulation, what are we being punished for?"

"What else? Human kind is corrupt and evil. Ours is the sin of Sodom, my friends. 'Pride, fullness of bread, and abundance of idleness was in her and in her daughters, neither did she strengthen the hand of the poor and needy.'"

"Either way," the first one argued, "we stand facing a great evil, and..."

"Food's ready!" Ken called from the kitchen, breaking Ben's concentration on the televised debate.

"And that's enough of that," Ben said, lifting the remote and turning the TV off again.

"Always nice to know we're headed straight for hell," George quipped.

"We've been headed to hell for a while now, if you ask the talking heads on TV," Ben muttered. "But I feel you. Ain't right to blame the Korovega on God. Ain't nothin' divine about those things. If they come from anywhere but here, they were cooked up in the mind of Lucifer himself."

"But if Lucifer..." George started.

Ben cut him off. "Ain't had enough coffee yet to get into a religious debate, leastaways with you. We survive a while longer and we might see to talking about God some day."

"What's the plan?" Owen asked, coming down the stairs. Sam was a few steps behind him. Both of them seemed to be doing fairly well, considering how rough Owen looked minutes before. Neither drug their feet and their faces even seemed freshly washed.

"Today we're all making supply runs, right?" Ken asked from the kitchen.

"Not everyone," George replied. "I'm staying here to survey the area and draft up some renovations and improvements."

"Same with me," Sam added. "I'm going to help design and plan for our logistics support. Food, water, storage, that sort of thing."

If anyone noticed George's brief flash of pleasure at being left alone with Sam, he seemed oblivious. The expression came and went quickly, though. As much as he looked forward to spending time with her, the last thing he needed was for everyone else to think he was staying behind only to do that.

"Who's driving?" Michael asked.

"Me, for one," Ben replied. "Probably Jessie and her jeep. Owen, you can drive a stick, right? Can you haul a trailer?"

"Yes and probably," he replied. With a laugh, he added, "you going to let someone else drive your precious Dakota?"

"I got to," Ben said with a shrug and an expansive hand gesture. "I'll be driving the 3500. Those are the only trucks we got right now, if you count a jeep as a truck. We got to haul as much as we can, so here's what I'm thinking..."

"Food first," Sam interrupted.

Ben laughed. "That's why I keep you around, woman."

Sam rolled her eyes, but laughed in return. "Glad I have some use."

* * *

Breakfast went quickly. No one wanted to get stuck in traffic and, even if traffic became unavoidable, leaving early would give them the entire day to get things done. Owen left first, driving Ben's smaller truck and pulling a trailer. Michael left after Owen, driving his Outback. Ben, driving a larger truck with an equally larger trailer departed third. That left Ken and Jessie, driving her jeep, as the final ones down the driveway.

To their mutual surprise, they encountered very little traffic. They drove through Andersonville, but the little town was nearly silent. The few little places that were still open looked packed, and so they drove on in search of larger stores. It meant more people, but Jessie hoped that the crowds would be a little less dense.

Ken insisted that they visit one of the myriad home improvement stores in the area, before stopping for food. Oak Ridge had several, giving them their pick. Most people were crowding the grocery stores, not the hardware stores. On the way, Ken explained that he wanted to get material to keep chickens. The egg-laying birds would be easy to care for, and ideal for their situation.

After packing the jeep with chicken-wire fencing, food troughs, and other materials, they made their way to a nearby grocery store. Oak Ridge had several of varying qualities, and they planned to hit as many of them as they could in order to bring back the most food possible. It was logical to assume, even this soon after the Korovega's appearance, that food was going to be rationed to a certain amount per customer. They could improve their chances by splitting up and going to different checkout lanes, but no single store would sell them enough food to pack a jeep, not with thousands of other people descending on them at the same time.

Snow days were bad enough. Jessie had no desire to see what an actual apocalypse did to the milk, bread, and egg stock here in the South, but she had a job to do. They parked and she shut the engine off.

Vultures, or something that loosed very much like them, circled overhead. Great black wings with vivid white markings dipped and soared overhead.

"Sounds like you and Ben go way back," Ken said, stepping lightly out of the jeep. He shut the small door with a thud after tapping the manual lock. The night's sleep and shaving that morning had done him well. He no longer looked like a fugitive, though the nervous look remained in his eyes.

Jessie nodded. "Yeah. I hauled ass back here when I got his call the other day. It felt like a movie, like Ben just stood out there and yelled 'assemble!' and we all came out of the woodwork."

"Not very many of you," he observed.

Jessie shrugged. "Maybe some people don't believe it. Maybe some of 'em think they can ride it out alone, or they're responding to someone else's call."

"Or they're turning to highway robbery," he growled.

"They're long gone."

"Damn well better be. I was," he paused, "less than thrilled when they showed up."

"I can imagine."

Ken smiled. "On the upside, it was kind of nice watching you guys kick the shit out of them. I'd wanted to do that for years, but I wasn't exactly in a position to fight them all, so I cut and ran in the middle of the night."

"No one else thought what you were doing was wrong?"

"Maybe, but we were all afraid of Boss." He laughed. "Hell, we couldn't even call him Robert. Call him that and you got a black eye. He was, 'Boss,' and that was that. That fucking psychopath is the reason everyone stuck together. He'd find you if you ran. All the damn way from Chattanooga, too."

"You walked that far?" Jessie asked, eyes wide.

"I drove some, walked the rest. I figured if I went far enough, they'd never find me. Guess I was wrong."

"What'd you do to piss them off so bad?"

He shrugged again. "Told them the truth; called them murderers and rapists and told them that I wanted out, had wanted out for years, and that they could stuff their macho bullshit where the sun didn't shine."

She laughed, not at him, but at the situation. "And they drove all that way. What was it? Hundred and thirty miles?"

"Close enough."

"All that way just to drag you back in."

"Drag me back, yeah," he grunted, "probably from a rope behind the truck."

Jessie suppressed a shudder. That was not a pleasant thought.

"I can't believe you're not worried about the crowd," Ken said after a long, tense pause. He eyed the parking lot full of cars.

"I am," Jessie admitted. "It's just that there's not much we can do about them except try not to touch off some kind of riot. Plus, right now people are going to be buying the same sort of things they go after when it starts to snow. We avoid that stuff and we ought to avoid most of the crowd."

"We need some of that, though."

Jessie nodded. "We do, but not in the sorts of quantities we need other things. Milk goes bad, bread molds, eggs break," she said, counting things off on her fingers. "We need things that will last."

The automatic doors of the supermarket slid silently aside in front of them, presenting the pair with a cacophony of conversation and a press of people denser than either of them had seen outside of predawn on Black Friday.

"So," Ken said. He took a deep breath and surveyed the hundreds of massed people. "Stick together or no?"

Jessie started to say, "no, we'll cover ground faster if we split up," then her mind went to every single disaster movie and horror flick she had ever seen. Reality was no movie, but in how many of them, she asked herself, had something terrible happened thirty seconds after a group split up, "to cover more ground?"

She realized the answer was, "all of them," and replied, "no, we stick together. I'm not expecting trouble, but that doesn't mean I'm not going to be prepared for it."

Most of the people in immediate eyesight were clogging the fresh food, the bakery, and the snack isles. Other perishables, such as dairy or meat, were out of sight, but the unceasing roar of heated conversation coming from all areas of the store made it clear that they were no less packed. The dry goods isles in the center were crowded, but nowhere near as badly as the outer edges.

Worried-looking cashiers scanned item after item for the seemingly unending horde of customers. Jessie hid a small laugh. It would take the apocalypse, she thought, to get a grocery store to turn on every lane at the same time.

The biggest problem was going to be navigating through that mess with two shopping carts full of food without hitting a chokepoint or having people steal from them before they even made it out the door.

Jessie grabbed the handle of the nearest cart, wondering idly exactly how many of the things the store actually had for there to be some left in the front. She pushed it in Ken's direction, then took hold of the one behind it. Jessie strode in front of him and, with a wave of her hand that told Ken she had no better idea at the moment, said, "keep your head down and shop."

"Right," he agreed. "Dry goods first?"

"Yeah. Get as much beans, flour, and so on as you can, then we'll see what else we can get before we have to hit somewhere else."

"Done and done."

* * *

The two of them spent the next hour filling both carts with hundreds of pounds of long-term foodstuffs. Most of it was dry goods, some cheese, and a few other things. The selection of canned food was sparse, to say the least. To their mutual surprise, some ice cream remained, and after a short debate where Ken argued that their group needed some sort of comfort food, they agreed to buy a a dozen and a half gallons of the stuff.

Halfway to the front, struggling with slow-moving carts loaded down with food, the ever-present noise of the crowd suddenly crescendoed. Jessie looked, but saw nothing that could have been the source of the noise. Too many people were pressed close around the cash registers—to say nothing of the slow trickle of people slipping between the cracks and making it out the door with stolen food—to see what was going on.

The obscuring crowd parted, apparently not of its collective free will, when one of the customers was thrown against a display table, scattering a dozen boxes of semi-stale doughnuts and pastries on the floor.

Another customer, wielding what appeared to be a can of soup in one hand, jumped on top of man he had just thrown down as people, torn between watching the spectacle and gathering up the precious doughnuts before they were squashed, ran in every direction. The nearest two cashiers were already on the phones, whether to their manager or to the police, neither Ken nor Jessie could tell.

"Should we...?" Ken asked quietly.

Jessie interrupted. "No. Keep your head down."

"But they could kill each other!" he hissed.

"We have a job to do," she replied. "We have to get this," she jabbed at her cart with a finger, "back to the house so that everyone else can eat. I don't particularly want to do that with a concussion because I got between a can of corn and its intended target!"

"But..."

"Not our problem," she said forcefully. "Come on."

Jessie turned and, after a moment, managed to get Ken to turn away from the rapidly escalating brawl and to head for one of the further away checkout lanes. He caught her facial expression, realized that leaving right then was not the move she wanted to make. She eyed the struggle again, cursed, and sighed. Ken followed—he realized how hard the decision was for her, and after a moment's consideration came to agree that their errand was too important to risk, no matter how much he hated knowing that people might die if he and Jessie did nothing.

None of that mattered a moment later when the small fight spilled out into a massive brawl. Jessie and Ken were, in a small way, fortunate because their carts were already in what amounted to a corner, stuck neatly between two display racks. Others were less lucky as carts, food, and people erupted into chaos.

Someone from the crowd, Jessie had no time to determine any of their features other than a moving fist, lunged at her. She sidestepped, grabbed, and threw them down, only aiming enough to keep them away from her buggy.

Out of the corner of her eye, she saw Ken fending off another attacker. A glint of steel flashed in his hand as he whipped a butterfly knife across the forearm of large, fat man. Ken delivered a kick to his middle, sending him back into the milling crowd.

Somewhere in the midst of the mob, Jessie heard a deafening bang, followed by the massed screams of the crowd. Stunned silence fell in the ringing aftermath of the surprise gunshot as people wavered between too stunned to move and too afraid not to.

She grabbed for Ken, to pull him safely to the floor, but he was already halfway to the tile. Her instincts screamed at her to get down, to avoid the angry asshole with the pistol, and she was on the verge of obeying those urges when the other man involved in the brawl pulled a pistol as well.

She was back on her feet, fight having overcome flight, in moments. A fistfight was one thing. Stupid people are going to fight over things instead of cooperating, she had told herself when the scuffle broke out. Her goals had been to defend and escape, nothing more.

When the first shot rang out "defend and escape" became "survive." The second gunman trained his weapon on the first and a pit opened in her stomach. Someone was about to die.

Unfortunately for any rational sense of self-preservation, she told herself that she could stop it. She had to stop it. Jessie stayed on her feet, despite her hammering heart telling her with every breath that she was insane.

Jessie herself had a small pistol tucked into the front pocket of her shorts. Her hand automatically reached for it, but she stopped mid movement as a person a few yards ahead of her, closer to the brewing gunfight, drew a third weapon. He held it at arms length, swaggering with more bravado than heroism.

Shit, she cursed mentally and drew her own pistol with a small, unobtrusive movement. Common sense hold her not to, that she would only add to the carnage about to erupt, but she hushed common sense and chose to believe the other voice, the one that told her that she knew what the hell she was doing with a gun in her hands and she could, if she was lucky, prevent tragedy.

She stood with her hands on her hips, projecting authority. Her pistol was small enough to hide the grip in her palm and the barrel behind the curve of her hip. To anyone in front of her, as the three would-be gunmen were, the gun was invisible.

She said a prayer so short and quick that it might have been nothing more than a single thought, and snapped, "you three! Guns down!"

For a moment, nothing happened, but the attention of the first two gunmen was on her now. The third, one who fancied himself ready to shoot the "bad guys" without trying to talk them down first, shot her a look over his shoulder that was equal parts confusion and indignation.

"Now!" she snapped. When none of them complied, she continued in the same stentorian tone of voice, "listen. Think! Do any of you really want to do this? It's not worth it. We've got Korovega trying to kill us off. Don't give them any help! Whatever started this, it's not worth it to kill each other. Because that's what will happen. Whoever fires first, assuming you both don't kill each other, is going to take two to the chest from this guy," she inclined her head at the third gunman.

"And if he doesn't drop you," she continued, revealing the pistol hidden behind her hip, "then I will. Put. Your guns. Down. NOW!"

The two men looked at each other, then Jessie, each other again, then to the mess their brief fight had caused. The fact that people were gathered around, and that their shots might hit someone in the crowd, finally seemed to dawn on them. They eyed one another suspiciously.

"You first," one said.

"No way," the other snapped. "You first."

"Drop it, you heard the lady." The first waved threateningly with his pistol.

"Don't you tell me what..."

"Both of you fucking drop your guns or I'll shoot you both!" Jessie snapped. They froze.

"Now, goddamnit!"

She held her pistol aimed between the two men, ready to shoot either of them should they make any more threatening moves. After an tense few seconds, during which her heart did its best impression of Khachaturian's Saber Dance, one of the two would-be gunmen slowly pointed his pistol at the floor. After a suspicious glance, the second one did the same. Together, they lowered their hammers and returned their guns to their respective pockets.

"You too," Jessie said. She was looking at the third man, but her pistol was already back in her pocket as well. Despite wanting to use force first, he had wanted to help the situation in his own way, and so she felt she had nothing to fear from him.

"Thanks," he muttered, slipping his pistol into his waistband.

"Next time?" Jessie said. "Words first, alright?"

He nodded. "Yeah. Sorry. I sorta expected something like this to happen. Guess I jumped the gun a bit."

"Yeah," she agreed, then, "stay alive out there."

"You too."

She turned, looking for Ken, but he was nowhere to be seen. "Ken?" she called. Suddenly afraid he had been caught in the rush of people and potentially trampled, she yelled again, "Ken!"

"Over here," he replied, waving to catch her attention. He stood with both carts of food near the door. As she approached, he said, "I paid while you were talking those two down."

She raised her eyebrows. "Seems like an awfully calm thing to do."

He looked away, but before he did, she realized that his face showed none of the adrenaline she felt. The butterfly knife was out of sight as well. "I needed something to do, so I took care of this."

She laughed with nervous energy. Now that her attention was once again on mundane things, her adrenaline was slowly fading and her limbs felt like wet noodles. "It's a good thing you did," she said, fighting the post-adrenaline shudder in her voice. "I'd just as soon not stick around here any longer than we have to.

"Agreed."

Together, they took their two carts into the parking lot, opened her jeep, and started to load. They had all of one cart unloaded and part of the second when a voice from behind slurred, "hey! Th' hell d'you think'y're d-th-oing-uh?"

They turned. The man who had spoken was only a yard or so away and staring at their food with greedy eyes. His clothes were dirty, he bore a think coat of stubble, and he smelled like he had been drinking nonstop since the Korovega torched Washington.

"We're just loading our groceries," Jessie replied. Mentally, she was thinking: just go away, you drunk bastard. I've had enough violence for today.

"Keepin' it all t'yerselves, looks like!" he roared.

"There's plenty more in the store, promise."

"I ain't want to go in here," he slurred. "They tur' t' turned me out yesterd'y. Said, they said come back when I was sober. I ain't gonna be sober! You hear? Fuckin' things blew up the White House an' they're coming for us. An' I ain't gonna be sober no more."

"If you're going to give up, can you do it in your own home, for God's sake?" Ken snapped. "Some of us are trying to survive out here."

Immediately, he regretted saying that as the drunk's body language changed and became threatening. He grabbed at his pocket with one hand and lunged for Ken with the other. Jessie, on the other side of the cart, was three steps too far away to stop the drunk from grabbing Ken's shirt with his hand.

And she was one step too far away to stop the knife in his other hand from going into Ken's ribs.

Ken staggered back, eyes wide, and clutched at the knife with one hand. His butterfly knife was in his other hand and he slashed several times before the river of blood from his chest forced him to his knees.

Jessie grabbed the drunk from behind, pulling him away from Ken and slamming him face first into the metal basket of the shopping cart.

He reeled, bleeding from Ken's knife and now from what appeared to be a broken nose. Jessie kicked his feet out from under him and he went down hard. The drunk struggled to his hands and knees just in time to receive a rib-breaking kick. Jessie, fueled by the adrenaline that never quite left her system, kicked again and again at the man's ribs and face.

She lost herself in rage and violence—She had only known Ken for a day and a half, but he seemed like a good man, and for him to be attacked like that for no reason filled her with the desire to hurt the person who had done it.

"Jess..." Ken managed. His breathing was wet, and gurgled in his throat.

She snapped out of her red-tinged haze with an immediate clarity of focus. "You're hurt," she said, then berated herself for stating the obvious.

"A bit," he replied with a grin. He grabbed at the knife in his side, partially withdrawing it before a coughing fit halted the motion. "Got any aspirin?"

"Hush," she said, pulling her shirt over her head. She held it in one hand, leaned in close and placed a hand on the knife in his ribs. The blade was dirty and it was cutting apart his lung with the way he had been shifting it. She told herself it had to come out. It would do more damage if she left it in. "This will hurt. Do you trust me?"

His head lolled to one side in response and his eyes refused to focus.

"Shit," she muttered, then counted to three and removed the knife from his side. As quickly as she could, she removed his shirt and examined the wound. Blood poured freely from it. Stopping the bleeding was her first priority.

She stared for a moment, then grabbed her own knife from a pocket and cut his shirt into ribbons which she wrapped around his chest. Blood soaked through the fabric in seconds and, cursing, she unwrapped the makeshift bandage. Another moment of thought and she pulled her own shirt off, wadded it up, and pressed it against Ken's side, then wrapped the strips of his shirt around his ribs again.

He did not move during the entire operation. Pulse pounding, Jessie wrapped his arm over her shoulder, and lifted him to his feet. Wordlessly, she shuffled him into the passenger seat of the jeep and buckled the seatbelt. She could get the blood out of the seat later.

She finished loading the food as fast as she possibly could, throwing most of it and leaving it to sit wherever it fell. She kicked the two carts away, not caring if they hit another vehicle as long as they were out of her way.

"I'm getting help," she said. "Don't you dare die on me."

She heard no reply. Ken's eyes remained closed and a knot of fear gripped her stomach until she saw the slow rise and fall of his chest.

"Don't you die on me," she repeated quietly, turning the key in the ignition.

Chapter 8

Sam's work kept her inside all day, though she had worked with the windows open until an unfortunate gust of air sent her papers flying. Thereafter, she remained buried in stacks of paper, only without benefit of natural air-conditioning. They would soon have a third refrigerator, possibly a second freezer, and seven mouths to feed. The lot of them were going to consume massive resources if they wanted to stay properly fed. Judging by dinner last night and breakfast that morning, it was going to be far more than she expected.

Sam looked over the chart again. She had become even more proficient at drawing graphs and charts by hand than she ever thought she would be, and still the answers refused to come easily. She realized early on that the biggest problem was that none of them had any experience farming. She had kept a garden, as had both Owen and Ben. She assumed the others at least knew how to keep plants alive, but it was a far cry from remembering to water the orchid to growing, maintaining, and preserving enough food plants to feed even seven people.

She tossed her pen wearily away from her. It bounced once, then rolled to the edge of her notebook and sat there, taunting her. Logistics, she understood. She even understood the architectural plans George had explained over breakfast, but crop rotation and soil maintenance were both beyond her. Without that crucial piece of knowledge, she was stuck, and she had no time to spend on the internet delving into the theories behind it.

Even then, the best plans for how to manage their resources were useless without plans to get those resources in the first place, she thought ruefully. She hoped Ben would know; he seemed to know everything else about living off of the land, anyway. However, the fact that he had left the land around his house unworked spoke to how difficult a task it would be.

Still, she thought, the lack of a food garden around his house might have been more an issue with scale than with knowledge. She reached for her pen once more. A task that would be impossible for one person might just be feasible for seven. Teamwork, she reminded herself, was going to keep them alive.

She looked up as the glass door to the deck opened and George came through. They made eye contact momentarily before Sam looked down at her work again. He had minded his own business for most of the day except for the occasional question as he went in or out.

"Birds out there keep freaking me out," he muttered. "Big black and white things. I get the feeling they're watching me."

She looked up without moving her head. He was surprisingly sweaty. The day had been relatively cool, meaning it had to be work sweat and not heat sweat. On the other side of the—still open a crack, she noticed with annoyance—glass door, she saw a spiral notebook that looked like it had been dropped in the dirt a time or two recently.

Sam lowered her eyes to the floor. George had muddied the doormat outside, but still had tracked in a few shoeprints' worth of dirt.

The chart in front of her caught her attention again. She wracked her brain. What was she missing? Letting her eyes cross and treating the chart like a hidden image puzzle proved fruitless.

There was something, she felt, right at the edge of her thoughts and if she just kept at it a little longer, she would find it. Perhaps a new approach would work.

"George?" she called. "Have a look at this."

He came over to the table and looked down at the notebook. Standing right next to her, practically leaning against her shoulder, she could smell the sort of sweat that came from working in the sun all day. She wished he might have chosen a spot a step or two further away to stand, smell or no.

"What am I looking at?" he asked.

She explained her plans, shifting through the stack of papers as she did so, then gave him a brief rundown of the problems she kept running into.

"We need to keep a running list of jobs, schedules, that sort of thing," he said.

Sam shifted papers around again. "Here," she replied, sliding it toward him. "I'm trying to come up with some way to turn this," she tapped the sheet, "into a rotating schedule that's fair to everyone."

"Let me get my notebook," he offered, standing up and heading for the door. "I was thinking about that very thing earlier."

He left his drink on the table and went back outside and picked up his notebook.

Coming back inside, he said, "the biggest problem with a fair schedule is how much weight do we give to each task. Is keeping watch more important than building walls and," he trailed off, standing suddenly upright and at attention. "...the hell?"

"What?"

"There's a car outside."

Sam checked the clock on her laptop. The others had only been gone for a few hours. No one was due back for at least another four. She could however think of several reasons why a car would be approaching the house; none of them were good.

Her pulse doubled, heart hammering in her chest. She pushed her chair back and stood up. Her pistol was a heavy weight in her hand as she withdrew it from her pocket, but her grip was firm. That gun had killed once already. While she knew it had been done in defense, the memory nonetheless remained. The feel of the gun in her hand brought it rushing back for a moment, but she banished it. If it came down to it, she could not afford any doubts.

"Outside," she ordered.

George nodded, following. To his surprise, Ben had trusted him with a pistol and insisted he carry it with him at all times. With fingers that were trembling far more than he would have liked to admit, he reached into his own pocket and shakily withdrew it.

He took a deep breath, held it, and let it out. It only shuddered a tiny bit. "Okay."

By the time they got outside, the car was much closer. On any other road, he would have been able to spot and possibly even identify whoever it was a long way away. But here, amid dense thickets of trees and bushes and with a view that was complicated even more by the switchbacks in the road, there might have been a quarter mile visible. Unfortunately, because of those same switchbacks, that equated to maybe a thousand feet of linear sight past the treeline.

He missed straight roads.

Just a little closer now, he thought, and he would finally be able to see whoever was coming. The part of his brain not screaming with adrenaline made a note: fixing the sight-lines around the house would be one of the first projects on their list.

Jessie's jeep roared into view, nearly coming up on two wheels as it rounded the second-to-last switchback. He felt a feeling of relief and started to drop the pistol back into his pocket. It was only when he saw Sam still holding hers that he kept a solid—or as solid as he could maintain—hold on his as well.

His subconscious realized before his brain did that Jessie being back so early was most likely a bad thing and his heart sped back up, possibly even faster than it was before.

Had something happened to her? Or to Ken?

"She's early," he observed, realizing even as he said the words how stupid they sounded.

"No shit."

The jeep slid, literally, into the driveway in a spray of gravel. The engine shut off and the door opened within three seconds.

"Sam!" came Jessie's panicked voice from around the house. "George! Anyone who's still here!"

"Here!" he replied.

"We're coming!" Sam shouted back. She broke into a run with George on her heels a pace and a half behind.

The porch ended with three small stairs. Sam cleared them in a single leap, landing lightly in the gravel driveway. Behind her, it sounded like George was having more difficulty with the sudden change in footing, but he managed to avoid falling as he hit the ground with a small skid.

"What's..." Sam began. She was startled to see Jessie shirtless, but assumed that there was a valid reason for it—most likely something bad.

"It's Ken," Jessie replied, adrenaline wavering in her voice. "He's been stabbed."

Sam's eyes went wide. "George!" she snapped, instantly shifting her brain into what Owen had once called "Command Mode."

He snapped to attention, taking his eyes off of Jessie and turning his attention wholly on Sam. "What?"

"Inside. Now. Clear the table off fast."

"I was going to help carry him in, and..."

"Inside, damnit."

"But..."

"Now!"

Despite his best effort to hide it, he crumpled ever so slightly. He ought to be the one giving orders and saving the day, he thought crossly. Still, the day needed saving and he had his part to play. If that part was, "George, clear the table," then it was going to be the clearest table she had ever seen.

Jessie jerked the jeep door open, reached in across Ken's unmoving body, and undid his seatbelt. He slumped limply forward.

"I'd carry him myself," Jessie said with a nervous laugh, "but he was stabbed in the ribs and I don't want to risk jostling the wound any more than I already have with the drive here."

Sam nodded, forcing herself to be the cool and collected one. "I understand. I'll take his feet."

Jessie swallowed and nodded in return. Working in concert, they maneuvered his body out of the jeep and into their arms. Sam, confident in her ability to not trip on the stairs while walking backward, led. They went around the hot tub and directly through the door which George had left open.

The table was not cleared off. George was neatly stacking her paperwork against the wall beside the table. She admitted, she appreciated the gesture, because if her work got jumbled, it would take hours more to put back in order again.

On the other hand, "I said fast!" she snapped.

"I was..."

"I know what you were trying to do, and thanks, but clear it off now! I can sort things after we've made sure he's still alive."

"He's still alive," Jessie said firmly.

"Let's hope," Sam replied.

George took one look at Ken's body, finally registering that he had nothing on above the waist aside from his and Jessie's blood-soaked shirts as tourniquets, and his face went pale. With three great, sweeping motions, he sent Sam's work to the floor and cleared the rest of the table in seconds.

Together, Sam and Jessie stretched Ken out on the table. George, still pale, left the room without another word.

"Ben's got a first aid kit," Jessie offered.

"Get it," Sam ordered. "Does it have gloves?"

From the stairwell, Jessie replied, "yes."

"Bring those first!" Sam shouted. She looked Ken over. He was pale, his skin cold, and the two shirts were soaked with a lot of blood.

First things first, she thought. She scrambled onto the nearest of the dining chairs and leaned in close to his face, putting her ear inches away from his lips. She felt nothing, no air movement at all in or out.

"Shit," she muttered, shifting her position and sitting on the edge of the table near Ken's shoulder. She looked him over once more. He was pale, that much was painfully obvious, but there was still color in his lips. They had yet to turn blue, which meant, she hoped, that he had only recently stopped breathing.

She lifted his wrist, noting as she did the complete and utter lack of tension in his muscles, and checked for a pulse there.

She found nothing.

Gently, she laid his hand back on the table, shifted around again, and pressed two fingers to the side of his neck. She thought for a moment that she could almost feel something. If there was anything there at all, it was weak, far weaker than any pulse she had ever felt, even during first aid training.

Sam checked his pulse again on the other side of his neck, and this time was confident that she felt nothing.

She wanted to curse, but she was so focused on her task that any other action seemed unimportant. She slid off of the table and shoved several chairs aside. After checking one final time, and after mumbling a quick apology for the trauma she was about to inflict on his ribs, she placed her hands on his breastbone and started compressions.

She counted silently, dimly aware of footsteps behind her.

"Thirty!" she said, and stopped compressions long enough to administer two short bursts of mouth-to-mouth.

"I brought the kit," Jessie said, behind her.

"Lay it all out," Sam ordered, starting compressions again. "And get me, fourteen, fifteen, a bucket, nineteen, no three or four buckets, twenty three, twenty four, of water."

Jessie said nothing, but her retreating footsteps as Sam gave another round of respiration told her enough.

Sam checked for a pulse again. She thought she felt one, but was still not sure. In first-aid, she had been warned against feeling her own pulse in her fingertips and attributing it to the other person. She started another round of compressions and respiration, then another. Two rounds after that, Jessie returned with the water Sam requested.

"Is he...?" Jessie asked, voice empty.

"I..." Sam said. "I don't know. Why did you bring him here, instead of a hospital?" she demanded.

"I drove past Methodist on the way here. It was packed full; I assumed the hospitals in Knoxville would be the same. I thought that whatever we could give him here would be better than nothing."

Sam checked once more for a pulse and once more found nothing. This time, she was completely sure. "Does Ben have a defibrillator?"

Jessie smiled bitterly. "You'd think he would. He'd got damn near everything else, but no. There's nothing like that here and it would take way too long to rig one up that wouldn't accidentally fry him dead."

"Jessie..."

"Keep it up," she interrupted. "Please."

"Once more," Sam agreed.

That round of compressions, like the others, failed to produce any results.

"It's not going to work."

"Again."

"Jessie..."

"Do it again!"

Sam did her best to keep her voice level. "There's nothing I can do. We can clean him up and sew up his wound for dignity's sake, but that's it."

"Can't you do anything?" Jessie demanded. She was angry, but she had no idea which one of them she was angry at.

Sam shook her head slowly. "Not unless he starts breathing on his own in the next few seconds."

Jessie slumped heavily against the bartop separating the kitchen from the dining area. Her tan skin had gone pale, and a cold sweat shone on her forehead. She closed her eyes. "Do whatever you can. I'll help."

Sam nodded. It was hopeless, she knew, but she could at least clean up the blood. "Bring me the scissors. We can't move him around enough to get that tourniquet off of his side, so we're going to have to cut it off."

There were steel scissors in her hand a moment later. A few seconds after that, she had the shirts cut apart, exposing a deadly amount of blood and a ragged slit in his side. The wound was nearly parallel to his ribs.

"How big was the knife?" Sam asked.

"I took it," Jessie replied and withdrew it from her pocket. It was wrapped in a bloody handkerchief. Her hands moved slowly, with methodical precision that failed to conceal the tremors plaguing her movements, as she unwrapped the blade.

Sam stared disbelieving at Jessie for a moment as her mask of calm slipped. She quickly got control again, shoving her shock back down where it would not, could not get in her way.

Jessie had removed the knife, likely before putting him in the jeep. That meant most of the bloody stain soaking his skin and clothes could have been prevented if she had simply left the knife in the wound; it was not ideal, but the blade would act like a plug to prevent traumatic blood loss.

She looked at Jessie. The other woman's eyes were fixed on the knife in her hands. The blade was easily four or five inches long, and almost entirely covered in blood. Some of it could have been transfer from the handkerchief, but she was afraid most of it came directly from Ken himself. Sam's heart sank.

Had she really not known? Sam asked herself. Her eyes darted across Jessie's tanned face, searching for something besides pain. No, Sam realized, she had no idea what she might have done by removing the weapon from his ribs.

She never would, either, Sam decided after half a heartbeat's consideration. No one would know. It was better that way.

She turned a clinical eye back to the body stretched out before her. A five inch blade was enough to reach the heart, even from the side, and Sam suddenly had even less faith that he might have survived. True, people had made it through worse, but not often.

And he had failed to breathe even once in the ten minutes since they had laid him out on the table.

"Hand me a wet washcloth," Sam commanded.

She heard a dull clatter on the counter behind her back, Jessie dropping the half-wrapped knife, and then her footsteps leading away. Between adrenaline, shock, and nearly forgotten Red Cross training, Sam's head swam. She barely noticed when Jessie pressed a damp cloth into her hand. With surprising economy of motion, and an even more surprising grip on the contents of her stomach, she started wiping the blood away.

"Aren't you being a little rough?"

Sam shook her head. "I'm trying to cause him some pain."

"What?" Jessie demanded. "Why?"

"Simple," Sam said, hoping her voice sounded more sure of itself than she felt, "if he's at all still alive, causing pain ought to provoke some sort of reaction."

Jessie nodded. "Did you check his eyes?"

Sam stopped momentarily. "No," she replied. "I was took busy checking for a pulse. Get a light and do that for me."

"Will do."

Sam looked down at the wash cloth and at her own bloody hands. This made twice in as many days she had another human being's blood on her hands. Ken was a friend, or was at least on his way to becoming a friend, which made the sight of his blood all the worse. She wondered if she would ever get used to it.

Sam had finished cleaning Ken's wound, though plenty of blood still remained on the table, when Jessie returned with the flashlight. While Jessie checked his eyes, Sam felt around inside the wound with one gloved finger.

No fresh blood flowed, another sign of a stopped heart, and the blood that did end up on her finger was cold, dark, and sticky. Everything about this blood was different from the blood that had splattered her from the man she shot the day before. That had been hot, wet, and full of life. Ken's blood felt like death.

Moving him around had left a smear of that cold, dead blood on the table. Sam hoped it could be scrubbed out, but it had had close to half an hour to soak in.

She withdrew her finger from his side and looked up. Jessie had finished checking his eyes. Her own eyes were sunken, distant. They locked gazes for a moment before Jessie shook her head slowly.

"I believe you," she admitted.

"I'm sorry," Sam said, for lack of anything else. "You should probably change."

Jessie looked down. Blood soaked into her jeans in spots and her bare torso was covered in smears of the stuff from where she had carried him inside. "You too. Hell, we both need showers."

"What are we going to do with his body?" George asked from the far side of the room, where Sam and Jessie blocked most of Ken's blood from his sight.

Jessie jumped. She had been focused on Ken's body, and on Sam, and had not heard George enter the room again. She had no idea how to answer his question, though, and simply shrugged.

"We'll take him outside," Sam said. "Digging his grave will be the first alteration we do here."

"Where?" George asked.

"We'll find a spot."

* * *

George waited at the far end of the flat area below the house. At his feet were three shovels, a pickax, and a mattock. He shifted nervously from foot to foot as they approached.

"I thought these," he nudged the mattock and pickax with one toe, "might come in handy."

Jessie nodded. "Good thinking. Sam? Over here. Set him down."

Sam followed, placing Ken's corpse on the ground as gently as she could manage. His head lolled to one side, which some detached part of her found very undignified, and so she straightened it with care.

"This is far enough away from the house," George said, pointedly not looking at the body on the ground. He spoke quickly, with a nervous energy Sam had not seen in him that morning. "I thought it would work. We probably won't use this space, at least not for a while."

Jessie picked up the nearest shovel, oblivious to the blood on her skin and clothes. "Well," she said, "let's get started."

"Wait a second," George said. He went to Ken's body, knelt, and felt around in his pockets.

"The hell are you doing?" Jessie demanded.

"One second," George protested. He found what he was looking for and took Ken's wallet out of his pocket.

"Seriously?" Jessie asked. "You're stealing from a corpse?"

George shook his head. "No. If we can use whatever money he had left, sure. Whatever. We have to survive. But this," he withdrew the dead man's driver's license with a shaking hand, "is what I was looking for."

Sam raised her eyebrows. "Why?"

George looked down at Ken's body, able to face it now that most of the blood was gone, and suddenly, briefly, his expression turned thoughtful. "So we've got something to remember him by."

Sam smiled, touched. "Good thinking." She said, then sighed. "We'll want to do that for everyone."

"Everyone?" George asked, he had been reaching for the mattock, but froze.

Sam nodded. "Yeah. When my time comes, I want to be remembered, even if it is just with a crappy driver's license picture," she replied, picking up the second shovel. She stepped closer to the spot George indicated, then stopped and said, "Jessie?"

"Yeah?"

"If we're out and something happens to me..."

"It won't."

"But if it does, if we're going to die, I'd rather die among friends than out there. Promise me that?"

"So long as you'll do it for me."

Sam forced a smile. "Deal."

"It's been three days since the Korovega and we're already burying one of our own," Sam said. It struck her that if he survived, Ken would have had to endure a lot more time and scrutiny before he became "one of them." Now, in death, he had become just that. By dying on their watch, he had removed any possibility that he might have been a bad person.

Sam wondered what that said about the human race, and if that said more about her perception of humanity than anything.

It took a little under two hours of constant digging to get a pit deep enough for a proper grave. They started in shifts, but the two not digging always found standing near a corpse to be disturbing, and so they all ended up working almost shoulder to shoulder.

For the most part, they all dug silently. The only sounds were their shovels in the dirt and their own heavy breathing punctuated by the occasional curse. The birds overhead provided a strange counterpoint to their morbid labor.

George eventually traded the mattock for the pickax after it became obvious that the ground was full of rocks. By the time they were finished, he had become rather proficient in breaking them apart.

Sam, fortunately, had the foresight to lower a plastic lawnchair into the hole. Otherwise, the six-foot deep grave would have been a real challenge to escape from. They tied a rope around it so that it could be hauled out after they all used it to vacate the pit. They did so, and brought the chair up after them, which left them with a corpse, a pit, and a rope.

"I need something to drink," George said, panting. He, like the two women, was dripping with sweat.

Sam felt like she too was about to die, a feeling that the mid-afternoon sun was not helping in the least.. Liquid refreshment sounded good right then, and she said as much amid her own gasps for oxygen. The air in the grave had been cool and moist but not humid, and the hot and humid air at ground level added yet another layer of unpleasantness. She envied Jessie's ability to work shirtless and not worry about the sun; Sam's own forearms and shoulders were a light shade of pink already

"Bring three," Sam requested.

"There ought to be Gatorade in the fridge," Jessie added.

"Gotcha," George replied, walking—limping would have been more accurate—toward the house.

"Let's get the rope rigged up under his body," Jessie said.

Sam nodded. "How?"

Jessie paused. "Excellent question. We've only got the one?"

Sam nodded. "Yeah."

"Damn it. We don't have the material to make a bier, so we'll make due with this. I just hope his spirit ain't watching when we do. Wrap the rope under his arms. We'll ease him in feet first."

Sam did as instructed and they slowly lowered the corpse into the pit. George returned with three ice-cold blue bottles. He carried Sam's and Jessie's in one hand. His other held his own, which was already half empty.

Sam took the first bottle and passed it to Jessie, and they both cracked the plastic seals and drank with relish usually reserved for five-star dinners. When they finished, they looked around for the first time since emerging from the fresh grave.

"George," Sam said. "Take the rocks we broke up and stack them somewhere. Maybe we can use them for material later."

He nodded, picked up the nearest rock. It turned out to be a head-sized chunk of Tennessee marble. He carted it toward the house.

"Was he religious?" Sam asked, picking her shovel up again.

Jessie stared into the pit for a moment before saying, "I don't know. But I am."

She picked up her own shovel, scooped up a load of dirt and held it over the grave, saying, "O God, whose property is always to have mercy and to spare, we humbly beseech Thee for the soul of thy servant Kenneth Cooper, which Thou hast this day called out of the world, that Thou wouldst not deliver it up into the hands of the enemy, nor forget it unto the end; but command it to be received by Thy holy angels, and to be carried to paradise, its true country; that as in Thee it had faith and hope, it may not suffer the pains of hell, but may take possession of everlasting joys: through our Lord Jesus Christ, Thy Son, who liveth and reigneth with Thee in the unity of the Holy Ghost, one God for ever and ever.

"Amen."

And the first shovelful of dirt cascaded into the abyss.

Chapter 9

"'Sup, kids?" Ben shouted, shouldering his way through the glass door with an armload of hardware store shopping bags. A moment later, he registered the bleak atmosphere in the main room of the house. Sam and Jessie were sitting on the couch, facing one another, absently playing some sort of card game. Oddly enough, from his perspective, the first strange thing he noticed was that they both had changed clothes since the morning. Sam's hair hung in wet, red strings around her head.

From where he stood by the door, Ben had no way to tell what it was that was bothering the two of them. Neither George nor Ken were anywhere in sight, but the door to the bedroom was shut. Owen and Michael had not returned yet, the TV was off, and there was no music playing. The house felt eerie.

"Who died?" he asked. Sam's head shot up and she fixed him with an icy, withering stare that made him profoundly uncomfortable. He instantly realized that was the worst possible thing he could have asked.

"Oh, shit," he whispered. "Don't tell me..."

"You didn't see it?" Jessie asked. She kept her back to Ben, but the tension in her shoulders told him as much as her facial expression might have.

"See what?" he asked. "I saw where you guys had done some digging but... not..." His eyes went wide at he made the connection. "Sweet Baby Jesus. Who?"

"Ken," Jessie said, finally turning around and looking Ben in the eyes.

Ben dropped his bags on the kitchen table. As he did that, his eyes fell on the dark stain in the wood. It had turned a rusty brown in the hours since Ken had been taken off and, despite everyone's best efforts to clean it, seemed like it would remain permanently.

He touched the stain with his fingertips, then pressed his entire palm against the tabletop and closed his eyes. He sighed. The sound would have been relaxing if the tension in his arms and shoulders had not been obvious from across the room.

"Who did this?" he growled, grating every syllable individually through his teeth. When no one answered, he slammed the side of his fist into the bloodstain.

The heavy table thundered under an impact hard enough to make the floor tremble. He stared at Jessie, eyes hard. Much louder, much angrier, he shouted, "goddamnit, who did this?!"

Jessie swallowed hard. Ben had only been that mad once in her memory and, though she knew it would never be directed at her, seeing the raw fury on his dark face was frightening. Slowly, she set her cards back down on the table. "There was a man in the grocery store parking lot. He was drunk. He said we were taking all of the food and leaving him to starve. He had a knife and jumped Ken before I could react."

"She brought him here," Sam added, her quiet voice cutting through the tension in the room like a razor. "We tried to revive him, but..."

"I'm afraid he died on the way here," Jessie finished.

Ben seethed. "And the bastard 'at did it?"

"I beat him," Jessie said, then turned her eyes down for a moment. "Don't know if he lived or died, honestly. But I beat him until he couldn't move and then I raced here."

Ben took a deep breath, held it, and made a zen rooting motion with his hands. When he opened his eyes again, the fury was gone, but the hardness that set in moments before still hung there.

Slowly, he crossed the room to where Sam and Jessie sat. He kept his eyes on the floor or the walls as he drug the ottoman away from the nearby chair and closer to the couch. Finally sitting down on it, he looked Jessie in the eyes again.

Ben reached out with one hand and touched her shoulder for a moment, then placed both hands on his knees. "It wasn't your fault."

Jessie smiled weakly. "I know it wasn't my fault up here," she tapped her temple. "That doesn't mean I don't feel like it was my fault in here," she added, tapping twice on her chest with one finger.

"Feeling ain't..."

"...got nothin' to do with it," Jessie finished. "Yeah, I know. Doesn't help."

"Jess, you gotta..."

"Gotta what?" she snapped. "Gotta move on? Get to work? Ben..." She looked away and squeezed her eyes shut as if to will the tears back inside. "Goddamn it, Ben, I dug his fucking grave! With my own fucking hands! Don't you get that? Ken's gone, six feet under, and he died on my watch! Mine! Just..." She never finished that sentence, because it was choked off by the first of many sobs.

Ben sat watching her for several long seconds before quietly getting up and walking away. He went to the kitchen, leaving the two of them alone again.

Sam glared at Ben's retreating back for a moment, angry that he would leave Jessie's side at a moment like that, then touched Jessie's knee. She sat there with her hand on the other woman's knee until Jessie got her breathing back under control.

When she could see straight again, Jessie reached for the cards between them and slowly gathered them up into a single deck.

"It's been a hard few days," Sam said, her voice quiet.

Jessie laughed much louder than she would have expected herself to. "That's a hell of an understatement."

A few seconds of tension passed between the two of them before Sam spoke again. "Where were you when you heard the news?"

"About the Korovega?" Jessie asked.

Sam nodded.

"Out driving, actually. It came across the radio." She laughed—a short, sharp sound. "I thought it was a hoax at first. You know, like when they first broadcast War of the Worlds on the radio a hundred years ago.

"I was just driving along with the top off, enjoying the weather after all those freaking storms we had last week, and it comes across the radio. They interrupted the music and all the normal stations, too, talking about how this army of monsters had marched on Washington and attacked."

Jessie smiled bitterly. "I actually thought it was a pretty good story and I was getting into it, you know, like it was a radio play. Hell, I thought it was a radio play. But then I changed the channel, because I still had an hour or so of road ahead of me and I wanted some music."

"And then..." Jessie turned to stare out the window. "It was on every station I turned to, the same thing. The Korovega slaughtering and burning, fighting the National Guard, beating them."

Sam nodded, listening. Jessie's posture suggested she was not done with her story, even though she now sat silent.

"They took out a tank, Sam!" Jessie exclaimed, eyes wide. "How do we fight that? I mean, really fight something that can do that?"

Sam shook her head. "We'll find a way," she whispered. "We have to."

"And if we don't?"

"We will," she said firmly, trying to force herself to believe it as much as she was trying to make Jessie believe it.

"How can you be so sure?" Jessie asked.

Sam gave a half smile. "Want to know the truth?"

"Not really," she admitted.

Sam grinned. "Then it's because Ben and I are secretly super heroes," she whispered.

Jessie laughed. It verged on a hysterical giggle, but never quite went there. "I wish I could be as confident as you are."

Sam shrugged. "I'm confident because it's the only option. It's that or die."

Jessie glanced at the table, then back to Sam. "But if we're going to die, I'd rather die on my feet than on my knees."

"If we die, then we die," Ben said quietly. He had come up behind the two women without making a sound. In his hand was a steaming ceramic mug. He continued, "but while we live, we fight. If the Korovega want our lives, they can't have them for free. If they want 'em so badly; let them come and take them."

Sam nodded approval, though her face remained downcast.

He extended the mug in Jessie's direction. "Here."

"What is it?" she asked, taking it. She looked down, noting the light brown color of the liquid, and finally realized what it was she smelled. She looked from the mug to Ben—who was trying hard not to grin—then back to the mug. "When did you earn to make this?"

"About two weeks after you left," he admitted with a shrug.

She smiled in return and took a long, slow sip of the frothy liquid.

"That explains what you were doing in there," Sam said, while Jessie savored the beverage. "What is it?"

"Mexican hot chocolate," Jessie replied with a momentary look of bliss on her face. "Extra thick and with just the right amount of chili added."

"She used to make it all the time when we were roommates," Ben said, taking his seat on the ottoman again.

"Good to see you were paying attention," Jessie said. The hot chocolate was already beginning to lift her mood, like Ben hoped it would. When they lived together years before, every time she had been down she had made hot chocolate for herself using a very specific recipe. To Sam, she said, "it was my abuela's recipe."

"You practically taught me how to cook," Ben replied sheepishly, "I was bound to pick up something."

Sam cracked a smile. "So there are things you don't know how to do."

"Just a few, though," Ben replied, feeling relief at the improving mood. "I'm still working on flight."

"And invisibility," Jessie added with a grin.

"Woman, have you seen me at night?" he asked, flashing a smile that was bright against his dark skin.

"Point taken." She turned back to Sam. "You asked where I was that day. Where were you?"

"With Owen," Sam said. "It came across the TV, just like you and the radio, but on TV you could," she paused, collected her thoughts, and continued slowly, "you could watch it happen. I saw the face of their king. He had these cold, yellow eyes, ash gray skin, and fangs, like a mannikin made up of nightmares.

Sam spoke faster as she went on. "I spent the night at Owen's apartment. Ben showed up the next day, then you, George, and Michael the day after."

As if summoned, Michael burst into the room from the "high side" of the house, panting like he had just run up the flight of stairs.

"Guys there's a grave outside, what the hell," he said, managing it all in one breath between pants and gasps for air.

"It's Ken's," Jessie said quietly, and retold the short version of what happened in the parking lot earlier.

Michael went pale as she spoke, and looked like he was going to be sick by the time she had finished. "I need to lie down," he announced, heading for the bedroom.

Sam warned him that George had taken the bed for a nap.

"I'll go downstairs, then. Lay on the couch for a bit."

No one moved to stop him. No one particularly disagreed with his desire, either, but the collective feeling was that the only thing worse than suffering was suffering alone. So the three of them sat together in silence for a few minutes before Jessie picked up the deck of cards and, without saying anything, shuffled them and dealt out five cards to everyone.

They played two hands of poker without saying a word to one another. A darkness still hung over the room, but most of the tension had dissipated. In its place was a pall of despair that threatened to swamp them and prevent the work that would ensure their survival.

"When's Owen due back?" Jessie asked once the third hand was dealt.

"What time is it?" Ben asked.

Sam stole a glance at her phone. "Almost five. He should have been here forty-five minutes ago."

"Should'a been here before me," Ben grumbled.

"Maybe he got stuck in traffic?" Sam offered.

"Or worse," Jessie muttered.

"Damn it," Ben cursed, laying his cards on his lap. "You just had t' say it. Hold up, I'll call him and we'll see where he's at, assuming I got signal."

"You weren't worried before?"

"Course I was worried before," Ben replied, swiping at his phone screen. "But Owen can take care of hisself. You're just making me worry a touch more, is all."

"I can too," Jessie muttered, "and you see where it got me."

Ben looked away, unwilling to make eye contact just then. He wanted to tell her to get over it, that it was nothing she had never seen before. But the cold knot, no matter how small or how much he ignored it, in his stomach reminding him of his own mortality kept his mouth shut as the phone at his ear rang.

Ben put the phone on speaker, assuming Sam and Jessie wanted to hear as well. It rang twice, made a weird noise, and then let out a busy signal.

"Didn't even know phones still made that noise," Ben muttered, jamming his finger against the screen again. The phone rang normally this time.

"I just made my last stop, what's up?" Owen asked, by way of greeting.

"Last stop?" Ben demanded with the slightest hint of a good-natured jibe.

"I thought you were going to be back at four," Sam said.

"Hey, Sam," Owen replied. "I got everything on the list and made a couple of extra stops of my own."

"Where at?" Ben asked.

"The sports store and the art store."

"Art store?" Ben asked, surprised. "Th' hell for?"

"Art," Owen replied, laughing.

"Art," Ben said, deadpan. "You serious?"

His replies were distracted. "Yeah. I'll fill you in when I get back. Traffic's a bitch right now. I went into Knoxville to get a few things and I've spent more time waiting for traffic to move than I've spent getting stuff.

"Oh," he added, almost as an afterthought, "I've passed more than dozen wrecks and what looked like a dozen or so more already being cleaned up. Let's say, 'domestic disturbances' were the order of things today. The police have had their hands full."

"I was afraid of that," Sam muttered.

"What?"

She repeated it louder, and added, "you've stayed away from it, right?"

"Best as I can, yeah," he replied.

"Makes one of us," Jessie said.

"Listen," Ben interjected. "Hurry your ass home. We've got, ah, some news that I don't want to go into over the phone."

"That sounds bad."

"Just hurry it up, a'ight?"

"Trust me," Owen said. "I'm hauling as much ass as I can in this traffic. See you guys in a bit."

"Later. Call if you run into trouble."

"You think I wouldn't?"

"Just making sure," Ben replied, ending the call. To the others, he said, "see? Told you he was safe."

Jessie smiled. "Sorry. I'm just worrying."

"Don't act like you don't have reason to be worried," Ben said firmly.

"What's that supposed to mean?" she demanded.

"A good man's six feet in th' ground. That ain't exactly cause to fly the flag high, hear?"

"I guess, but..."

Ben sighed. "Grieve, woman! It's your right. You were there."

"And what then?" she snapped.

"Then," Ben replied, echoing the sentiment Jessie started to give voice to earlier, "we keep going. We move on. We don't forget."

Sam nodded agreement. "There's too much to do to give up. Too much worth fighting for to let death intimidate us like this. We're going to see a lot more of it in the coming days."

"That ain't terribly comforting, you know," Ben pointed out.

"But it's true," Jessie said. She took a deep breath, then, "alright. So that's our lives, then? Every day we wake up and we tell death, 'not today?' That doesn't much seem like living, but it'll do."

Sam nodded. "It's all we've got right now."

"We beat the Korovega and we can worry about other things," Ben added. "In the meantime, what are we going to do until Owen gets here?"

"I'm thinking food," Sam replied. "I haven't eaten much since breakfast. We got busy digging and, well, I didn't want much to eat for a while."

"I can understand that," Ben said. "So. Food."

"What's in the fridge?" Jessie asked.

Sam laughed. "What isn't in the fridge? With the food we unloaded from the jeep, we've got even more food shoved into coolers and packed in ice right now than we had before dinner last night."

"Help me unload the two I brought home and get some of this mess straightened out and we'll talk," Ben said.

"Two?" Sam asked.

"Two," he replied. "One full-sized fridge and one full-sized freezer. I eat a lot."

Jessie smiled the first genuine smile since bringing Ken's body inside. "That's an understatement."

* * *

"I'm guessing the grave outside has something to do with the news you didn't want to go into," Owen said as he slipped through the glass door beside the kitchen area. The mood in the room was somber, he sensed that much as soon as he took a look around. The smell of dinner being prepared improved things some.

"Hi to you too," Ben said, looking up from the skillet he had been carefully tending.

Owen managed a small smile. "That too." He paused, then, "what happened?"

"I made some tea," Michael said from the couch across the room. His voice was hopeful, just a touch short of plaintive. "It's in the blue pot on the table. You're," he paused, "ah, you're probably going to want some."

If we are already digging graves, Owen thought, I could use a stiff drink. But the day there is booze in this house is the day Ben rests in the next grave over, and I probably will be close behind him. Aloud, he replied, "tea sounds good. What kind?"

Michael shrugged. "No idea. Something Indian, I think? I just picked one that smelled good."

Owen grinned. That was as good a way to judge tea as any, he thought. "Can someone pass me a mug?"

Absently Ben reached across the counter with his long arms and handed Owen a small one taken from an IHOP years ago and still bearing the faded logo on the side. He accepted it and poured it full of the dark, vaguely rose-scented tea. By the time he was done and had set the pot back on the table, the frustration from his drive had mostly melted away.

After a few minutes, Sam joined him at the table.

Without preface, she said, "it's Ken."

With a harsh sigh, Owen set the mug down on the table in front of him. He cursed under his breath. "Is Jessie ok?"

Sam nodded. "It wasn't Ken's doing, though. They were shopping and..."

The whole story took less than five minutes, even including what Jessie had told the rest of them about what had happened inside the supermarket prior to the fighting in the parking lot. Sam shook her head as she finished. "It just bugs the hell out of me that this is already happening."

"Sturgeon's Law applies to people too," George grumbled, dropping heavily into the chair beside Owen. He fidgeted, not looking in any one direction for more than a moment at a time.

Owen raised an eyebrow. "Which is?"

"Ninety percent of everything is crap," George replied. "People too. Eight billion people on this planet and most of them are trash."

"That's not true," Sam argued. The fire from before was gone, at least temporarily. Her voice sounded tired. "We've been over this."

George glared momentarily before looking away again. His eyes were fixed on something in the trees outside, or perhaps on the trees themselves. "Isn't it?" he asked. He rambled. "I kind of liked Ken, you know. Barely knew him, but he seemed like a good guy. And now I don't know if I'll ever wash his blood out from under my fingernails."

"People are scared right now," Sam said. "That doesn't mean they're evil."

"If it doesn't," George said, turning back to where Sam and Owen sat, "then why are they already murdering each other? Hm? Owen, how many road-rage 'incidents' and fights on the side of the street did you pass on your way here?"

Owen thought for a moment. "Six or seven?" he estimated.

"Six or seven!" George echoed. "And that's on one stretch of road in one metro area in one state. What do you think the rest of the world looks like?"

"That's not a pleasant thought," Owen mused.

"It's not a pleasant world right now," George countered. "And you went out in it! You all went out in it!"

"That doesn't mean we have to bring that unpleasantness in here," Sam said. "If the world is going to hell..."

"Which it is," George interrupted.

"...then we have all the more reason to keep our spirits high," she finished, unfazed by his interruption.

"Alright," Owen said, setting his now-empty cup on the table. He started to recite a list of things that needed to be done before they went to sleep that night when his eye fell on the blood stain left from the failed attempt to save Ken's life. He pointed at it, as though there might have been something else strange he would have been asking about. "The hell is that?"

"A reminder that you can't save everyone," Sam replied quietly. "That's Ken's blood. From where we tried to do CPR."

Owen let a tense breath out through his teeth. "That's a lot more immediate than a grave somehow."

Sam nodded. "Yeah. We did try to clean it, but it had soaked into the wood by the time we got the grave dug and came back inside."

"Our very own memento mori," Owen said. "Comforting."

"'Terrifying' is more like it," George added. "I tried to get the women to scrap it for construction material, but they wouldn't let me."

"The women," Sam said the words with contemptuous sarcasm, "thought we needed the reminder that our lives are going to be hanging by a thread for the foreseeable future. 'The women' also pointed out that it's the only table we have big enough for everyone."

Owen nodded slowly, then let out a short, bitter laugh. "I know seeing a bloodstain first thing in the morning every day for the rest of my life is certainly going to put things in perspective."

"'We're all going to die' isn't exactly the sort of perspective I would have wanted," George growled.

"Quit your bitching," Ben yelled from the other side of the room, where he and Jessie were still busy preparing dinner. "Without Owen's help, you'd not be worrying about being about to die, you'd be about to die."

"I can take care of myself, thank you!" George snapped. He knew Ben was right, but there was no way he would let him win the argument.

"Yeah," Ben snorted, then turned back to the stove.

"What's that supposed to mean?" He demanded.

"Nothing," Ben replied with a wave. "Just saying that you need to watch whose bad side you get on."

George glared, rapidly turning red, and stood up. "Just a minute, I'm trying to keep this thing together, and..."

Ben turned in place, practically spinning on his heels. "Cool it," he warned. "It don't matter here, understand?" He made a motion with the spatula indicating the two of them. "Least it doesn't matter between you and me. You wanna fight about it, fight with them two. They don't need me to put you in your place."

"And what 'place' would that be?" George snapped, starting to make his way around the table.

The spatula in Ben's hand suddenly looked more like a weapon than a cooking implement as he shifted his stance and grip on its handle. "Your place," he said, "is the same as my place, or Owen's place, or Sam's place. We're all in this together. Nobody here's a hero. Nobody's desires come 'fore anyone else's. Got it?"

"Tell that to him!" George snapped, pointing an accusing finger at Owen.

Owen stood, turning fully to face George. "I went out and risked my life to bring back things we needed."

"You drove out there because you wanted to be a hero more than you wanted to be smart," George growled.

"Guys," Michael said. "Can we not do this now?"

"Let it go," Sam added, turning in her chair to eye both of the arguing men.

George ignored them both. "Without me, you wouldn't know how to redo the landscaping outside to make this glorified vacation house into something we can defend! I'm going to give us clean water once the pipes are shut off! You don't have a clue..."

Ben interrupted by slapping the counter hard with his open palm and leaning across the rib-high divider. "You really want to do this now?"

George quailed at first, but just for a moment as the big man invaded his personal space. He did his best to stand firm as he said, "and if I do?"

"Then today's your lucky day," Ben growled. "'Cause I've got more important shit to do than beat you until you smell colors, hear?"

"Don't you threaten me!" George yelled, fighting the wobble in his voice.

"Don't dish out what you can't take," Ben grated out through clenched teeth.

"You started it!"

"You threatened our supply of drinking water."

"The hell I did!"

"Anyway," Ben said, forcing a calm mask down over his seething face. "You're right. We do need you 'round here. But we don't need your attitude. I said today's your lucky day and I meant it. Mouth off like that again and I'll put your ass through that window, understand?"

George said nothing.

"Understand?" Ben asked again, leaning forward once more.

George understood perfectly. He understood that Ben, Owen, perhaps all of them, did not care much for their own survival. He understood that the more he stood up for himself, the more Ben would try to beat him down. Of course, now that Ben admitted that he was important in front of the others, George felt like he scored a small victory.

Aloud, George said, "yeah. I get you."

"Good." Ben forced a smile that would have looked fake on a game show host. "Now sit back down and relax. Dinner's almost ready, assuming you didn't make me burn the churros."

George bristled, but he knew when to fold his hand and bide his time. He sat back down without another word. Inwardly, he seethed as anger and frustration warred with the knowledge that he could not make it on his own.

* * *

After several minutes of tense silence broken only by hushed words between Ben and Jessie in the kitchen, Michael said, "I'm going to turn the news on if that's alright."

"Go for it," Ben said. All traces of his anger from before were gone.

The TV clicked on.

"...eyland Drive and Gay Street are on fire this evening after a Korovega soldier attacked earlier."

The entire room went deathly still. That was in downtown Knoxville, at the riverfront, and was only thirty or so miles from Ben's house. Owen's frustrations from the drive back were completely forgotten. Ben and George's brewing fight was forgotten. Even the food was momentarily forgotten as a wave of absolute terror, cold and sharp, washed over the room in the wake of a few short words.

"Turn it up," Ben whispered.

The TV grew louder.

"...is on the scene at Market Square, which has been evacuated by local police, firefighters, and EMTs. Alex?"

The screen, which had been half split between the newsroom and the live feed from Knoxville, went still as the feed was recalibrated. A moment later, the view of Market Square filled the large screen. Emergency personnel milled around in the background in a chaotic mix of policemen in normal uniforms, heavily armed and armored SWAT troops, firefighters, and paramedics. Behind them, the sky was filled with roiling black clouds still licked by tongues of orange flame. Off to one side, a team of firefighters wrestled with a large hose, dragging it around a mound of fallen debris.

"Thanks Joan," the reporter, presumably Alex, said as the feed caught up with the reality. He wore a flak vest emblazoned with "REPORTER" across the front in large, white letters. A charcoal-filtered respirator hung loosely under his chin. The skin that had been underneath looked strikingly clean against the layer of dust covering the rest of his face and hair. His eyes looked hollow, but none of the fear he had to have been experiencing showed in his posture or his voice as he spoke.

"At approximately 2:43 this afternoon, reports began coming in about a strange flock of eagles. Descriptions and photographs match animals seen in Washington and other major cities. Thirty minutes later, a single Korovega scout emerged from the river. Some of the survivors described it as though it was looking for something, like a predator. Whatever its motives, we have extensive video footage from cellphones and security cameras and easily a thousand photographs of the Korovega."

"Figures that people would stand around like idiots and take pictures instead of fighting," George mused aloud.

"Or running," Sam said. "You saw what they did to Washington."

George nodded. "Running is probably the only thing to do against them."

"Hell," Owen added. His tone wavered between angry and scared. "Look at all that smoke. That was one Korovega. Just one. Alone."

Ben shushed them.

On the TV, the screen had split again. On the left side, in the newsroom, the anchor spoke. "What started it?"

After a second's delay, Alex replied from the right side of the screen. "According to witnesses, Joan, several people in the crowd, civilians and police alike, were carrying handguns at the time and opened fire on the Korovega."

"Can you give us an estimate of how many people that was?" Joan asked.

"Witnesses said that at least a dozen people were shooting at the Korovega while others fled the scene. Most of the reports we have are wildly divergent, which I can understand, given the impact of this attack."

"Have you been able to get any closer to the scene of the attack?"

Alex shook his head. "No," he replied. "I've been getting periodic updates from the fire department, though. They say all of the survivors have been safely evacuated and, while the fires are still burning, they've managed to stop them from spreading any further.

"It's estimated that at least two dozen people are dead, including the ones who engaged the Korovega."

"Survivors?" Joan asked.

"I spoke with the Chief of Police earlier. He said that, while it was tragic that so many people died, he estimates that the actions of the men and women who tried to fight delayed the Korovega's initial attack long enough for everyone else to escape."

"Thank you, Alex," Joan said, "now we go to..."

"Food's ready, if anyone's still hungry," Jessie said quietly.

Michael turned the TV off. "Might as well enjoy it while it lasts, you know?"

"It's going to last," Ben countered. "We're going to eat, then we're going to train. Tomorrow, we're going to build, then eat, and train some more. When the Korovega show up here, we'll show them what for!"

"How?" George asked weakly. "Seriously, three days ago, the Korovega were in Washington. Now, there's one in Knoxville. That means they could be here before we know it. Hell, there could be one outside right now!"

"And you're gonna go fight it on an empty stomach?" Ben asked.

"Well, no," George admitted. "I was kinda thinking you would."

Ben smirked. "Me? You trying to get rid of me that badly?"

George shook his head. All of his bravado from earlier was gone, or at least very well hidden. "You're the strongest one here, so I just assumed..."

"Yeah, well," Ben said, leaning on the counter between the kitchen and the rest of the space. "Pretty soon all y'all are going to be just as good as I am when it comes to fighting."

"And if we can't keep up?" George asked.

"Then you're going to feel bad when I can knock Big Ben flat and you can't," Sam said with a small grin.

"Every defense has a weakness," Ben asserted. "We've got until one shows up here to figure out what that weakness it. But right now, we've got food to eat."

"And then?"

"And then we unload my truck," Owen replied.

Ben quirked an eyebrow. "Your truck?"

Owen rolled his eyes. "Your truck. The one that's full of the stuff I hauled through thirty miles of Armageddon traffic."

Ben grinned. "That's more like it. Still want to know why you was screwing around the arts an' craft store for."

"I needed to get out of the traffic," he said, then shrugged. "It was the first parking lot I found that was empty enough for me to park easily. I went in to use the bathroom and, while I was inside, had a thought. What are we fighting for?"

"Survival," George quipped.

"Friends, loved ones," Sam said. "Humanity."

Owen nodded. "If we forget art, music," he gestured to Michael, "then we forget the humanity that we're trying to protect."

Ben clapped his hands together. "Amen. Let's eat."

Chapter 10

"Sam, you wanted to talk first?"

She nodded and stepped out of the lineup to stand next to Ben. She turned to address the others. They had just finished unloading Owen's truck, and the sun was well on its way to the horizon. The exterior lights of the house were all on, illuminating the yard better than the dying sunlight was able to. Solar shadows mixed with man-made ones, throwing everything and everyone into front-lit relief.

Behind Ben and Sam was the open-sided carport attached to the ground floor of the house. The cars had been moved out and parked in various places that theoretically would allow any or all of them to be driven away at a moment's notice. In their place, two heavy punching bags had been hung from the rafters at one end. For the time being, they were the only things present, but, with George's help, Ben had drawn up a plan to fill the carport with equipment.

"Three days ago," Sam began, "the world as we know it came to an end. The Korovega attacked the world's capitals, burning them to the ground. They had surprise. They have what for all practical purposes is magic. They're coming for our lives, but do you know what they don't have?"

"Human ingenuity?" George offered.

Sam shook her head with closed eyes. "I'm sure they could build nukes if they wanted to. But they don't appear to want to do that. What they seem to want is fear!"

"They got it," Michael mumbled.

"No," Sam snapped, voice tight. "We will not let them scare us. Do you know why?"

Silence.

"Because we're better than that! If ten thousand years of human history has taught us anything, is that we will survive this." She indicated Ken's grave. It stood behind them, on the far side of the yard, far enough away that its oppressive fatalism could be ignored unless it was deliberately pointed out. "Three days since the end of the world and we've already lost one friend."

Sam paused for a moment, looked over the small line of people, and sighed. "I'm not going to tell you that you're all going to survive." Out of the corner of her eye, she saw George roll his eyes. She chose to ignore it. "I'm not going to lie to you like that. There's a very real chance that any of us could be killed at any moment. Does that mean we're going to roll over and die?"

Oppressive silence hung for a moment before Owen spoke up. "I don't plan on it."

"Me either," Michael agreed.

"So," Sam said, then repeated, "are we going to roll over and die?"

"No!" Owen replied.

Again, Sam repeated her question. This time the reply was a unanimous, "no!"

"So what are we going to do?" George asked. There was a trace of condescension in his voice, but not much. He clearly held Sam's attempt at motivation in low regard. At least, she thought as she recognized his tone, he has the good sense to keep it to himself. He folded his arms over his belly and waited for her reply.

Sam waved her hand in Ben's direction and he took a single, measured step forward that put him even with her. Standing next to one another like that, their difference in height was startling, but it was still clear who held the authority at the moment. Ben's shoulders were relaxed, hands clasped behind his back, while Sam stood straight and made every movement with precision.

"I'm glad you asked," she replied with a smile, then took a step behind Ben. As he straightened his shoulders, he seemed to grow another several inches.

Whether practiced or not, the way they traded off authority made it was clear that the two of them made a formidable team.

Sam quietly resumed her place in line. She stood next to Owen, and they exchanged a brief, mutual smile as Ben began to speak.

"Alright!" he barked. "Listen up! I'll repeat myself if I have to, but I'd rather not. Makes me kinda cross, hear? What you see behind me," he indicated the carport with a sweep of his hand, "is what's going to form the beginning of our training area. You're all going to learn to fight like your life depends on it, because it does! You're going to learn to shoot, to box, to wrestle, and once you've proven to me that I can take my eyes off of you and you won't die, I'll hand you over to Owen and you're going to learn to use a sword."

George snorted with repressed laughter.

Ben looked down his nose, literally as well as figuratively, at George. "Somethin' you want to share with the class?"

"It's all so ridiculous," he said quickly and derisively, apparently before his mental filter could stop it. In a more normal tone, he continued a moment later with, "normal human beings with sharp metal sticks taking on the army that burned down our nation's capital? It's insane. What hope do we have, really?"

"It's fight or die," Jessie, standing in the middle of the line, growled. "What part of that don't you get?"

"Oh, I get it," George replied. "But if we're going to die anyway, then why bother doing any of this? Why bother being here?"

"We fight and we risk dying on our feet or we give up and we die on our knees," Owen said, interrupting. "So I don't know about you, but I'm going to fight until I can't fight anymore. Besides," he added with a smirk, "training like this is going to give you the chance to hit Ben in the face." Owen grinned. "Seems like that's something you might want to consider."

George scowled for a moment, then grinned in return. "That idea does have a certain appeal," he admitted.

"Now if you kids are done, let's get down to brass tacks," Ben said. "I can fight and Jessie can fight. Owen can take a punch and might be able to fight worth something, even without a sword."

"Thanks for the vote of confidence," Owen interjected. He grinned though, and added, "I'll still beat you with a sword."

"When we get to that part, you can try," Ben replied with an answering grin. Waving to indicate Sam, he added, "Sam can shoot. She might be as good as me."

"Who won those skeet shooting metals?" Sam asked, smiling. The serious mood from the speech was gone, but the lightheartedness that replaced it felt just as motivating.

"You cheated," Ben accused.

"I am left handed," Sam replied.

"True," he said, then turned to Michael and George. "Either of you two know how to throw a punch?"

"Kinda?" Michael replied, with a doubting look on his face. Hearing the others talking about their skills, though, served to inspire him in a way.

"We'll work on it as much as we have to," Ben said. "More important, I s'pose, can you take a punch?"

Michael shrugged. "Probably not," he admitted. "Hardest thing I ever did was drumline."

"To be fair," Jessie interrupted, "that's kinda badass."

Michael smiled. "Thanks. But, no, I probably couldn't take a hit. Especially not from someone like you." He gestured toward Ben with one hand.

Ben nodded, making a mental note to assign Michael a lighter-intensity training schedule to start off with and to keep an eye on him as they progressed. He turned to George, "now, you," he said, with a wide grin, "you can take a punch, right?"

George sighed. "I took some basic Karate, yeah. But A, that was watered-down, American karate, B, it was over ten years ago, and C, you already knew that."

"Just checking." Ben looked over the entire small group again and was silent for a moment. Suddenly, loudly, he clapped his hands once and said, "so! Here's the plan. Tonight, we're going to go over the basics. We're going to cover a lot of info, but I won't expect you to remember all of it for at least a day or two because you'll get it all again and again, as many times as you need it.

"Tomorrow, we'll start the proper schedule. Sam, you got that plotted out, right?"

She nodded and replied with a simple and definitive, "mhmm."

"Good," Ben said. "So, everyone's going to have a pretty strict schedule. That includes me, so I don't want to hear any bitching about having to do specific things at specific times. If you don't like it, take it up with Sam. She's in charge of the clock."

Ben continued, "everyone's going to have work, sleep, guard duty, and training in your schedule. When you're training, you'll be working with someone more skilled. Otherwise, everything's going to be the same, just a bit more regimented."

"I notice food wasn't listed in there," George pointed out.

"We're going to try and get everyone together at mealtime," Ben said. "I feel like that's something we all need to do together."

"What about guards while we eat?" Michael asked.

Ben sighed. "Unfortunately, we still need 'em. That means that one or two of us is going to miss out on eating with everyone else once in a while. It can't be avoided if we're going to keep watch."

Michael nodded. "I understand."

"Now, if there's no more," he trailed off for a moment. His face assumed a thoughtful, or confused, look. He said, "'s that an engine, I hear?"

Owen looked around the yard. "I hear it too."

"Same," Jessie added. She withdrew her pistol from her pocket and thumbed the safety off.

"You really think that's necessary?" George asked. His mocking tone was a thin veneer over his sudden attack of nerves. Holding a gun had been hard enough earlier; he had no desire to do it again.

She snapped at him. "After what happened earlier?" With a tilt of her head in the direction of Ken's grave, she added. "Yeah. It's necessary. Now draw and get ready or get out of the way."

"It's inside," George admitted, almost sheepishly.

"Then get the shotgun from under the downstairs couch," Ben ordered, drawing his own pistol. "Everyone else good to go?"

Owen nodded, drawing the small pistol Sam had given him when they packed up her apartment. He carried it constantly since then, and the weight in his pocket had quickly become an accepted part of his day-to-day life. He hoped he would not need to fire it, but deactivated the safety just in case.

Silently, he asked himself, is this really how we are going to treat people now? As though any stranger might be coming to kill us, so we ought to be prepared to defend ourselves if necessary?

Then he remembered Jessie's description of Ken's wounds, how they had happened so suddenly and without provocation after he fought so skillfully against the crowd, and he decided that a touch of paranoia might not be out of place during the apocalypse after all.

Sam looked around, wondering if the others realized how much power they held in their hands. She shook her self mentally. Of course they did, she chided, reminding herself that she understood that as well, despite what her adrenaline-shocked nerves were trying to tell her.

She exhaled slowly and drew the revolver from her pocket. It still had black soot around the back of the barrel and cylinder. Sam realized not only that she never cleaned it, but she never even replaced the spent round, limiting her to five shots if they had to fight.

Owen crossed the yard slowly, approaching the edge that overlooked the switchbacks that led from the main road to the house.

"Where you goin'?" Ben asked quietly.

"I kinda thought that knowing what was on its way would help. You coming?" Ben shrugged. "Might as well."

* * *

Owen and Ben left the others to guard the house while they went around to the edge of the yard. Four turns of the switchback down the hillside—about a quarter mile of road covering a tenth of that distance as a straight line—was a small, black coupe. In the lingering half-light, something gold glittered on the car's hood as it raced around one of the tight curves. Bags and suitcases were stacked high on the trunk. The shifted dramatically as the car banked around the switchbacks.

Owen laughed and lowered his gun. He left the safety off just in case he was wrong, but his posture relaxed considerably.

"I miss something?" Ben asked, quirking an eyebrow.

"You ever see Smokey and the Bandit?" Owen asked. "Came out in the late '70s?"

"Yeah," Ben replied. "What about it?"

Owen pointed with his free hand at the car slowing down to take another of the switchbacks. "That," he said, "is a 1977 Pontiac Firebird, unless I'm mistaken."

"Since when can you ID cars on sight?" Ben asked.

"I can ID 1977 Firebirds on sight," Owen countered, grinning slightly. "Mostly because I know someone who has one, or I did. I haven't seen him in six or seven years, though. Remember Will?"

Ben's blank look said that, no, he did not remember such a person.

"About yay tall," Owen said, indicating an inch or so above his own head. "Joined the Army halfway through college when his scholarships ran out."

"Wait," Ben said, holding up one hand. "Monday?"

Owen's face brightened as the car made the second-to-last turn. "That's the one."

Ben grinned. "Smarmy bastard. I liked him. What ever happened to him?"

Owen shrugged. Will had started college a year behind Owen, then enlisted in the military halfway through when his scholarships ran out. They kept in touch for a while during his deployment and afterward, but he moved to Arizona less than a year after finishing his term of enlistment. They still spoke now and then, mostly exchanging comments on social media, and the last time Owen remembered talking to him had been weeks before. He had no idea how Will had found him—or, truthfully, if that was Will in the car at all—but Owen was glad he had.

Owen finished the short version of the story as the Firebird crept around the last turn. Unlike the previous sections of the road, which the car had roared around, he took this last one with the care of a man trying not to startle the guards in front of him. Owen realized that, given the way the car had abruptly slowed down halfway through the final turn, the driver probably had not seen them until just then.

The sudden realization of the possibility that the driver of the car might not be his friend sent a quick burst of adrenaline through Owen's system and he tightened his grip on the pistol just in case.

The car paused in front of them.

"You sure about this?" Ben asked quietly. He held his own pistol loosely at his side, creating an effect which was more more intimidating than Owen's white-knuckled clamp.

Owen nodded, despite the adrenaline snaking its way through his muscles. "Someone trying to rob the house would have run us over."

"You think?"

Owen sighed. "After today? Yeah, I think."

Ben shook his head slowly. "Shit. Demons burn down the capitol and three days later people go all kinds of nuts." He grinned as though it were a joke. Owen could still see the complex byplay of fear, anger, and bravado that never quite left his old friend's eyes, even in the gloom, but he admitted that it did lessen the tension somewhat

"Not demons," Owen replied with what he hoped was an equal measure of humor, "just monsters."

"Oh yeah, big..." Ben started to say, "big difference," but Owen's gesture toward the car silenced him. The mechanical window had rolled down.

"Owen?" a familiar voice called.

"Will? That actually you?" he replied.

"Who else?" Owen could practically hear the grin in his voice.

"I dunno," Ben exclaimed, dramatically shading his eyes with his empty hand. "The headlights make it kinda hard t' tell if I should shoot you or not!"

"One moment," Will replied. True to promise, a moment later there was a click and the bright headlights shut off. The Firebird's engine continued to purr, however. As their eyes recovered, Ben and Owen saw at least one more person in the car with Will.

The car door opened and Will's feet hit the ground with the relieved thud of someone stuck in a car for hours. "Mind if I come say hi?"

"Long as you leave them lights off." Ben grinned.

"Big Ben Stuart!" Will exclaimed. "I thought that black hulk beside Owen was you."

"Laugh it up," Ben said. His voice was gravely serious, but—provided Will could see that well at night—his face was split by a wide grin. He thumbed the safety on his pistol back on and dropped it into his pocket, holding out his free hand. "Com'ere, you sumbitch!"

Will did, holding out his own hand for Ben to shake. "It's been a while," he said. "How've you been?"

Ben shrugged. "Not too bad, on the whole. Still running around with this yahoo," he jerked a thumb at Owen, "but we're doing pretty decent aside from that whole 'apocalypse' thing going on."

Will laughed. "Right. Right. Whose idea was it to schedule the apocalypse for this week anyway?"

"Not me," Owen said.

"You guys holed up here?" Will asked. He gestured up the hill the rest of the way to where Ben's house sat illuminated from within.

Ben nodded. "Yeah. Seemed as decent a place as any. We're away from all the people trying to kill each other."

"Yeah. I know how that goes," he replied. "Drove my ass out here from Arizona because of it."

Owen's eyes went wide. "Why?"

"No one closer I'd trust my life with, to tell the truth," Will admitted. His voice had suddenly gone terribly grave. Owen wondered what he had seen in Arizona, or on the way to Tennessee, but decided not to ask. Will then smiled again. All humor returned to his face, and he extended both arms, wrapping Owen in a friendly embrace.

"Better question," Ben interjected, "how?"

After a moment, Will allowed Owen to breathe again, turned to Ben, and said, "there were two of us. Three after I stopped in New Mexico on the way here. We took turns, switching out every four or five hours.

"Took two and a half days to get here," he continued. "I went to your apartment first, Owen, but no one was there and the place looked ransacked, so I figured—hoped—that you'd moved here."

Owen held up a hand. "Why didn't you call first?"

Will turned to Owen with a look that said, "seriously?" Out loud, he said, "I did. You didn't answer your phone. So I came up here to make sure you weren't dead."

"Owen."

"Yes, Ben?"

"Did you leave your phone inside?"

Owen thought for a moment. He remembered having it that morning and checking his messages when they got up, and he remembered having it on the road because he used it to communicate with the others when he was stuck in traffic. Once he got home, he also remembered taking it out of his bag and laying it on the bed.

"It's on the charger in the loft," he admitted.

Will rolled his eyes, but Owen could see the relief in his posture. On any other day, Owen would have made fun of him for worrying so much. But given how quickly he world had gone bad, he supposed he could not blame his old friend for worrying when he failed to answer his phone.

"I'm impressed you still remember how to get here," Ben admitted, cutting through the sudden awkward tension.

Will grinned. "The Army taught me how to memorize maps. I checked a map at a gas station once we passed Nashville, found Clinton, and could more-or-less remember my way from there once I realized Owen had left town."

"Impressive," Ben said.

Will shrugged. "This was the only other place I could think of that you'd go."

"Still," Owen added, "that was good thinking."

Ben turned, looking at the car. He squinted in the dim light. "You got more people in there?"

Will nodded. "Yeah. I'll introduce you after we park."

"Fair enough. Owen, head back and let the others know not to shoot this guy when he pulls up, will ya?"

"Going."

"Others?" Will asked, returning to his car.

"House ain't full yet," Ben said, then looked at the car again. "Yet."

Will laughed. "Alright, hombre. Show me where to park."

"Pull into the yard," Ben instructed, indicating a spot at the edge of the driveway where his Charger had driven into the grass. "I wanna keep the driveway clear as possible."

"Done and done," Will replied, then returned to his car. He waited for Ben to move out of the way, and flicked his headlights on again. A moment later, the car was once again in motion, maneuvering off of the edge of the driveway and sliding up next to Ben's car.

* * *

"Cancel the red alert, guys," Owen said as he came back into sight of the house. He held up his hands to show that they were empty.

Sam, Michael, and Jessie were in the driveway, near where they had been standing before Will's arrival distracted everyone. Sam held her revolver firmly gripped in both hands. She had reflexively pointed it at the approaching footsteps, but relaxed—slightly—when she realized it was Owen. She also stood with one of the house's floodlights directly at her back. It looked like a deliberate decision, and a sound one from a tactical perspective. She would be hard to aim at with that light directly behind her.

All three stood with a tense readiness, but only Sam and Jessie looked like they had any idea what they were doing. Sam stood with her feet slightly apart, knees relaxed, and the gun held lightly in her hands. To Owen's eyes, it looked like whatever bout of anxiety that had gripped her before was gone, replaced once more by the calm and collected determination he was used to seeing her radiate. If not for her shorts and tank top, she would have looked every inch the part of a proper security guard.

Jessie stood off to one side, out of Owen's immediate field of vision. She knelt on one knee, elbows braced on her leg. Unlike Sam and Michael, she was out of the floodlight's area of illumination and nearly invisible in the darkness between her black hair and dark clothing. Her gun gave more away visually than she did.

Michael, on the other hand, was not so intimidating. He held a large, fancy-looking shotgun with a dark wood stock that Owen immediately recognized as Sam's. He looked as though Sam had given him the thirty-second version of how to hold and fire the thing, because even Owen could tell that his form was less than stellar.

Though physically he was much larger than Sam, and the shotgun he held was a much more intimidating weapon than her short-barreled .357, he exuded something more along the lines of, "bewildered conscript," rather than, "armed guard." His feet were apart, likely modified after seeing how Sam stood, but his knees were locked straight and, while his shoulders were erect, his arms hung limply down under the weight of the heavy shotgun held in front of his waist. Perhaps if it actually came to shooting, he would have been able to pull the trigger, but Owen would not put any money on that possibility.

Owen searched for a moment to find George. He doubted George would have hidden from any potential danger—especially not when it would mean leaving two women and his untrained friend alone to defend the house—but he was nowhere in sight.

Looking up, he finally saw George standing like a statue on the upper deck. He cradled a long gun in his arms with the barrel pointed toward the ground. A moment later, Owen realized that the gun in George's arms was one of Ben's shotguns, which might have been a problem. He had no idea how skilled George actually was with guns, but Owen hoped he had loaded slugs into the gun rather than pellets. Standing on the deck like he was, he would have been lucky to hit his target with conventional shotgun shells.

Worse, Owen realized and made a mental note to speak to him about it later, the spread of shotgun pellets at that distance stood a chance of hitting one of their own if any attackers came too close.

"Who is it?" Sam asked.

"You remember Will Monday? Guy I used to hang out with in college before he joined the Army and moved to the middle of nowhere out in Arizona?"

Sam nodded for a moment, searching her memory. She remembered him, but had not spent nearly as much time with the former soldier as Owen had and so most of her memories were of group outings to the movies and dorm parties. He had seemed a decent sort back then, though, and if Owen was not worried about his unexpected arrival, then she felt she had no reason to be either.

She relaxed slightly and smiled. "Yeah. I hadn't thought about him much in the last year or two. What's he doing here?"

Owen shrugged. "He said this was where he felt safe. He's got two others with him, too. Apparently they drove for two days straight to get here."

Sam raised an eyebrow, slightly on guard again. "How did he know we were here?"

"He didn't. But he went to my apartment first. When we weren't there—oh, and the note was gone, by the way—he took a gamble and came here."

Beside her, Michael relaxed more obviously and completely. His shoulders slumped. He looked sideways at Sam, lifted the shotgun, and asked, "can I take this back inside?"

She nodded. "Go ahead. Just set it on the upstairs bed. I'll put it away."

"Okay," Michael said as he turned back to the house. Owen watched him for a moment, then looked back to Sam.

Out of the corner of his eye, Owen watched Jessie stand up. She still held her pistol ready, but the barrel pointed to the ground now instead of straight ahead. She made no move to step into the floodlight.

Owen decided not to draw any attention to her on the off chance that they still needed a guard for something. Paranoia seemed to be the order of the evening.

"So there are three of them?" Sam asked.

Owen nodded. "I caught a glimpse of the guy in the passenger seat, but I didn't recognize him. Will said one was from Arizona and the other from New Mexico."

"Should be interesting," Sam mused.

"That's what I'm thinking."

She laughed. "Of course, this means I have to redo my entire schedule."

"I don't think it's all that necessary right now, is it?"

She shrugged. "Maybe not right now, but we've got more people than we do beds, so we're going to have to do something about that, first."

Owen grinned. "Maybe next time we do a supply run, we'll stop by the bed store."

Sam nodded, apparently unaware that his comment was meant as a joke. "Might not be a bad idea. We've still got yours we can set up, too."

Owen covertly rolled his eyes. He could already see the wheels turning in her head, though, and he felt sure that whatever solution she came up with would be the most effective use of their resources—both literal and human.

"Well," she said, "the night is young. Sounds like we ought to get acquainted with our new guests."

Owen gestured toward the house. "Shall we?"

"Lead on," Sam said, then turned her head and called over her shoulder as she walked away, "Jessie, you coming?"

Jessie fell in beside Owen a moment later. "So you know the guy?"

He nodded. "Yeah. Old college buddy."

"He's good people?"

Owen nodded again. "Unless something's seriously changed, yeah."

Sam smiled. "Don't worry. I'll put one of us with them at all times."

"I assumed you would," Jessie replied.

Sam shrugged. "Just being paranoid."

"'Prepared' is more like it these days. A week ago I would have thought six people drawing weapons on an approaching car would have been insane, now..."

"Now it's different," Owen agreed quietly.

"I'm just glad it didn't come to anything," Jessie said.

"Yeah," Sam agreed. Her voice was barely above a whisper, but the night had stilled considerably since Will silenced his engine. "Me too."

* * *

They entered through the sliding glass door on the bottom floor and filed silently up the stairs. In contrast to the stillness outside, the main floor of the house was a bustle of activity. Everyone was busy unloading the bags and boxes taken from Will's car and chatting away as though the horror of the day was, at least for a few fleeting moments, far away.

Now that everyone was in the light, they had a chance to actually look at the people Will brought with him and, especially in Owen's case, a chance to look at

Will himself to see how he had changed. Of course, he had seen photos online; they had kept in contact through most of Will's deployment and time after, but simple photos did little to convey the ways in which a person's physicality could change over the years.

His face looked the same, a little squarer perhaps, and his sandy hair was much shorter than it ever was in college. Near as Owen could tell, his shoulders looked to be twice as broad and Will held them with much more propriety than he remembered. His movements as he unpacked were fluid, without a hint of wasted energy, not the spontaneous and spastic jerks of the hyperactive goofball from years before. His eyes, however, held the exact same mischievous spark which told Owen, more than anything else, that this was indeed the same person he had come to know before he joined the military.

Ben was with him, along with one of the most handsome men any of them had ever seen. His skin was a few shades darker than Ben's, and he stood between him and Will in terms of height. Where Will had allowed some civilian softness to dull his military edges, this man looked as though he just stepped out of a recruitment poster. He had sharp cheekbones and piercing eyes, but it was his infectious smile that, Owen suspected, was the root of the way he, Ben, and Will stood around laughing like old friends.

George and Michael stood helping a blond woman unpack a small stack of suitcases. Given that they were purple rather than the overwhelmingly military mix of black, tan, and olive drab of the rest of the luggage, Owen suspected they were her personal bags.

Michael, Sam noticed, seemed to be doing more watching than anything. She suspected that George had roped him into helping the woman unpack only so that his attentions would not be so terribly overt.

Sam shook her head slightly, wondering what went on in his head. He seemed decent enough, and he was certainly intelligent, but every time they spoke to one another, she could not quite shake the weird feeling he gave her, like she had been forced to work with a used car salesman.

The day before—Christ, she thought, was that really only yesterday?—Ben had hinted that they had an unpleasant history. Whatever history it was, George certainly shared an animosity for Ben that rivaled Ben's own animosity for George himself. It would be a cold day in hell, she thought, before she put those two on any crew together. Even now, they stood on opposite sides of the big room.

She had to admit that Ben's attitude had piqued her curiosity, and she thought she might set up the first watch that night for the both of them so that she could ask about it. With Will's three new people, they could afford to have two people on watch duty at any given time, which she found to be a vast relief.

She shook her head again to clear her wandering thoughts, focusing on the woman again. She caught a name, "Katrina," but little else. She looked bewildered, a feeling that Sam suspected they could all share.

Sam went to help Katrina, who looked like she was sorting through her things more than she was unpacking them.

"I got this," she said. "You two go help with the big stack of bags and the heavy stuff."

George looked like he was about to protest, but a quick glare from Sam silenced that possibility before he could. More importantly, Michael took the hint and gently, if physically, ushered George away.

"I'm Sam," she said, sidling in next to the blond.

"Katrina," she replied. She held out a hand. She had the strange sort of accent that someone born to German parents, but raised among Americans, often had. "Nice to meet you."

Sam smiled, shaking her hand. "You too." She gestured to the small pile of stuff and the three suitcases. "Having trouble unpacking?"

"Trying to figure out what I need to unpack, honestly. I threw a bunch of stuff in here and my personal things are all mixed in with things for everyone."

Sam made a show of dramatically looking over her shoulder at the others. "And you didn't want George nosing through your lingerie," she said with an expression that was half eyeroll and half smirk.

Katrina giggled. "Something like that. Is he always so eager to help?"

Sam took a deep breath, biting back the urge to correct that phrasing into something more along the lines of, "eager to impress every woman he meets," but kept silent for a moment. It would be bad form to send the new person running into the night, she reflected. Instead, she said, "yeah. He's usually pretty good about wanting to be in the middle of things."

"I want to keep everything that's personal in here," Katrina said, holding up the smallest of the luggage set, which was empty. "I just have to find it all."

"I know the feeling."

In her head, Sam failed to suppress a wave of annoyance at this woman. In contrast to Jessie and even herself, she seemed scattered, unorganized. She should have planned better, Sam thought, then chided herself.

She had no idea what the woman had been through, or if anything noteworthy had happened to her at all, but that did nothing to change the fact that three days ago the unthinkable had happened and now she was literally on the other side of the country from where she had been living.

More importantly, she should be building bridges, not putting up walls. No matter how soft she seemed, Will had brought Katrina here for a reason, even if that reason was only that she was his friend.

Over the next ten minutes, the two of them systematically went through the other two suitcases, only talking as much as they needed to. Sam's occasional, "this yours or for everyone?" when something was not necessarily clear-cut was one of the few things that broke the reverie, which suited her just fine.

Katrina, on the other hand, looked about ready to fall asleep on her feet.

Someone tapped her on the shoulder. Sam turned slowly. To her annoyance, Katrina's drowsiness had started to affect her as well. She came back alert quickly enough when she saw Ben standing next to her. Behind him, a line of people carried empty duffel bags and suitcases to the basement.

"All done?" she asked.

He grinned. "All done."

"That was fast."

"When you got seven people, this kind of thing don't take no time at all."

"What's the plan tonight?" Will called, returning from the basement and threading his way past the others.

"You're asking me?" Sam questioned.

He nodded. "Ben tells me you're in charge around here."

That's news to me, she thought. Aloud, she said, "I want two people to keep watch tonight, rotating every three hours."

"Three?" Will asked, eyebrows raised. "That's a kind of random number."

"Honestly, you three arriving is making me throw out my schedule. Tomorrow, I'll write up a better one, but I think three three hour chunks is best tonight. That means everyone on watch gets at least six hours of sleep, too."

Will nodded. "Fair."

"That means only six of us are on watch," Ben pointed out. "Who're the lucky bastards who get to sleep all night?"

Sam pointed over her shoulder to where Katrina was already drowsing on the couch. "Her, for one."

"I kept telling her to sleep in the car," Will explained, "but I don't think she ever did for more than an hour or so at a time, and it's a twenty-three-plus hour drive from where we picked her up to here."

Sam glanced at her, reevaluating her initial opinions ever-so-slightly. She might be soft, but maybe there was something buried there. She certainly had determination to spare if Will was right.

"Sheesh," Ben said. "Yeah. She gets to sleep. Who else? You?"

Will laughed, but shook his head. "No thanks. I slept a good six hours about four hours ago, so even if I'm not on first watch, I'll probably stay up anyway. Put me on second watch 'officially,' if you would. Marcus would probably be good for last watch." He gestured vaguely in the direction the handsome black man had gone. "That dude makes a mean breakfast."

"I'm alright with that," Sam said. "So?"

"Let's let George and Michael sleep," Ben said. "I don't think Michael's feeling up to it tonight, not after what happened this afternoon, and let's not give George a reason to complain any more today."

"What happened this afternoon?" Will asked.

Ben sighed. "Man, oh, man. That's a story..."

Chapter 11

Most of them had gone to sleep an hour before. Jessie took the downstairs bed, with Marcus on the couch. George and Michael claimed the two couches on the main floor, leaving Katrina sprawled out on the bed. Owen slept in the loft bedroom, under Sam's strict orders to get as much rest as he could. Will, still awake, had stretched out on a lounge chair in the master bathroom—the only room where he could easily keep a light on to read. In two hours, they would wake Jessie so that she and Will could take the second watch and, three hours after that, Owen and Marcus would take the last watch.

From Sam's perspective, the first watch was the hardest. She had never exactly been a night person, preferring instead to get up with the sunrise and go to bed relatively early. It had made for some tense living arrangements when Owen, the would-be night owl, had been her roommate and was one of the reasons they eventually rented separate apartments. She knew she needed to learn to function on limited sleep, or on strange sleep patterns, or on any one of a wide variety of unpleasant possibilities, so she had scheduled herself for a rotating watch shift. Tomorrow, she would take the second watch, and the day after she would take the third and so on.

She also reasoned, and she hated that it even had to be a consideration, that rotating everyone through the same shifts would prevent any feelings of favoritism. Not only that, but with the three additional people Will brought with him, she hoped that everyone would be able to have a "free day" at least once each week where they would be able to sleep the entire night.

Charts and calculations filled her head as she busied herself in the kitchen, making the first of several pots of coffee she expected go through that night. She shuddered to think what would happen when the local grocery stores ran out of coffee beans. East Tennessee was not exactly prime coffee-growing real estate, and if the Korovega stuck around—or left them all alive—long enough for the supply to run out then things would be bad indeed.

Sam smiled to herself. It seemed silly to worry about such small, trifling things when the fate of the human race was at stake, but in the face of such absurdity, what else was she expected to do?

Ben stepped inside through the open deck door. To cut down on noise, they left the main deck door open so that they could easily come and go as they needed to. George, who had taken the third watch the previous day, had been the first to come up with the idea, and Sam was happy to continue doing it.

He moved slowly to avoid bumping into anything in the darkness. Aside from the light over the stove, the same light Sam was using to see the coffee pot, all the lights in the house were off. With people asleep on every floor, including in the main room where the kitchen was, keeping light and sound down to a minimum was a top priority.

It also made navigating the stacks of boxes and supplies still strewn around the house rather difficult, Ben reflected as he kicked a cardboard box with a dozen boxes of Cheerios packed inside. He winced as the noise rattled loud against the still night, but the only disturbance of the sleepers around him was a muted grunt from one end of the couch that George had claimed as his own for the night.

Slowly, and much more carefully, he crept into the kitchen area.

"Th' brain juice ready?" he asked, stopping an arm's length from where Sam stood. Ben's voice was barely above a whisper, but his deep rumble carried far. He tried to keep it down as best as he could, though Sam still glanced at the two sleepers on the other side of the room to make sure their conversation was not disturbing them.

She turned and leaned against the counter where the coffee pot was obviously still gurgling. "Does it sound ready?" she whispered.

"It's a coffee pot, woman. Pour two cups now and let's get out of this glorified bedroom before someone starts snoring."

Sam barely suppressed a laugh. "Fine," she said, "but don't complain to me when it's not brewed right."

"Brewed right?" The amount of incredulity Ben managed to stuff into a barely audible whisper was impressive. "Th' hell do I care about that for? It's coffee. You make it hot an' you make it strong."

Sam rolled her eyes. "Go back outside, you big lunk. I'll bring you a cup. How do you want it?"

"The usual," he replied, edging his way out of the kitchen. Ben managed, to his surprise, not to hit anything in the floor on his way out.

Despite her own misgivings on the matter—coffee was serious business, after all—she pulled the coffee pot and quickly poured two mugs full before too much could drip onto the burner. Ben liked his with sugar, but no milk—"black as hell and sweet as sin," was the phrase he often repeated in her hearing—which was easy enough to do in the dark. She considered doctoring hers up properly with cream and sugar and perhaps even a little bit of nutmeg but she had no desire to rattle around the kitchen for another five minutes while the coffee cooled.

Sam settled for black coffee. Dealing with cream, or even milk, in near pitch darkness would have been more trouble than it was worth, and she had no love for cream-free sweet coffee. If it was going to have things added to it, she might as well add enough to make it a proper beverage. If not, she took it plain and black.

She took one mug in each hand and carefully made her way through the open door.

Ben leaned against the deck's railing where it overlooked the small valley below the house. A large, black rifle with a night-vision scope and light hung loosely in front of him.

Sam, for all that her revolver had induced feelings of anxiety earlier, had begun the watch by finally cleaning and reloading it. When Will was still a mysterious unknown, the uncertainty reminded her that the gun was a tool for defense. It only worked when she willed it to, and it only killed when she made it kill. Yes, she had taken a life the day before, but that life had belonged to someone evil who wanted to hurt her and her friends.

Now, the weapon was a comforting weight hanging from her belt as she set the twin coffee mugs on the rail. Her shotgun, an overly embellished, engraved Italian weapon, rested against the wall behind her. She had originally leaned it against the rail, but that was open and the thought of it dropping the twelve feet to the ground was an unpleasant one. The gun, a gift from her grandfather after winning her first skeet-shooting tournament, was worth far more than she would have ever spent on herself. It had no magazine, but the expensive gun had been expertly made and was far more accurate than cheaper, shorter shotguns she had fired. To make up for the lack of reserve ammunition in the gun, she wore a cowboy-style belt that held three dozen shells within easy reach.

Ben would see anything coming long before she would, though—perks of having a night vision sight on his rifle. She made a mental note to track down and purchase some night vision goggles for general use. By the time they ran out of batteries, maybe they would have some alternative figured out.

"So," Ben said, breaking her concentration, "how 'bout today?"

Sam smiled and shook her head. Ken's grave was relatively far away, but the cool moonlight overhead turned the makeshift cross into a ghostly shape at the edge of her vision. "Hell of a day. And it's only going to get worse."

"You think so?" he asked, turning slightly to look at Sam and rest one arm on the deck railing.

She took a sip of her coffee. The heat killed the feeling of cold in her belly, but the dread was still there, and the acidic drink did little for that. She did her best not to let it show for the moment. She trusted Ben almost as much as she trusted Owen, but she had no intention of letting the conversation turn dark so quickly.

Finally, Sam replied, "yeah. But we've got three more people, which is something."

"'Something' is a word for that crew, all right."

"You seemed to hit it off with Marcus and Will well enough."

Ben shrugged. "Owen trusts Will and Will trusts Marcus. I'll reserve judgment..."

"Of course," she interjected.

"But they seem like good people, capable people. Plus," he continued, "he and I've got some stuff in common that makes starting a friendship a bit easier, if you catch my drift."

"Marcus, you mean?"

"Same one."

Sam nodded, thinking. "Katrina's nice."

"I agree. Thanks, by the way, for clearing the vultures away."

"Michael's not bad, he..."

"Just follows where ever George leads? Yeah."

"Speaking of vultures. Have you seen any more of those eagles?"

"The black an' white ones?" Ben asked. He shook his head. "Saw a bunch of 'em out over Oak Ridge and toward Knoxville, Owen said he watched a dozen of 'em circle and then dive at something, but that's it. Ain't seen 'em here."

"Yet."

"Yeah." He grunted. "Kinda felt like they were following m'truck, you know?"

Sam nodded. "George said he saw some early in the afternoon."

Ben grunted. "Shoot 'em if you see 'em."

"That's the plan. Now, speaking of everyone's favorite person..."

"Aw, crap."

"Yesterday morning, you told me that you and he had some history. Care to elaborate on that?"

"You're gonna drive me to drink, woman." A grin flashed across his broad features.

"Don't joke about that," she warned. "Owen told me how hard you fought to sober up."

"He only saw the tail end of it," Ben said. "Jessie, now, she helped me through some bad shit."

"So she's said," Sam replied. Then she grinned, and added, "but you're not getting out of telling me the story about George."

Ben sighed. "I don't have much choice, do I?"

Sam shrugged one shoulder. "Eh. Maybe. Keep it to yourself long enough and I might give up."

"Seriously?"

"No."

Ben laughed. "Thought not. It's a long one. You sure you're up for this sort of bedtime story?"

Sam smirked. "We've got two hours."

Ben rolled his eyes dramatically. "I was afraid you'd say that. Alright, Samantha Jean," he emphasized her full name for, she assumed, the sole purpose of annoying her, "you win. I suppose you put up with his ass all day today, so you've earned the right to know why I hate him so much."

"I'm all ears."

Ben took a long sip of his coffee, then shifted his position again so that he could look out over the valley below the house. Sam inched closer beside him, close enough that they could speak without worrying about their voices carrying very far. She leaned her back against the rail, watching for any approach from the uphill side of the house.

"I used to be hot shit in the MMA circuits, you know that?"

Sam nodded. A moment passed and she realized her head was out of his peripheral vision, and she said, "you've mentioned it time or two."

"Or twelve."

"Or that," she agreed. "You'd think you were proud of it or something."

"Something like that."

"Anyway," Sam said, trying to steer the conversation back on track.

"I fought for six years, and I won a lot of medals and trophies in the first four."

"What happened?"

He turned towards her again. When Sam looked, he was mimicking drinking something, holding an invisible glass in front of his face and tipping it back and forth. He gave her a self-mocking half-grin but said nothing

As Ben turned to gaze out over the railing again, Sam asked, "how long?"

"How long was I like that?"

"Yeah."

He laughed. "Too long. Five years, maybe? It didn't get too bad until later on. But I lucked out and met Jessie. Known her for ten years now. She whupped my butt back into shape and probably kept me out of the gutter while she was at it. Hell, that woman probably kept me out of the ground, truth be told."

Sam had heard that part of the story from Jessie earlier. Not that the story itself was anything less than amazing. From what Jessie had said and, if her version of the story was accurate and Sam was inclined to believe it was, she had done a lot more than talk sense into Ben's head. It had taken her the better part of two years to help him kick the habit. And it seemed to have worked. In all the time Sam had known him, she had never seen Ben take a drink, or even act like he wanted one. He had talked about drinking in the past, but always with a reference to how he "used to be."

But that was not the story she wanted to hear. "Where does George come in?"

"Two years into my career as a fighter, I met a girl..."

"Should I already guess where this is going?" Sam interrupted.

Ben chuckled. "Might as well. It's the same damn story you hear all the time. I'd be sick of hearing about it if it hadn't happened to me."

"So go on," Sam said. She could already guess the outcome, given how much Ben seemed to hate George. But she had asked for the story, and it would be impolite to stop it now. Plus, she reflected, Ben's tone made it clear that he needed to tell it, however much he might deny that fact, as much as she had wanted to hear it.

"I was twenty, hot shit in the ring like I said, and she was twenty-two. I was doing the local circuit, nothing major, but I'd driven about an hour for the fight and she'd driven about an hour from the opposite side of things to watch it."

"A fan of yours?"

Out of the corner of her eye, she saw Ben shake his head. "Not when she sat down, but she was when the final bell rang, I can tell you that! Man, I beat the tar out of that guy," he paused, "what was his name? Something goofy, like Earl Rutherford, or something.

"Anyway," he continued, "I beat the fire out of him in the fourth round. He put up a good fight, though. Busted my jaw up so I talked funny for a week afterward."

"Ben?"

"Yes."

"Focus."

"Sorry." His tone sounded anything but. "Reliving good memories. But I was talking about Izzy." He stopped for a moment to see if Sam wanted to interrupt and, when she said nothing, kept speaking. "Isabelle Harrison. I still remember everything about her, even though I wish I didn't, most days."

"It can't still be that raw after all these years," Sam said pointedly.

"It ain't," he admitted. "Time heals all wounds and all that trite crap. We had a lot more good times than we had bad, that's for sure. She was funny, energetic, loud, and she looked damn good, too."

"How long were you two together?"

"Three years," Ben replied. "Used to be, I could give you the months and days too, but all that ain't important anymore. I stopped keeping score long ago."

Sam spared a glance inside where George slept relatively soundly amid his pile of blankets and pillows on the couch. Somehow, she suspected Ben's assertion of having moved on was not quite as true as he wanted to believe. Of course, he had refrained from punching George's teeth in when they first met at Owen's apartment, so perhaps there was some truth to it.

"Thing was," he went on, "we lived two hours apart. We'd meet each other's friends when we could, but a couple of times we'd go months without any face-to-face time."

"That had to be rough."

He shrugged. "Off and on."

"I can't imagine a relationship that far apart."

"We made it work for a while." He paused, thinking. "Not all that long, though, when you think about it. Three years with her, thirteen without."

Sam did the math in her head. "So she was gone before you met Jessie?"

"Yeah. Jessie never even met her." With a grin, he added, "she did threaten to knock her teeth in for me if they ever did cross paths. Wonder if she remembers that."

"Probably."

"Yeah. Anyway. You keep letting me get off track."

Sam laughed. "I'm not letting you do anything. I'm trying to keep you on track!"

"Yeah, well."

"So go on."

"I met George at the gym of all places. He was trying to get in shape, you know. We got to talking and I learned he knew some karate, so I took him to my gym. My real gym."

"How'd that work out?"

Ben shrugged. "So-so. He never got good or nothin', but one day he decides to go with me to a fight, hear, and Izzy's there..."

"Oh crap," Sam muttered.

"What?" Ben asked, turning around and reaching for his rifle. Before the motion was complete, his face was set in a stony glare as his eyes searched the darkness for whatever it was that had suddenly rattled Sam.

"Hmm? Oh, not that," she said hurriedly. "I was 'oh crap'ing your story."

"It's not bad yet."

"No?"

"Nope. See, we'd worked out an open relationship during the first year we were together. We only saw each other a couple of times a year, so why not? It worked for a while. She met a few people. I met someone during that time—which also did not last."

"That's," Sam started, then thought about it. "Well it's unusual, but I suppose I can't blame you in that situation."

"Like I said, it worked for a while." With a surprisingly heavy sigh, he continued. "They'd been dating for about two months, Izzy and George. Now, see, before this, we'd call each other every day and talk for hours. If not every day, then every other day. Even when we 'had' other people, we'd always make time for each other. With me so far?"

"I think so."

"But after she and George got together, all that slowed down. I'd not hear from her for a few days, then a week at a time. George quit coming to my gym, too. And she'd lie about where she'd been, 'cause he'd tell me the truth."

"Wait, what? George..."

"Yep. I thought he was lookin' out for me, see." As he went on, his voice grew steadily angrier, though he never did raise his voice. "That he knew she and I were having issues, let's say. I found out later, in the same conversation where he told me she told him she never wanted to see me again, that he wasn't doing it t'be nice. He was doin' it so that he could separate us. Always figured he was lying to her, too, making her think what he wanted her to think."

Ben put his index finger against the side of his head and made a twisting motion. "Bastard's all screwy up here."

After a long pause, Sam said, "that... isn't quite what I had in mind when you said it involved a woman, but yeah. I could see that putting a damper on any potential friendship between you two."

"Her," Ben said, "I eventually forgave. Eventually. It look a long damn time, but I did. That bastard in there on my couch, though, part of me still would beat him half t' death just as soon as look at him."

Sam stood in silence, processing his story for a few minutes. Breakup stories were always biased by the teller, and something continued to nag at her the more she thought about it. Parts of it felt off, and she knew she was only getting one side of the story. It had been a long time ago, though, and he seemed to have put most of it behind him.

"Had you run across George since then?" she asked.

He shook his head. "No," he said, then, "well, once. Owen met him through something in college, I think. George was running some kind of architecture program a buddy of Owen's did. So they met, and I only found out about it later."

Sam laughed quietly. "I imagine that went over well."

Ben's echoing laugh was almost pleasant, but still carried a small tint of bitterness. "Oh, yeah. Real well. He invited a bunch of people to this bar in Knoxville. Nice place. They had live music, brewed their own beer, not that it meant anything to me at that point. I'd stopped drinking long before then.

"Anyway, I come in a bit late 'cause I had to work that afternoon, and I see that pudgy, smug bastard in there," he jerked a thumb at the living room couches through the glass, "sitting at the table, although," Ben laughed again, and this time it was genuine mirth, "the look on his face when I strolled over to the table was priceless. I thought he was about to shit his pants right there in the bar."

Sam shot him a questioning look.

"I'll have you know I behaved myself quite well, or at least as well as you'd expect."

"Which means," Sam interjected, "you didn't paint the sidewalk with his blood?"

"Pretty much," he replied with a grin. "But I took Owen aside later on and told him in no uncertain terms that I wouldn't have any part of having him around."

"Did you ever tell him the story?"

Ben shrugged. "A few months later, yeah. Damned persistent, both of you. But he's a good sort—like you need me to tell you that, you two are practically joined at the hip most of the time—and I never did see ol' George again until day-before-yesterday."

"And that was that?" she asked, somehow unable to believe, if the story ended in such a relatively clean way, that there was still so much bad blood between the two of them.

"That was that then, sure."

"But that wasn't 'that,' was it?"

"Like I said, I forgave Izzy for her part in everything before I ever met Owen. It was George, the way he had to have manipulated her, that I kept hating. Oh, sure," he went on, oblivious for the moment of whether or not Sam was still listening, "I still loved her for a long time after she up and vanished. Then I hated her. Then I loved her again."

"Again?"

He sighed ruefully. "Yeah. After all the bad memories and anger faded away, I started remembering the good times. Bad decision. I thought about her too damn much for a year or so. Can't move on if you can't forget, you know?"

"I'd imagine."

Ben chuckled. "Sorry. I don't mean to bore you with all my crap."

Sam shrugged, smiled. "Don't worry about it, I asked."

"But, yeah," Ben said, looking over his shoulder at the living room yet one more time. "If it were up to me alone, I would have tossed him out as soon as he showed up Monday. Hell, I wouldn't have called him in the first place, not even if he came packaged with a lifetime supply of free bacon."

"But he's useful."

"But he's useful," Ben echoed in exasperated tones.

"So even if you hate him..."

"I can't kick him to the wolves," he finished, interrupting her. "No matter how much I want to."

"I'm not his biggest fan, either," Sam admitted, then, "he's abrasive, sure, but he's smart. I'll give him that."

"Just don't go givin' him too much, or he'll think you mean business, if'n you catch my drift."

Sam shrugged. "I've made it clear where I stand. If he doesn't take 'no,' for an answer down the road, then I'll remind him that I'm proficient in, as you put it, 'foot-to-ass communication.'"

Ben laughed. "Fair enough. That's why I keep you around."

Sam grinned, leaning on the rail. "I thought you kept me around because I reminded you to eat."

Ben shrugged. "Y'got lots of talents. Don't blame me if I appreciate 'em all."

Sam laughed. For a moment, at least, the stress of the day was gone.

* * *

Sam's dreams that night were bloody.

She stood at one end of a dark alley. Film Noir rain beat down on her head, punctuated by the occasional too-bright flash of lightning. Somewhere in the distance, the ubiquitous "other place" where car chases always happened off screen in movies, a police siren wailed. She wore a black jacket over a white shirt, which had absorbed just enough of the rain to be interesting, but not enough to make the damp, clingy fabric uncomfortable. She wore makeup, and it ran as the rain beat down, dripping into puddles of incongruous color on the wet ground at her feet.

Had she been aware of the fact that she was dreaming, the sheer absurdity of the situation would have elicited more than its fair share of laughter. As it was, though, her dreaming mind perceived everything as being real, right down to the revolver with one last bullet in the cylinder and the hard brick wall at her back.

Five bodies lay unmoving in the alley in front of her. Five steadily spreading pools of blood mingled with the rain and the dirt and filth of the street to make her only-in-a-movie heels even less practical to move in, but move she did.

She heard the footsteps; there was someone else coming. Despite the rain noisily hitting the metal awnings and stone walls around her, the newcomer's footsteps echoed loud and clear. Like the others, he was outside the alley and coming closer

Sam was tired of hiding, waiting for the danger to come to her. She crept around the bodies on the ground, never once slipping or even losing traction on the slick concrete. Her heels clicked a counterpoint to the heavy thuds of the newcomer, whose footsteps had quickened as soon as Sam went into motion.

Fortunately, he had been far away, or had he?

Sam tried and failed to shake the feeling that he had been exactly as far away as he needed to be so that no matter how quickly either of them walked, they would meet at the exact same place: right around the corner to the alley.

She stepped out into the neon glare of a thousand street signs and there he was. He wore a brown leather jacket with a ripped white t-shirt underneath and a pair of jeans. He wore those clothes in a time and a place where everyone around him wore suits and cocktail dresses, and the better dressed members of the faceless crowd that milled about the two of them were in tuxedos and ball gowns, all oblivious to the rain.

And he wore jeans, a t-shirt, and the same face as the five men laying face-down in the alley behind her. His face was indistinct, blurry, but Sam could not shake the feeling of deja vu at seeing him again.

No one payed the two of them any heed. The crowd simply parted around them when either tried to make a move.

"Who are you?" Sam grated. Even angry and tired, her voice seemed to be perfectly level. There in the rain, she felt a strange sense of control, even fearlessness.

He only grinned.

"What do you want?" she demanded.

He lunged for her. He moved just like the others had—clumsily, angrily, with hands outstretched to grab and seize rather than to strike and injure.

Sam fired her last bullet. It struck him in the stomach just as it had done the others, only this time he did not die. Unlike the others, he did not fall to the ground. He simply stood there, gushing blood from a fatal wound to the stomach as the crowd milled around them.

Then his eyes went wide and he screamed. But what came out of his mouth was not pain or even anger. Whatever he was shouting sounded like an alarm.

He shouted again and the well-dressed crowd started to disappear into puffs of smoke and fog, drifting away on a cold wind.

He screamed again and Sam's eyes slammed open. She was in Ben's house, in the loft, sharing the bed with Owen. Her heart thundered in her chest as Owen jerked awake next to her.

Then the voice, Will's voice, screamed again, and she realized what he had said.

"KOROVEGA!" the shout this time was punctuated with the ear-splitting crack of a rifle round.

* * *

Sam was on her feet before even realizing that she was moving. Her mind was slammed instantly awake, shocked into immediate and full functionality. On the other side of the bed, Owen threw the sheets off and dropped both feet heavily on the floor. She followed suit, not particularly caring that at the moment she was only half dressed. Some base instinct told her to move and so she went with as much speed and coordination as her stunned brain could manage immediately after waking up. She reached for the nightstand and palmed her pistol.

"Owen!" she called.

He stopped with one foot still on the stop step and turned, wide-eyed. He was barefoot and shirtless, wearing nothing but a pair of pajama pants with a corny flame print. He looked about as panicked as Sam felt, she thought. She realized he was unarmed.

"What?" he snapped back.

"Gun!" She tossed the revolver onto the bed in what was probably he least safe thing she had ever done.

Owen nodded understanding. His own pistol, the one Sam had given him two days before, was still in the pocket of the pants he had been wearing that day. He had fully intended to transfer it to the pocket of his next pair of pants when he awoke for his turn at the watch, but in his panicked state, the weapon slipped his mind.

He dashed back to the bed and picked up the pistol. Instinctively, being friends with Sam and Ben for as long as he had had taught him a few things after all, he checked the cylinder and found it clean and loaded. He snapped the cylinder closed. A half-dozen speed loaders, each with six rounds, waited in the drawer of the bedside table and he scooped them all up, dropping the heavy ammunition in his pajama pocket.

Armed, he sprinted down to the main floor, taking the hollow, wooden stairs two and even three at a time.

Sam was moments behind him. After her watch with Ben had finally ended, she simply stripped off most of her clothes and crawled into bed for what she hoped would be a reasonably restful night. Her brain was still running on instinct, giving her tunnel vision and rendering her incapable of thinking about anything other than moving forward.

If Will was sounding the alert, that meant less than three hours had passed. She groaned, ruing the lost sleep.

Fortunately, her body seemed to be working on autopilot while her mind finished waking up. She snatched her leather ammo belt from the pole of the headboard and buckled the three-dozen shells around her waist. One hand tightened the belt, while the other picked up her shotgun.

She raced down the stairs. The living room was already empty when she got there. Through the door, she saw Will dash by, headed for the upper driveway. He spared a half a moment to look inside as he passed the door, but otherwise his stone-faced, if pale, attention was focused solely on the world beyond the deck.

Thankfully, Will and Jessie had been leaving the door open like she and Ben had. Sam doubted, given how pumped full of adrenaline she was, that she would have had the mental faculties to fool with the door handle just then.

Out on the deck, she rounded the corner of the house right as Jessie let off a pair of shots in rapid succession from her pistol. Her target was somewhere in the dark, somewhere where Sam could not yet see. Out of the corner of her eye, Sam saw Owen at the far end of the deck with her revolver in his hands. He took aim and fired into the darkness as she rushed to the railing.

Sam impacted the railing with the force of her half-stopped charge and leaned out over the darkness. She brought the gun to her shoulder and let her finger rest on the trigger. Something was down there, something that moved with a blue-white glow, but her eyes were still too blurry to make it out.

Someone on the floor below fired a shotgun. The bright muzzle flare dazzled her eyes and silhouetted the inhuman creature out there. At almost the same moment, the sparking flare of the pellets impacting the Korovega's energy shield lit up the area like a strobe.

She exhaled, and only then did she finish sighting the gun. As she dropped the little dot of the sight over the pale figure in the yard below her, a cold void opened where her stomach should have been.

There it was, right in front of her: a Korovega soldier. Awareness of it had been one thing, but to actually see it froze her blood. Even in the darkness, its ash gray skin stood out. In person, the thing was infinitely more horrifying than it had been on TV, not least because it was so close. It looked human at first glance, but as two and then three seconds ticked by, the subtle wrong-ness of the creature glaring up at the humans on the deck tied her stomach in knots. Its eyes were too large, too close together. Its teeth were too pointed and every one of its limbs was just ever so slightly too long. A glowing blue-white shield hung in the air in front of the things left arm.

She fired. The recoil from the shotgun slammed into her bare shoulder like a brass-clad fist. She let the impact move her shoulder but kept steady on her feet despite the growing feeling that her knees would give out any moment. Competition shooting calmed her down; this was having the exact opposite effect.

The Korovega turned angry yellow eyes on her as its hand flashed up. The shield flared with a buzzing snap where it stopped the pellets from her gun. It opened it hand, and the shield vanished. A little ball of white light flashed into existence in the center of its palm and replaced the shield. In that moment, Samantha Jean Bennett knew she was going to die.

She fired the other barrel from her shotgun. The Korovega's eyes flared slightly wider and then narrowed in what she would have called, "annoyed surprise," in a human. Its hand clenched, dissipating the energy in a small flash as the shield came alive again and stopped every one of her gun's pellets—all in a fraction of a second.

From far to the left, a shot rang out. It impacted the edge of the glowing disk in front of the Korovega. The creature turned, dropping the shield once more and preparing to use whatever came from that white spot of energy that replaced it.

As Sam fumbled, jittery with adrenaline, to reload her shotgun, Jessie fired again, followed by three extraordinarily loud bangs from under the deck that took what little hearing she had left.

Jessie's shot caught the edge of the Korovega's shield and it growled. It turned with inhuman speed, alerted by Jessie's gunshot, just in time to stop the first two bullets from the burst. The third seemed to have missed completely.

Owen fired and it moved its arm, intercepting his shot.

Sam's eyes went wide as she realized what it was doing, but she had no time to communicate her thoughts to anyone else because the Korovega had been inching closer with every blocked shot. Soon enough, it would be close enough that it could use the sword sheathed at its belt. Sam had no idea if it could use the sword and that energy shield at the same time, but she had no desire to find out. Because if it could, then all it had to do was wait them out. Eventually someone would miss or it would get close enough to strike.

"Cover me!" she shouted, pushing away from the rail and running to the stairs that led to the lower deck and then to the yard.

Jessie complied immediately, unloading four more shots at the Korovega, none of which seemed to do any good.

Sam sprinted down the stairs in the darkness. Her heart pounded, but she never missed a stair on her descent toward the devil itself. At the bottom, she fired a shot with the bare minimum of aiming as she ran. The Korovega blocked it easily, but its attention was on her now as she immediately reloaded the single spent shell.

Out of the corner of her eye, she saw Ben's eyes go wide as he saw her, but his attention was only diverted for a fraction of a second. He looked almost comical, a huge man in smiley-face boxer shorts holding a short-barreled shotgun, pumping shell after shell at the demon in his yard. Beside him stood Marcus. He looked equally out of place clad likewise in pale blue boxers and holding an AK-47 to his shoulder. It boomed again, coughing ineffectual thunder and fire at the Korovega.

Michael crouched beside them. He had a shotgun cradled in his arms, but seemed too profoundly terrified to use it. George and Katrina were nowhere to be found.

Sam reached a point that she hoped was past Will's line of sight to the Korovega from the other side.

"Kill it!" she screamed, raising her shotgun to her shoulder and firing the first barrel. The brass plate of her shotgun thudded into her shoulder, but the adrenaline in her blood walled away everything but herself, her gun, and her target.

As one, as if prompted and inspired by her shout, six guns including hers spat fire at the Korovega. It was fast, inhumanly so, but so long as they kept it occupied defending itself Sam believed that it would be unable to attack them. She was willing to stake her life on that assumption, not that she had any real choice.

So far, her assumption seemed to be right. It was still keeping up with the incoming fire, but it seemed to be lagging behind with every movement. There were simply too many threats operating at too many semi-random intervals for it to follow perfectly. Here and there someone would fire slower or faster, or have to stop to reload, or any of a number of things that altered their firing speed and changed the pattern. Each time something different happened, the Korovega lost ground.

Sam reloaded for the seventeenth time. The only way she knew the number was that her belt would only have two more shells left after she fired the two now in her gun.

Across from her, Will fired his rifle, which the Korovega barely intercepted. It swept its shield through its high lines, defending solidly against the shots from Jessie and Owen it had been allowing to impact the edge of the shield, as it brought it around to deflect against Sam's shot.

It was successful, but the burst of fire from Marcus and Ben's guns almost caught it as it pivoted toward them.

What it had not counted on, though, was that Sam's double-barreled shotgun allowed her to fire a second shot very quickly after the first. The recoil was hell but she was fighting for her life at the moment; a little bruise on her shoulder would mean nothing if they were unable to keep the Korovega in front of them from simply killing them all.

Part of the second burst of pellets from her gun made it past the shield as the Korovega swung the energy projection back around. It made a noise that was equally growl and scream, and started to say something in its language when a bullet from Will's rifle ripped through its calf. The bullet kicked up a clod of dirt between Sam and the Korovega.

Now, it screamed. The sound, like everything else about the Korovega, was inhuman. It roared and warbled, spitting curses in a language dead for millennia. The sound echoed in everyone's bones, reminding them of some fear so deeply ingrained in their genetic code that no one knew it had existed until they were face to face with abomination itself.

And it screamed again as Ben and Marcus opened fire on it. The shield, shimmering a dark blue now, expanded into a dome around it. The dome was made of energy like the smaller shield, but much darker in color. It looked somehow thinner as well; the world was less distorted through it. Bullets from Marcus's AK47 and Will's rifle made it though after hanging in the air for a moment, but by the time they struck their target they were moving so slow they were barely more dangerous than an airgun pellet. The shotguns and pistols impacted almost as harmlessly against the dome as they had against the shield.

The Korovega screamed another curse as it turned and ran and the triumphant shout that followed in the wake of its departure would have awoken the dead. The cheers were so loud and continued on for so long that Sam had no idea what anyone was saying after the first few seconds. After the first minute, she had no idea what she herself was saying either, but she still shouted herself hoarse, hurling mockery and insults at the retreating demon that had tried and failed to kill them.

The shouts slowly died down as the giddy rush of victory retreated. Sam approached Ben and Marcus. She already sounded hoarse from yelling, but that was the least of her worries. "So the bastards can bleed, after all."

"Damn straight," Marcus replied.

Sam panted. "We did good. Thank God my plan worked."

Ben nodded and folded his arms across his massive chest. The shotgun hung from a shoulder sling, momentarily ignored. "We're alive." He nodded once, then looked at Sam. "Now, I just got one question."

"Hmm?" Sam cocked her head slightly.

"Why the hell are you naked?"

Chapter 12

Sleep was elusive the rest of the night. The few able to get some rest spent their sleep tossing and turning. Katrina, who never went outside and so never saw the Korovega in the flesh was the first one back in bed, but even she spent as much time awake as asleep. George claimed the couch as his bed again, but the constant creaking as he shifted around and the occasional footsteps as he would get up and pace, or simply stare out the window, made his mental state clear. Michael nodded off in the chair in the bedroom, intending to keep Katrina company in case she needed anything, but eventually fatigue took over from adrenaline and he sank into profoundly restless sleep. Owen had tried to at least take a nap in the loft bed, but found himself unable to sleep at all and so he rejoined the others still awake in the basement.

When he came down the steps, he found Ben sitting in his chair. Will sat in the opposite chair. The lights were dim, and against the black leather of the chair, Ben seemed swathed in shadow. Sam was sprawled out on her back on the couch, obviously fighting some combination of fatigue and residual panic. Jessie and Marcus were nowhere to be seen.

Will was still dressed like he had been before the Korovega appeared, while Ben had thrown on a tattered, white t-shirt and a pair of jeans over his boxers. Sam, he saw, had dressed in a tank top and shorts. The bottoms of her bare feet were stained green.

Owen looked down at his flame-print pajama pants. They were all he wore; a shirt was not worth the time it would have taken to put on so late at night. Compared to the others, though, he fit right in.

"Somebody keeping watch?" he asked, reaching the bottom of the stairs.

"Jessie's upstairs and Marcus is right outside," Sam replied from the other side of the couch.

"Couldn't sleep?" Ben asked.

The red rim around Ben's eyes and the shell-shocked expression told Owen that he was not the only one who had tried and failed to sleep. Will seemed less perturbed than Ben, but he had an unfamiliar set to his eyes and his jaw that Owen had never seen before.

Owen shook his head. "No. You guys can't either?"

Sam sat up on the couch, leaning heavily on one of the thick arms. Her legs were still stretched out along half of the couch's length, but the shift opened up enough room for another person to sit. She waved to the now-empty end of the couch.

"I tried," she said. "It didn't go well."

"Down here?" he asked, sitting down heavily.

She nodded. "Not by choice. I stretched out here to try and decompress my muscles after you went upstairs. Didn't intend to fall asleep at all, but one moment I was listening to these two talk," she waved at Will and Ben, then shuddered despite the warm, close air, "and the next moment I was staring down that damn Korovega again."

"Clothed, I hope?" Owen asked with a grin.

Sam rolled her eyes. She chose to ignore the tinge of pink that crept across her pale shoulders. "Yes. Clothed. Trust me, these two have already taken the liberty to remind me of that fact."

Will shrugged. He grinned, but the steely set never left his eyes. Owen noticed that his eyes seemed to dart back and forth around the room, as though he were hearing things no one else could hear. His conscious attention was fixed in one place, but still he kept looking around.

"I thought I might have been dreaming then," Will said. He laughed. "Beautiful redhead comes storming out of the house with a shotgun, and she's not wearing anything but an ammo belt?"

Sam flushed, for real this time. She was not embarrassed to have gone nearly naked in front of everyone. The situation had called for immediate reactions, after all, and immediate meant some steps get skipped when running out the door. Rather, it was the way in which Will, and to a lesser extent Ben, were making it out to be some badass feat that flustered her. She had simply done what needed to be done, nothing more and nothing less.

"I was wearing underwear," she protested.

"Same periwinkle blue as Marcus had on, too," Ben added, amid guffaws of laughter.

"Since when do you use words like periwinkle?" she asked, trying to divert the subject.

Ben took on a mock-haughty look and said, "what, I ain't allowed to know fancy colors?" Then he grinned, laughed again, and added, "naw, periwinkle is what Marcus called his. Said you wearin' the same color panties as his shorts was funnier than you runnin' out there naked."

"Not naked," she said again and stuck her tongue out at Ben.

Will laughed quietly. "Hell, I thought my time was come and you were a Valkyrie come to take me to Valhalla."

Owen laughed.

"It's not that big a deal, guys," Sam said. "I heard you yelling and I grabbed my shotgun. If it'll make you feel better next time, I'll stop to get dressed before staring down humanity's worst nightmare."

Ben grinned. "No, no, I think you were fine the way you were."

She rolled her eyes. "Thanks."

"Seriously, though," he said, "when you came barreling down them stairs like some sorta red-haired war goddess I didn't know what to think. But when you went out to distract it that was damn good thinking."

"It made sense at the time. I knew I could've been killed running out there like that, but that thing was slowly getting closer."

"No two ways about it," Will said. "That monster was keeping up, somehow, with every shot we made. I don't know how it knew when we were going to fire, but it did and it blocked every one of them until you went out there and we got a crossfire going. No," he repeated, "there's no two ways about it. We'd be dead if not for you."

She flushed once more. In an effort to distract them, again, from praising her, she said, "I was watching its eyes when it was out there. Truthfully, I could barely look away. It was like staring down a snake that could do higher math."

That elicited a small peal of laughter from the group.

Sam sat up a little straighter. "Seriously, it was watching us. Its eyes were constantly moving around. I don't think it has any special powers or anything. It's just really damn good at being observant."

"What do we do next time?" Owen asked.

"That's what we were talking about before you came down," Sam said.

"Give me the short version?"

Ben shrugged. "Same as it was before. Only now we got more people to train and to help. Will," he pointed with one finger, "and Marcus," he turned his hand over and pointed to the door with his thumb, "can fight. But if your theory is right and we have to kill these things with swords one-on-one, then we need to teach them how, and fast."

"Still sounds crazy," Will said. He sighed, then, "but I saw how one of those things almost killed the six of us with guns because it had that shield. If one or two people can get up in its face and stab it to death without it frying them, then maybe it's not such a crazy plan." He trailed off for a moment, lost in his thoughts.

The others chose to let him think, giving him a moment to collect his thoughts.

"But do we know that it's even possible?" he finished after a moment's silence.

"I think so," Sam said. "We hurt it. Before that, we pissed it off. So why didn't it fire that beam we saw them use in D.C.?" Before anyone could answer, she continued, "It kept its shield up with one hand, but never did anything with the other. The one time it tried to do something, it created this ball of light in its palm. I think that was the beam weapon. I think it was charging somehow. It had to drop the shield, though. That's got to be important. I think that's why it never used the beam. It can't do both."

Owen held up two fingers. "So now we know two things about them."

"Two?" Ben asked.

Owen nodded. "One, what Sam said. Two," his eyes narrowed and he growled, "we know those bastards can bleed!"

"Goddamn right!" Will exclaimed. "Hooah." He cupped his had around an invisible glass and raised it in the air in salute. "But," he put the nonexistent glass back down on the arm of his leather chair, "what are we going to do?"

Ben snorted. "Kill 'em."

"But," Will repeated, "what are we going to do?"

"In the short term," Sam replied, "we've got a construction project to work on."

"Several projects," Owen corrected.

Sam nodded. "Right. He," she pointed at the ceiling in the general direction of where George was trying to sleep on the couch, "apparently has quite the brain between his ears. He's drawn up a half-dozen or so projects for us to work on as time goes on."

"What's first?"

"We need to build a workshop," Ben said. He jerked his thumb at the storage room adjoining the basement. It was now filled with additional boxes from their supply run earlier that day: extra material, spare parts, and nonperishable food that would not fit into any of the three refrigerators around the house. "That ain't cutting it no more. Not with nine of us here. We need that room for storage and not much else. I'd like to turn it into a walk-in cooler..."

Will held up a hand to interrupt. "Let's not get ahead of ourselves. What did you have in mind for the workshop?"

He had addressed the question to Ben, but Sam answered. She explained the general idea, a simple, single-room building with a large door at one end to allow machinery in and out and enough windows for light and heat. It would have to be wired for a fair amount of electricity, she said, but one of George's less grandiose plans called for a water wheel which could provide enough energy to power anything they had in mind.

"I assume we have the material?"

Ben nodded. "We picked up some of it today, and I've had some quick-drying concrete laying around for years. Always meant to pave that spot under the deck where I used to park. The," he made air quotes with his fingers, "'new and improved,' training area."

"Why not lay down come cement there, anyway?"

Ben almost replied, stopped, then said, "it's on the list. You volunteering?"

Will spread his hands apologetically. "You guys saved my life tonight, I'm happy to render whatever assistance I can."

"You were Army, right?" Sam asked, seemingly out of the blue.

Will nodded. "Yes'm. Marcus, too." He grinned. "Helps explain how I didn't shoot you by accident."

"Thanks for that, by the way."

"I make it a point of habit not to shoot naked, shotgun-toting redheads who're actively trying to kill the same thing I am."

Sam rolled her eyes again. At least, she thought, he was obviously joking around. The same line coming from, say, George would most likely have carried enough overly-interested undertones to make her profoundly uncomfortable. As it was, she just felt like Will was being a bit of a goofball as the adrenaline high wore off.

"That happen often?" she asked, smirking.

"Once, so far," he admitted. "But it's probably a good habit to have."

"Probably," she agreed.

"Anyway," Ben said with a loud mock sigh. "We're going to teach everyone who lives here how to fight. That means starting with fists, going to knives and swords, and stopping at guns."

"We ought to start with guns," Will offered.

Ben disagreed. "I was going to do it that way before, but now that I seen the Korovega up close, seen just how guns really don't do shit-all against them, I don't know."

"We wounded it," Will said. "That counts for something."

"We used up a lot of bullets, too," Ben observed. "I reloaded six or seven times, so thirty or thirty-five shells. I watched Marcus change out twice too, and that AK holds thirty."

"I reloaded twice," Owen added, almost ashamed of the numerical difference, "so maybe I shot it fifteen times?"

"I went though all but two shells in my belt," Sam said. "So right at three dozen."

Will sat in thought for a moment, steepling his fingers in front of his face. "The military'd call that acceptable, but we don't exactly have an armory and five hundred thousand more rounds to burn."

"No." Ben said. He chuckled. "I ain't got that big a collection."

"Damn," Will muttered. "Even if we only went through a quarter what we did for an actual kill, we'd still run out fast."

"People are already making runs on the gun stores," Ben agreed. "Just a matter of time before it's all gone."

"So why not just skip firearms training completely?" Will asked.

"Sometimes you have to kill things that don't have energy shields," Sam muttered.

"Ah, yeah," Will said. "Owen told me about that."

Sam looked away. After a moment, she turned her eyes, and only her eyes, toward him again. "It ever get easier?"

Will sighed. He looked at Owen out of the corer of his eyes. He said, "you don't want to know the answer to that."

Neither Sam nor Owen was sure who, exactly, he was addressing, but she replied. "Yes. I do. I just," she paused, took in a deep breath. "I just need to know."

Will closed his eyes. "Yeah." He paused for a moment. "It does, after a while." He shook his head slowly, sadly. "After a while, it gets pretty damn easy."

Sam let out a tense lungful of air. "Good."

"No," Will countered firmly. "Not good."

"Easy means I'll eventually be able to sleep at night."

"No," he said. He sat upright in his chair. "It gets easier to kill, but that doesn't mean you forget. I see things when I close my eyes, in here," he tapped the side of his head, "that I pray you guys never have to see."

"And when you don't have a choice?" Sam asked, softly.

Will sighed. It was a slow, deliberate sound. "You live with it," he said. His eyes were focused elsewhere and his voice had taken on a gravely tone that Owen had never heard before. "Doing it, pulling the trigger, thrusting the knife, throwing the grenade, it all becomes so very easy after a while. Eventually, you maybe don't even think about it."

Tense silence fell for a moment. No one, not even Sam, wanted to interrupt.

"When it starts to get easy," Will said after a moment, then, "you don't want to be that kind of person."

"I just don't want to feel," she groped for words, then simply thumped her chest with the side of her fist, "this anymore. This hole."

Will sat silent for a moment. "It helps, for what it's worth, to have someone to talk to."

Sam sighed, then smiled. "I'll keep that in mind, thanks. Now if you three don't mind, I'm going upstairs to try to sleep again."

She started to stand as Ben said, "hold up a minute. You got tomorrow's schedule done yet?"

Sam, despite her fatigue, laughed. "Actually, yeah. It just took some shifting around after everyone got unpacked."

"And we're all still alive, so we don't have to redo it," Will said with a grin.

Sam shot him a withering look, but relented when she saw what was in his eyes. His face was grinning, but that hard set his his eyes from before still remained. Finally, she thought she understood where it had come from. She had seen that look on Will's face for a moment when Ben hold him about Ken's death, and she finally realized that, had the Korovega killed one of them earlier, it would not have been the first death of a friend he had seen.

And that, she thought to herself, would be the hardest thing to get past.

She returned his grin with a wan smile and sat back down. "Yeah, there's that."

"Care to fill us mere mortals in on it?" Ben asked.

She did, explaining the system she came up with. Everyone had a something to do, either working, training, or guarding the house. At lunch, they all would switch to something else, except for Owen and Will, whom she had tasked to make another supply run.

"I'm sure that'll be lots of fun," Ben muttered.

"Being stuck with me all day?" Will grinned. "I can see how that would get old."

Ben laughed. "No, he's going to love going back out in that mess of traffic right now."

"Oh, yeah, that," Will replied with an exasperated sigh. "Why do you think it took me so long to get here?"

"I dunno," Ben replied with a laugh, "because you were driving all the way from freaking Arizona?"

"Well, yeah," he replied, "but after that."

Owen shrugged. "We'll manage," he said, interrupting Will. "Sam and I already talked about it and I've got copies of George's material list and the list Sam wrote out for me."

"To go back to what we were talking about earlier," Will said, "Marcus has a bayonet for his AK, but I don't have one for my AR on hand. Would it be worth learning to use?"

Ben thought for a moment. "Could be. If you need something with a bayonet, I've got one on my Nagant..."

"That's got to be a beast," Will interjected.

"It is," Owen said.

"Keep it in mind," Ben offered. "Only thing is I'd be about that fancy gun of yours if we stuck a bayonet on it. What happens when a Korovega busts it up? One good smack with a sword and that sight's gone. Might even take the receiver with it."

"It's something to consider," Will replied. "At the very least, somebody with a gun could provide covering fire.

Ben nodded. "Yeah. I imagine it's not too different from spear fighting, really."

"It isn't," Owen added. "We did some a few years back before you joined the group, but no one wanted to keep it up. It'd be good for people who might not have much time to devote to learning to use a sword."

"Good point," Ben said. "Let's talk about it some more once we get people started learning how to fight. Then we can figure out what weapons work best and all that jazz."

Owen nodded. "Yeah. One step at a time."

"Not that you all aren't good at improvisation," Will said.

Owen laughed. "You do what you've got to to survive, I suppose."

"Ain't that the God's-honest truth," Will muttered. "Anyway, she's nodded off again." He pointed toward where Sam lay slumped against the arm of the couch. Her eyes were closed and her breathing was shallow and steady.

For the moment, anyway, it seemed to Owen that she was not being plagued by the nightmares she had before the Korovega attack. Thinking about dreaming produced feelings of dread when he imagined the sort of things his mind might conjure after the night's events.

"I'll take her upstairs," he offered. He nudged her shoulder. "Sam?"

"Wasn't sleeping," she protested, but her body's automatic wake-up stretch told the truth better than she did.

"Sure you weren't," Owen said. "Come on, let's try and get some sleep. Tomorrow's going to come a lot earlier than any of us want."

She nodded, standing groggily to her feet. "Alright."

"They're cute together," Will said, once the duo was safely out of hearing.

"They still ain't together," Ben replied.

Will's eyes went wide. Then, with interest, "really?"

"Don't even think about it."

"I wasn't. Yet. Anyway. No, I figured those two have known each other forever. It still seems weird that they're not, you know, 'together.'"

Ben shrugged. "Ain't the weirdest thing I seen today."

* * *

When the two of them reached the top of the stairs, they saw George step through the open deck door. His clothes were mismatched and looked like he had tried to put together some sort of "security guard" uniform out of what clothing he brought with him. He had on a pair of black jeans and a light blue, short-sleeved dress shirt. He had one of Ben's shotguns—one of the lighter ones, Sam noted—slung across his back.

Owen pointed to his retreating back and the two of them slipped into the kitchen area to listen in on whatever conversation they could hear.

George stepped almost out of view. They could see one shoulder and part of the back of his head. "Figured I'd let you try and sleep."

"What time is it?" Jessie asked. Her voice carried clearly enough through the open door.

"Almost four," he replied.

"I'm fine."

George shook his head. "We change watch at four, remember?"

"I couldn't sleep right now if I wanted to. You try and get some more sleep."

"I'm in the same boat," he admitted. "Hell, I wasn't even supposed to be on watch at all tonight. Sam decided to do me a favor," at that, Sam grimaced, "and let me off the hook tonight. But I can't sleep, and I only saw that damn thing through the window."

"I noticed," Jessie replied, tense.

"I'm sorry, alright?" he said. To their ears inside, he sounded genuine in his regret. More than that, he almost sounded upset that he had flaked out on everyone. "I was on my way out, but I had to find a gun, then Karina started freaking out, and I..."

"Don't worry about it," Jessie replied. "Just don't let it happen again, hear?"

He nodded. "It won't. Promise."

"If you like that gun, ask Ben if you can keep it," Jessie offered. "Might make it easier next time."

At the mention of a possible "next time," George blanched, but he held his back straight. He wavered slightly, but that was all. "I don't know if I like it, per se," he said, trying his best to sound relaxed, but his voice betrayed the fear that his posture hid, "I never got to use it earlier, but if he doesn't mind parting with it, I can... no, why don't you ask him? I expect that if I asked him, he'd tell me 'no,' just to spite me. There's no reasoning with that man, you know."

"I'll talk to him." Jessie's tone of voice that communicated that, she would talk to him, but she refused to play into George's feud.

"Who's on watch downstairs?" he asked, changing the subject. If he was annoyed that Jessie refused to take his side against Ben, he kept it to himself. The only thing he radiated at that moment was relief.

"Marcus," Jessie replied. "He was supposed to take last watch, but he said since he was up already that he'd go ahead and put in the extra hour or so."

"Well," George said, "try and get what sleep you can."

"I could tell you the same thing."

"I did, earlier. Then I tried to again a little bit ago, but every time I'd doze off I'd start dreaming. Right now, I think being awake is the best thing I can do."

Jessie snorted. "You think it's just you?" Owen wondered if she meant that to come out as harshly as it did.

He almost said something, but stopped. After a moment, he spoke again. "But you and Ben and the others are tough. I'm, well, not. Michael made it out the door before I did, for Christ's sake. But I'm working on it."

A moment's pause stretched into a long tense silence outside. George rocked on his heels, obviously waiting on Jessie to say something. Sam wondered if Jessie was about to tear into him; she knew she probably would have right then, but she was still feeling the jittery after effects of adrenaline.

"Give me ten minutes," Jessie said after a minute. "Coffee's almost all gone. Make yourself a fresh pot and then come get me, alright?"

"Deal," he said, turning to go back inside while Owen and Sam made a show of having just stepped into the kitchen for a snack. When he saw Owen and Sam, everything about his bearing changed. He forced his shoulders straighter and a serious, even angry, expression flashed across his face before he covered it with a smile. "Hey, you two."

"You going on watch?" Sam asked.

"Yeah," he replied. He waved one hand over his shoulder. "Dunno if you heard any of that, but I'm going to take over from Jessie here in a few minutes. Try and make up for not helping out earlier. Though," he looked at Sam for a moment too long for her comfort, "I hear I missed more excitement than just a Korovega attack."

Inwardly, she cringed, but outwardly she refused to give him the satisfaction of a reaction of any sort. Her earlier assessment was correct: a comment from Will was amusing, because he obviously meant nothing by it and, more importantly, they had known one another long enough to joke around some. An identical comment from George was enough to make her skin crawl.

Owen gave a dismissive shrug. "Not really."

"Well, not to you. You've seen it before," George shot back.

For the moment, still riding on the traces of her adrenaline high, Sam decided to play ball with him and said, "and now everyone else has, too. Except you. I hear I looked pretty good out there when I," she temporarily adopted a Hollowood-esque pirate voice, "wearing naught but me skivvies," her voice returned to normal, "finally put a handful of lead through that thing's shoulder."

"Sorry I missed it," George said. "That sounds," he groped for the right word for several awkward moments before finally saying, "pretty awesome, actually. Jessie told me you and Will actually managed to wound it."

She nodded, willing to continue the subject so long as his thoughts did not seem to wander where they did not belong. "We did."

"That's... that's good."

"You don't sound convinced," Owen said.

George sighed. He turned to the coffee pot and opened the machine to empty the basket. They were saving the grounds, and he dumped them into a small bowl nearby. With his back to them he said, "yeah, we hurt one, but what happens next?"

"What do you mean next?" Owen asked.

George's shoulders twitched with a suppressed shudder. "Yeah. Next. When he brings a dozen of his buddies back and burns this damn place to the ground."

"That might be a while. Until then, we live and we prepare," Sam said.

"Or it might not," George countered, turning to the sink and filling up the empty coffee pot. "I don't know if being here is the best idea, not when we pissed it off by shooting it in the leg."

"We scared it," Owen said. "You didn't see its face, but when we hurt it, we scared it. It won't be back."

George turned back to the coffee pot. He was, they noticed, very carefully avoiding eye contact with either of them. "That just means they'll come back with more. You know what they say about a cornered animal."

"This one's not cornered," Sam said. "It's more like a wolf stung by a bee. It didn't expect us to be able to hurt it, but we did. Owen's right, that frightened it. I was close enough to it to see that for myself."

"So what good's that do for us?" he hissed, careful to keep his voice down to avoid waking the few of them who found themselves able to sleep.

"I think we confused it," Owen said.

"Do tell," George replied, clearly unconvinced.

"It's like Sam said. It didn't expect us to be able to hurt it, so when we did..."

"...it retreated to figure out how to deal with us," Sam finished.

George glowered for a moment. In the dim light, even his roundish face, clouded with troubles, seemed threatening. "You're not doing a good job of convincing me we're safe."

"We're not," Owen admitted.

George rolled his eyes. "Yes. Thank you. I've been telling you that for days now!"

"No one ever said we were safe," Sam added. "But what we've got is time."

"Either we squander it or we use it," Owen argued. "We know they're going to be back, just like we knew they were going to come in the first place. That's why we had guards out tonight and, realistically, why we're all still alive. So when the next one comes, we'll be even more prepared."

Sam placed her hand on George's arm. The gesture seemed to calm him somewhat, though his face was still dark and the tension in his shoulders caused his hands to shake as he switched the coffee pot on.

"We're all getting through this," she said.

George sighed, shook his head, and chewed on his lower lip for a moment. Another deep breath, another sharp exhalation, and he said, "alright. Alright." He managed a smile. "What next?"

"For me?" Sam asked rhetorically. "Sleep. If I can."

"Same," Owen said, turning and heading for the stairs to the loft.

"The schedule's on the table." Sam gestured with one hand to where a manila file folder lay open on the dinner table. "Wake everyone up on schedule, alright?"

"Even if you've only slept an hour or so?" he asked. Sam thought he showed genuine concern for a moment.

She had to admit, the temptation was strong. She had stayed up late to take he first watch, then slept all of two hours, and had been awake for another hour or so.

168

That left precious little sleep, and the thought of it drug on her eyelids. Still, she nodded firmly. "On schedule."

"Yes, ma'am."

* * *

Owen waited on the edge of the bed in the loft for Sam. When she came out of the bathroom, he took a moment to look her over for any injuries from the encounter with the Korovega. Her eyes were sunken, her hair a mess, and she seemed to be favoring one shoulder ever so slightly. Otherwise, she had gotten off as easily as the rest of them—at least physically. Owen doubted that anyone who saw the Korovega—everyone but George and Katrina—would ever sleep soundly again, and the encounter had already produced a few small changes in people's personalities.

Sam, though, just looked tired. He felt as tired as she looked, and he suspected he looked even worse yet.

Still, she managed to smile. "Remind me never to sleep in just my underwear again," she said, laughing.

Owen, despite his fatigue, laughed too. "I'll try. I'd been out for a couple of hours when you came to bed, though, so I can't quite be much help on nights like that."

"No, I suppose not." She climbed in on her side of the bed and sat leaning against the headboard. A moment later, Owen joined her. A companionable space lay between the two of them, but Owen was the glad of the physical proximity nonetheless. If nothing else, now he had someone to talk to for the few hours remaining until "tomorrow" officially started by Sam's schedule and they would have to be awake again and ready to work.

"I'm glad you didn't stop to get dressed, for what it's worth," he said, after a minute of silence.

"Why's that?"

He shrugged. "Who knows what those extra few seconds would have cost us. Maybe it could have gotten too close for your plan to work, or, I don't know."

Sam laughed. "It wasn't exactly a plan," she said, and sighed. "I had a flash of an idea that seemed a few percent less likely to get us all killed and I took it. I'm just glad Will's such a good shot."

"Yeah."

"Owen?"

"Hm?"

"We did good out there."

He nodded. "Yeah, we did. George is right, though. We have no idea what the Korovega will do now that we've managed to hurt one. Maybe a dozen or more will come calling tomorrow night. Or the day after, or..."

Sam reached over with one finger and held it next to his head. After a moment, they made eye contact and Owen laughed. Sam poked him in the side of the head. "Hush."

"But it's true."

"We can't do anything about whether or not it's going to happen."

"We can make plans for when it does happen," he countered.

She nodded, looking up at the ceiling. The fan overhead spun slowly. She said nothing.

"We've got better odds now than we did last night, but I don't know how much they're going to help."

Sam looked back at Owen and held her finger threateningly, prepared to administer another poke if needed. "Pessimism is my job and you know it," she said with a grin, then sat back against the headboard. With less enthusiasm, she added, "it takes too damn much energy to be optimistic, but we've got to, hey?"

Owen tried to smile, but the gesture came out as a lopsided smirk. He picked up on something different in her posture. "Alright, Miss, 'we're all going to die.' What's changed your mind?"

"What do you mean?"

"The other day you were talking about how unlikely it was that we'd survive, just being realistic, I'll grant, and now you're the one putting on a brave face, and hurting the damn Korovega while you're at it, and I'm over here trying not to freak."

"Same reason you're all confidence and 'attaboy'-this and 'good show'-that," Sam said, affecting a bad British accent. She gestured toward the floors below their loft with one hand. "It's for them."

Owen realized she was right, but had nothing to say. He had not planned for it, certainly. If he was being honest with himself, part of him liked being in charge and having authority, but that part was overshadowed by the conviction that they all were, in fact, going to die very soon and he had no real idea what he was doing.

"At least we can put the masks down from time to time," he said, turning his head toward where Sam sat.

She nodded. The impassive, stern face that she had put on for George was different from the carefree mask she had shown Will. Before he arrived, without anyone other than Owen or Ben around, she had let that mask down as well. She barely knew Will Monday, and so upon his arrival the mask went up once more. Alone in the loft, though, Owen could see every thought, care, and fear written on her face as plainly as if they had been his own.

"Sam."

"Yeah?"

"When this all goes to hell, I just want you to know there's no one I'd rather have watching my back."

In the darkness, she gave a warm half-smile. "Same to you." Finally, she turned away and reached for the bedside lamp."Goodnight, Owen."

Silently, he settled down into the sheets. The sounds of Sam doing the same a foot away were comforting. This time, he felt, he might be able to sleep.

"Sam," he said. "I don't think I like the apocalypse very much."

Chapter 13

Seven AM came far too early. For George and Marcus, who had taken the last watch, it felt like it came far too late. After taking over at four from Jessie, George went through an entire coffee pot simply to stay awake in what remained of the calm, quiet night. As his adrenaline crashed, he found himself dozing more than once, but he had a job to do, and so forced himself to stay awake.

Marcus, too, had been awake far longer than anyone intended. After keeping watch in the hours after the Korovega attack, he stayed awake as well. Unlike George, this sort of interrupted sleep schedule was nothing new for him. It had been a few years, granted, but old talents hung around for a while.

When he first heard that George was going to take over the last watch upstairs from Jessie, Marcus was rather ambivalent. He had caught most of the conversation in the basement, including referencing the fact that George had stayed inside with Katrina during the Korovega attack. Ben and—the redhead, what was her name? Marcus had never been good with names and struggled to remember for a moment before it came back to him—Sam seemed to hold the man's actions against him personally, but he picked up from their tone that Ben had some sort of other grievance with him as well.

Marcus understood what must have been going through George's head, though. Between Will's alarmed shout and every one else's panicked assemblage, the atmosphere earlier had been less than pleasant. Certainly, he thought, it had not been easy to make rational decisions—not that charging toward an enemy was ever a truly rational decision, he reflected.

But whatever his reasons had been before, he seemed perfectly willing to stand guard in the last few hours of the morning and that earned him a positive note in Marcus's book. He had seen enough men run for cover during their first gunfight that, quite honestly, he was unwilling to judge George on that fact alone.

As it happened, not only was he willing to stand watch without being asked, George had turned out to be a rather skilled chef. Their stock of food was eclectic to say the least, obviously the end result of several people all mass-buying whatever they could get their hands on that they might need. It was significantly better than an Army kitchen, though, for which he was grateful.

"Food's gonna be an issue, long term," George observed. He seemed surprisingly bright and cheerful for someone who had barely slept that night. He lifted the lids off the two coffee pots and nodded satisfactorily at one while giving the second an impatient grimace.

Marcus gave a sigh as answer, then, "tell me about it. Just feeding everyone breakfast is using almost twenty bucks worth of food. We can't keep this up for long, even with," he peeked in the refrigerator to confirm his memory, "five dozen eggs left. That's not even enough, if we make breakfast like this every day, to last until next Monday."

"Ken wanted to get some chickens, but I have no idea how many we'd need so that everyone stays fed," George admitted.

"Ken's the one who was killed yesterday, right?" Marcus asked. As the words came out of his mouth, he realized how totally nonchalant they sounded and silently hoped that no one in earshot would be offended by his tone.

George nodded solemnly. Like several of the others, he had yet to make up his mind about the man they met on the side of the road before he had been killed, but afterward George thought of him relatively fondly. He had had a good sense of humor. All he managed aloud was, "yeah."

"Sucks," Marcus replied. He was no stranger to the feelings he suspected were running through George's head. Multiple deployments across the globe to fight people who wanted him and everyone in his uniform dead would do that.

Marcus, for lack of anything else to say to diffuse whatever was going through George's mind, said, "it's a good idea. Will and... Owen?"

"Yeah."

"They're going on a supply run, so hopefully they'll bring some back. Means we have to get a coop built before they get home, though."

"Sam's got you digging most of the morning," George said.

Marcus rolled his eyes. He had done his share of that in the Army, he thought, but at least that meant he would be used to the work. He hoped he could share relatively evenly, but he suspected, especially if Owen and Will were going to be gone all day, that he and Ben would be shouldering most of the work that called for a strong back.

Aloud, he asked, "what's she have you doing?"

George made a none-too-excited face and replied, "combat training. Miss Santiago gets to spend the morning kicking my ass around the yard."

"Santiago? You mean Jessie, right?"

George nodded. "Yeah, her. Used to fight Ben for fun. I can feel the bruises already."

Marcus laughed. "You'll learn quick then."

"Hopefully," George said, and the coffee pot that he had been waiting on puffed dramatically. He lifted the lid to check on it, nodded. He thought waking everyone up himself, but the last thing he wanted to deal with was Ben first thing in the morning. "Everything's ready. While I start getting things out and on plates, can you go make sure everyone's awake?"

"Can do," Marcus replied.

* * *

Katrina jumped and flailed her arms as a touch on her shoulder shocked her into sudden wakefulness. She sat bolt upright, pushing instinctively away from the contact and against the bed's headboard. Half a second later, she snatched at the sheet, forgotten for a moment in her fright, and jerked it to her shoulders.

Her wide eyes scanned the darkness for a moment before settling on a figure silhouetted against the dim light coming through the doorway. For a brief moment, she forgot where she was, where she had been, and panic gripped her heart. A conscious reminder that she was at Ben's house, across the country from where she had lived her entire life, did little to still her nerves right then.

The shadowy figure smiled, teeth white against the early-morning gloom. As her pulse slowed, she realized the silhouette belonged to Marcus. The house creaked around her, shifting in the morning's humidity, and she twitched at the sudden noise.

Katrina laughed, quietly, at the absurdity of it. There were Korovega out there, hellbent on killing all mankind, and here she was jumping at shadows and freaking out at the creaks and groans of an old house.

She took a deep lungful of air, forcing herself to slow her shallow, panicked breathing. She held it for a moment, then let it out in a burst. The feeling was still there, but she felt her nerves slowly calming down. She rubbed her eyes, forcing the sleep out of them as well, then shook her head, letting blond ringlets fall in front of her face.

Taking another deep breath, she smoothed her hair back out of her face, looked back up at Marcus, and smiled. His was a comforting presence, a friendly face.

"What time is it?" she asked, speaking quietly.

"A few minutes past seven. Breakfast is ready."

"Oh," she relaxed even further. "Okay. I'll be ready in just a minute."

"Take your time," Marcus said with a smile and a wave. "I've still got two more floors to wake up."

"I'll just be a minute," she repeated. A small upward tug at the sheets still clutched at her shoulders conveyed the rest of the message, and Marcus nodded and left the room.

Alone, she let the sheets fall back down and slid out of bed. There was a small mirror mounted on the wall next to the bed and she faced it for a moment. Katrina had gone to sleep in the clothes she put on the middle of the night when she had almost gone outside to help the others. Despite her best efforts, she had been unable to get farther than the bedroom door, and so had sat and watched helplessly as gunfire lit up the night outside.

She stripped off the oversize tshirt she slept in and tossed it at her suitcase. It fell into a small lavender pile atop the purple luggage.

Katrina sighed and turned back to the mirror, running her hands through her hair.

"Wer bin ich?" Who am I, she asked, addressing her reflection as much as anything.

She gave a half smile in return. Her reflection seemed small in the darkness, all wide eyes and narrow shoulders. She looked at her arms, shoulders, and chest in turn, remembering the sight of Sam and Jessie the day before with their sleeves rolled up.

Muscles like steel cables ran under their skin and she, Katrina looked hard at herself in the mirror, had no such strength. She tried to flex, only to end with a vaguely amused smile when the effort produced no result.

She crossed her arms tight across her chest, imagining for a moment that the swell of her breasts was muscle instead.

A few seconds passed and she continued to stare at her reflection. She tried to put on the hard sort of expression she had seen on Jessie's face when they first met, but it looked out of place on her features. A try at the determined set Sam got in her eyes when working on a problem also came up short, but perhaps there was something there.

She tried again, this time trying to simply project confidence instead of aping someone else's expression. Staring at her own face in the mirror helped, seeing the growing confidence on her face helped her to put more out there until, after a minute, it felt a little less forced.

Katrina took a deep breath and closed her eyes. She put her hands on her hips and opened her eyes again. The expression on her face had changed, softened a little, but there was something strong in it that had not been there the day before.

She nodded once, pleased with what she saw.

* * *

Will greeted Marcus with a wave as he descended the carpeted stairs to the basement. He was already awake, sitting in the less worn of the two leather chairs. In his lap was a thick crossword puzzle book, the same one that he had carried with him all the way from Arizona. Will looked the same as he had the night before, except that he had exchanged his old tennis shoes for a pair of sand-colored boots— one of the few things he had kept since leaving the service.

He looked up and Marcus instantly recognized the look in his eyes. "Breakfast?" he asked, and Marcus nodded. Will smiled, a gesture that stopped short of his eyes. "I've been smelling bacon up there for twenty minutes now."

Marcus laughed and gestured to Ben who was stretched out on the couch. As with most couches, he was taller than it was long. Even with his head resting on one armrest, his feet hung over the end. One muscular arm had fallen to the floor.

"He alive?"

Will nodded. "Yeah. We stayed up a while talking."

"I noticed," Marcus replied with a grin.

"Right you were outside." Will tapped his forehead once in a, "duh," motion. "Sorry, it's been a long couple of days."

Marcus laughed again. "You think?"

"I'll get Ben and Jessie up. I was trying to let him sleep as much as possible. I don't think we shut up until almost six."

"That was a bad plan."

"Tell me about it. We'll be up in a few."

"Don't wait too long, otherwise the bacon's mine."

Will smirked. "Just try it, see what happens."

"Bacon's serious business, man. Move it or lose it."

"Yeah, yeah," he said, waving dismissively in Marcus's general direction.

Marcus laughed and headed back up the stairs. When he reached the main floor, he saw Owen and Sam had already come down from the loft. They were milling lazily around the living room just then. Sam nursed an exceptionally large mug with a skull-and-crossbones on it. Next to her, Owen cradled a much smaller cup. Both mugs steamed with freshly brewed coffee.

Sam seemed alert, but Owen drug somewhat. Neither of them seemed particularly like they had been troubled by poor sleep or bad dreams, but fatigue hung over them like it hung over everyone else. Marcus suspected that, no matter what was on the schedule, tonight was going to be an early night for everyone. Some of them—himself and Will, who had experience going without sleep from their time in the military—might be able to take first watch that night, but he suspected that there would be a fair amount of napping in the evening after the day's work was done.

"Ah, you're awake," he said, looking across the room at the two of them, "good."

Sam nodded. "Yeah. Michael came and woke us up while you were downstairs."

"Hope you don't mind," Michael said.

Marcus laughed. "I don't see why I should. You saved me a trip up the stairs and got everyone to the table that much faster. Nothing wrong with that. You guys sleep alright?"

"I'm drinking coffee willingly," Owen replied.

Sam smirked. "That means 'no.'"

"I was going to turn the TV on and see if there was any news, but no one else liked the idea," Owen added, gesturing toward the flat screen.

He had addressed Marcus, but George spoke up. "I didn't think everyone needed to be getting worked up before breakfast two days in a row, is all."

"So it's going on after we eat," Sam finished.

"So we're all gonna sit around the TV with our coffee and our tea and pretend we're civilized folk," boomed Ben from the top of the stairwell.

"Something like that," Sam said.

"Where's the coffee? I was promised coffee and bacon," Ben said.

"And pancakes," Marcus added.

"Will didn't say nothin' about pancakes," Ben replied. He turned to look over his shoulder where Will was still mounting the stairs behind him. "You holdin' out on me an' trying t'Bogart all the pancakes?"

From the stairwell, "wouldn't dream of it."

Jessie staggered up the stairs last. By the look on her face, she had possibly slept worse than anyone else. Unlike some of the others who found their dreams troubled by nightmares, Jessie lacked the wide-eyed, fearful expression that would have pointed to that as the cause. Instead, she simply seemed to be tired; what little sleep she had managed to get, at most three hours before her watch and then perhaps two afterward, had clearly not been enough.

"Food's ready," George announced. He gestured to the counter that separated the kitchen from the dinner table. Unfortunately, that table only had six seats. They could fit eight people by extending the table and adding a leaf to the middle, but the leaf had so far eluded everyone's attempts to find it. Those not sitting at the table occupied a set of tall bar stools types on the table side of the counter. Between the two, everyone could share the room well enough.

The counter had been laid out with a large glass dish full of scrambled eggs, a pile of bacon, and a smaller pile of breakfast sausage. At the end of the spread was a tall stack of pancakes and two gallon jugs of juice—one apple and one orange. The only thing missing from the visual was a meeting-room-style electric carafe for the coffee.

"Dig in," George said.

The nine of them spent a few minutes jockeying for food and then for seating positions. A few piled everything on one plate, but most made several trips to and from the counter after claiming a place to sit. Some of the pancakes and eggs were left by the first pass, but none of the bacon or sausage survived very long. Both juices and one entire coffee pot were emptied as well as the swarm of people settled in to eat.

Despite the magnitude of food, breakfast itself went relatively quickly. Everyone ate as though they were starving, which was understandable given how much excitement and adrenaline had been shared the night before. Plus, for those who had seen Sam's schedule, they ate like people who knew they would be spending all day in the hot sun either working or fighting.

* * *

When breakfast was over and everything had been cleared from the table, they retired to the TV area. Ben claimed the large chair; George, Michael, and Marcus took the couch; and Will and Katrina shared the loveseat. That left Sam to drag the ottoman to one side and sit on it. Jessie and Owen volunteered to handle kitchen cleanup.

Ben picked up the remote and the TV clicked on. It still showed the news station they had left it on the day before, which made finding something with coverage easy.

In the days since the attack on DC, most of the non-news stations had started slowly resuming their regular programming in an effort to assuage whatever anxieties their audience had. Ben suspected that people were already starting to turn away from the news in preference for entertainment television. Not that he could blame them, he thought. Entertainment, anything to get their minds off of the tragedy unfolding around them was emotionally preferable to a constant onslaught of bad news.

"...fate of the President," announced the reporter on the screen. His face was under tight control, betraying absolutely none of the emotion he must have been feeling.

"Turn it up," George ordered.

Ben did so as the feed went black for a second. It stayed that way as the news anchor announced, "technical difficulties, please be patient." Ben suspected that the truth was that the feed was being routed through three dozen encryption layers and bounced across a thousand false locations.

When the feed went live again, the scene appeared to be inside of a bunker somewhere. A man none of them recognized sat behind a table draped with a white tablecloth printed with the Presidential Seal. A large flag had tacked onto the concrete wall behind him.

His face was lined with worry and anxiety, and it showed in his eyes past whatever training and preparation he had undergone. His hands were absent from view, but the tension in his shoulders sent a clear message that his hands were most likely clenched into white-knuckled fists in his lap. His eyes were red from lack of sleep, but otherwise he seemed to be in good health. If he had been injured, it was well covered-up.

"Ladies and Gentlemen of the American public, for those of you who do not know me, my name is Kevin Dean," he began. He spoke informally. If there was a teleprompter or notecards on the other side of the camera, he gave no indication of it.

He looked down, then to one side, closed his eyes and bit his lower lip for a moment before speaking again, "I am, or I was, the Republican senator from Idaho. As of this broadcast, I am the senior surviving member of the United States government."

"Mutter Gottes," Katrina muttered.

Ben added, "holy shit."

"I'm sure you all have seen the footage of the Korovega attack on Washington DC. I can't tell you what state I'm in, but know that those of us who have survived are doing everything in our power to combat the Korovega menace. At this point, footage from across the globe has also been released. I would like," he paused, "no, I wouldn't like to, but I have to. I can confirm that the Korovega attacked every world capital simultaneously with nearly the same result.

"There are simply not enough of us left, not even to enact Martial Law. As of twelve noon, MST, today, I will be signing authority over to the state and local governments.

"Korovega have also been sighted in several large cities around the country. Please, if you see a Korovega: do not engage. They are indescribably dangerous. Instead, call your local police or emergency services. Until we discover a weakness, the best way to stay safe is to stay away.

"And, please," he fixed the camera with an intense stare, "please, Ladies and Gentlemen. Citizens. Americans. Please be safe. We'll keep you updated as soon as we learn anything."

The TV switched back to the newsroom, but now the newscaster from before had been joined by two others. Dramatic red text across the bottom of the screen read, "KOROVEGA MENACE: ARE YOU AT RISK?"

"Yes, dumbass," Jessie snarled, "everyone is."

"This looks like typical, 'discussion panel,' junk. What say we either find a different channel to watch or get a jump start on today's work?" Marcus asked, hoping for the latter. He hated TV news, especially after the way they had handled the "military action" that was his and Will's last deployment.

"Fine by me," Ben replied. He put his hands on the arms of the chair and started to stand.

"I think we ought to wait a little longer," Sam said.

Ben shrugged. "You made the schedule."

Sam nodded. "And I don't know about you, but after everything I just ate, I'm not ready to let Jessie run me around a boxing ring just yet."

Jessie laughed. "I'm not ready to chase you, either."

"Sounds like it's decided," Ben said, settling back into his chair. "Time to find something what ain't quite this crappy."

Two channel changes later, they found something that seemed like it would actually provide coverage of events around the country rather than airheaded fearmongering.

Things did not look good.

* * *

After some searching, Sam managed to find what purported to be a real-time projection of Korovega sightings online. Several other websites claimed the same. Using a nearly identical set of data, they differed only in their presentation. She brought the map up on one of George's spare devices and connected it to the television.

Seeing the map so large did not encourage any comfort or feelings of safety, but it told them a lot. Namely that the Korovega were spreading out systematically from Washington. They traveled fastest down rivers and over bodies of water, but their progress was logical, which made it predictable.

The map was also zoomable, with data down to the county level. The sighting in Knoxville was there, as were a half-dozen others along the river.

The existence of the map spawned a fierce argument over whether or not to report their encounter the night before, adding one more dot to the map. Will, backed up by George and—initially—Michael and Katrina, argued that they needed to keep the sighting secret. It would only incite panic, they said.

Will argued that the National Guard had several armories in the area, and, "they'll handle it."

"How'n the hell are they gonna handle it if they don't know one's here?" Ben demanded.

"If people think there's no Korovega presence here, they'll take stupid risks," Owen asserted.

"That won't stop people like you from doing dangerous, stupid shit," George growled.

"Cap—I mean Owen's right," Michael said, breaking the tense silence. He kept his voice level, talking more to George than anyone. "People need to know. You know? I'd want to know that someone saw one of those things."

"I don't want the damn Press coverage!" George snapped. "They learn we saw one and next thing we know we've got newsies so thick around here that we can't work. We bring more people here, people that screw up our plans, and that Korovega's going to come back for us."

"Man's got a point," Marcus said. He spoke quickly, trying to get his thoughts out before the yelling started up again. He had been backing Ben's point of view that knowledge was power and people, as Michael said, had a right to know. He seemed reluctant to agree with George's argument, but could not fault the logic. Without a break, he added, "the last thing we need is a bunch of targets milling around if that thing brings friends next time."

George paled. "Next time," he stopped and collected his thoughts, "there better not be a next time. We stay hidden and we stay safe! No one talks!"

"You think them eagles we keep seeing ain't tied to the Korovega som'wheres?" Ben growled.

"He's right, too." Marcus nodded. "If those birds are flying recon for the Korovega, then they already know where everyone is."

"'If,'" George snorted. "They're fucking birds, man. They're not drones or spy planes. How the hell are a bunch of eagles going to, 'fly recon,' for them?"

"How the hell should I know?" Ben demanded. "Do I look like I'm in on their secrets?"

"My answer is still, 'no,'" George growled, deliberately not looking at Ben.

"Come on, man," Michael pleaded, "don't you think..."

"No!" George snapped. Michael recoiled at his tone. "In fact..."

"So we don't tell them where we are," Sam said. Her quiet voice, heavy with authority, cut though George's comment, effectively silencing it.

Even sitting directly between Ben and George, she had managed to avoid the rush of emotions and the flash of tempers that had gripped everyone else. She had not spoken in some time, instead watching and listening as everyone else spoke their piece, almost as though she was taking notes. She went on with, "of course we give them a general area, but we don't have to tell them our address. 'North of Andersonville' or 'south of Norris Lake' will do just fine. We tell them a lone Korovega appeared in our yard last night, but we frightened it away."

"And when they ask how?" George snapped. He immediately, and quite clearly, regretted it when Sam turned a steely glare in his general direction.

"We tell them the truth," she said, voice level. She spoke slowly, enunciating every word. "We tell them that there were several of us who shot at it, protecting the others inside. We surprised it and it ran."

"One scout burned down half of Downtown-fucking-Knoxville!" George shouted, anger steamrolling over good sense and decorum. "And you seriously think they'll believe that a half-dozen assholes and one naked chick with guns scared one away? Are you insane or just stupid?"

Sam shrugged. She turned her head away and watched the outdoors through the large window behind the television for a brief moment to keep him from seeing the absolutely withering expression on her face.

In her reflection, she watched eyes the color of honey blaze with fury. Maybe if Ben held him down and I beat—No, she thought. He's too useful, I can't kill him. Now I know how Ben feels, though, her thoughts continued.

She was, however, ready to tear him a metaphoric new asshole, if not a literal one. Still looking out the window, she was about to allow her temper off of its leash for a moment when Jessie caught her eye and gave an almost imperceptible shake of her head.

And Sam remembered that she and George were both scheduled for a training session with Jessie as soon as they all went to work on their various jobs. Sam locked eyes with Jessie and just smiled.

That realization let her reign her temper back in as well, which was probably a good thing. If she crushed his windpipe in the middle of Ben's living room, they might break something. Plus, continuing the verbal fight would drive group morale even lower.

Temper under control after a few tense seconds during which everyone in the room expected her to leap for his throat, she spoke. Every word, every breath and motion was carefully controlled. Fury brimmed just under the surface, that much was visible from her eyes alone, but her voice contained nothing but iron.

"Our responsibility is to convey the information that we have, in fact, encountered a Korovega. What they do or do not do with that information is not my concern. My concern is keeping everyone here alive. If that concern is best served by letting the authorities, whose job it is to ensure the safety of the civilian population, know that there has been a Korovega sighting here then we damn well will tell them that.

"If you cannot handle that," she continued, "if you will not help me keep us all alive, no one is forcing you to stay here."

After several tense seconds, long enough for everyone in the room to get their bearings again, a time in which George ranged from dumbfounded to apoplectic and back again, all the while opening and closing his mouth as words and sentences came to him and then were chased away by another new emotion and retort, Will spoke up.

Quietly, though without much of Sam's control, he said, "she's right. There's still a chain of information here. I don't want to expose ourselves any more than we have to, but we've got a duty to make sure information flows."

"I think that about settles that." Ben was unable to keep his voice as level as the others, and so laid a thick covering of semi-forced laughter over it. "Sounds like it's about time t' get to work!"

George's expression shifted from anger to embarrassment and back several times as they all stood up. Thoughts moved under his skin, but he found himself unable to even decide how he felt right then, let alone what to say.

"You," Jessie said, pointing at George. He ignored her. "George!" she snapped. He turned his head, grating, "what?"

"Outside. Now. Need to get you familiar with the training."

"I've taken karate," he said, and his voice dripped with sarcasm. "I know how to fight. Spare me the condescending attitude, if you don't mind."

"We'll see." She sounded unconvinced. "Either way, outside. If you know what you're doing, head downstairs and start warming up on the punching bag. I'll be down in a minute. I'm going to mix up something for us to drink."

George started to protest, but Jessie cut him short. "Now!"

Grumbling, he left the room.

* * *

Without George's seething temper heating up the room, things cooled down quickly, but the mood of camaraderie was broken. People stood and drifted in different directions, some alone, a few in pairs. Ben took his work crew and led them downstairs as Owen and Will prepared for their supply trip. In minutes, the only person left in front of the cancerous red map was Katrina.

She looked around and found Sam.

"I'm on guard duty, right?" she asked, still feeling shaken by the abrupt downturn in the morning's mood. Katrina had taken the time to brush her hair and clean up before coming for breakfast, which only made the frightened expression on her face stand out more.

Watching her, Sam wondered how much of that was instinct and routine and how much was a desire to wash away the memory of the demon from the night before. In a way, she pitied the blond woman. Katrina was not a fighter like Sam or Jessie, and yet she had been thrust into the middle of an unending series of fights.

Sam hoped Katrina could survive, but, if she was honest with herself, she had her doubts.

Sam took a deep breath, pushing the anger George had stirred out of her immediate consciousness. She forced a smiling mask onto her face and turned toward Katrina. "Yeah. Let one of us know if you have any questions."

"Shouldn't I start with the training you're doing downstairs?"

Sam shook her head. "Ideally, you would be. You'd be trained to shoot and fight before we put you on guard duty alone, but there's going to be six of us hanging around in the yard doing various things. We'll have shovels and picks on hand, if not other weapons, too."

"So my job is...?"

Sam smiled, trying to make it sound more important that it really was, given her lack of training. "You're keeping watch for anything unusual around the house. You see anything, you yell and we'll take care of it. Sound doable?"

Katrina nodded. "I think so." She looked like she did not, in fact, think so. With wide eyes, she asked, "do I get a weapon?"

"Have you ever shot before?" Sam asked.

"Once or twice?" she replied, embarrassed. "I'll understand if you don't want to give me one, though."

Sam sighed. "We'll fix that soon enough. We'll get you something easy to use for now."

Katrina smiled. Her face seemed to brighten a little. "Thanks," she said. "I want to help however I can. I promise I'll take my training seriously and I'll do everything I can to..."

Sam squeezed her shoulder reassuringly. "Trust me, you're helping. Go downstairs and talk to Jessie. Ask her to get you one of the sixteen-gauges. If you can rack it, take it. If not, grab one of the break-opens. Jessie will know what else to tell you."

Katrina nodded, smiling. "Thanks, Sam. I," she took a deep breath, "I'm going to do my best. I can't promise I'll be able to do what you do, but I'm not going to give up. If you think I can handle a gun, then I'll handle it, and..."

Sam interrupted. She felt Katrina's nervous energy infecting her, but in Sam it resulted in a strange kind of cheer. She smiled. "Do your best."

"I will, and..."

Sam interrupted again, taking her phone out of her pocket, "talk to Jessie."

Katrina nodded, waiting a moment as Sam put the phone to her ear and climbed the stairs to loft. As vociferously as they all had argued, she felt like she needed to know what Sam told the police. Katrina caught snippets of the conversation as Sam paced.

"...yes... Korovega.... Yes... Korovega. No. Just one. ...night, around four AM."

Satisfied that Sam had things under control, satisfied more importantly that Sam was the sort of person who could deal with the responsibilities that had been forced upon her, Katrina made for the stairs. If she could be half as capable as Sam was, Katrina thought she might just be able to come out alright.

Chapter 14

Owen drove through Clinton, and past his apartment first. Will was right; the complex was nearly empty and many of the units, including his, looked like they had been ransacked. Elsewhere, few people roamed the streets. Most of the large stores were already closed, empty, or both. After driving through that town, they headed for Oak Ridge, which was large enough that something there should still be stocked. If Oak Ridge had been picked bare, they could always drive out to Knoxville, but neither of them wanted to deal with that level of traffic.

The sun had yet to burn off the early morning fog, and the roads were nearly empty, lending everything a surreal quality. The roads grew more congested as they got closer to Oak Ridge, but even that was light compared to the utter standstill Owen had found himself trapped in the day before. The hardest part of the trip had simply been leaving the driveway. A large truck compounded by a large trailer also did not play well with the tight curves of the switchbacks leading from Ben's house.

Owen wondered how Ben managed to make the drive, and make it look so easy as well, and he dreaded the return trip up those same switchbacks with the big truck and trailer loaded down with, perhaps literally, tons of supplies.

When Owen complained aloud about the tight turns in the backroads ahead, Will asked, "isn't there a more direct route?"

He nodded. "Yeah, but there's also probably more people that way."

"Good."

Owen cocked his head to the side, shifting his gaze between Will and the road. He could not quite make out the expression on the other's face. "Good?"

Will nodded once. "Yeah. We want there to be as many people around as possible. Safer that way."

"Unless things go bad," Owen muttered.

"Even then. If things go bad, we want witnesses who might bring the police over."

"That why you didn't bring your rifle?"

"Police are going to be on the lookout for anything that might spell trouble, and an out-of-towner packing a tricked-out AR15 spells 'trouble' for people trying to keep the peace. Plus," he paused, "I don't like carrying my rifle around groups of civilians. Makes 'em nervous, you know."

"People are already nervous."

"That's my point. Hell, if things go bad in a crowded area, we might discover some new friends."

"Or not," Owen countered.

"Think positive, man."

Owen processed the idea for a moment, then nodded. "Of course, if things go bad in the middle of BFN, there might not be any help for hours."

"Not only that..."

"But people are going to be less likely to turn violent if they know they're being watched," he said, finishing Will's thought. Thinking of Ken's murder the day before, he added grimly, "the sane, sober ones anyway."

Will nodded. "Right. There's risks either way, but I'd rather take my chances with people than risk being stranded and face-to-face with a Korovega."

"Fair point."

"Besides," Will added with a grin. "If I die alone, I won't get another chance to hit on Sam."

Owen rolled his eyes. "Just be glad she puts up with you."

Will laughed. "I am. Trust me. She's a hell of a woman, you know."

"That 'hell of a woman' is going to keep us alive."

Will looked over at Owen and thought for a moment. "You're doing a lot too, you know."

Owen made eye contact briefly, and Will nodded once. Owen looked away. He had been feeling a lot of things since they woke up that morning, but praiseworthy was not one of them.

Still, arguing that point was one of the last things he wanted to do just then. He was proud, in a way, of what he had managed to accomplish in such a short time. Will knew it, and Owen knew that he knew it. False modesty was no good, but the compliment still made him uneasy, and so he simply dropped the subject.

The big truck rumbled on without problems until they came to the edge of Oak Ridge itself. The main road ran under a bridge, then past a park before splitting off in two different directions. On one side was a small park on the land where the eastern checkpoint sat during the Manhattan Project. When Oak Ridge had been the site of Top Secret nuclear research, towers and gates protected every entrance. With the Korvega prowling around, that area was host to an impromptu, but armed, checkpoint once again.

Just past the park was a large intersection. The main road continued to Oak Ridge, while a road to the left went towards the Bull Run steam plant, and thence to

Knoxville or back to Clinton the long way around. To the right sat a few small shops and, behind them, a recently-emptied National Guard Armory.

A SWAT van sat in the parking lot between the little shops, watching the intersection. Three police cruisers were parked at the corners. Six police officers, dressed in full SWAT gear rather than their normal uniforms, stood at various parts of the intersection, two for each direction.

"Well this is fun," Will muttered.

"Still got your military ID?" Owen asked. He laughed, without humor.

Will shook his head with an answering laugh that actually sounded rather amused. "Hell no. It's probably sitting in the bottom of a box somewhere in Arizona right now. Good riddance. I haven't seen it since six months after I got out. Besides, I don't think it would help any right now. If Oak Ridge is still hurting for numbers in the police force, they might even try and draft me on the spot!"

Owen grinned. "There is that. I've got my badge, though, so we should be fine."

He slowed the truck down. Three vehicles idled ahead of him at the intersection. The SWAT officer was talking to the driver of the first one, a bewildered-looking teenager, underneath the blinking yellow of the disabled traffic light. After a few minutes, the officer waved the car forward and through the intersection and Owen inched the truck forward some.

"This is going to be an absolute blast when we come back through here loaded down with supplies," Will said sarcastically. He flexed his arms in front of him in mockery of a cop from a cheap movie. He adopted a bad Southern accent and said, "What're you kids doing with all that stuff, eh? Where'd ya steal it? I don't like how yer lookin' at me. You want trouble? I'm'a gonna 'rrest you boys!"

Owen laughed. "I doubt we'll be in it quite that deep, but it just might take some explaining."

"It's gonna take some explaining now!"

The car in front of them moved. The woman driving had flashed a badge, and the officer let her through with a curt nod of his head.

Owen pulled the truck forward. "Let's hope he likes mine that much."

"Showtime," Will said.

"License and registration," the officer requested, holding out a gloved hand. From the bored expression on his face to the lackadaisical way in which he held his hand out, it seemed clear to Owen that he did not want to be there. Owen sympathized. Fencing kit was hardly SWAT gear, but he had been out in the hot sun in full gear enough times to know how quickly it became uncomfortable.

"Both of you," the officer added as an afterthought.

Owen fished around in his pocket, struggling more with the seatbelt than anything. After a moment, he withdrew his wallet, opened it, and fished out two cards. He handed them, along with Will's driver's license, across to the officer before searching the glovebox for the truck's registration. Luckily, Ben was serious about caring for his vehicles and the registration was easy to find. He passed that across as well.

The officer glanced at the IDs, paying a few extra seconds of attention to Will's out-of-state license, probably trying to determine if it was real or fake. He paid significantly more attention to Owen's badge, checking both sides and shifting the holographic emblem to make sure it was legitimate. Satisfied, he handed the three cards back and said. "Lab's still closed. What's your business in Oak Ridge today?"

"Buying food and supplies," Owen responded quickly.

The officer eyed the trailer attached to the truck's bed. "Uh huh. Gonna need an awful lot of 'food' to fill that up, won't you?"

Owen nodded. Being truthful would, hopefully, result in less suspicion on the part of the armed man in body armor. "It will," he agreed. "We also need to get some building material. Wood, cinderblock, brick, that sort of thing. If there's any left to be had."

"Gonna wall yourselves in, eh?"

"Building a workshop."

"Hmmph. You're good to go. Don't cause no trouble, now."

"Thanks," Owen replied.

"Fair word'a warning, though," the officer said, after taking a step back. "This ain't the only checkpoint 'round the city. You start loading down with all sorts of stuff, and you can expect to be stopped and searched. Just how it is right now, nothing personal.

"And you should know," he went on, "that the Guard's been called out as well. I can't say how they'll react if you start flashing that Q around, so keep it quiet. Lots'a people been leaving town lately and they're looking real close at anyone coming in."

Owen nodded again. "I understand."

"Carry on." He waved the truck through.

Owen pulled forward and through the intersection. A car from the other road pulled in shortly behind them.

"That went easier than I thought it would, actually," Will observed.

"I assumed it would be like that," Owen admitted.

"Well, yeah, you've got a Q Clearance," Will said. "Speaking of, when the hell did you get a DOE badge?"

Owen shrugged. "I've had it for a while," he admitted. "It's not for anything fancy; I worked on the computers at the Labs before, well, before this week."

"And you never told? I don't believe you!" Will accused. The grin on his face told his true feelings.

"If I told you," Owen began.

"...I'd have to kill you," they both finished, grinning, and then dissolved into laughter. They sat in amicable silence for several minutes before Owen piped up again. "What I'm not looking forward to is the checkpoints after we start loading gear and material in the back of the truck."

"As long as we're not trying to smuggle drugs or bombs, I honestly don't think they're going to care right now. And besides, you've got that fancy, big-kid badge you can scare them off with."

Owen laughed. "Point. I still don't really want to be searched every other block."

Will shrugged. "Those cops are there for show, honestly.

"You think?"

He nodded. "Yeah. They're just there to make everyone feel like they're being taken care of. You know as well as I do that they won't be able to do any better against the Korovega than we did, or than the Guard did in DC. I may not like seeing police everywhere, makes me feel like I'm an extra in Judge Dredd, but they're probably going to be doing a lot to prevent 'disturbances' around the area."

"Yeah. 'Disturbances.' Like riots."

"I don't particularly want to be caught in a riot," Will countered. "Right now? I'll take a few checkpoints if it means that a thousand people, all drunk on mob violence, won't trample me just for being in their way."

"And if a riot does start?"

Will's face darkened. "I plan to be way the hell away from the city, and any large masses of people, before that happens."

"We'll be..." Owen started.

"Don't even," Will said. His tone was firm, but he grinned. "Don't say 'everything's going to be alright.' Alright?"

"But you just said it."

"I said it because I'm telling you not to say it."

"Seems like that'd still have the same effect."

"It doesn't."

"I don't think jinxes play fair like that."

"Don't care."

"Yeah, but what if it did?" Owen asked. The lighthearted banter was lifting his spirits considerably. Being clear of the police blockade was doing that as well, but the road ahead of them, empty at a time when it should still be packed with the morning rush, was trying hard to drag him back down.

"It didn't," Will countered. Owen saw it in his face as well. A severity had settled over Will's features after their encounter with the Korovega, but now that pall was starting to lift. His eyes still darted around, taking in all of the changing details around him, but he no longer seemed ready to fight any unexpected noise.

"Yeah, but what if it's like Macbeth?"

"You mean 'the Scottish Play?'"

"Yeah, that. And you can't tell people not to say Macbeth because you can't say Macbeth in the first place."

"Dude, I'm pretty sure curses are different than jinxes."

"Mhmm," Owen replied. "If you say so."

"You were the one about to say it anyway."

"But I didn't."

Will sighed dramatically. "Fine, if we catch fire in the next five minutes, it's totally on me."

"I'll try and remember that amid all the burning."

"I hear, as an experience, it's overrated."

"That's what they tell me."

They continued bantering back and forth for another ten minutes as they neared the hardware store. It had been built on a series of caves and the area around it was constantly sinking at a slow rate which made the street leading up to the store feel more like a mild roller coaster than a road.

They parked and stepped out of the truck.

"Got the list?" Will asked, slamming the heavy steel door. Owen had taken up two spaces, end-to-end, right in front of the doors. On a normal day, he would have been forced to park at the far end of the lot to find a space large enough for the truck and its trailer.

Owen held up small notepad. He had the list on his phone as well, but notepads did not crack when dropped. "Right here."

"You think someone should stay with the truck?"

Owen looked around the empty parking lot and shook his head. "No. We should be fine. Even if there were a lot of people, it's really only going to be the food I'll be worried about, and that's our last stop.

"Good deal," Will said, smiling. "Let's do this."

* * *

The punch that sent George Sinon to the ground hurt his pride vastly more than it hurt his jaw. Unfortunately for his pride, the blow delivered quite a bit of pain as well as embarrassment. He sprawled on the ground, thankful for the soft puzzle-piece floor that Owen bought at the art store the day before. It was thin, and it had a tendency to shift underfoot, but the alternative was to fall directly on the gravel.

George was not about to give Ben the satisfaction of bleeding on his driveway.

He felt his lip. He would, however, give him the satisfaction of seeing him bleed on the safety mats, no matter how much he had tried to avoid it. They had been instructed not to target the nose or eyes, and Jessie had explained why a straight punch to the teeth was a bad idea, but slugs to the jaw were well within the short list of rules she laid down.

He grit his teeth.

Sam stood over him. She was panting, yes, and her face dripped sweat that could only tangentially be blamed on the rising humidity and temperature, but she was still standing. He resented how smug she looked; despite being barely over five feet, she had thrown or pushed him to the ground four times since they started. Equally frustrating, especially due to his inability to do the same, she had been able to stand up to Jessie for short periods of time. Neither of them managed to land a solid hit on their instructor, but Sam had proven over and over to be able to take several hits of her own before Jessie could knock her flat.

Watching Sam go toe-to-toe with Jessie, and then turn around and put him on the ground, all while wearing nothing above the waist but a black sports bra, was not exactly doing anything good for his state of mind either. Her pale body glistened with sweat, and he found himself distracted more than once. Sprawled on the ground, he suspected he hardly looked competent, let alone attractive. Sam doing so well in their fights, and looking so damn good doing it, did an excellent job of fueling his frustration.

"On your feet, Sinon!" Jessie barked. She had been running them ragged almost since they had started. They had been given one water break in the hour and a half they had been "practicing," which was about three too few as far as George was concerned.

He grumbled, pushing himself away from the mat. He had heard that phrase too many times in the last hour and was growing very tired of it. He had to admit, though, as her words filtered through his brain, that when Jessie sent Sam sprawling, she gave her neither more nor less pity than she gave him. He could deal with "tough" so long as "but fair" was tacked onto the end.

George came to his feet slowly. The previous two times Sam had knocked him down, he had simply adopted the guard Jessie had taught him, which turned out to be nothing like the watered down karate he had learned years before, and waited for the start of the next round—a unit of time that so far had mostly been defined as "how long George can stay on his feet."

This time, however, he had other plans in mind. Jessie had constantly been harping on him to improve his attacks, to make more of them, to, as she put it, "fight like she's trying to fucking kill you, damn it." He wiped the blood from his mouth with the back of one hand, looked at it in a detached manner, and launched himself toward Sam.

He took three large steps, the last of which was more of a lunge than a step. Truthfully, two steps would have put him within striking distance for a straight punch or a kick. The third step put him so close so quickly that his shoulder would pass her at the same time as his fist.

The blow was sloppy, horrendously telegraphed, and never would have worked if she had even a second's advance warning. Sam's eyes went wide with surprise and she tried to move to one side. The evasion was almost successful, but she had neither enough space nor enough time. Yet the movement was not completely in vain; it positioned her perfectly to sink her fist into George's solar plexus.

George's blow hit hard as he added a torso rotation to his lunge. His fist caught her just under the left collarbone, sending her sprawling to the ground. Fortunately for her, he missed her sternum and impacted muscle and breast tissue which absorbed much of the force.

Her counter came just as hard as George barreled into her with all of his momentum. He gasped and his knees buckled. As he fell, the conscious part of his brain watched with satisfaction as Sam fought to stay on her feet. She staggered back and hit the ground a few seconds later and about a yard away.

Never before had he been hit quite so hard, and some dim part of his brain realized that it was his own fault. The pain spread from his ribs down to his crotch and his eyes watered as he gasped for breath. George had never realized that having the wind knocked out of one's lungs was literal, but for the first few panicked moments after Sam's fist struck him, his body refused to inhale.

Finally, his diaphragm obeyed him and he sucked in a huge lungful of air, only to cough and choke on half of it.

Sam, he saw, was already on her feet, and he struggled to join her. His legs and arms all worked just fine, but he was still having a hard time breathing and his vision kept trying to go gray at the edges.

"You lose," Jessie said. "You hit nice and hard, I'll grant, and Sam looks none too happy about it over there, but you let her lay you out good in the process."

George grunted.

"What's rule number one?" Jessie demanded.

"De," George started, then coughed, "defend first," he stopped, panted, and finished, "then attack."

"And did you do that?"

He shook his head, but said nothing. The pain in his gut was answer enough, as far as he was concerned.

"What did you learn?"

George eyed her quizzically.

Jessie repeated, "what did you learn?"

"Don't do that?" he asked, managing a rueful grin.

"That's a start."

"Sam hits hard?"

"Almost."

"Liver shots fucking hurt?"

Jessie chuckled. "Closer."

"What am I missing?" he demanded. He hated feeling like he was in the dark about something. He felt like Jessie was lording it over him, which, surprisingly, only made him want to get back into the ring and fight more. His breathing was clearing up, but the ache persisted. Sweat beaded on his face, threatening to run into his eyes, and his hair stuck to his forehead. He wiped it away with the back of his hand.

Jessie pulled a smaller handkerchief with a red lace border out of her back pocket and wiped her forehead. "You always get back up." That was the second time he had heard her use that flat tone—the first had been when she imparted "rule number one" to the two of them when they started.

"But you said I lost," he accused.

"Yeah," she replied. "You lost this round. Maybe even lost the match, depending on how hard you got hit. But in a real fight, you don't lose until you're dead. So you get back up every damn time you get knocked down. More you get knocked down, the better you get at getting back up. Understand?"

"Yeah," he replied, actually respecting the way in which she had delivered that bit of knowledge.

"Good," Jessie said. She turned to Sam. "Now you. You know what you did wrong?"

Sam blinked. After the dressing down Jessie had given George, she fully expected to be praised for how she handled his reckless attack. "What do you mean?"

Jessie lifted her chin and looked down her nose at Sam for a moment. A bright-red, fist-sized blotch stood out around the straps of her sports bra. "How's the chest?"

"Stings," she replied, "but I'll manage."

"Shouldn't have to."

"I should have gotten out of the way."

Jessie shoot her head. "Sometimes you got to take a hit to give a hit. But the way he was coming at you? The way he was all bunched up?"

Sam nodded. Like all of the exchanges so far, she had been replaying it in her head, trying to determine if there was anything she could have done better.

"Coming at you like this," Jessie mimicked George's tucked-arm stance, then proceeded to give a brief lesson on countering reckless attacks. When asked why she had not started with that, Jessie told them that they had to learn to fight right before they could safely deal with someone with no regard for their own safety.

The lesson morphed from there from a strict stand-and-punch routine to grappling and control of the fight. George had to admit, despite the glee with which Sam had been throwing him around, he was fascinated by what he was learning.

"Got it?" she asked, allowing George to stand up straight again.

Sam nodded, watching. "I think so."

"You're always learning," Jessie pronounced. She wiped her forehead with the red-lace handkerchief again. Her tanned skin was significantly drier than either of her students', but even Jessie had been sweating heavily in the Summer morning's heat. "Never forget that. Now. Water break!"

Earlier, they had brought out a cooler full of ice and stuffed it with various bottles. Some had sports drinks, others had juice or water. A similar cooler held drinks near the shallow pit where Ben, Marcus, and Michael were digging out the foundation for their workshop.

Katrina paced unsteadily overhead. The deck had a roof over it, but the morning sun still slanted between the slats at a steep angle. Her feet and legs cast strange, long shadows on the wall of the training area as she walked the length of the house and back.

Away from Jessie for a moment, George approached Sam where she stood watching Ben and Marcus take turns hammering on a particularly stubborn rock with their pickaxes. Michael was, for the moment, simply staying out of their way. Michael kept a shirt on, though it was long since soaked through with sweat.

Marcus and Ben, on the other hand, had removed their shirts as soon as they started to sweat. Ben was a good ten years older than she was, but his conditioning had kept him in excellent shape. Marcus, on the other hand, was nearly her age and his chiseled torso still looked like he had only left the military yesterday. She took a moment to appreciate the way the sweat glistened on their muscles.

"Hey," George said. He waved, a small and halfhearted motion, with his free hand. The other still held a bottle of what appeared to be apple juice.

Sam nodded at him but said nothing. She continued to watch Ben and Marcus hammer away at the stubborn boulder. Both of them were cursing heavily under their breath at the steadfastness of the stone. From where she stood, it looked like a chunk of Tennessee marble much like every other rock they had uncovered. That would have explained the trouble they were having breaking it, anyway. Finally, with one last great swing, Ben split the boulder into three large chunks—plus a handful of rock chips and dust. Grunting, he and Marcus levered the pieces the rest of the way out of the ground and threw them aside.

Finally, she turned her attention to George, and asked simply, "can I help you?"

"Look," he said. He stopped, softening his facial expression and tone as if by will alone, and continued, "listen. I'm sorry about what I said earlier. I was pissed off and I said something stupid. Don't hold it against me?"

He offered a seemingly genuine smile and held out his hand. She eyed it distrustfully and kept her own hands clasped firmly behind her back.

George dropped his hand awkwardly to his side.

Sam nodded. "Apology accepted."

George bit back a heated reply. With forced calm, he asked, "that's it?"

Sam cocked her head to one side and looked him up and down. He looked tense, she thought, ready to spring one way or the other. She felt just as tense, but she was also kept it under better control. Between the anger that still rolled under her surface and the burst of adrenaline his apology brought on, she felt ready to snap as well.

Instead of letting her anger out, she channeled that feeling into a dispassionate focus. Watching the three men working gave her something other than George to focus on. She could keep her attention on them, letting her displeasure spill over the sides of her expression rather than turn the focus of her anger directly on him. She did not care much about offending him with her dismissal, but she did harbor concerns about what it would do to the group's cohesion if she deliberately antagonized him.

"What else is there to say?" she asked.

"I don't know," he replied, voice dripping with sarcasm, "maybe, 'that's alright,' or at least say 'thank you'?"

"The first one would be a lie," Sam said, "and the second implies that you didn't have to apologize and I should be grateful that you did."

"You should," he muttered.

"You shouldn't have tried to start a fight earlier. I get that we're all stressed, but that's no excuse."

"I didn't..." he started, but Sam continued speaking as thought he had said nothing.

"I'm not about to forget what you said, but there's no point to dwelling on it."

"What do you mean, exactly?"

She shrugged. "You apologized; we move on. It's as simple as that." Finally, she turned to face him. Eyes narrow and voice firm, she said, "but don't do it again."

"I'll behave."

She nodded and a hint of a smile crossed her face. "Good. Now, let's get back to training."

He laughed and, with a grin, asked, "you're not going to try and break my arm again?"

That time, she did smile, though to call it "friendly" would have been a stretch. "No promises. That's what we're learning to do, after all."

Chapter 15

After lunch, Marcus led everyone through an hour-long yoga session. He claimed that, between the back-breaking work required to put in the workshop and the high-intensity sparring and training they were doing, everyone was going to need as much relaxation and flexibility as they could manage. The routine proved difficult for Michael and Ben, neither of whom could have listed "flexibility" among their strengths. George and Sam found it somewhat easier, only struggling on the more complicated positions. While Jessie had no trouble keeping up with the pace Marcus set, even she found some of the more unusual movements a challenge.

During a break in the routine, George commented to Ben about Jessie's flexibility. He even made the classic comedy routine elbow-nudge and eyebrow-wiggle as if his point was not obvious enough.

In response, Ben had simply said, "we tried that. I had reach, but she had flexibility. Didn't work out."

The latter half of the routine was mostly slow movements as Marcus took them through a long series of relaxing stretches that hit every muscle and joint they had been using that day.

After the session ended, Sam approached Marcus. She had to admit that she felt better than she had not just since the Korovega attack, but in weeks at least. "Where'd you pick that up?"

"I started leading sessions in the army," Marcus replied. "Took some doing, but I eventually got all the guys in my squad into it."

Sam grinned. "I imagine there was a bit of push back against it."

"'I ain't doing that! Yoga's for women and nancy boys!'" he said, mimicking the voice of every Hollywood Drill Sergeant to appear in a movie. He laughed. "They came around pretty quickly, though, when I showed them some of the stuff I could do because of it. The guys on base apparently thought it was pretty cool when I could do inverted poses with a full combat load of gear strapped to me." He shrugged. "But I learned the moves in the first place when I was a kid. Well, teenager, really. I did competitive gymnastics for the better part of a decade."

Sam thought for a moment, trying to reconcile those two things. "What made you stop? Going from a gymnast to a soldier doesn't seem like the most normal career progression."

Marcus laughed. "Gymnastics wouldn't pay for college. Putting on a uniform and yes-sir-ing my way around the world for a few years did, though."

"Whatever works, right?"

"Yeah. Pretty much."

She waved briefly toward the pit that would soon be their workshop. "How's the work coming?"

Marcus smirked. "You'll see for yourself soon enough."

Sam rolled her eyes. "I know that much. I'd kinda like to know how nice the pit is before I jump in it, though."

"It's a nice pit," he said. He grinned. "Well, maybe not right now. The dirt down there's nice and cool, but it's too shallow for shade.

"That's good to know. I'll put on some extra sunscreen before I head that way. Gingers burn in direct sunlight, you know."

Marcus laughed, a deep, genuine belly laugh. "Anyway, there's a ways to go before we can pour the floor. Speaking of, I ran a few things through my head and I don't think the mixer we have is large enough to mix up enough concrete for one solid floor down there."

"I assume you're telling me this because you have an idea?" Sam asked.

Marcus nodded. "You're not going to like it, though, because it's going to make this thing take a lot longer unless everyone pitches in."

Sam sighed again, closed her eyes, and cursed her luck. Opening them again, she said, "alright. Lay it on me."

He outlined a fairly simple plan that would make more efficient use of their materials. The downside was that it would take twice as many people and probably fifty-percent longer to put it together.

From where he was standing nearby, George said he agreed with the plan, claiming that the only reason he had not designed it that way was time.

"That settles it, then," Sam said, then, louder, "everyone over here, I've got some changes to announce."

The others slowly formed a semblance of a line and Marcus groaned inwardly in reflex. Not that he had any illusions about their training, but he and Will had spent enough years perfecting their concept of "standing in a straight line" that a ragged line still bothered him on some level. He managed to ignore it and went to stand with everyone else in what was rapidly becoming more of a semi-circle than a line anyway.

"What's the plan?" Ben asked, leaning against side of the basement door frame.

Sam outlined Marcus's idea, ending with, "it's probably the best chance we have of getting this thing done and sturdy in short order."

"How much of a hurry are we in, exactly?" George asked.

"None," Sam replied, then before he could say anything else, "right now. But it still needs to be done as quickly as possible. The longer it takes, the longer until we get a space where we can build things, like your water wheel, and the longer until we can get the extra refrigerators and freezers hooked up in the storage room. Even if we hurry, it's still going to be Sunday or Monday before we get it finished unless we seriously buckle down and work around the clock.

"Any other questions?"

Katrina politely raised her hand.

Sam pointed her out. "Yes?"

"Um," she started, "I've never built anything bigger than a birdhouse. I don't' really know what I'm doing..."

"You and me both," Michael said with a self-deprecating laugh.

"Are you alright to stay on guard duty, then?" Sam asked. She had planned for someone else to take the second shift, but if Katrina was going to be second-guessing her carpentry while they worked, it might be better to ease her into another project later.

"I-If that's alright." Hesitation shook her voice. "I don't want to throw off the schedule and make everyone else work extra. I can pull my weight around here, I promise. I'll just need..."

Sam raised a hand to stop her midsentence. She then placed that hand on Katrina's shoulder, leaned in slightly, and in the most comforting tone she could manage, quietly said, "don't worry about it. There's plenty of people down here. You just worry about keeping an eye on things. Ok?"

"I can do that."

"And Katrina?" Sam said. "If you see any of those Korovega eagles? Practice your shooting."

Katrina nodded. More accurately, her head jerked up and down twice in a nervous emulation of a nod. It made Sam wonder just how much the stress of not only a new place and unfamiliar circumstances, but having encountered a Korovega as well was getting to her. The rest of them had their various jobs to bury themselves in—that was why she wanted to rotate people through guard duty quickly. The lone guard during the day would be alone with their thoughts for hours at a time.

She shook herself back to reality, aware that getting lost in thought while there was still work to be done was bad. There would be time for that later. Plus, she thought, if she was just standing around thinking, she had no moral authority to make anyone else work through their tiredness. They had all slept poorly the night before, and the day was dragging on everyone equally.

Back in the real world, Sam realized that everyone was still watching her. She had only been silent for a few seconds, but the intent stares of those gathered around her was surprisingly uncomfortable, and not just because of the tension in the air.

They are all waiting on me to turn them loose, she realized. They are waiting to see if I have any additional instructions.

The realization was subtly disconcerting. Objectively, she knew where it had come from. She had been ordering this group around for a day and a half, and now they expected her to continue. She had always enjoyed the challenge of organizing things, but the actual carrying out of her organization, the actual commanding, was better done by other people.

The unsettling thing, she realized, was that part of her enjoyed being the authority. Still, the fact remained that five people waited intently for her next orders, heedless of how she felt about it. Time was one thing they did not have to waste. Desired position or not, that responsibility had been heaped on her shoulders and it was her job to bear it.

Sam clapped her hands in front of her once, firmly, and did her best to project confidence. Oddly enough, it was easier than she expected. Having everyone waiting for her signal lent her a sort of confidence all its own. Scanning the crowd, meeting their eyes one-by-one, gave her words a strength that they would not have had otherwise. Whatever she thought of her abilities to lead, they seemed to think that she had it in her, and so she spoke.

"Katrina." She nodded to the deck above their heads. "Back upstairs."

The blond nodded, but stayed put as if waiting for more instructions.

"Now, if you please."

Katrina nodded again and this time turned and strode as confidently as she could manage up the exterior stairs to the upper level.

"George, Michael. You guys know your away around a hammer?"

George have her a look that rather clearly communicated that he thought the question was a silly one. Of course he knew how to use a hammer, his sarcastic glance said.

Michael, to his credit, nodded. "Yeah." He grinned. "That's one thing I do know how to use, anyway."

Ben let out a short bark of laughter. "You didn't do so bad with that pickax."

Michael grinned, but it was equal parts embarrassment and humor. "If you count having to stop every few swings to catch my breath and get pointers as doing well."

Ben grinned. "Yeah, but you didn't quit."

"There is that, I suppose," Michael admitted with a sheepish grin.

"Anyway," Sam interrupted, "get with Marcus. It's his plan; He's in charge. Got it?"

They both nodded, Michael more emphatically than George, but neither argued.

"Ben..."

"Let me guess," he interrupted. "You're sticking me back in th' pit?"

She nodded, and apology showed on her face. "Yeah. We need your muscles."

He rolled his eyes and hid a grin. "If'n you sweet talk me like that, I suppose I can't say no."

Jessie elbowed him lightly in the ribs. "We like watching you work."

"You just like making me sweat," Ben replied with a grin.

Jessie laughed. "I ain't admitting anything."

"Alright, you two," Sam interjected. "Let's get to work, why don't we?"

"Tools still over there?" Jessie asked as they approached what would soon be the foundation for their workshop.

Ben nodded. He flexed his knees and dropped the three feet into the wide pit.

"How deep does it have to be?" Jessie asked.

Ben shrugged. "Half a flight down, so three an' a half, four feet, plus eighteen inches or so for the foundation."

"So." Sam slid into the pit, falling lightly on her feet. "Deeper than this."

Ben laughed. "Yeah. And as level as we can get it. Concrete's gonna be liquid when we pour it in here, so we level the top before it sets, but the flatter it is down here the stronger the slab's going to be."

"So...?"

Ben laughed. "We dig."

"You're having fun," Jessie accused, "admit it."

"Nope," he replied, swinging his pickax at yet another stubborn chunk of Tennessee marble. He grinned. "Not a bit."

Jessie laughed. "Uh huh."

"Less talk, more shovel," Sam said, forcing herself not to laugh as well.

Ben gave in and laughed again. "I'm tellin' you, Jess. This one's mean."

* * *

The line of cars that stretched ahead of their truck seemed endless. It would disappear on the far side of one of a dozen gently rolling hills only to reappear on the upslope of the next hill. Their line of sight varied from short to long to short again as the heavily laden truck crept its way down the road. The pattern continued as far as they could see, with only small variations here and there as some lucky—or impatient—driver pulled out and took to one of the side roads and subdivisions that lead back toward Oak Ridge proper. A dozen or more cars had pulled off the road, either overheated or simply unwilling to endure traffic any longer.

Worse, at least for Owen's state of mind, those black Korovega eagles circled the sky overhead. They moved in regular patterns that reminded him more of a search grid than a circle of vultures.

The towers of the Bull Run steam plant rose a short distance away. The shorter of the two towers—the only one to actually function after the larger one was decommissioned but left standing as a historic monument—stood tall in the sky. It puffed a steady stream of white vapor into the clear blue sky, in idyllic contrast to the jam of cars at its feet.

"Have I mentioned I hate traffic?" Will grumbled.

Owen chuckled. Despite his own frustration, and the steadily dropping needle on the gas tank as they sat in traffic that was going practically nowhere, he was grateful to have company. The fact that he shared Will's opinion of their situation, though, did not exactly offer any consolation.

"A time or twelve, yeah," Owen replied.

"This shit sucks," Will said, lolling his head dramatically to one side.

"Tell me about it."

"I thought we took Edgemoor to avoid this crap."

Owen looked at the clock on the truck's dash. It read "4:17." He shrugged. "The rush hour backup shouldn't have started in this direction for another half hour or so. On any normal day, this road would have been clear at least as far as Bull Run."

"Would have, should have," Will retorted, rolling his eyes. "I mean, don't get me wrong. Ben's kept this beast in good condition, so it's not as bad as it could be."

"By, 'good condition,' you mean the AC works and the seats are in one piece," Owen interjected.

Will laughed. "Well, yeah, but I rode in some pretty shitty Humvees in my day. Seats with cushions are still a luxury so far as I'm concerned."

"Fair enough. You were saying?"

Will shrugged. "Nothing. I was just going to say that it didn't suck as bad as it could," he replied, then jerked a thumb at one of the cars on the side of the road. White smoke billowed out from under the hood as a bewildered-looking couple ineffectually fanned their overheated engine. "We could be them."

"I'm keeping a close eye on the gauges, trust me."

"Didn't say you weren't."

"Just making sure. You watching the trailer?"

Will nodded. "Yeah. A few people have looked kinda interested, but no one's willing to jump out and try and play pirate."

"Well at least one thing's going well right now," Owen replied with a sidelong grin.

"By the way, back at the hardware store," Will began, and Owen suddenly felt a rush of adrenaline. The tone of Will's voice indicated that whatever he was about to say was not pleasant. "Since when do you spell your name with a K?"

Owen sighed. He had been afraid Will would bring that up first. Owen had spent most of the ride thus far trying to come up with a way to work it into the conversation. From that perspective, he supposed he was glad that Will said something.

"Since Kenneth Cooper died with thirty thousand dollars in the bank."

Will glared sideways. "That's fucking dirty, man."

"Woah. It's not like that."

Will raised an eyebrow.

"Ok, fine, it's like that. But it's what we all agreed to on Tuesday."

His voice was skeptical, but only slightly accusatory. "That you'd rifle through each other's pockets when you died?"

Owen nodded. "Pretty much."

That stopped Will in his tracks. "Wait, really?"

Owen laughed. "Did you honestly think I'd stolen his card off his dead body?"

"Desperation makes people do stupid stuff," Will muttered. "But I ought to know you better than that, hey?"

Owen smiled. "I'd hope so."

"So you really made a bargain to keep spending, even if one of you is killed?"

"Yeah," he replied. "He's not legally dead anyway. No one knows he's gone but us."

"No friends?"

Owen's eyes darkened. "Who do you think tried to kill us on the road Tuesday afternoon?"

"That's harsh," Will muttered. Louder, he asked, "you in on it too?"

Owen nodded solemnly. "Yeah. Everyone but you and the two you brought with you are in on it. Nothing written, but a verbal contract's good as anything else right now."

"I know how that goes," Will said. "Over in the sandbox, if you promised something to your buddies, you'd better keep it. They know where you sleep."

"That's about how things feel right now."

"Anyway," Will continued, changing tone to something brighter. "Count me in. I'm sure Marcus and Katrina would be willing, too. Are we trying to spend as much as we can, or what? Because that," he jerked a thumb over his shoulder, "was damned expensive."

"That's the idea. When the Korovega start burning banks and credit unions, anything to do with modern money's going to fizzle up."

"You sound like a prepper."

Owen rolled his eyes. "I know. Don't remind me. But that's the situation we're in."

"You don't think banks and whatnot will hold on?"

"Oh they'll hold on," Owen replied, "but not for long."

They rode along in relative silence for another ten minutes. The radio played quietly in the background. Early in the day's work, they had had it on a short rotation of local news stations, but after a while they started to repeat themselves. This one talked about how dangerous and scary the Korovega were, that one talked about ways to fight them—none of which seemed like they would work on the beast that interrupted their sleep the night before—and this other talked about anything other than the Korovega. After lunch, they set the radio to one of the classic rock stations and left it on for background noise. It did a decent enough job of filling the silence when they ran out of things to talk about.

The truck crested another small hill and Will suddenly sat bolt upright in his seat. Owen watched his eyes go wide, not in fear but in the sort of alert expression he had seen the night before.

"What is it?" Owen asked. Urgency inspired by Will's sudden reaction crept into his voice. He made no attempt to hide his concern.

Will's eyes narrowed. "People are moving around up there."

"Moving around as in...?" Owen make a few questioning motions with his hands, mimicking the patterns of people moving around calmly, "or," he added, then made two fists and bashed them together once.

"I see at least three people on foot. Two on the left side of the road and one," he paused and shifted his head right and left as though trying to get a better parallax on whatever he was seeing. "The third one's in the middle of the road. Maybe there was a wreck? Or something happened? I can see people, but I can't see what happened from here."

Far ahead of them, the two figures on the left side of the road moved hesitantly. Even as as far away as they were, tension showed in their movements. They were jerky, moving first fast and then slow, as though they had no real idea what they were supposed to be doing or how to proceed. Now that Will had pointed them out, Owen could at least see that much.

The figure on the right side of the road seemed to be ignoring the other two. The truck crept a few car-lengths closer as the figures milled about and he wondered if there had been a wreck that led to a fight.

"Maybe the two on the left are cops?" he offered.

Will squinted again. "Could be. They look bulky. Might be kitted up like that riot cop that stopped us earlier."

"Keep rolling?" Owen asked, hand hovering over the manual gearshift in the floor between them.

Will made a noise that was half scoff and half laugh. "What other choice do we have? If we try and turn this trailer around, we'll just make traffic even worse both both sides."

"It's thinning out on that side," Owen said, pointing to the oncoming lane. True to his observation, there were very few cars in the oncoming lane.

"So it is." Will rolled down his window and leaned out. He cursed, came back inside the truck, unbuckled his seatbelt, and leaned most of his body out of the truck as it inched forward a few more yards. He slid back inside and said, "yeah. Whatever's happening up there has stopped traffic. People are still going this way because whatever-it-is is on this side of that left-turn ramp-thingy. So we can still go, and the people on the other side of the light can turn right, but no one else is moving."

Owen rolled his eyes. "Great. When the drivers on Melton realize that, they're all going to u-turn and clog everything right back up even worse."

"Tell me about it."

Owen laughed. "That's my li—"

A sharp crack like thunder, but octaves higher in pitch split the air.

"What th—"

Will interrupted him with a sharp, "quiet!"

Owen's face registered confusion at the sudden change in tone. He felt even more confused at the sudden influx of tension radiating from the right side of the truck's big cabin. The noise had set Will on edge immediately, and Owen mentally ran through a short list of things that might possibly have that effect on him.

Traffic ground to a halt, a real and true halt and not just the inch-by-inch creak of a traffic jam as another crack split the air. Owen's eyes went wide as he realized what was going on. The riot police ahead of them were firing at whoever the other figure was—perhaps it was the other way around, but if the stranger had fired first, Owen suspected that the riot police's reaction would have involved a lot more than one shot.

Will unbuckled and leaned out of the side window again as several more shots rang out in quick succession. There were only a few dozen cars between them and where the altercation was going down. Owen could see very little of the riot police other than movement. Between the intervening cars and the haze from heat and exhaust gasses, his vision was rather limited.

Owen fidgeted in the seat as Will shifted and dropped gingerly back into the cabin. His face was white as a sheet.

"Did they shoot him?" Owen demanded. That was the only thing he could think of that would have unnerved Will so thoroughly. He reasoned that whoever had been up there—perhaps he was threatening bystanders as well as stopping traffic?— had proved to be enough of a threat that the riot police felt compelled to use lethal force to stop him. Owen found that thought unsettling, but there was nothing he could really do about it one way or the other.

Will shook his head. "No," then, "well yes. They shot but..."

"But...?" Owen prodded.

Will shook his head again and swallowed hard. "Yeah, they shot, but that's not a man they're shooting at up there."

Owen started to ask, "then what are they shooting at," but the realization came to him as the first words were coming out of his mouth. The silhouette he had seen moving up there had been humanoid. He thought it had been human, but Will's eyes were sharper than his at such a distance, and he believed what the other man had seen. That left only one other possibility.

"Korovega," Owen breathed.

Will nodded. "Yeah."

Owen blanched. He was trapped in a truck, dozens of miles away from the house that had become their safe haven, and without a weapon. His mind went to the pistol in his pocket and he corrected that condition: without a weapon that would be useful. It would have been bad enough had the thing that trapped him been human, but it was far from it. Fear, anger, and a cold emotion he had no name for fought for supremacy in his gut as he sat there in the unmoving truck.

Far ahead, the two officers came close to one another, apparently in conversation. They kept their guns trained on the Korovega, or where Owen assumed the Korovega was. It stood on the other side of the line of cars blocking his vision. After a moment, one of them backed slowly away and out of sight.

Owen assumed he was going for help, not that it was likely to do any good.

The other riot cop kept his rifle trained ahead of himself, seemingly fixed on one spot. Owen was leaning out of his own window now, as were dozens of other drivers. The officer and the Korovega stood at what appeared to be a stalemate for the better part of a minute.

On the other side of the truck, Owen became aware of Will softly counting to himself. "Eight. Seven. Six."

"What are you counting?"

Will nodded grimly toward the cop. "He's about to lose it. His gun's shaking. Three. Two. One..."

The policeman fired, then fired again twice more. Owen heard a sizzling crack, like a bug zapper taking down a particularly large moth, as bullets hit the Korovega's shield. There was a moment's pause where he presumed the poor man in the riot armor sweated away half of his weight in fear.

He backed up a step, then fired again. Again the dull zap of a bullet on the thing's shield echoed down the road. People were getting out of their cars now. Even Owen could see that he was panicked—a judgment he made mere seconds before the man emptied the rest of his magazine in a hail of bullets.

The Korovega's shield buzzed and sparked like a high tension wire, throwing off arcs and flares of light. From a distance, it was surprisingly beautiful, like the corona of the sun writ small and out of blue fire.

Owen watched the cop's hurried reload. To his credit, he never faltered or missed the receiver, despite the fear causing the gun to shake. But Owen knew what was about to happen, and the officer's apparent skill only made that knowledge sit all the colder in his stomach.

Owen's mind raced. Surely, he thought, there was something he could do to help. Because if that Korovega attacked, none of them within a mile or more of that spot would be left alive after it finished its slaughter. More importantly, they were right next to one of the largest power plants in the area. If the Korovega destroyed Bull Run, it would leave thousands of people without power.

For a brief second, area ahead lit up with a brilliant blue-white flash. It called to mind a photographer's flash and the light from an arc-welder all in the same instant. Like the shield, Owen might have considered it beautiful if he did not know exactly what it meant and his heart sank in his chest.

When the beam cleared, the cop in riot armor was gone. No Hollywood-esque smoking boots, no action-comedy spinning helmet; nothing remained of him or the trees that had been behind him.

Owen heard an engine rev and saw, across the intersection, the lead car shoot forward. The Korovega turned, pivoting on one heel like a dancer, and sent a second beam of blinding blue light into the passenger-side fender from less than six feet away. A large chunk of the car vaporized instantly. What remained of the vehicle spun out of control and smashed, burning, against the car at the head of Owen's lane.

A lightbulb went off in Owen's brain and, before whatever rational part of his mind still remained could stop him, he turned to Will. "There's a pair of bolt cutters behind your seat. Hand them to me."

"What? Why?"

Owen held his hand out. "Just do it. Please."

Will twisted around as the sound of another exploding car washed over them with the concussive force of a boxer's punch. He retrieved the bolt cutters and handed the heavy tool across the cab. Owen took them with one hand and unbuckled his seatbelt with the other.

Owen opened his door and slid out of the tall cab in one movement. He absently swatted at the door behind him and it half closed, but failed to latch. He ignored it. He had other things on his mind.

"What the hell are you doing?" Will demanded, fighting with his own door and then sliding to the ground a few seconds after Owen. "I repeat. What the hell are you doing?"

Owen lowered the tailgate and reached into the hollow of one of the cinderblocks. He pulled out a pieces of the rebar they had bought. It was almost as long as the truck bed. He hefted it from the middle with one hand, then with two, swinging the heavy piece of iron in a lazy arc.

"You're not doing what I think you're doing, are you?"

Owen eyed the piece of rebar a moment longer, acting as though he had not heard Will's voice. In truth, he had, and he knew exactly what he was doing, but he had no intentions of sharing that particular piece of information. Will would only try to stop him. He would tell Owen the truth, that the idea in his head was insane and he should stay in the truck. Instead of listening to that voice, Owen simply extended one end of the rebar to Will and said, "hold this."

Will took it, but the look on his face was far from happy. "Don't you do this. This is insane," he growled, echoing Owen's own thoughts.

Owen positioned the bolt cutters five feet from the end of the rebar. He held them at such a sharp angle that most of the cutting surface lay across the steel pole. For cutting supports, it was a terrible idea. The resulting piece would be wickedly sharp and unsafe for use.

But Owen was not cutting something to use for support.

He clacked the bolt cutters together and the free end of the rebar fell to the asphalt. Owen bent to pick it up and held it in his hand. It was poorly balanced, too heavy for its length, and generally made a worse weapon than anything he would have had at home, but it was what he had on hand and so it was what he was going to use.

"Don't. Do this," Will said forcefully. Worry crept into his voice. "This is stupid. We get in the truck. We get it turned around, and we get the hell away. Don't do this!"

Owen shook his head. "I have to."

"What the hell for, man?"

Owen gestured toward the other cars with the crude spear he had just made. "I can't leave everyone to die."

"You don't owe them anything!"

"I..."

"If you die, what do I tell Ben? What do I tell Sam?"

That thought hit harder than the previous one had. Of course he owed the people in the cars around them nothing, but that had no bearing on whether or not they deserved to die. No one deserved to die at the hands of the Korovega, and if he could somehow prevent another hundred or so from having that same fate, then he would.

Thinking about how Ben and Sam would take his death shook him. They would be furious at him for getting himself killed. He wondered if he really was that important to them, and then imagined Ben calling it a, "damn fool plan." He imagined them putting on a brave face for the others, but breaking down in private. He and Sam would have each other, but they had never been terribly close. Perhaps his death would change that, but he would not be around to see.

He shook his head. He would have the same reaction if they were killed. They were his friends. He and Sam were more than friends; he knew exactly how he would react if, one day, Sam were not there by his side. Without her, he would be diminished, more like losing a part of himself than losing a friend. Yet, he also knew that if he abandoned these people, that she would never forgive him.

Owen weighed the rebar spear in his hand and made a decision. No, he did not have a choice. If he died, then he died, but at least he would die on his feet. And if he lived, if he somehow won, then that would make it all worth the risk.

"Owen! Damnit!" Will hissed as Owen walked away, toward the Korovega.

"Watch the truck for me. I'll just be gone a minute," he said. Somehow, Owen kept the fear and uncertainty out of his voice.

* * *

The Korovega was still hidden from his direct view by a half-dozen cars and a rapidly thickening cloud of smoke. He could hear Will's exasperated shouts behind him, but he ignored them. He ignored every sane impulse he had, especially the ones that told him to go back and run away. He filtered everything out of his mind but his weapon and his enemy. For all he knew, people in the cars he was passing were saying things to him as well, but none of them were moving, neither toward nor away from the Korovega. He heard nothing except the crunch of his own shoes on the asphalt and the bowstring sound of the Korovega's energy beams.

He reached the end of the line of cars. What remained of the car that had tried to ram the Korovega had smashed into the front car. Owen stopped to look inside it. The airbags had deployed and the two occupants seem to have mercifully passed out. He went on.

Inside the burning car, it was far worse. The beam had burned though the car diagonally like a drill. Fortunately, no one was in the back seat or the passenger seat, but the beam had struck the driver. It looked like it hit his right arm, right hip, and the entire right side of his torso. Where the ravening energy burned its hole through the car, nothing remained. The man was dead, eyes staring at his own missing parts with wide-eyed shock. A little trickle of blood colored his forehead where it looked like he had slammed into the steering wheel, but the energy had cauterized the damage from the beam itself, a fact for which Owen was profoundly grateful. Despite his readiness to do battle, running across a blood-smeared car would have had unpleasant consequences for the contents of his stomach. As it was the stench of burning flesh was bad enough by itself—a human being should not smell like undercooked steak and burnt plastic.

The Korovega's back was to him. It had apparently decided that the other lane's cars were to be punished for the one that had tried to ram it. So far, more than a dozen cars lay in burning wrecks as the inhuman beast walked its energy beam down the line one car at a time. Further down the line, cars were trying to flee, but they only got in one another's way. The occupants, most of them anyway, seemed to be getting out and running.

The Korovega made no move to chase those who fled. It was not carrying out a slaughter, Owen realized. The Korovega had turned things into an execution. It was methodical in its movements. While it could have destroyed them all with one shot from the front, it seemed to take pleasure in systematically annihilating people one by one.

Fortunately, the black smoke from the burning car next to him gave Owen a bit of concealment as he crept forward. He moved in a deep crouch that any fencer would have appreciated, spear at the ready. His movements were slow, deliberate, until he reached the edge of the makeshift smokescreen.

Owen stopped. The Korovega was on the far side, at least fifteen or twenty feet away. Owen could cover than in a few seconds, he knew. But he also knew that the Korovega was fast and that his shoes would make a hell of a lot of noise on the asphalt. He had no choice, though. If the Korovega turned while he was still creeping around and decided that he was next to die, he suspected that no amount of quick lunges would cover the distance fast enough.

He sprang into action, covering the ground in long, loping strides. He moved as fast as he could without losing his balance. Closing the distance would do him no good if he tripped and fell over his own feet or careened headlong into the Korovega itself.

The monster turned and humanlike surprise showed on its wrong-featured face. It raised one hand, the hand that burned with energy, but Owen was too close. The Korovega's fist clenched and the swirl of half-charged beam energy became a shield as its other hand reached for the complex-hilted sword at its side.

Owen had no desire to let it finish the draw, and lunged. The wicked point of his spear impacted the translucent energy of the Korovega's shield. The jarring impact was painful, and the spear threatened to skid out of control. There was no way he was getting through the blue disk. He struck again, and this time the Korovega's sword was in the way.

Owen backed up half a step and the Korovega dropped its shield. The glow of a beam in preparation replaced it. Owen mentally cursed more violently than he ever had and stepped back in for another strike with his spear. The Korovega caught it with its sword and the familiar shield once again replaced the ball of energy in its other hand.

The Korovega swung its sword. Some distant corner of his mind, the corner that had not yet realized his life was at stake, admired the monster's perfect form. Every part of the thing's arm uncurled exactly as it should, and it shifted its shoulders and hips to maximize its power and speed. Humanity's best swordsmen would have been impressed, he thought, as the blow came down like a hammer on his rebar spear.

They traded blows for a dozen seconds, each as long as an eternity. Owen's heart was racing as he jabbed his spear high over his head in a descending thrust. It scraped past the Korovega's shield and, despite the creature's best attempt to dodge, left a bright red streak across its shoulder.

"See!" Owen shouted. He was unsure if he was shouting for his own benefit, for the benefit of the people slowly gathering around them, or in an attempt to intimidate the Korovega. "They can bleed. They can bleed!"

He almost missed the blow coming from the Korovega's sword. He caught it with the bottom half of his spear, but the angry strike knocked him off his feet. That was better than letting the Korovega's sword hit him, he reflected as he shook his head to clear the daze of hitting the pavement.

The Korovega glared and somehow smirked at the same time, and dropped its shield to ready the beam again. Owen, though, had sparred with Ben. Big Ben, as he was called in their fencing group, was not shy about using his huge frame to knock his opponents around, Owen included. Over the years, he had been knocked to the dirt more times than he could count by the big man, all of which had taught him the one skill that kept him alive right then.

Owen was on his feet a moment later, spear high, and yelling something incoherent even to himself. The Korovega—was that panic on its face?—reactivated its shield and raised it, but Owen had no intention of letting it block him again.

He feinted high and the Korovega moved its shield high and cut with its sword at Owen's legs. Owen pivoted, slamming the Korovega's sword with all the force his heavy stick of rebar could deliver. He carried the motion through into a high thrust on the other side.

The Korovega yelled a curse, and barely brought its shield up to block in time. Owen's spear bounced off of the edge of the energy disk, ruining his balance. It pivoted, bringing its sword forward for a thrust that would have skewered him like a pig had another hard smack from his spear not sent the blade wide.

Its legs were exposed, Owen realized, and he struck out with the blunt end of the spear. He connected with its shin, but failed to draw blood. What he also failed to do was notice the Korovega's shield as it crashed down against the side of his head.

Owen spun through the air, clinging desperately to consciousness. He had a second to reflect on his mistakes before his shoulder slammed into the pavement. He slid then flipped twice. Right at that moment, as thew stinging pain in his shoulder set in, he knew he was dead. The spear was nowhere to be found in his half-second of desperate groping and the Korovega's footsteps were coming closer. He had no idea why it had not simply killed him with a beam yet, but right then he was in no position to object to a few more seconds of life.

The Korovega lifted him into the air with one hand. Its other hand held its sword, which meant that the hand holding him by his shirt collar was the energy-projecting hand. Its breath smelled of strange spices, almost pleasant. It certainly was not the carrion and death that he would have expected from such a monster. It drew back its sword for a thrust and placed the tip against Owen's chest.

Owen spat blood at the Korovega, leaving a pinkish-red streak down the thing's ashen face. "What," he managed before having to struggle for a breath. The pain was almost overwhelming. He closed his eyes for a moment, just breathing. Then, "what do you want?"

It grinned at him as though savoring the moment before ramming its sword through his ribs. Owen refused to close his eyes, staring back into its face as its arm tensed for the killing blow.

A gunshot sounded from nearby and the Korovega threw Owen heavily to the side. The tip of its sword scratched across his chest, but did little more than draw blood. Of course, between the pain in his head and shoulder, Owen was unsure whether he would have even noticed another injury.

The Korovega turned toward the direction of the gunshot and brought up its shield as a second shot buzzed past it and thunked into a tree. It grimaced and kept its sword trained on Owen as it scanned the smoky scene for the gunman.

Owen located his spear and picked it up. He realized he was about to trade people's lives for the seconds he needed to get his weapon back, and his heart sank. The cold pit in his stomach told him that he was just as bad as the Korovega, sacrificing people so that he could live, but he also knew he had no choice. He had to move quickly, to do what he came there to do, otherwise those few deaths would turn into many deaths, and that was a far worse alternative.

A third crack and its shield flared with white light. It retaliated by dropping the shield and lancing a beam of energy in that general direction.

For Owen, that was all he needed. Pain screamed at him, but adrenaline fueled his muscles. He hurt, but that only made his movements more precise. When every action hurt, any wasted effort was just more pain.

Owen pushed off of the hot asphalt and came to his feet in a single springing movement. The action sent him forward, toward the Korovega. The monster saw him moving and started to turn, but because its attention had been on the man shooting, it was a moment too slow.

He thrust into the Korovega's ribs, realizing only as the spear connected that he had picked it up backward. The impact from the dull end knocked the Korovega off balance for a moment, and Owen twisted around, lunged, and struck out with the lethal end. The sharp tip caught the side of the Korovega's skull and blood flew as its head was knocked to one side by the blow.

The Korovega pivoted, reflexively striking out at Owen. He shifted backward, barely out of the way.

"What do you hope to accomplish, ash-man?" The Korovega growled. It spit blood at its feet. Its English was perfect, but with an accent that had never been heard during human civilization.

Owen stared, panting. There was no way he could go another round with the monster in front of him. An idea came to him and he shouted, "I just showed all these people that you can bleed, motherfucker!"

The Korovega turned fully toward him, shield ready and sword forward. "You are defiant. I find that amusing. But you fought well for vermin. Perhaps you have earned a warrior's death, after all. Come to me, perz-manus and we will end this."

"They can bleed!" he shouted at what he thought was the top of his lungs. Then, somehow ever louder, he shouted again. "THEY BLEED!"

The mob moved. First one, then another, then five, then ten, then twenty-plus people all rushed the demon from beyond time.

The Korovega knocked the first one sprawling with its shield. It spitted the second one with its sword and slung blood across the faces of two people to one side of the dead man, blinding them for a moment and effectively taking them out of the fight as well. A dozen panicked and ran before they could get close enough to fight. A dozen more stayed; some even carried knives, tire irons, or other tools.

Owen kicked at the Korovega's exposed knee and it went down. Blows rained down on it over and over again and it growled. The growling grew louder, then turned into a scream, then a roar as it threw them off all at once by creating a dome of energy that pushed them all away like a strong wind.

The dome was less solid than the shield and people were already forcing their way through it. The Korovega snarled and cursed in its ancient language. It looked around, swiped at one of the nearer people with its sword, leaving a bloody gash on the woman's arm, then turned and ran.

Owen held his spear over his head. Swept up in the triumphant emotions of the crowd, he yelled, "they bleed! They can be beaten! Fight back! While you live, you fight!"

The crowd cheered and, for the first time in four days, Owen felt hope. And, as he stumbled back to the truck, he felt pain. His back was hot and, he assumed, bloody, and the dull throb in the side of his head was quickly becoming a distraction.

Back at the truck, he went straight for the passenger side. At Will's questioning glance, he said, "you're driving for a bit."

Will shook his head. "You're a damn fool." He found himself unable to suppress a grin, though he hid it from Owen's sight. "But you came back alive."

"Something kinda like 'alive,' anyway," Owen replied with a small laugh.

Sliding into the driver's seat, Will muttered, "I've driven a Humvee. How hard can this thing be to drive?"

Chapter 16

Owen and Will made it back to the house shortly after sundown. According to Sam's original plan, that was several hours after they were supposed to be back. Two phonecalls had done little to assuage everyone's nerves but, as Owen had explained after his phone rang a second time, force of will was not going to make traffic, nor police checkpoints, move any faster. More to the point, their entire truck and trailer had been searched not just once but twice as they passed the roadblocks surrounding Oak Ridge. That, more than anything, had added to the time they spent in the truck.

Owen had, of course, declined to mention his injuries on the phone. He was already late, he reasoned; there was no point in making them worry more than they already were by telling them that, "oh, by the way, I fought a Korovega outside Bull Run while I was out." There would be plenty of time to tell the story later.

"You look like hell," Will commented, watching Owen grit his teeth as the truck hit a pothole that had been hidden in shadows. He had retaken his seat on the passenger side of the truck after getting out of the traffic jam and reluctantly admitting that he really had no idea how to maneuver the heavy trailer.

Owen grinned. "It's not so bad. The blood kind of sucks, but it's all shallow. You know, road-rash."

"And road-rash isn't bad?"

Owen shrugged, grimacing slightly as the motion rubbed his shoulders against the towel he had placed on the seat. Said towel had been clean before he used it, but now it kept trying to cling to his back as the shallow scrapes clotted and dried. "I'd rather have road rash and a migraine than end up with a foot of Korovega steel through my chest."

"Fair point," Will said, holding up one finger as though marking off lines on a chalkboard. "You still haven't actually talked about it, you know."

Owen coaxed the truck through the last switchback before the road leveled out into Ben's driveway. Maneuver finished, he spared a moment to look over at Will.

Will had seen that expression before. Hell, he thought, he had worn that expression before. Owen had the look of someone who could barely believe he was still alive. Will knew, or at least he suspected, that Owen had been running hypotheticals in his head ever since the fight was over. Thoughts like, "what if I had done this?" or, "what if the other guy had done that?" would be running though his head. He knew Owen was a fighter and that sort of thought process was normal, but with the enemy he had been up against, most of his "what-ifs" were going to end with him dead.

"I mean it. I," he paused, "I know how you're feeling. Let me put it that way. You need to talk, come find me, ok?"

Owen nodded once, but kept his attention on the driveway. "Yeah. I know. The danger isn't even what's bothering me, though."

After a moment's silence, Will asked. "So?"

Owen turned the truck into the lower driveway, pulling as far forward as he could to make unloading easier.

"So," Owen echoed. "So that thing was damn fast. I mean, I know I only had a shitty piece of rebar to fight with, but still. One mistake and you're dead. I mean," he stopped and laughed, "ok, so it is the danger."

"But now we've got intel on them, right?" Will asked, smiling. "You made contact with the enemy and now you know first hand what they're capable of."

Owen unbuckled, stopped, and said, "yeah. I guess so."

Will shook his head. "No way. None of that."

"What?"

"Me? I saw that thing toast a couple of riot cops. I saw it blow a half dozen cars to hell and gone. I watched people die. Them in there?" He pointed to the house. "They didn't. Even if they see the aftermath on the news, or if somebody had a camera going and the TV gets a hold of the video, all they're going to see is a recording. Got it?"

"I think so?"

"They," he pointed toward the house again, "are only going to know what we tell them. And they're going to feel about it how they think we feel about it."

"Um..."

Will shook his head and laughed. "Listen. You go in there and start in with, 'I almost got my ass killed by a devil and it was horrible,' and they're going to be afraid. Think, man. What was it you said that got that mob in motion?"

"I said the Korovega can bleed," Owen responded, then a grin spread across his face. "I didn't tell them how badly it hurt me, or that I was barely conscious right then. I just told them it could be beaten."

"You gave them hope, smart guy."

"I," he started, then, "oh. Yeah, I get what you're saying. So when we go in there..."

Will interrupted, "when you tell the story, remind them that you won. Show off your back if you want, but..."

"Sort of like saying, 'this is the best it could do,' yeah?"

Will nodded. "Something like that," he agreed, then opened his door. "Come on, they're going to wonder why we're just sitting here if we don't hustle. We're already late."

Owen tapped on his pants pocket where he kept his phone. "Trust me, I know."

Will laughed. "Well, let's not give them a reason to call again. Though they'd probably just send Ben to throw rocks at us or something."

"And scratch up his truck?"

Will looked over the truck with a dubious eye. It had more dents, dings, and repainted scratches than he could count right away. "You mean the truck that looks like he drives it through the woods on a regular basis?"

Owen shrugged. "Don't look at me. I don't get it either."

"The hell you two been?" Ben boomed from the upstairs porch.

"Same hell that I told you about when you called me," Owen shouted back.

"Better not have busted up my truck."

Owen laughed. "Trust me, it wasn't the truck that got busted up." He carefully kept the bloody towel in his hands out of the porch's floodlights.

"Sam said some story about Korovega in Oak Ridge came across the news on her laptop while you were gone. Least you didn't get caught up in that."

Owen just grinned and shook his head.

Ben's eyes narrowed. In the stark floodlight, the simple motion closed off his face and turned it into a thing of brooding shadows. "You did stay away from it, didn't you?"

Owen raised the blood-soaked towel into the light with a halfhearted smile. "Not really."

"You son of a bitch," Ben swore quietly. "You alright? Where's Will?"

"I'm here," Will replied. "Downstairs door unlocked? We'll tell you everything over some food."

"Should be," Ben said. He turned toward the upstairs door. "I'll meet you down there."

Will headed for the door, but Owen turned aside and walked further out into the yard. He came to the edge of the pit that held the foundation for what would be their workshop. The concrete seemed solid, but it was too dark to tell for sure and he had no plans to poke at it to see if it was fully set.

A cinderblock's width of open space remained between the concrete and the ground. Tomorrow morning, they would pour another sheet and set the rebar, minus the spear, into it to solidify the walls. After that, the real work would begin. Cinderblocks would be stacked against the steel poles, followed by building a second floor, a roof, and wiring. The real challenge would be to finish the whole project before next week.

Owen laughed to himself.

"What's funny?" Will asked. His boots crunched in the loose dirt and broken pieces of rock strewn about. As he came up behind Owen, apparently having abandoned his original plan to go straight inside.

"Just thinking that if anyone who saw us today comes to find us, we're going to need more buildings than this."

Will made a noise that was half scoff and half laughter. "Let's hope not. We might be able to fit a few more people in here if we hot bunk and sleep during the day, but I don't really want to deal with that."

Owen looked sidelong at Will and grinned. "It's not like it's the end of the world or anything."

Will sighed. "Point taken."

"The hell did you do?" Ben asked, voice rising in pitch as he took in the sight of Owen's back. Owen had heard that tone countless times before, usually when Ben was presented with something that he would have considered unbelievable had the truth not been right in front of him.

Owen turned, and Ben's jaw dropped as the massive bruise on the right side of Owen's face, and the torn collar of his shirt, came into the light.

"I repeat," Ben said. This time his voice was serious—rather stern, actually. "The hell did you do?"

"I..." Owen started.

"Stopped a bunch of people from getting killed," Will interjected, patting Owen on the back. He was careful to try and miss the spots that had been torn up from his tumble on the pavement.

"And almost got his own self killed in the process, looks like," Ben countered. His drawl thickened when he was frustrated or angry at something.

"But not quite," Owen countered, managing a smile.

His muscles had finally—or perhaps already, which meant he was going to be in a world of pain in the morning—started to ache from his ordeal. Between adrenaline and keeping his mind busy, he had kept the worst of it at bay until Ben's comment. Now, as though his sarcasm had opened some sort of gate, all of the aches and pains from his fight twinged at once. His muscles hurt, certainly, but the dull burning in his back vied with the jackhammer throbbing in his head for the rank of worst pain.

And, yet, the worst thing, beyond the pain, was the twin memories of the smoking hole where there had been a policeman and the burnt wreck with its erstwhile human driver that hurt the most. Those clawed at the pit of his stomach, threatening to make him throw up the hamburger he had eaten for lunch.

He had seen people die, nearly everyone with family had seen someone die at one time or another, but he had never seen anyone actually killed before. Even Ken's death had happened long before his arrival. Ken's death was motivation, not horror. Rather than repulse him, knowing how Ken died made him angry.

The other cars that the Korovega had destroyed, each with its own driver and possibly passengers, had been merely a backdrop, a smoking prop reminding him how evil the creature he set out to fight really was. He had not seen the death there, only the destruction, and it affected him little more than a natural disaster would have.

But the smell of burnt human flesh and the acrid tang of fresh blood would haunt him forever.

"Yeah," Ben said, stepping closer and scrutinizing the discolored patch on Owen's face. "Not quite." He grinned. "What'd you do though, see how close you could get?"

Owen managed a grin. His head pounded but, despite the location of the bruise, his face itself felt fine by comparison. "Something like that."

"What'd you use?"

Will held up the piece of rebar where Ben could see it in the limited light. He twirled it in his hand once, turning the sharp end toward himself and offering the other end to Ben.

Ben took the makeshift spear in one hand. He brought the tip close to his eyes, turning it in the light. The cut portion glittered against the matte finish of the rest of the bar. Yet the most interesting thing was the dull-colored stain running from the tip, down one edge of the cut portion and smeared a few inches down the side.

"Looks like you nailed it pretty good," he said approvingly.

"Twice," Owen said.

Ben made a brief figure-eight in the air with the rebar. "This thing's a piece of shit, you know."

Owen laughed, then grimaced as he discovered a bruised rib that he had, somehow, been unaware of until just then. "I didn't exactly have a saber on hand right then."

Ben shrugged and handed the spear to Will. "Just means the story's even more impressive," he said, and held his hands up in a classic, "picture this," pose. "I mean, which sounds better? 'Man fights Korovega with perfectly designed saber and barely walks away,' or 'man fights Korovega with shitty piece of sharpened rebar and manages to hurt it.' The choice seems pretty clear to me."

Owen laughed again. "I'll be sure to fight the next one with an equally crappy weapon. Just you watch."

"The hell you will," Ben growled. "Next time, you use a real weapon and you kill the damn thing. You just do the stupid thing once. You know, for the story."

At that, Will laughed. "This definitely qualifies as stupid, that's for sure."

Owen rolled his eyes. "Thanks."

"Hey, I told you to stay in the truck."

Owen grinned. "Yeah, and then that Korovega would have blown up the truck. Assuming we survive that, then Ben kills us for messing up his truck."

"Damn straight," Ben said, nodding with mock severity. "Anyway, let's get you inside and cleaned up."

"I like that plan," Owen said. He held up the bloody towel. "What do you want done with this?"

Ben eyed the towel for a moment before turning a grin that was half amusement and half concern toward Owen. "Better not be any of that shit on my seat."

Despite the stinging in his back and the lingering shakes from the adrenaline, Owen laughed. "Your seat's fine. Would I bleed on your truck without permission?"

Ben laughed. "Wouldn't be the worst thing that's happened to it. Now," he took the towel and balled it up in his hands, heedless of the mostly dry blood. "I'll rinse this off, get it clean as I can in the sink, and throw it in the laundry tonight."

Will laughed. Unlike before, where he had been simply laughing at a joke or at the situation, this time his laugh was full of genuine mirth and amusement.

"Something you want to share?" Ben asked.

Will continued laughing for another minute before finally getting a rein on himself and catching his breath. "Oh, I was just thinking. 'Huh. Laundry. That's an awfully mundane thing to be concerned about after seeing a Korovega roaming around Oak Ridge.'"

Ben smiled, then laughed. "I feel you there. But, hey, if we don't keep up with laundry and showers and shit, then we start to smell funny, and that's bad for morale."

"As long as I don't have to scrub a uniform on a metal washboard in a tub full of rainwater, I'm happy," Will replied.

Ben shrugged. "You guys brought the rest of the stuff we needed to set up George's water wheel. We pipe that water through some filters after it passes the wheel and we'll be good to go if, when, our water gets cut off. Won't even miss civilization when it's gone."

Will laughed. "Me neither."

"Come on." Ben motioned for Will to follow. "Let's head upstairs and let everyone else know you ain't dead. Oh, and Owen? Sam's on her way down, so don't you go nowhere."

"Sounds good," Will said. "I could do with some food, too."

Ben grinned. "Nope."

"Nope?"

"We ate it all. Not my fault you missed dinner."

"Don't blame me, blame the end of the world. Makes traffic even worse than Black Friday," Will quipped.

Ben laughed and clapped him on the back. "Come on. We'll heat it back up for you."

* * *

Sam met them at the door, pushing past Ben and Will with a determined, even harsh, look on her face. The two of them quietly made their way upstairs as she stormed across the yard and stood in front of Owen. For a moment, she looked like she was about to tear into him, but then she saw his condition. Her eyes widened as she took in the bruise on his face, and her expression softened considerably.

She waited until the others were upstairs before doing or saying anything. Wordlessly, she wrapped her arms gently around his shoulders and stood there, heedless of the blood and dirt, for several long moments.

"Alright," Sam said, once she was confident she had her voice under control. "Let me look at you."

"I look the same as I did this morning," he replied with a grin, "promise."

"You weren't covered in blood this morning."

He grinned. "Ok, so I'm missing a few bits."

Sam stepped closer, almost close enough for a second hug. She even reached one arm around his back as though she were about to do just that, but instead lightly slapped one of the fresh scabs covering his shoulders.

He flinched and let out a hiss of surprised pain. "Ow! What was that for?"

Sam stepped back with a smile and a small shake of her head. "Come on," she said gently. "Ben's right. You need to wash up. Even if you are fine, which you are not, you need to change clothes and rinse all the road dirt off of you."

Owen let out a huge, mock-exasperated sigh. "If you insist."

"I do. Upstairs. Now."

Owen went. The basement never had a lot of open floor space, and the boxes and suitcases from Will's car still sitting out made it even harder to navigate.

"The workshop's foundation looks good," he said, for lack of anything else to say. After his ordeal, silence felt somehow oppressive. He was sure Will had tired of talking long before they made it back to the house, but talking let him focus on something other than how much he hurt.

Behind him, Sam replied. She sounded pleased. "It does, yeah. We got a lot more work done on it today than I thought we would. Marcus improved on the initial plans a lot. We ought to have it ready for use early next week."

Owen laughed quietly. "Don't make promises we might not be able to keep."

She stopped, halfway up the first part of the staircase. "What's that supposed to mean?" she asked.

Owen turned to see her with her hands on her hips, staring up at him. He laughed again. "A week ago," he said with a bitter shake of his head, "everything was normal. Now..." He made an exasperated noise, and spread his arms to either side in a gesture of confusion.

She stepped up another riser and motioned for him to continue upward as well. "Now," she said, picking up where he had trailed off, "things are different, yeah. But if we don't have plans, then what good is trying to survive? So what if we have to remake those plans every day? At least we've got something."

Owen shrugged slowly; the motion hurt. He took another few steps, then stopped again. He craned his neck around to look over his shoulder. "I really am alright, Sam."

She smiled. "I know."

He finished ascending the stairs in time to see Will, surrounded by people at a reasonably safe distance considering the sharpened piece of rebar he was swinging around like a baton, say with great panache, "and then the bastard sucker punched him in the side of the head with its shield! He hit the ground hard, but he was back on his feet in a flash!"

Will stood in front of the TV with everyone else circled around him, mostly facing away from the side of the room with the stairwell. Owen had no idea how Will managed to convince everyone to let him tell the story, but he was thankful he had. Owen found his flair, and the embellishments he was likely to be adding, to be rather embarrassing. On the other hand, having everyone following him and asking about his injuries and wanting to hear the story from him would have been worse.

From the delicious smell permeating the room, the dinner that Ben was reheating was some sort of soup or stew. He made a mental note to come back down and get some after bathing. If it tasted half as good as it smelled, he felt like it was just the thing to assuage the aches in his muscles.

The two of them skirted the edge of the group as Will continued his story. He was making it out to be a much longer, and much more intense, fight than it really had been. Owen was in no real position to voice his objection at being made out to be some sort of action movie hero.

At the top of the stairs to the loft, he stopped again and listened to Will's story for a moment.

"...with one mighty blow, struck it upside the head!"

Owen smiled and shook his head slightly. The story had gone far into the realm of fantasy at that point, but Will's audience was listening with rapt attention. Only George looked profoundly uncomfortable as Will spoke. Katrina and Michael were completely absorbed in the story, while Marcus and Ben seemed interested, but had been in enough fights themselves to tell when Will started embellishing things.

Try as he might, Owen failed to muster any resentment at the amount of attention they were paying to a clearly made-up story. He supposed, had it been Ben or Sam or Jessie who happened upon a Korovega and barely managed to survive pissing it off, that he would be right down there with everyone else.

Hell, he thought, he would probably be the one telling the story.

"He really can work a room, can't he?" Sam asked, coming to stand next to him.

"Will? Yeah."

"So, now, Mister Hero, what are you going to do?"

Owen laughed, but that quickly turned into a frustrated sigh. He gestured toward Will with one hand. "Try to live up to that."

"That's about all you can do at this point," she replied.

"I didn't tell him to do this."

"I know. Seems like it's bothering you, though."

"It's not bothering you?" he asked.

"This is how you inspire people," Sam replied with a small shrug. "Like it or not."

He shrugged. "Yeah. I mean," he paused, groping for the right words, "it is. But..." He stopped as words failed once again.

"But?"

"On the way in, Will told me that I needed to play up what I did, you know? Act like I just stepped out of some nineteenth-century Romantic painting of a medieval knight. Ben said the same thing." He shook his head and sighed. "I don't know if I can do it. I mean, he's right, but I don't know if I can live up to the sort of legend he's trying to build."

Sam laid a hand on his shoulder, touching one of the few bloodless spots. The muscles underneath were sore, but her touch was a welcome comfort. "Honestly, it's not hard to play it up like that," she said. "It's a good story."

He turned a sidelong glance toward her for a moment, then sighed. "I know. That's the problem."

She grinned. "I'm talking about him, not you."

Owen gave her an inquisitive look that communicated more of a question than words could have.

She returned it with a grin. "They're scared. With the Korovega that showed up last night and then hearing about one in Oak Ridge..." she trailed off, then resumed after a moment, "and then we hear that not only was there one in Oak Ridge, but the guy who brought everyone out here was dumb enough to try and fight it."

"Sorry," he said, lamely.

Sam squeezed his shoulder. Her grip was firm, but she was again careful to avoid putting any pressure on the road rash. She also made sure to squeeze the deltoid muscle itself, which was sore enough after swinging around a piece of rebar.

Owen grimaced.

"Don't be hard on yourself. Sure, you did something crazy, but calling everyone you knew and moving all of our important worldly possessions to a house in the hills wasn't a little nuts?"

Owen laughed. "I suppose you've got a point."

She smiled. "Of course I do," she said, then her expression turned stern. "Just promise me something, next time."

"What?"

"Next time," she said, squeezing his sore shoulder again, "you decide to take on something that a hundred bullets barely managed to hurt with nothing more than a pointy metal stick, take some backup."

He smiled. The unspoken implication, he knew, was that she wanted in on the fight the next time around. Unfortunately, he was sure Sam would get her wish because the odds of never fighting the Korovega again were somewhere below the sun suddenly going black. And, he thought, to be fair to her, if he had a choice, he would have taken some backup into that fight. The idea of facing down a Korovega again was frightening enough, but the idea of doing it alone was enough to make the blood freeze in his veins.

Sam stared at him for a long moment as Owen, in turn, stared through the wall-sized window fronting the living room. She could tell that his mind was so far elsewhere that Will's story, now finally winding down, barely made it into his notice—assuming it made it past his ears at all. His face had gone pale, and a heavy tension had settled around the edges of his eyes.

She slipped her hand into her pants pocket. The empty shell casing from the round that killed the biker on Tuesday was the only thing in there. She turned it over in her hands, feeling the contrast between the smooth brass of the sides and the sharp metal of the open end. Such a small thing, she thought, to have so much power over life and death.

She dropped the shell back into her pocket and shifted her hand on his shoulder, turning him toward the bathroom and gently propelling him that direction.

"Hm?" he asked. "Oh, yeah, shower."

"I was actually going to suggest a bath," Sam said.

He stopped. "What for?"

"Because one of us needs to see how badly you're actually hurt, and you can't exactly do that while you're showering." Her tone indicated that she had both thought it out and would brook no disagreement.

Owen sighed and, where she could not see, rolled his eyes. Sam had done this before, though Owen's injuries had not been quite so bad. In college, Owen had, through a series of events that would have been slapstick gold with the right sound effects, severely cut up his back while working on a construction project. They of course had access to a real doctor and real medical care to stitch up the worst of the damage, but Sam had insisted on cleaning the cuts and scrapes herself first.

He had done the same thing for her when she wiped out on her previous motorcycle. The bike had been totaled, which had been when she decided to buy Big Blue, the high-powered machine currently parked against the back of the house. She had not been badly hurt, "only my pride," as she said at the time, but ironically, she had suffered extensive road rash. Her leather jacket had stopped the worst of it, but her back and large parts of her arms and legs looked then about how Owen's felt now.

The scars were still there, he knew, but only barely. Her skin was naturally clear—a fact that frustrated him to no end during their teenage years—and the abrasions healed up with minimal residual scarring. He could still feel the scars on her arms at times, but even they were faint enough that someone who had never known about them would likely never find them.

Owen made his way around the boxes and suitcases that still held things from his and Sam's personal belongings that had not been unpacked yet. Between them, the huge bed, and the dresser, there was very little room to walk. Of course, there was very little room to walk anywhere just then. The house may have been spacious, but it was still designed for, at most, six people to have a comfortable vacation. Space for nine people and all of their important possessions had never been part of the design plans.

The loft was relatively small, despite all of that. The floorplan was the same size as the master bedroom directly below it, but the sloping ceiling it shared with the living room limited usable space, and the bed took up most of it. That left just enough room in the recesses of the walls for a closet and bathroom on one side and a attic on the other. Fortunately, it did have windows of its own, even if they opened to nothing but tree-studded hillside. Sam had set up a tray table with her laptop in front of those windows, further limiting available floor space.

Owen slowly pulled his shirt over his head, painfully aware of the way his skin hurt every time what little remained of the fabric brushed against it. "What do we do with this?" he asked, holding out the tattered and bloody shirt.

Sam took it gingerly and rolled it up. The blood was dry, but she was careful to set it on the bathroom counter with the cleanest side down. She shrugged. "Bleach it and use it for bandages."

"I liked that shirt."

Sam laughed softly. "Yeah, well, consider yourself lucky that most of the front side survived, then."

Owen sighed. "Most of us aren't going to be wearing t-shirts much longer, anyway."

"What do you mean?"

"Just a thought I had today. We ought to get used to wearing something sturdier. I mean, a fencing jacket or a motorcycle jacket won't stop a bullet, but..."

"It won't stop a sword, either," Sam added, turning on the hot water in the bathtub.

"No," Owen agreed, "but it would slow one down."

"I suppose that's important."

He nodded. "And it'll protect against grazing blows and..."

She interrupted. "I get the picture; you don't have to explain it to me. A heavy jacket would have helped a lot against this road rash, that's for sure." Sam pointed to the tub. "Now. In."

Owen laughed. "You're relentless."

"It's one of my many admirable traits," she replied with a straight face.

He grinned, removed his jeans, and stepped carefully into the rapidly-filling bathtub. The water was hot, which meant it felt positively burning to the scrapes on his back. Thankfully, the pain was temporary as his body temperature adjusted to the steaming water.

Sam rolled up the hems of her pants and carefully stepped into the tub behind him. She sat on the rear edge, leaving her feet in the hot water.

Owen took a deep breath. "This is going to hurt, isn't it?"

"Probably."

He chuckled, then winced as she ran a warm washcloth across the scrapes on his shoulders. "You're supposed to say, 'no, of course not.'"

Sam wiped the cloth across his back again. She barely put any pressure on it, but shallow wounds tended to hurt even more than deep ones. Deep wounds meant dead nerves, but shallow wounds meant that all of the nerve endings were still functioning. She would have to go over the damage multiple times too, cleaning the wounds a little more thoroughly each time. Having been on the other end of road rash, she knew it was better this way.

His hissed and flinched, trying hard not to do both of those things.

She grinned, but said nothing. The almost-laugh that escaped her lips was enough to convey her dubiousness at his comment. She failed to recall a single time where, "this won't hurt, I promise," ever helped when real pain was concerned.

As she continued washing away bits of road dirt and blood, Sam felt the muscles in Owen's back start to relax. Either the pain was lessening with the warmth, or he was doing a steadily better job of gritting his teeth and bearing it.

She looked over his back. The scabs from their fight Tuesday were still there, partially. Those wounds had been shallow, not even as bad as a skinned knee, and were already well on their way to normalcy. Some of the scabs had been torn off, revealing the pink hue of the lower layers of skin, but none of those wounds bled, at least not badly. One or two of the worse-looking ones wept a little blood on the way home, it looked like, but they had stopped bleeding before he got into the bath.

The ones from that afternoon's fight, on the other hand, were worse. One entire shoulder looked like a ten-year-old's knee after falling from his bicycle. Nothing was terribly deep, but an area the size of her palm was torn and bleeding. Little rivulets of blood ran down his back and into the water as she washed. It would heal up quickly, she thought, assuming he could refrain from anything terribly violent for a few days.

After several minutes of relaxed quiet, Sam asked, "was it the same one we saw last night?"

Owen shook his head. "No. We put a bullet through that one's leg. Unless they can heal freakishly fast and do it well enough that the wound didn't scar, this was a different one."

Sam sighed, but kept the rhythm on the washcloth steady. "Then there's two of them in this area."

"At least. Probably more. There have to be more."

"Why?"

He shrugged. "Because if there's only two of them here, then it means they're coming after us."

"Aren't they?"

"No, I mean us specifically," he replied. Owen started to gesture with his hands, but Sam pushed his arms back down by his sides. "Think about it. We've seen two in two days."

"That doesn't mean they're coming after us."

"If they're not, then that means there's enough of them around that chance sightings are going to be common, and that map you found only shows ours from last night," he argued. "And I saw more of those eagles overhead today."

"You think Ben's theory is right?"

Owen nodded once, slowly. "Yeah," he replied. "They didn't tail us here, but I kept seeing them circling the whole way home."

"Coincidence?" she asked, playing devil's advocate more than anything.

"Could be, but," he sighed, "I don't buy it. That Korovega I saw today, why did it pick Bull Run?"

"Maybe it was going to attack the plant?"

Owen shook his head. "It was in the wrong spot for that. I mean, sure, the road was full of people, but it could easily have gone after the Turnpike or Solway or some other place with even more people if that was its goal."

"It's not hunting you, Owen."

"Isn't it?" he demanded. "Can you really be sure of that?"

"I," she said, then, "no, not really. But why us?"

"Because we hurt that other one," he said, "and I swear those damn birds were watching us. Will and I never went more than a few minutes outside without seeing one."

Sam nodded. On the surface of it, having a small platoon of Korovega prowling around the area was terrifying. A lone scout had torched much of downtown Knoxville the day before and, from what she understood of the real version of the events outside Bull Run, the scout Owen fought had killed at least a dozen people already. Knowing that there could be dozens or even hundreds of them around the area made her skin crawl.

On the other hand, the idea that the Korovega might be deliberately targeting them was a hundred times more frightening. Unfortunately, they had wounded two Korovega at this point. The news had yet to make it to the TV or radio, but surely others had managed to hurt them as well. The Korovega were not stupid, and they had to know who had hurt them and where and when.

So, in reality, not only were there likely hundreds of them working their way through the so-called "Greater Knoxville Metropolitan Area," but she, and Owen, and everyone else in the house were all on the Korovega's kill list. Worse, if Owen was right and those black eagles had been tracking him all day, they knew exactly where they were.

"I don't like it," she said, "and I don't want to admit it, but I can't think of any reason why you'd be wrong."

Several tense seconds passed before Owen asked, "you alright?"

Sam became aware that she had gotten lost in her thoughts and stopped moving the washcloth. She resumed. "I'm fine."

"I believe that about as much as you believed it when I said it earlier," he retorted, grinning.

Sam laughed. "I was just thinking."

"That's dangerous."

She laughed again, this time with a touch of bitterness. "Yeah. Right now, I suppose so. It just struck me that we've pissed them off, so we probably are going to be targeted."

Owen sighed. "Wonderful. So what?"

Sam rinsed the washcloth off, stood up, and stepped out of the tub. "Right now, you're going to let that water drain, refill the tub with clean water, and relax in here."

"What about you?"

"I'm going to go help unload the truck."

Owen shifted in the bathtub and started to stand up. "I'll help."

"You will not. You're hurt, even if you're only hurt a little bit. You're going to stay there and rest. Right now, we can spare the manpower to let you take it easy for half an hour. Save that energy for when we're all getting two hours of sleep at night, and working and fighting for twenty hours straight."

He nodded. He hated feeling useless, but she was right. He needed to relax, especially since he had been a ball of tension and nerves ever since traffic started to back up on Edgemoor, long before he knew there was even a Korovega there at all.

And the water felt nice, he thought.

Sam, satisfied that he was going to stay in the bathtub and relax as instructed, left the room, closing the door behind her. She dried her feet off, put her shoes back on, and headed downstairs.

Chapter 17

Summer in East Tennessee meant that, even at five in the morning, the heat never quite abated. Fortunately, the humidity had dissipated near the start of the third watch, leaving the night warm but pleasant. A cool breeze came off the water, turning what had been a muggy and miserable night into something comfortable. It had started raining just after midnight and only stopped shortly after three, leaving the air damp.

"Isaiah Clarke?" Jessie asked, leaning one elbow on the deck railing. She turned slightly toward Michael, who stood beside her, but kept the majority of her attention on the yard. All of the floodlights had been turned off to minimize visual "hot spots," areas that were so bright they lost their night vision, and the only light came from the moon and stars overhead and the radio tower blinking in the distance on top of a hill. They carried flashlights but they too were turned off unless needed.

Michael nodded. "Mom and dad couldn't decide what which middle name to give me, so they gave me both."

Jessie grinned. "Michael Isaiah Clarke Campbell. I like it. Sounds like you're a British nobleman or something."

"Scottish, if you must know." He kept a straight face for a few seconds before laughing.

"Name like that and you must be next in line for the throne, Mister Isaiah Clarke Campbell."

"Oh definitely, yeah," he said with mock severity. "If the three hundred million people in line ahead of me all die off, I'll be ready to go."

Jessie grew silent. She knew that he was joking, but given the present condition of the world, that was not an impossibility. Of course, the selection process for the British throne would not take into account someone some three hundred million places down the list, but it was entirely possible for the death toll to reach those kinds of numbers before everything was said and done.

"Everything alright?"

She forced a smile. "Yeah," she replied, wondering how many people were telling that same lie. If she was honest with herself, she knew she was not alright, but she had little choice. No matter how bad she felt, the world itself was worse off.

Of course, when she thought about it, things really were much better than they seemed, at least for the people around her. They had their issues, but those were working themselves out. Proximity, and the knowledge that they had nowhere better to go, did a lot to bring people together. Ben and George were tolerating each other to an extent, and he had even apologized to Sam for his outburst that morning. Will and his friends had been there for a day and a half, but they had already integrated rather well.

Michael adjusted the shotgun slung over his back. It was one of the weapons Will's group brought. Michael thought it had belonged to Marcus, but he never knew for sure. The spare guns, essentially everything that had not been claimed by anyone for permanent personal use, were kept in a small cleaning closet just outside of the master bedroom. Michael, like George and Katrina, had had no weapons of their own and he had picked his watch weapon from the closet when Owen woke him up. Jessie had showed him how to carry it, but the unfamiliar weight still felt strange.

Of course, what felt even more strange was the short cutlass-like machete hanging from his belt by the sort of clip usually reserved for keychains. Despite getting less than an hour's practice with blunted swords earlier in the day, he felt like he needed to have it with him. He knew Will's story was mostly made up, but there had to be a core of truth to it. Owen had come back far too beaten and bloody for nothing at all to have happened. They had fought, and unfortunately killed, two people so far, and Will would not have made the story about a Korovega if they had simply been jumped by a human.

He looked over his shoulder. Before bed, Ben had rigged up a simple rack out of a pair of hooked pieces of pipe and nailed it over the door. In the crook of the pipes sat the rebar spear Owen made. Hanging from the spear by two short lengths of twisted wire was a sign that read "THEY BLEED" in blocky lettering. According to Will's story, that was the phrase Owen had used to rally the people around him into attacking the Korovega.

Michael doubted the veracity of that part of the story. It simply sounded too much like a fantasy story for Owen to have simply shouted a single throwaway line and convinced a dozen people to help him fight the monster that had, minutes before, been killing everyone in front of it. He had to admit it did make a good story, though. Whatever the truth of the events were, the spear and the blood on its tip were real and they made one hell of an inspiring totem.

Jessie's laugh brought his attention back on his duty. He yawned and leaned against the railing, resting his bearded chin in one hand.

"Fair's fair," she said. Her eyes were still on the dark yard, but Michael knew she was paying at least some attention to him. "Carmen."

"Carmen?" he asked. "Oh, right. Your middle name."

She grinned and her brown eyes flashed with amusement in the dim light. "You'd forgotten already? This game was your idea."

He laughed. "I know. When I said I was a morning person, I meant six or seven o'clock not," he motioned toward the still-dark sky, "this."

Jessie sighed. "Well, get used to it. Things will be like this for a long time yet."

Michael nodded. "Yeah."

"Want some more coffee?"

"That'd be awesome."

Jessie smiled and headed back inside. Like the other nights, they left the kitchen door open a crack so it would stay silent rather than making noise each time it opened or shut. Everyone needed as much sleep as possible, given their watch schedules, and no one wanted any noise that would risk waking anyone.

Not that her desire for silence was reflected in reality. Like everyone except Ben and Owen, Jessie was not used to wearing a sword around. She had used knives in the past, and even taken some Olympic fencing classes years before, but none of that had involved strapping a cavalry saber to her belt and navigating a darkened house filled with furniture and boxes.

The scabbard banged noisily against one of the dining chairs as she turned the corner into the kitchen proper. She froze for several seconds, but if anyone woke up at the noise, they were quieter than she could manage to be.

Jessie poured two cups of coffee. More accurately, Jessie poured one cup of coffee and one cup of cream and sugar that had a little coffee in it. With a little effort, she picked both mugs up with one hand. She rested the other on her saber to keep it quiet and away from furniture, and made her way back outside.

Michael's laughing smile greeted her as she rounded the corner.

Jessie handed over his mug and asked, "what's funny?"

"Your last name's Santiago, isn't it?"

She closed her eyes, muttered something that sounded something like, "oh boy," and made a noise that was half exasperation and half laughter. "Yep. It is."

"Jessie..."

"'Jessica,' if you're going to use the whole thing."

"Jessica Carmen Santiago, eh?"

"Just," she said, "if you've got any decency, don't start humming the theme song."

Michael grinned. "Aw, but I had all of the jokes lines up."

"Trust me," she countered, "I've heard them all. And, for the record..."

He shushed her. "What was that?" His voice was barely above a whisper.

"What was what?" she asked, equally quiet. Something in his tone had put her instantly on alert. One hand went to her gun and, a second later, the other went to her sword as her eyes scanned the darkness. The coffee sat forgotten on the deck rail. "I don't see anything."

"Me neither," Michael whispered. "But I hear something."

"Good ears."

"I'm a musician. Now, please, hush," he replied. He fumbled for the shotgun on his back. After a few seconds of flailing at it with one hand in which he failed to effectively grasp it even once, Jessie set her pistol down and helped him swing it around in front of him and made sure his grip was solid.

They locked eyes momentarily and she gave his shoulder a firm squeeze. The brief contact seemed to restore his nerves and his hands stopped trembling.

He leaned on the railing. His eyes darted around uselessly and, seeming to realize the futility of trying to locate something by sight with his bad eyes, he closed them and listened. For a brief moment, the tension in his shoulders abated as he simply absorbed the sounds from the night around him.

Jessie was security-minded enough not to disturb him when he was trying to pinpoint whatever it was he heard, but her heart raced nonetheless. She tried to listen, but she heard nothing out of the ordinary. At the start of their shift, he had jumped at every sound, asking her to identify everything he heard. Most of them she was unable to ID beyond, "it's an animal," and he had quickly stopped asking. She never was sure if he stopped asking because he gave up on her knowing what he was hearing or because he finally learned what, "it's an animal," sounded like. She had suspected it was the latter, and his reaction now seemed to back that up.

After a tense minute, she could stand it no longer. "Where?" she hissed.

Michael opened his eyes. "Toward the water, I think. I heard a splash, kind of a, 'bloop,' noise, but that's been it."

Her mind raced. From what Will had told her, he thought the Korovega the night before had come out of the water too. Everything else they knew supported that as well. Of course, it could be a fish jumping, or an animal could have gone down for a drink and gotten too close to the edge and fallen in.

There were literally dozens of things that could explain the noise Michael heard. It frustrated her that she had not heard it as well, but there was nothing she could do about that other than pay closer attention. She relaxed her eyes, taking in the entire scene in front of her in an old martial artist's trick that allowed her to see everything, but focus on nothing. If anything moved out there, that was the best way for her to spot it.

"Hear anything else?" she whispered.

"No."

Jessie wondered if she should send Michael to investigate, but instantly realized that was a bad idea. He might have good ears, but going out closer would require good eyes and his eyesight was useless at night. That meant if anyone was going to investigate, it should be her.

But what good would it do, she asked herself, if she went to investigate with no real idea of what was out there or where? That was how guards in bad movies got killed. No, the real question, she realized, was, was it important? If so, should she wake the others?

She was leaning heavily toward not waking the others. It was probably a fish. There were plenty of large fish in the water around Ben's house, and several varieties liked to jump for one reason or another. That would explain any "bloop" noises. If an animal had fallen in, it likely would have thrashed around in surprise and even she would have heard that.

And yet...

"Go inside," Jessie hissed, drawing her saber. Her pistol had been in her hand ever since Michael told her the sound he heard had been a splash. "Wake the others. Tell them to bring weapons."

"But..."

"Now!"

* * *

The stair creaked and Jessie's heart skipped a beat. Suddenly, she was thankful that she had put a light on her pistol. Unlike the tiny pocket pistol she carried daily, the weapon she picked for guard duty was a robust, large caliber handgun. Most importantly, right then, it had a flashlight attached to the rail under the barrel.

After coming up and down those stairs dozens of times in the last few days, Jessie knew exactly where that creaky step was. Fortunately, it was near the bottom. Unfortunately, wild animals heavy enough to set off a creaky board did not usually climb stairs. The list of things that did was short, and Jessie was not sure if she would rather it be a Korovega or a bear.

Bears did not go out of their way to creep silently across the yard.

Slowly, praying that one of the others would arrive to back her up before whatever was creeping up the stairs made it up, she took a step toward the staircase. Nothing made a sound, but deep down in the human brain was the part that had endured through millions of years of evolution. That part, responsible for fear, told her that something was coming.

Jessie kept close to the wall of the house, away from the open railing. She crouched low, minimizing her profile as much as she could without sacrificing her ability to move.

Jessie was right-handed and carried her pistol in her right hand instinctively, which meant her saber was in her left hand. That fact alone probably saved her live when the Korovega sprang out of the darkness at the top of the staircase behind a flashing blur of steel.

She reflexively slapped the creature's sword out of the way with her saber, fired a shot from her pistol into the darkness, and stood up. The bullet made the same blown-capacitor sound as the hail of bullets had on the previous Korovega's shield. She hit it, then. That was good. As it stepped closer, she could see the disk of its shield glowing, a faint, blue fire in the darkness.

It swung again and some dimly remembered piece of fencing training brought the guard in between her and the incoming blade. It hit like a hammer, sending a jarring shock up her arm. She doubted even Ben hit that hard in a fencing match, but the creature attacking her was not trying to fence her—it was trying to kill her and swung with a force that communicated its intent clearly enough.

She switched on her pistol's light and directed it at where she knew the Korovega had to be, somewhere a few inches above the glow of the shield. Under the little light, its yellow eyes shone like those of a cat, turning its ash-gray face into a Halloween mask of horror. Only this Halloween mask was real and attached to a body that was actively trying to kill her.

The Korovega hissed and threw its shield hand in front of its face in a reaction so instinctive that no amount of training or skill would have prevented the momentary lapse in its guard.

Jessie swung her sword, but her form was poor and the creature was able to block her blow with its own sword, despite its momentary shock. It lashed out with its shield as well, inadvertently, or perhaps deliberately, intercepting Jessie's next shot and knocking the pistol out of her hand.

The Korovega turned its hand to strike with its sword when a voice behind her boomed, "get down!"

That voice roared with the tones of command and she dropped flat to the deck as a clap louder than anything a dozen thunder gods could have produced split the air. The Korovega's shield popped like a firecracker. The flash of energy it left behind was bright enough that she was seeing spots afterward, as though the ringing in her ears was not enough. Another crack—this one much quieter, and she wondered if the first one had deafened her or if this was a second gun—split the air, followed by another bright pop of light against the Korovega's shield. The second shot, she noticed, came close to throwing the Korovega off balance.

Jessie stole a glance backward to see Will take a step while his hands worked the bolt of an absolutely massive rifle. The gun was enormous, far longer than any modern combat rifle, with a full wooden stock and a bayonet that had to be a foot long at least.

She looked back at her enemy and cursed the idiocy that drew her attention away from it in the first place. Its shield was still held high, defying Will's shots, but its sword was three-quarters of the way to her face. She screamed profanities and threw herself to one side, away from the Korovega. In the same motion, she flailed her sword in the general direction of the demon-like creature.

Her parry was partially effective. Rather than splitting her skull, the Korovega's sword merely slashed a bloody gouge down her arm.

Behind her, the Mosin-Nagant boomed a third time. The Korovega intercepted this shot as well, but the impact of the heavy bullet on its shield knocked it ever-so-slightly off balance. Jessie knew what the rocking motion of its heels meant. She had seen it a thousand times in fighters who tried to soak up a punch or kick that was too hard for them.

The beast was off balance, giving her an opening. In an instant, she was moving. Rather than come to her feet, Jessie rose just enough to grab the Korovega by the knees and lift. Behind her, she was dimly aware of the sound of rushing feet as Will closed in to bring his fearsome bayonet into striking distance.

Two things happened simultaneously.

First, Jessie lifted the Korovega up off of the ground and threw it heavily onto its back. It hit the deck with a hiss and a curse in its inhuman language. It still had its sword, but was in no position to use it just then. For the moment, and she was not about to let this opening get away like she did the last one, its guard was down and it was vulnerable.

Second, while she was lifting, she heard a clang of steel. Out of the corner of her eye, she realized that Will's bayonet was less than a foot away from her head. She was ready to turn a string of curses on him that would have drowned out the Korovega's own cursing when she realized why his bayonet would have been right there right then.

He saved her, she realized, parrying the Korovega's sword before it could take her life.

"Thanks," she panted.

Will sprang forward, holding his rifle above his head like a spear. "Don't talk, just kill," he snapped, bringing the bayonet down in what should have been a coup de grace.

The Korovega struck the bayonet aside, then again as Will stabbed at it a second time. Jessie spared a look over her shoulder, but her pistol was several feet away where it had fallen. The flashlight was still on, but pointed out into the yard for all the good that would do anyone in the fight.

She looked back to the Korovega as it came to its feet and slashed out with its sword. Will parried with the bayonet, then thrust the butt of the rifle at the Korovega's rising face. It jerked its head out of the way, striking out with its sword again. Jessie lunged, intercepting the attack and allowing Will to thrust his bayonet over her arm.

Its wrist twisted and it turned its sword against Jessie's to get a better angle without allowing her to attack again. When it looked like Will's thrust might actually hit, the Korovega flipped its wrist around, brought the sword over Jessie's, beat Will's attack aside, and turned a new attack toward Jessie's head.

There was no way she could parry. Her sword was hanging out in midair, too far away to be of any use. Even if she tried to dodge and counterattack, the creature's shield was still in play. She mouthed a curse and took several quick retreat steps to bring herself out of range.

Will swung the bayoneted rifle down hard in a motion more like an ax than a spear, but the Korovega caught it, barely. The force of the heavy rifle almost proved too much for the creature to stop, but it did. The weapons met, pushed toward the Korovega, then it raised its hand and out-levered Will's rifle.

The creature pushed Will's bayonet out of the way, down toward the deck, and relit its shield. This time it came on as a small, bright buckler, not the large diffuse shield from before. It thrust the buckler toward Will's head. He dodged backward, but the attack continued anyway, slamming into Will's torso and crossed arms. His feet left the ground and he hit the wooden planks with a heavy thud.

Jessie sprang forward as she heard rapid footsteps coming from behind the Korovega. There was another way down at the far end of the deck, and she nearly froze in place as the thought that more Korovega might be coming crossed her mind. The master bathroom also had a door that opened onto the deck, and relief washed over her when she remembered that fact.

She traded blows with the Korovega for several moments before whoever it was rounded the corner. With each attempt on her life she stopped, her motions grew more confident. She had done this before; it was only a matter of getting her muscles to remember that fact. Swords had never been her forte, but she had done enough unarmed martial arts that she had the speed and strength to hammer at everything in front of her. Nothing was coming close to hitting the Korovega, but what she was doing was good enough to keep herself alive, at least.

Ben rounded the corner and her heart leapt with joy. Behind her, Will struggled to his feet, but he groaned with every movement. She questioned how helpful he would be for the rest of the fight. Seeing Ben, however, was an almost literal breath of fresh air. She was keeping pace with the Korovega for the moment, but she knew it would not last. She was running on adrenaline and speed, and when she started to wear out and her speed slacked off, her more skilled opponent would kill her.

In Ben's hand was the enormous sword he called "The Beast." The look on his face and enraged glint in his eyes lent some truth to that name. His footsteps thundered across the deck as he charged forward, swinging the huge sword.

The Korovega turned halfway and took a step backward, trying to avoid being caught directly between Ben and Jessie. It worked somewhat, but its two opponents still forced it into a position where it could only defend against Ben's attacks with its shield. Jessie was hammering too hard and too fast on its other side for it to take its sword away long enough to attack Ben.

Its eyes darted back and forth between the two of them. Jessie could see the thing's face clearly and the expression, even on such an alien visage, with unmistakable. It may not have been afraid, but it was certainly surprised and possibly a little concerned.

When Owen came around the corner behind Jessie, the Korovega's eyes went slightly wider, though not with fear. In the dim light, Owen saw a thin red line across the creature's face, exactly where he had hit the Korovega he fought with his spear.

"Oh fuck me," Owen cursed quietly. The point of his saber drooped perhaps a fraction of an inch.

"Ash-man!" the Korovega hissed. Its face twisted in what might have charitably been called a smile. "Our battle was not finished!"

"It's finished now," Owen said, dashing forward and lunging with his sword-arm outstretched. As he passed her, Jessie thought the bruising on the side of his face looked like a domino mask.

The Korovega parried the attack, and Jessie's followup attack, with a single sweep of its arm that bound Owen's and Jessie's blades together. In turned on its heels in time to catch Ben's sword with another sweep. It stepped forward, dropped the shield, and clamped a vicelike hand on Ben's sword wrist. With the same movement, it pivoted and started the motion that would have brought its sword through his neck.

Ben instinctively headbutted the Korovega, catching its nose with his forehead. It screamed and flung Ben towards the others. Owen's fast reflexes saved Ben's life by beating Jessie's sword out of the way with his own, knocking it out of Ben's path just before he plowed into the two of them.

The Korovega turned. Inhumanly bright blood streamed down its face from its nose. It cursed in its own language before saying around, "I will enjoy carving your skulls into trophies for my children! The black-winged hrel will have the rest!"

"To hell with your kids," Ben roared, coming forward again. He and the Korovega traded blows back and forth, neither giving ground, while the others got their bearings.

Sam came around the corner. She had a machete in one hand and a pistol in the other.

Owen turned. "Check on Will," he barked.

Sam nodded, coming to a quick stop and dropping to her knees next to where Will had drug himself out of the way of the fighting.

Owen turned his attention back to the fight as Marcus came around the corner leading to the master bedroom. He carried his AK47 with the bayonet. He thumbed the safety on, not wanting to risk his finger landing on the trigger during the fight and a stray bullet hitting someone. Jessie was three steps ahead of him, closing on the Korovega again.

Ben swung.

The Korovega blocked with an upward flourish of its sword, raised its buckler to block Ben's remise, and turned on its heels. Sword still in the air and buckler held out behind it, it turned to face Jessie. It brought the sword down and she reached out to block it.

In a flash, Owen knew what was about to happen. He had fenced for too many years and done the same thing himself too many times not to know what was coming next. Jessie's arm and weapon were too far away from her body. She was too committed to defending against the blow she thought was coming to defend against the blow that actually came.

The Korovega turned its wrist mid-swing and shifted its aim slightly. The creature's sword slipped past the end of her saber and continued its downward journey.

It bit into her shoulder, cutting through her trapezius and sternomastoid muscles. The blade severed her external and internal jugular veins, parting tendons and muscle with equal ease, and sliding deep into her flesh like a razor. It only slowed to a stop when it impacted the hard bone of her cervical vertebrae. It might have missed her carotid artery, because the mess that erupted out of her neck poured in a steady stream of dark, veinous blood and not the energetic spurts of a severed artery, but that meant very little. Her head fell to the opposite side as the shock and pain froze the scream in her throat, turning it instead into a wet and strangled sputter.

Jessie's eyes went wide in disbelief. It hurt, of course, but the Korovega's sword was so sharp and so cold that the pain seemed only a distant mirage. Much more real was the surprise. The feint had taken her completely off guard. She was, in some distant way, impressed at the skill the Korovega displayed and its mastery of its weapon.

But she was also mad. The thing had hit her. That was not supposed to happen. She was supposed to hit it instead. But it had hit her, and it had hurt her.

The pain was all gone now, but so were other sensations. The cool morning breeze was gone. The shouts of Owen and Sam and the furious bear-like roar that came form somewhere in Ben's direction never made it from her ears to her brain.

Everything, in fact, was going away.

"Give 'em hell, Ben Stuart," she whispered as her eyes closed.

* * *

Less than three seconds had passed between the moment when the Korovega's blade touched Jessie's neck and when she closed her eyes for the last time. Sam rushed to her side, but she had barely fallen to her knees next to her when she died.

Owen stared, open mouthed, in disbelief. His stomach turned to stone and he sank to his feet as his knees went gave out. He hit the floor hard. He had been running, and he tumbled through a full somersault, clutching his saber to his chest in an attempt to avoid killing himself in the process. He stopped on his back at the Korovega's feet.

The monster grinned and turned its bloody sword toward Owen's face. Out of his peripheral vision, a great black shape shot through with flashing silver slammed into the Korovega with the force and ferocity of a battering ram. The silver streak flashed out again and again as the air rang with the bells of hell.

The Korovega went back a step, then two, before Owen got to his feet. His knees were still shaky, but he managed to keep them under him. Marcus came up next to him with his rifle and bayonet as Ben drove the Korovega backward again.

"Shit, it's going to jump," Marcus said He dashed toward the stairs down. "Heading down. I'll stop it if it goes over."

Owen saw the same thing. It was turning slightly, searching for the rail behind it with its free hand while it sought to protect itself from Ben's berserk onslaught. In the process, it actually landed two glancing blows to Ben's arms, but he never slowed. Owen wondered if he even felt the pain.

The Korovega, like the other one, was clearly trying to flee. It had done what it came to do, had killed one of them, and now it had every intention to be on its way. Owen was not about to let that happen.

Owen made two fast cross-steps forward, closing the distance with the Korovega. Ben's arms and weapon were much longer, but he had pressed very close to the Korovega in his rage. Owen was faster with his lighter sword, but Ben was fueled by unbridled fury and lashed out with everything he had. Owen knew from personal experience, that the amount of force Ben was putting into his strikes would come back to hurt him later in the form of muscle pain, but he understood.

The Korovega that killed Jessie was going to die there.

Its face betrayed none of the fear Owen knew had to be there. He knew because its movements were not as fluid as they had been. The Korovega's arm moved in jerky patterns full of beats and swats rather than the elegant expulsions and manipulations that it had been doing earlier. Its eyes were narrow. It looked angry, focused.

Owen and Ben fought the ash-gray demon with everything they had. Will was on his feet again, but there was no room for him to join the fight and so, like Sam, he waited behind Owen and Ben, ready to step in if they were knocked down—or worse.

But reprieve was something they never needed. Ben bled from another three or four cuts on his arms, and the Korovega had managed to land a hit on Owen's arm as well. From Sam's perspective on what amounted to the sidelines behind them, none of the wounds looked serious despite the blood—though she now had a new definition of serious after seeing what happened to Jessie. What she was worried about was the blood soaking Owen's back from the broken scabs of his road rash.

Ben cut, but the Korovega blocked the blow. As it happened, Owen's blade was in the perfect position to strike and he landed a long slicing cut to the Korovega's upper arm. It flinched, breaking the rhythm of its attacks and defenses, without actually stopping moving.

It snarled and lashed out in pain and anger, nearly making contact with Ben's ribs in what was almost a second killing blow. Luckily, between a strong parry and a deep back bend, Ben was able to keep the deadly blade away.

As he came back upright, he pressed his blade into the Korovega's and turned the fleeting contact into a solid bind. His wrist writhed like a snake, twisting the swords around one another until the Korovega's blade was out to one side and Ben's own sword was in position for a thrust to the stomach.

Ben let out a primal scream as he plunged the schiavona's blade into the Korovega's belly. He pushed in farther and farther, until his sword embedded itself in the wooden railing behind the creature. It lashed out with its sword, but Owen parried as Ben brought his fist up and slammed it into the Korovega's face.

Owen grabbed for the creature's wrist, missed, beat its blade away again, and grabbed a second time. That attempt was successful and he latched onto its arm just long enough to bring his saber down in a swift cut that severed the Korovega's hand and sword from its arm.

Ben continued to beat the Korovega until his hand bled and the creature was clearly dead. He then jerked his sword out of the body and decapitated the corpse.

The Korovega's head dropped to the deck with a wet squishing sound and only then did Ben stop attacking. His breathing came in great heaves and he was covered in his blood: his own, Owen's, and the blood of the Korovega.

He looked at Jessie, feeling an ache in his heart. He crossed the short distance to where she had fallen and sagged to his knees. His sword fell forgotten from his hand, clattering to the deck.

Ben gathered Jessie's body up in his arms and held her close to his cheek, heedless of the blood.

"Leave," he muttered.

Owen stepped closer and placed his hand on the larger man's shoulder. "Ben..."

"I said leave." Ben's voice was anything but firm, but it also clearly conveyed that he would listen to no arguments.

Owen squeezed his shoulder once and stepped away. As he took Sam by the elbow and led her inside, he tried to pretend he had not seen Ben's tears.

Chapter 18

Ben refused to come out of the basement bedroom until long after breakfast. When he never came to eat, Owen took a plate of food and coffee downstairs for him and left it on the countertop of what used to be the bar. He knocked on the bedroom door, told Ben there was food waiting on him, and went back upstairs. Owen had no idea if he was even awake, but he needed to eat and leaving food right outside his bedroom door was the closest thing to forcing him to eat that they could do right then.

Before sequestering himself alone, Ben moved Jessie's body off of the deck. Owen and Sam offered to help, but he refused, lifting her across his great shoulders like a fireman carrying a smoke victim out of a burning building. They wrapped her body in a white sheet, secured it with paracord, and laid it in the empty trailer still hooked to his truck.

Before locking himself in his bedroom, Ben said he would decide what to do with her body. Other than Owen, no one had ventured downstairs since then.

"You think he's alright?" Michael asked. He, Owen, and Sam were sitting on the couch in the living room. Owen's torso and one forearm were wrapped tightly in bandages. The side of his face and head had turned a nasty shade of purple. His saber leaned against one arm of the couch, next to the cutlass Michael had carried that morning. Sam's shotgun and her cutlass-like machete leaned against the other arm.

For several long moments, no one replied, then Owen said, "right now? No. Long term, he'll live, but..." In lieu of anything else to say, Owen waved one hand in an, "I don't know," gesture. His palm made a dull thump as he dropped it heavily onto the arm of the couch.

"They knew each other a long time," Sam added. She had caught Jessie as she slumped to the ground after being struck, and held her while she died. Sam knew she went quick, probably so quick that she never felt any real pain, but knowing the departed went without pain did very little for the pain the survivors felt.

That put three deaths on her conscience, because she still felt deep down inside that she should have been able to save Ken's life. He was likely dead before Jessie even brought him into the house, but that meant nothing to her. Jessie had trusted her to save the man's life and she had failed, just like she failed to save Jessie.

The third death on her conscience was the man she killed on the way to Ben's house in the first place. He was a threat, an evil man, and meant to hurt her and her friends. She knew that killing him had been the right thing to do and that, because she had, an untold number of men and women had been spared his cruelty.

Yet, she had still killed him. She pulled the trigger, and it was she who watched his guts explode across the pavement. It was she who still saw his face in her dreams.

Sam turned toward Michael, leaning slightly against one arm of the couch. Her eyes and limbs felt heavy as though the oppressive mood that affected all of them controlled gravity as well. There was a subtle disconnect between her brain and her body, almost like being drunk, that had set in almost as soon as the adrenaline began to wear off.

"How are you taking it?" she asked, turning slightly to face Michael. "You were on watch with her."

Michael's eyes were blank. There was no obvious pain there, but neither was there anything else. From the outside, it seemed as if he had simply shut down, only functioning as much as necessary to communicate with the others and to move around. Either he felt nothing at all, literally nothing and not just an absence of pain, or his emotions were buried so far down beneath a layer of deep depression that not even he knew how he felt.

"I dunno. I just," he said. His voice was flat, uninflected. His eyes widened a little. "I heard a noise and I guess she figured out what it was. She told me to come get you guys and... and..." he rubbed his face with both hands. "And when I got back..."

Owen put his hand on Michael's shoulder and squeezed tightly. He held it there for a moment before quietly saying, "there was nothing you could do."

Michael stared blankly at him for a moment before a grin, small and pained but genuine nonetheless, spread across his face. "That's such a cliché."

Owen, with a little effort, returned the grin. "Did it help?"

Michael smiled a little broader as his shoulders relaxed a touch more. "A little, yeah. I mean, if she hadn't realized it was a Korovega, we'd all be dead."

Owen took his hand back and folded both of them in his lap. "Yeah. There's that to be thankful for."

"We're all going to die here anyway, so what the hell's it matter?" George demanded from the loveseat next to them. Where Michael's voice was flat, George's was hollow. He sprawled across both cushions, unwilling to share his space with another human being. His face showed every bit of the fatigue Sam felt but, instead of her pain or Michael's shock, a wildness had invaded his visage. His wide eyes roved constantly around the room, searching for something that he never quite found. Ever since breakfast, he had jumped at every sudden noise.

Owen's voice came out with the inflection of a teacher repeating the same truth for the thousandth time. "We're not going to die."

"I'm going to train even harder," Michael said. For the first time since that morning, emotion was starting to come into his eyes. He spoke with a fiery intensity. "I'm going to practice and train and work until I'm as good a fighter as Owen and Ben are. I'm not going to let anyone down again!"

George laughed, a raw and hollow sound. "You sound like an anime character, man. Give it a rest. The Korovega know we're here. When that one doesn't come back, they'll send more until they burn this place to the ground. We shouldn't stay here."

"What do you think we should do, then?" Michael asked. The fire in his eyes had not dimmed. "We can't just run forever!"

"Can't we?" George shot back. He sank further into the cushions.

"I think this morning pretty much proves that we can't," Michael retorted. "They'll find us! We've got to take the fight to them. At the very least we need to tell the rest of the world that," he searched for a the words, "that killing one is possible. You heard how the crowd reacted when Owen fought that one yesterday."

George scoffed. "You actually believed that bullshit? Owen just fell off the damn bed of the pickup in some parking lot in Oak Ridge and they cooked up that stupid story so we'd all fall on our faces and worship him as a hero."

Owen glared across the small divide, but Michael spoke first.

"So explain the spear then."

"Props are easy. The blood's probably just from some roadkill they stabbed so they'd have 'proof.' And..."

Owen leaned forward in his seat, resting his elbows on his knees. He made eye contact with George and held it. His face was hard when he spoke but his voice cracked like a whip. "You're going to want to think long and hard before you finish that thought, George."

"And what are you going to do if you don't like what I have to say? Beat me up?" he demanded, waving a hand in Sam's general direction. "That's her strategy."

"If necessary," Owen growled. His tone conveyed that he was not joking. He realized he, too, was scared and lashing out, but the proverbial die had been cast. The words were out and could not be taken back. Besides, there was one thing he needed an answer for.

"The hell's that mean?" George demanded.

"Where were you?"

George shivered at his icy tone and sat up a touch straighter, continuing to look defiant. "Looking for a weapon," he said. "Did you want me to go out there unarmed?"

"You know where the weapons are kept," Owen said.

"Yeah, and it takes a minute to get there from the basement!"

"Why didn't you have one nearby?" Michael asked. His voice had none of Owen's fury, but there was still an undercurrent of judgment in it.

"Shut up! I was asleep! After you came to get me, I went downstairs to wake Marcus and Ben up, then I had to come back up here to get a damn weapon and I didn't get out there in time!"

He looked hurt, Owen realized. Whether he was telling the truth and felt shame or whether he was simply upset that his actions were being called into question, Owen had no idea. Perhaps he was angry at himself for deliberately avoiding the fight and now feeling regret. He also seemed afraid of what might have happened to him, not that Owen could blame him for that.

Right at that moment, though, he did not much care. George insulted him and, perhaps more important as far as Owen's anger was concerned, called him a liar.

"Three times," Owen said.

"Three times what?" George snapped.

"I've been right in front of one of those things three times now in three days. In the yard, in Oak Ridge, and on that goddamn deck," he snarled. His voice rose in volume and dropped in pitch as he grew angrier. "I shot at the first one while you hid in the basement. And I fought the second one with a pointy stick while you sat here safe. And I helped kill one right out there. And where the fucking hell were you?"

George sank back visibly shaken by the intensity in Owen's voice. He took a breath and gathered his strength before replying. "I told you I was getting a weapon. Why don't you ask Will where he was? Or Katrina? Or Michael?"

"Because I know good and goddamn well where they were. Will and Katrina were with Marcus on the ground, waiting to catch the Korovega if it tried to run. Michael went around to the driveway at the other end of the deck to try and stop it if it pushed past us that way. I saw them.

"Where. Were. You?"

"In here, getting a wea—"

Owen angrily jabbed a finger at the wall behind the TV. "We can see inside from the deck." He pointed again. "We fought it right there! Right! There! I looked inside. I looked right at the weapon closet and didn't see you. And if you were on your way out, why didn't we run into you on the way back in or even after the thing was dead?"

"You want to know the truth?" George demanded.

"Yes!"

George fought to get a hold on his anger, looked down at the floor and, without making eye contact again, said, "I stayed in here to try and throw all of the design sketches and important paperwork Sam and I worked on into a backpack so that if we had to run, we wouldn't loose them."

Owen took a deep breath. For a moment, he felt his own fury turned back at him as George's confession deflated his anger. He dropped heavily back into his chair, only managing to say, "oh."

"Yeah."

"I'm sorry."

George shook his head, but refused to meet Owen's gaze. "Don't be. I know I'm a shitty roommate and I'm tough to live with. But I want to live just as much as you do, alright? Maybe more. Probably more, the way you go charging off. But I'm no good in a fight. I just wanted to make sure we'd be able to rebuild if we had to abandon the house."

"So why'd you lie?"

He gave a self-deprecating half-smile. "I didn't want you to think I was leaving you to die or going to run out on you in the middle of the night," he said, then looked up. "That would be stupid."

Owen took another deep breath, held it, and let it out. "Just let someone know next time, alright?"

"Next time," George said as the wide-eyed look of fear returned, "yeah. Yeah, next time'll be different. Next time, yeah."

"Owen," a graveled, tired voice said. It came from the stairwell, emanating from the dark hulk that might have been a man in better light.

Owen was instantly on his feet, all but vaulting over the back of the couch to cross the room. He went to the stairs. "Yeah?"

"Come down here, we need to talk."

The Ben-shaped bulk turned and retreated down the stairs, and Owen followed.

Silence fell across the rest of the room as the others held their breath to see if Ben was actually going to come upstairs or not. When Owen disappeared down the staircase, there was a sound like everyone in the living room simultaneously releasing the breath they had been holding.

"So he's still alive," George said. He might have been discussing the weather.

"Of course he is," Michael replied. "Why wouldn't he be?"

George shrugged.

Michael said, "he didn't get hurt that badly." He stole a quick glance at Sam, who had cleaned up Owen's wounds after the fight. He assumed she did the same for the cuts Ben received on his arms. "Did he?"

"Not that I know of," she replied. To George, she added, "what are you implying?"

"He seemed pretty broken up, that's all. That's the sort of thing that can drive a man to drink."

Sam started to retort, but bit it off before she said anything. He was trying to bait her like he had done Owen. He wanted someone to fight with so that he could have an outlet for his anger and shame, someone other than himself to blame for how he felt. Owen had given it to him, and Ben had given it to him simply by being Ben and having a part in the history they shared, but she was not about to rise to that sort of bait again.

Instead, she just shook her head and vowed not to speak to him for a while. A moment later, she pushed angrily away from the couch, leaving Michael and George alone. Those two had known each other for years, she thought, so perhaps Michael would find some way to talk sense into George's head. At the very least she hoped Michael would be able to calm him down enough to function.

Sam briefly contemplated going upstairs and losing herself in a book, or the internet, or even in paperwork. With Jessie gone, she would have to revise the schedule she put together for work and for the watches at night. Without her around, there would be one less set of competent hands to help fight and help build.

With Jessie gone, she had lost a friend.

Sam fought down that train of thought. She hurt, and she already missed Jessie in a way she never thought possible. They had never met before she arrived at Owen's apartment, though after meeting her Sam finally had a face to apply to the name Ben had talked about so often. But in that short time, especially after spending most of the previous day training together and working on the workshop, they had become friends.

Perhaps, she thought, had she not actually seen Jessie die, it would be different. Had she been like Will or Marcus, who went to the basement level to form a perimeter against the Korovega's escape, she might have felt differently. She still would have seen the body and the blood, but perhaps, she wondered, had she not been right next to her, she might not feel responsible. It might not hurt as much.

She forcibly ignored that thought, too. It was the fourth or fifth time since watching her die that the thought, and the weight of responsibility, crossed her mind. If she was to get anything of use done that day, she needed to ignore it. She could grieve later—either alone or with Owen, it mattered little. For the time being she needed to stay focused.

* * *

While the others sat and argued in the living room, Will, Marcus, and Katrina remained around the dinner table. Remnants of the breakfast they had all shared still were still scattered around. Sam headed their way.

Will and Marcus sat beside one another with Katrina opposite them. Their weapons were leaned against the end of the table, within easy reach. She had a look on her face similar to the one George wore, only where his was full of hateful recriminations, Katrina's showed an edge of iron peeking out from under her fear. Marcus and Will both had a hard set to their jaws and a distant look in their eyes. They had helped themselves to seconds of nearly everything they had eaten and were picking idly at what little was left while engaged in quiet conversation. Will's biceps and upper chest were already bruising an impressive shade of purplish-red, but otherwise the three of them seemed physically unharmed.

Sam had only gotten three steps away from her seat when she was suddenly conscious that she left her weapons. Without them nearby, she felt vulnerable again. She stopped and retraced her way back to the living room side of the large space and retrieved them. Weapons now in hand, she went back to the breakfast table.

"Owen alright?" Will asked as Sam leaned her machete and shotgun against the table next to the other weapons. For an open room, sound did not carry very well from one end to the other and so he likely everything but Owen's shouting.

She nodded, slipping into the seat beside Katrina. "Yeah. He's just on edge."

Katrina laughed nervously. Her hands, folded on the table, fidgeted. "Aren't you? I mean, you were right there when it happened. Darausend mit dem Korovega. Outside, I mean. You'd gone out to fight it with Owen and Ben and Marcus, and Jessie was already out there. And she was fighting it allein so that Michael could come warn us. I tried to help, I really did."

Sam put her hands over Katrina's, trying to still their nervous movement. When the other woman finally took a breath, Sam quietly shushed her, then, "it's alright. You went out there; that's all I can ask."

Sam's presence acted as a comfort, allowing her feelings to come flooding out. Katrina cried tears she had been holding in since the fight. German and English muddling together amid her emotional turmoil. "Nein! But it's not. Don't you see? It came for us and now Jessie's gone," Sam felt another pang of guilt at that, "and we're not safe and I tried to help, I promise! Ich weiß nicht was zu tun, und..."

Sam interrupted again. "Katrina." She paused. "It will be alright. Jessie," she stopped again, barely for for half a breath, to put her thoughts together. Any longer and she suspected Katrina would begin rambling again. She said, "Jessie would have wanted us to go on, right?"

Katrina nodded. Tears still streamed from her eyes, but she had her breathing under control again. She sniffed hard and pulled one hand from under Sam's to wipe her eyes.

She smiled.

"Jessie gave her life to protect the rest of us," Sam said. Absently, she realized she was talking to herself as much as she was talking to the hyperventilating half-German. "She knew what she was doing when she sent Michael to get the rest of us."

Will nodded once, firmly. "Because she did that, the rest of us are still alive. That's a debt we can only repay by continuing to live."

"Hooah," Marcus muttered so quietly that Sam barely heard it. His attention was, ostensibly, on the glass of apple juice in his hands but Sam had no illusions that he was ignoring the rest of them.

On the opposite side of the room, Owen came up the stairs from the basement with determination in his step. He went around to the other side of the staircase and headed up to the loft without a word.

"Owen?" Sam called. "Everything alright?"

He leaned over the railing at the edge of the loft, where they had listened to Will's embellished version of his street fight, and replied, "actually, yeah. Ben's got a plan."

Owen ducked out of sight, leaving only the sound of boxes and bags being rifled through at high speed to remind them where he was. From the sounds of things, he knew what he was looking for and had a general idea where it was. Sam heard a lot of boxes and such being moved around, but only two or three actually being opened.

"Not going to go check on him?" Will asked.

Sam shook her head. "Sounds like he's handling it."

"But you're not curious?"

"I am, but whatever plan he and Ben are working on will be," she made a dramatic gesture with one hand, "revealed in due time."

Will laughed. Despite the hard set to his face and the taught tone in his voice, the sound was warm. Having something else to focus on was helping all of them in different ways. "I assumed as much."

Owen came back down the stairs with two large, black duffel bags slung over his shoulder.

"Need help?" Will called.

"I'm good."

"Just let us know if this plan of yours requires us to do anything."

"Will do," he said, disappearing down the basement stairs again.

"Those looked like gear bags," Sam observed.

"Gear?"

She nodded. "Protective gear for when he and Ben and their club would fence. I don't know how effective some of it would be against a real sword, but," she shrugged, "I guess we'll find out."

"Somebody told me that people wear leather jackets when they, you know, when they go into seedy places at night," Katrina added. She seemed much calmer, Sam noted. Having other people around to calm, or at least displace, her fears seemed to be helping. Both of her hands were folded tightly on the table, but they had stopped trembling. With a hopeful smile, she added, "maybe it's like that?"

"A leather jacket won't stop a knife," Will observed.

Marcus spoke up. His voice was quiet, but carried. "Right, but it will slow one down a bit and protect you from weaker cuts, especially if you've got some stab-resistant..."

Marcus's next words were cut short by the sound of feet stomping their way up the stairs. There was only one set of footsteps, which made Sam worry. After the better part of three hours, she would have expected Ben to be out and social once more. He had been hurt worse than anyone by Jessie's death, no matter how he tried to hide it, but she had never known him to shut everyone out so completely. Sam hoped he was alright, especially mentally.

Owen came to the top of the stairs. "Everyone come down here." His tone indicated that it was not a request. "We've got work to do and we need to go over a few things."

Sam stood, followed by the others at the table with her. Marcus was last to stand, not from any apparent reluctance, only from seeming to be lost in his own thoughts. He took a moment to process what was said, then stood as well, and headed for the stairs.

Across the room, Michael stood quickly. Sam was surprised to note that he did not wait to see if George was following when he went for the stairway. George did follow, though only after a few moments of thought where he seemed to be weighing exactly how much he wanted to get out of his seat and converse with other people.

Sam noticed with a sort of grim detachment that everyone, even Katrina and Michael, picked up their weapons as they went. Yesterday, the weapons had been kept close by, either in the living room closet or in some specific location for personal weapons. Now—though the upstairs closet was packed with their stock of spare rifles, pistols, swords, and knives—everyone kept some sort of weapon within arm's reach. Even George had a Bowie knife thrust through his belt and, Sam assumed, a pistol in his pocket.

Sam slung her shotgun over her shoulder and picked up the machete next to it. Carrying her "personal" shotgun would be a bad idea for a patrol weapon. It was large, heavy, and only held two shells at a time. So she, like many of the others, had borrowed a gun. The short-barreled shotgun on her shoulder belonged to Ben, but he was more than willing to share.

The machete, on the other hand, was hers. It had never been bought as a weapon, merely the sort of brush-clearing tool that every self-respecting person who spent more than a few minutes in the woods would own. However, it was sharp and it would serve the purpose of weapon well enough until she had something better.

The lot of them made an unlikely sight trooping down the stairs. The house had been built to have the feel of a hunting lodge with wood paneling, wide open spaces, and animal-themed decorations that included a giant stuffed black bear that Ben always left on the loft bed, and so having rifles and shotguns around never felt out of place. But now the two men preceding her down the stairs carried large, military-style rifles fitted with wicked bayonets rather than hunting rifles. Behind her, Katrina carried another military rifle with a bayonet.

A hunting party would have fit right in with the décor, but they were armed for battle. Of course, Sam thought, even being armed for battle they looked strange. Bayonets were a rare sight on the modern battlefield, to say nothing of the swords that rattled around among their group. They were hardly dressed for combat either, with a profusion of tshirts, jeans, shorts, and other such clothing that anyone walking in off the street might have been wearing.

* * *

Sam rounded the corner at the base of the stairs. Owen and Ben stood on the far side of the basement's bartop counter. She glad to see Owen, but relieved beyond words to see Ben up and about.

Will and Marcus leaned their rifles against the back of the couch and went to the bar. Sam did likewise, and the others followed suit.

"Alright," she said, "what's the secret plan?"

Owen held up something that clanked. In his hand was a collection of curved and flat pieces of metal riveted to sort sort of leather. "This."

Sam stared at it for a moment, unable to shake the feeling that she should know what it was. Two large pieces of metal, one slightly larger than the other, formed a circle with buckles on opposite sides. From the larger half hung two overlapping metal plates riveted to a strip of leather. The other half had a similar single plate attached. It looked sturdy and well-worn, whatever it was.

Michael gave voice to her thoughts. "What is it?"

Finally, the lightbulb went off and Sam said, "it's a gorget."

"A gor-what-now?" Michael asked.

"Gorget," Sam repeated. "It's what they," she gestured to Ben and Owen, "wear around their neck when they fence."

"I saw what happened to Jessie." Ben's voice was rough. It had the sound of someone who had been screaming for hours, but the house was not that soundproof. They would have heard something if that had been the case. He sighed. "T'tell the truth, she screwed up. Parried wrong," he closed his eyes, took a deep breath, and continued with, "and I ain't gonna let any of you assholes die the same way, hear me?"

"Between the two of us," Owen added, "we scrounged up six of these. One's mine and one's Ben's, so that leaves four for the rest of you."

"There's six of us," George accused. "Who goes without?"

"I'm aware," Owen replied, "but until we can get the workshop finished, it's all we've got. Anyone on watch automatically gets one. Anyone running errands automatically gets one. Beyond that, we'll try to outfit everyone as best we can."

Michael raised his hand.

Owen nodded towards him. "Yeah?"

"Where will the extras be kept?"

"Same place as the weapons for now. By the end of the day, Ben and I plan to rearrange the coat closet to only store the weapons and protective gear."

"If we're gonna have an armory, that's all that spot gets used for, understand?" Ben asked.

Heads nodded around the room.

With a sweep of his long arms, Ben pushed the pile of neck armor to one end of the bartop. At the same time, Owen slid out four bulbous objects made of wire mesh and leather. The ones on the right of the line were significantly larger than the other two.

"We've only got four masks," Owen said. "And, like the gorgets, two of them belong to me and Ben. But that leaves two, and as long as we've got two people on watch, that's fine. Now..."

George interrupted. "Isn't all this for, you know, play fighting?"

Owen narrowed his eyes, but ignored the intended insult. "They're not exactly helmets, if that's what you're getting at, but I've seen these things take hits from real swords and knives and come out alright. And it's better than nothing, right?"

Reluctantly, George nodded. Owen had been watching him since the others came to the basement. He had stayed near the middle of the group at first, but had slowly drifted backward as they talked about the equipment he and Ben had laid out. He made a mental note to talk to Sam when he got a chance—if George was as unwilling to fight as he seemed, Owen wondered how good of an idea it would be to have him on watch at all. That would make the burden on their gear easier and free him up to do more desk-oriented work. They could give him weapons to defend himself, but someone else could be given his mask and gorget.

"Cap," Michael said. "Can't we just buy more gear? I mean, the stores are still open, right?"

"That's possible," Owen agreed, "but I wouldn't bet too strongly on it. It would have to be shipped, so we're relying on a whole chain of people to come in to work. And, really, the smart ones are already," he waved a hand to indicate the group of them and the house itself, "you know, not working."

"But it can't hurt?" Michael asked.

Owen shrugged. "I suppose not. The worst thing is that we'd be out some money, but unless the Korovega give up and go home, what George said the other day is right. The economy is going to collapse as the death toll rises." A chill swept the room when the mention of "death toll" reminded them all too much of Jessie's death only hours before. "Money's going to be worthless pretty soon. So we buy what we can and if some of it never makes here, then I hope someone's using it."

"Why didn't we do this sooner?" George growled.

"We was gonna give out gear as y'all learned to fight," Ben said. "We didn't get there fast enough."

George grunted. "Clearly."

"A gorget might have kept Jessie alive. I can't say. But I got t' live with that decision. Don't the rest of you blame yourselves none. Now where was I?"

They covered the rest of the protective gear Ben and Owen put together quickly. Owen had two heavily padded jackets. He claimed one as his own, and put the spare, along with a pair of unpadded ones into a pile for the others to use. Ben wore a large jacket-like coat called a gambeson. He had an unpadded jacket as well, but it was far too large for anyone to use without extensive tailoring. Sam had her motorcycle riding jacket, two of them in fact, and she donated the spare to the group pool in case anyone else her size came along. All together, they provided almost enough jackets for everyone to have one of a permanent basis.

Sam also had her motorcycle helmet which, while it was not designed for fencing, would be just as protective as one of their masks. She would wear it while on guard duty, she said, which freed up another mask for general use.

Like the other pieces of gear, Ben declared that some sort of heavy jacket would be mandatory for anyone on watch. "Yes," he added, growling, "it's going to be hot, but you know what? Would you rather be sweaty and drink a little extra water or would you rather have a Korovega cut your god damned neck open because you don't put your sword in the right place?"

Sam wondered how much of the fire in his voice was simply anger at Jessie's death, if not at Jessie herself. She hoped his grief would not cause him problems.

"Besides," Owen added, forcing a smile, "we've fought, not just stood around, but fought and sweated in these things in the middle of August. Standing around and keeping watch is going to be easy once you get used to it."

"And how long will that take?" George asked.

Owen wondered why it mattered to him. He had expressed his doubts that the gear would be effective multiple times already. Yet the question was still a valid one, Owen decided, and he said, "that depends on you. When you're wearing it for a few hours at a time every day or every other day, you'll get used to it quickly."

"Any questions so far?" Ben asked, but there were none, nor any further objections from anyone. He and Owen had made their case for the gear, laid down the rules, and, so far as Ben was concerned, been rather reasonable about it.

And if forcing them all to wear fencing gear and patrol the house in a mask, jacket, and gorget would keep even one of them safe from what happened to Jessie, it would be worth it in his eyes. He missed her terribly, but her death had been a lesson and he intended to honor the message that lesson taught, no matter how painful the memory.

"There is one last thing," Owen said.

He bent down behind the counter and came back up with a sword in a beautiful green and gold scabbard. The hilt was a shining mass of curving bars and rings surrounding a black leather grip. The belt wrapped around the scabbard was a matching emerald green color with a brilliant gold buckle. Sam had never seen it in Owen's collection before, but she was unable to shake the feeling that she knew it from somewhere.

He withdrew the sword, holding the tip up and reflecting the overhead light from the mirror-polished steel. The blade was long, not as long as Ben's schiavona, but longer than the saber he had been carrying that morning. It was also rather wide at the base, tapering sharply into a wicked point.

"This," he announced, "is my new sword. Up until a few hours ago, it belonged to our early morning visitor."

Sam's stomach dropped now that she recognized the sword. It the was weapon carried by the Korovega that attacked them. There was nothing inherently evil about the weapon, at least she assumed that whatever magic the Korovega used for their beams and shields came from something other than the sword, but she wondered how he could stomach holding the sword that had taken their friend's life.

Around the room, she felt the tension subtly increase as the identity of the weapon set in.

Owen continued talking. "I'm keeping it because, first off, it's a really nice sword. Second, more importantly, the thing that used this sword killed my friend. It killed your friend too! And I think it would be a fitting sort of justice to use that same sword to kill a few Korovega."

Abruptly, the tension vanished, replaced by cheers.

"Now get to work!" Ben ordered. "Take all this upstairs. I'll put it away in the closet. Everyone see Sam for your assignments. Those of you on watch, come see me next."

As the crowd dispersed, most carrying pieces of gear upstairs, Sam slid through the moving mass of people. Once she was sure no one other than Owen and Ben was within range of her voice, she asked, "so what's the plan today?"

He looked surprised. "Honestly, I was assuming you had one."

"I had one." She emphasized "had."

"But now things have gone all to hell," Ben observed.

"Yeah," she replied quietly. "You alright?"

Ben was quiet for a moment, waiting for the others to file up the stairs. When the three of them were completely alone, he let his shoulders relax and slump slightly. "No," he said, voice pitched not to carry more than a foot or two. "I ain't."

Sam offered a half-smile. She reached out and touched his arm across the countertop. "If you need anything..."

"What I need is for that to never happen again. It was dumb what got her killed, and she'd know it if she was still here."

Sam nodded. "Yeah," she said. She had no idea what else to say. She had been there, too, but telling Ben that he was not at fault would work about as well as telling her the same thing. "I'm sure Jessie would be proud."

He sighed. "I hope so. It ain't even just this that I got to thank her for. I told you the whole sad story the other night, remember?"

Sam nodded. Jessie had helped Ben get sober after long years of alcoholism. After cleaning himself up, he had met Owen and joined his fencing group. In a very real way, Sam realized, Jessie was to thank for everything that had keep them alive and safe over the last few days.

Chapter 19

The eight survivors stood around a vaguely human-shaped mass of white sheets. Underneath the sheets was a stack of kindling, dry twigs and small tree branches mixed with pine needles, dry leaves, and grass clippings. The sun was climbing progressively higher in the sky but if anyone was aware that they were losing valuable work time, no one seemed bothered by that fact.

Half of those present wore a heavy jacket of some sort. Most of them, the notable exception being George, who had vocally refused one, wore a gorget as well. Weapons in profusion hung from belts or off of shoulders.

The half who had no jacket had been assigned the first shift of building the walls for the workshop. Because they would have less protection than the others, their job in case the house came under attack would be first to clear out of the way. Those with both weapons and armor would engage first.

Ben, wearing a great, charcoal-gray gambeson and a gorget of blood-red leather stood at the body-shaped thing's head, a red metal gasoline can at his feet. His sword hung from one hip, a large pistol rested on the other, and his rifle hung from a sling across his back. He was a great gray-black monolith speckled with reds and silvers in the early morning's light.

Owen stood to his right, equally armed with the Korovega sword, a pistol, and a shotgun. Michael, Katrina, Marcus, George, Will, and finally Sam stood at Ben's left. Each of them, even George, were armed. Those tasked with working on the shop carried smaller weapons, but even they had something strapped to a leg or a belt. The faces around the circle bore a wide range of expressions varying from open sadness to anger and everything in between.

"If anyone wants to say any words, now's the time," Ben said. He wore an expression of deliberate nonexpression on his face. No emotion showed itself through the steel mask that was his eyes and mouth. He stared straight ahead, neither at the body in front of him or at Marcus on the opposite side of the pyre. In fact, since gathering them all around what was about to be Jessie's funeral, Ben had not made direct eye contact with anyone.

There was a tense moment of silence, and Sam said, "thanks," and nothing more. Her eyes were on the sheets.

Another few seconds passed before Michael spoke. "Jessie showed me what it meant to be a hero. She could have done a thousand things to save her own life this morning, but she didn't. She... yeah. I'm alive thanks to her."

Ben's eyes slowly swept the circle.

"I barely knew her," Will said, "but I can agree with Michael's sentiment. The night before last, when we were on watch together, we had several quiet hours to talk. She was a good person and the world is worse off without her."

Marcus nodded, but said nothing.

"I want," Katrina began. When she felt everyone's attention on her, she stopped, then stuttered out, "I want to be like her. She was such a vibrant person, but she wasn't afraid to fight or get her hands dirty."

Another moment passed and everyone looked towards Ben. He shook his head. "Ain't nothing I've got to say I haven't already said. Y'all know how we met. Y'all know what she did for me. Saved my life. Helped me clean up. Anything else I've got to say ain't for anybody but her."

Silence fell again except for the croaking of a frog in the nearby water. Ben motioned everyone back, then picked up the gas can. He undid the stopper and slowly circled the pyre, splashing fuel generously as he went. After a full circuit, he took the red can to a safe distance and returned. He fished a matchbook out of his pocket, struck a match, and tossed it onto the gas-soaked sheets.

The pyre erupted with a roar as the gas caught instantly. It burned with a brilliant yellow-white flame that climbed dozens of feet into the morning air. In a moment, the day went from mild warmth to oppressive, hellish heat as the funeral pyre raged.

Everyone but Ben took several steps back in near-instinctive unison. He stood at a technically safe distance, but much closer to the heat than anyone else was willing to stand. Within a minute, sweat beaded on his brow, but he still stood there with his hands behind his back.

As the gasoline burned off, the fire quieted down to more normal levels. Owen could see that Ben's eyes were closed and he was mouthing something, too quiet for anyone to hear. He wondered if Ben was praying, talking to Jessie's spirit, or simply giving voice to thoughts he wanted no one else to hear.

Black smoke roiled up from the pyre as Ben finally stepped away. He wiped the sweat from his forehead with a handkerchief taken from his pocket. It bore a border of red lace, and disappeared as quickly as it had appeared.

* * *

The group had dispersed somewhat. Owen stood alone, watching as people milled about. Sam was off to one side, talking to Michael and Katrina in hushed tones. Will and Marcus were under the deck, already arranging the supplies and tools for the day's work on the shop and George was—Ben scanned the yard—surely somewhere to be found. He would turn up sooner or later.

The heat and humidity crept ever higher in the East Tennessee morning, and they all stood around in several layers of heavy fabric. Owen wore an athletic shirt underneath his jacket, the sort made of quick-drying compression fabric designed to keep the wearer cool, but it was still a far cry from anything he would call comfortable. The leather gloves on his hands, the additional layers of dense foam padding, rigid plastic, and metal he wore as armor all contributed to his overall discomfort.

He felt like a soldier, or at least what he imagined a soldier would feel like. In addition to all of his protective gear, Will's twelve-gauge shotgun hung from a sling across his back and the sword he had taken from the dead Korovega hung from its green-and-gold belt. Waiting for him inside were a canteen on a long shoulder sling and a backpack that held everything from tools, batteries, and ammunition, to two spare sandwiches and drink mixes.

Of course, he remembered Will's tales of the gear they had to carry on a daily basis. Even hauling a backpack around, he suspected that his lot was still physically much easier than Will's or Marcus's ever had been.

Ben caught his eye and joined him. "You good to go?"

Owen nodded once, scanning Ben's face for any sign of emotion. The mask was still there, but the edges had softened somewhat. No longer did it seem like he was actively keeping anyone out. Rather, Ben seemed oddly at peace. Owen wondered again what Ben had been saying to the fire and resigned himself to most likely never finding out. Whatever it had been, though, it looked like it had helped.

"What about you?" Owen asked.

Ben sighed and pointed over his shoulder with his thumb as though that was all the answer he needed. A moment passed and he said, "that's going to be burning for a while, but we've got plenty of room to work. It probably won't burn down for the rest of day, not all the way. We'll bury what's left of the ashes when we can."

Owen nodded toward the fire as well. "What made you want to do it this way?"

Ben shrugged. "'S what she told me she wanted. Long time ago, we talked about it. Both of us wanted to be cremated. You remember that, hear?"

Owen nodded slowly, despite the sinking feeling he got from the implications of that statement.

Ben went on, "and this is probably the closest thing we got to cremation, yeah? I suppose it ain't so bad, going out Viking-style."

"Where's the boat?" Owen grinned a little bit, trying to lighten the tension that remained.

"I ain't burning m'boat. Not even for Jessie. She'd shoot me."

Owen laughed. "Fair enough."

To Owen's surprise, Ben laughed too. "Come on," he said, clapping Owen on the shoulder. Between the still-healing road rash and the cuts from fighting the Korovega earlier, the gesture sent a sharp stab of pain down his arm and back, but he gritted his teeth and chose to ignore it. Ben added, "we all got work to do. Has Sam already done those orders?"

Owen nodded. After going over their gear, and realizing that they had more people than armor, Sam hit the internet and spent several thousand dollars on more, hoping that the businesses would still be running. "Yeah. While you were preparing..." He gestured feebly toward the still-raging pyre.

"You can say it."

Owen nodded. "While you were preparing Jessie's body."

Ben nodded, pleased. "Good, good."

"She paid for overnight shipping, too. I had them send it to the PO box in Clinton."

For the past several years, he and Ben had split the cost of a Post Office box. They both had keys to it, but Owen mainly did the pickups. In recent years, it had seen much less use, but there was a time when both of them were keeping unusual schedules and the PO box had been an easy way to have fencing gear shipped without worrying about expensive things going missing after sitting on the front porch for hours.

Like so many other things, Owen knew it would not last much longer, but the space had been paid for through the end of the year. If the Postal Service, and the Clinton branch more importantly, was still around at that point, he would consider whether or not to renew it. If civilization still stood in some form, it might come in handy. If not, he supposed a rented aluminum box had a limited lifespan of usefulness in the face of the genocidal army creeping across the globe anyway.

"Alright," Ben said. "Get to it. Call me if you run into trouble."

Owen nodded. "You know I will. Try not to call me a dozen times if I don't check in, alright?"

"I'll think about it."

"I don't want my phone ringing while I'm trying to sneak around."

Ben grinned. "Put it on silent, then."

Owen laughed. "Fine, fine. Seriously, though, I'll do my best to keep in touch."

"Good."

Eager to be out of the sun for even a few minutes, Owen went back inside to finish getting his things ready. Getting caught unprepared the day before had brought up a paranoid streak in his packing. He and Will could easily have been stranded with nothing but whatever the two of them had in their pockets while that Korovega torched Bull Run. He was running no such risks on this mission.

He went for the stairs, being careful to avoid knocking into anything. Between the sword, the shotgun, the backpack, and the canteen, he had a hard time moving around the crowded house. Balance was no issue; Owen had had less physical room to work with before. Rather, nothing attached to his body wanted to stay still as he walked. He was somewhat used to carrying a sword around on his belt, but that had only been done for fun. In the fencing world, his swords usually stayed in a bag or case and were carried by hand to and from the practice area. With the other things banging around, he felt like his equipment was much harder to control.

The shotgun bounced heavily against his back for the third or fourth time since coming inside, and he gave a frustrated sigh. He hoped that it would become easier with practice.

* * *

Sam, George, and Michael were inside when he came out of the stairwell. Sam and Michael sat opposite one another in the living room area of the space while George peered intently at a spread of papers on the kitchen table. The stack was much smaller than usual. George was taking things in and out of a large backpack to work on them rather than leaving them on the table like he had been doing before.

Owen approached George first, quietly thankful for the sudden neatness. He leaned against the table, careful to keep the shotgun from banging into things, and asked what he was working on. He decided, for the moment, not to ask where he had gone so quickly after the lighting of Jessie's pyre. He would leave that particular confrontation to Ben, should Ben wish to pursue it. He and George had butted heads enough for one morning.

George held up an incomplete sketch. To Owen's eyes, it seemed little more than a collection of lines and curves.

"I've been drawing this out so that we can have some clean water when the sewer system goes down," he said, before Owen could give voice to the question in his eyes. At Owen's confused look, George rolled his eyes and added, "it's a still."

"Like for moonshine?" he asked, wary.

"Not for mo—ok, yes," George said, waffling between the simple answer and the answer that would actually satisfy Owen. "Technically, it's the same apparatus."

"You know how Ben feels about alcohol."

George shrugged. "First, not my problem. Second, even if it were my problem, this is only for water. You know, distilled water?"

Owen nodded as the pieces came together in his mind. The idea should have been clear when George called it a still. In retrospect, it was. His mind was still fuzzy, though, unable to fix on things very clearly.

"How long will it take to build?" Owen asked.

George shrugged again. "It's maybe an afternoon's work. We've already got the rain barrels and if this," he waved a hand at the large window behind him and the blue sky, "continues for much longer, we can get water from the river out there. It will be harder to clean, but we can do it easy enough. The work crews should have no problem putting it together as soon as we get the tubing."

Owen pointed to a second sheet beneath the design for the still. It looked vastly more complicated. "What's that?"

George pulled it out of the stack. Without another sheet on top, Owen could see more clearly. Off to one side was what looked like an exploded view of the still on the other sheet, but with a few modifications. On the other side, which had previously been covered by the diagram of the still, was a similarly exploded view of the water wheel George had drawn up the day before.

Realizing what the plans were for, Owen asked, "you're thinking of combining them?"

George nodded. "Yeah. I'd build this one," he tapped the first sheet, "first and use it to clean rainwater. This," he laid a hand on the combination water wheel-still, "will come after you build the wheel for power. You can take some of the water that runs through the generator and filter it for drinking or washing or whatever. Only problem is the wheel is going to be a bitch to build."

"I thought you designed a simple one."

George grunted. "I did. But it's still a water wheel. Hydroelectric power, even small stuff like this, requires a lot of moving parts that have all got to stand up to a lot of stress."

Owen nodded and stole a look at the clock on the wall. "Looks like you've got ten minutes before the hard work starts."

"Don't remind me. I'd rather work on this, alone, than the workshop."

"Yeah, but the workshop's got to get done. One project at a time and all that," he said. Unable to resist the jab, he added, "but if I had it my way, I'd stay in here with the air conditioning, too."

"Right," George said. He seemed not to be bothered by the joke, if he thought Owen was joking at all. "When are you leaving?"

"Here in a few," he replied. "Just as soon as I finish packing."

"I'd call you lucky," George said, "but you're probably going to charge headfirst into danger again."

Owen laughed and rubbed at the sore muscles in his shoulder "Trust me, if I can avoid danger, I will."

"Just remember that if it comes down to you or a bunch of strangers, your own life is a hell of a lot more important."

"I'll," Owen paused, "keep that in mind."

George nodded and went back to sketching on the unfinished still drawing, which Owen took as his cue to leave the conversation.

* * *

On the other side of the room, Sam and Michael seemed to be wrapping up their conversation as Owen sat next to them. The process of sitting took much longer than was comfortable because his gear required a ponderous amount of care to arrange.

Sam sat at one end of the couch, holding Owen's saber—the one he would have been carrying if he had not claimed the Korovega sword—in her hand. Michael was in the chair next to the couch. It sat at ninety-degrees to the couch itself, allowing them to use the ottoman as a sort of low table. His shotgun and pistol lay at one end of the ottoman surrounded by a small pile of ammunition. Sam's guns lay at the other end amid a similar pile of bullets and shells.

"Like this?" Michael asked. He held his cutlass aloft. Owen instantly recognized a dozen small ways in which his guard could be improved, but stayed quiet. Sam was doing the teaching just then and interrupting her would only confuse her impromptu student.

Sam made her own corrections to Michael's positioning, moving his hand herself rather than trying to explain things in words that could easily be misinterpreted. Her correction was still not perfect, but it would do its job of keeping his head attached to his neck.

"And then cut like..." Michael said, then extended his arm forward and flicked his wrist out. The motion was much cleaner than his parry had been.

Sam nodded. "Just make sure to keep your edge pointed at your enemy and when they attack you..." She held up her own sword with the guard close to her face and the blade sloping over her head. She tapped the base of the blade with her other hand. "Keep this part between their sword and you."

Michael nodded and grinned. "I got this."

"Good. Head on outside. Ben's going to want to start work on the shop soon and that means you're up for guard duty."

He nodded and stood up. It took a moment's finagling, but he slipped his cutlass into its scabbard and picked up the pistol. Under Sam's watchful eye, he reloaded the magazine he had emptied, placed it back into the gun, and slid the gun into its holster on his belt. The shotgun was easier for him to reload and, like Owen's, it went on a sling on his back.

Between the weapons, his borrowed jacket, and the pieces of armor he wore, he seemed as ready for guard duty as he could be. Modern weapons hanging next to swords and laying against gear designed to keep the wearer safe when sparring in a tournament all meshed together to make something that looked more like he walked out of a video game than a real security guard. Owen supposed he looked just as ridiculous, but looks were secondary to staying alive—function triumphed over style.

Regardless of how his clothing looked, Michael himself seemed more relaxed than he had on his previous stints guarding the house. He also seemed more self-assured and ready to fight if necessary. Owen supposed that was partially the doing of the gear he wore—it did have a way of making the wearer feel rather martial—but it just as easily might have been some mental change that had come over him since early that morning. Either way, the Michael who stood festooned with weapons and armor almost seemed a different person than the Michael who had awakened Owen and Sam in a panic a few hours before.

Owen nodded at him as they made brief eye contact.

"See you tonight, Captain."

"Keep everyone in line, alright?" Owen responded.

Michael nodded emphatically. "I will." He then turned to head for the deck door.

"He getting some last minute tips?" Owen asked, gesturing to Michael's back as he exited the room.

Sam nodded. "Something like that. He," she stopped for a moment, thinking, "doesn't want what happened to Jessie to happen to him. He's afraid, Owen."

The absurd understatement touched the bitter part of his sense of humor and he half-laughed. "Aren't we all?"

Sam stole a look across the room at where George was still sketching away at the table. She suspected it would take one of the others coming and physically guiding him downstairs and outside before he would leave.

Looking back at Owen, she said, "Michael's using that, though. He's turning his fear into something better. Sure, he's afraid of the Korovega, but he's more afraid of failing."

"Jessie didn't die because she failed," Owen countered. He felt a hotter retort on the tip of his tongue, but stopped it.

Sam was silent for a moment. Her face looked pained, but then it passed. "I was there, Owen. I talked to Ben. Jessie," she stopped again, then continued more slowly as she weighed each and every word she was saying, "Jessie died because the fight wasn't fair. She made a mistake, and..."

"And nothing," Owen interrupted. "Making a mistake doesn't mean you have to die."

"Sometimes," Sam said. She kept her voice quiet, trying to avoid being overheard. "It does."

"Bullshit."

"It shouldn't, but it does. Making a mistake when you're fencing means you lose a point. Making a mistake now," she sighed, "when you're fighting for your life, a mistake means you might very well die. What do you think would have happened if I missed that shot Tuesday? Or if Will missed his shot Thursday morning? Or if you, that afternoon, had missed a single parry with that spear?"

Owen fumed. He knew she was right, but he still did not like it. Jessie's pyre was still burning and they were discussing the mistakes she made that led to her death. He felt like she deserved more time than that. Perhaps that evening, or even the next day, they could discuss what she had or had not done well in her fight, but doing it so soon made him more uncomfortable than he wanted to admit.

But still, Sam was right as usual. If—no, he corrected himself, when—he had to face down another Korovega, it would not stop the fight to discuss technique. The Korovega trying to kill him would not pull a blow to turn it into a "teachable moment" nor would it explain, after gutting him, how he could have parried differently.

He sighed. "You're right. I don't like it, but you're right."

"I don't like it either, but it is what it is."

"Are you alright?"

She looked at Owen for a long moment, searching his face to see what he felt right then. She saw pain, anger, frustration, fear. All the things she felt, she saw mirrored in his face, hidden from anyone who did not know how to see past his mask.

She nodded. "As alright as you are," she replied, knowing that said enough.

Owen adjusted his posture to something that displayed a touch more confidence, watching Sam for her reaction.

"We ready to go?" she asked.

"Almost. I need to check over the bags."

"Already done."

"Really?"

Sam nodded. "Yeah. While Michael was getting the hang of reloading magazines I went over everything."

She stood up and adjusted her sword belt. Rather than a fencing jacket, Sam wore an antique-styled long motorcycle jacket. It had four pockets on the front— two breast and two on the front of the thighs. It buckled at the waist and zipped above that, but the lower part moved freely. It also had buckles at the wrists and neck that snugged the black leather tight against her skin. Normally, of course, she only wore that jacket for relaxing rides because it was much heavier than a more modern jacket would have been. Now, it was that heaviness that prompted her to wear it. With the addition of a semi-rigid breastplate and armored inserts under the jacket, she was easily as protected as Owen was, if not more so. Under the neck of the jacket, she wore a simple steel gorget.

Sam seemed to be having no easier of a time of maneuvering with her weapons than Owen. Unlike Owen, Sam had never carried a sword on her belt outside of the theater. Her interest in fencing had always been limited, too, but it seemed she remembered enough of what he had taught her over the years to have given Michael a rudimentary lesson in the basics.

The shotgun she handled with much more ease. She picked it up and settled it against her front side where she could easily reach the trigger. Owen almost adjusted his to match hers, though he had no idea if that position made it any easier to use the gun. Shortly, it would be a moot point because he would be on the back of her motorcycle and jamming a shotgun between her back and his belly did not seem comfortable.

Their backpacks were waiting against the end of the bartop counter that separated the kitchen from the dinner table. Owen lifted his and instinctively slipped the heavy bag onto his back where it drove the side of his shotgun into his kidneys. Cursing rather vehemently as the weapon smacked against his road rash, he dropped it on the floor, adjusted the gun for the dozenth time so that it now sat against his hip, and picked the backpack up once more. Sam carried hers by a grab handle on the side, holding it like a misshapen briefcase.

"Lead on." He gestured toward the door.

* * *

Earlier, while they cleared the area for Jessie's pyre, Sam took her motorcycle from its resting spot against the basement wall of the house and propped it up on the kickstand in the driveway. It sat ahead of Will and Owen's cars, as well as Ben's charger. The trucks had been moved further into the yard when they were being unloaded. Now, the large bike stood like a lone, blue sentinel, awaiting their mission.

Sam stifled a laugh as she thought of how many cars were clustered around the admittedly large house. To her eyes, it looked as though it would be difficult to maneuver them if they needed something like George's van—parked in front of Jessie's jeep—or either of the big trucks again. Counting her motorcycle, there were twelve vehicles for the eight of them who were still alive.

She swallowed hard at that thought. The memory of Jessie racing home and rushing inside, frantically clearing the table still stuck with her. Jessie had been so convinced that something she could do would save Ken's life, but it had been a fool's hope from the beginning. Sam thought that, at some level, Jessie knew that, but she forced herself, and by extension Sam, to try everything in their power.

Fresh memories burned in her mind, but there was nothing to be done for them except honor the memories of the ones they had already lost and do her best to prevent any others from meeting the same fate.

She felt Owen's hand on her shoulder and realized she had stopped in place and was gazing at, without really seeing, the landscape below the house.

"You alright?"

Sam inhaled deeply, held it, forced the bubble of emotion back down where it belonged, and relaxed. "I'm alive."

Owen smiled. "Good to hear."

"Besides." A smile spread across her features. "Shouldn't I be asking you that instead?"

"I'll live," he replied.

"You were actively bleeding last night and you tore most of the scabs open less than six hours ago." Her voice was flat, matter-of-fact.

"I had a good doctor." He grinned. "I'll try not to bleed on Big Blue's seats."

Sam laughed. "Make sure you don't. They're leather."

Owen laughed as well, but inwardly wondered exactly how many times he would need to wash his rashguard before the blood came out of it. Perhaps it was adrenaline, but his back itself had stopped hurting before he had gone to bed for the brief sleep he was able to catch after the fight. He only knew there was fresh blood because he could feel it—either that or it was sweat—on his skin. The part that actually hurt was his forearm where the Korovega cut him. That was hot, and throbbed in time with his pulse.

Sam handed Owen his helmet. Her head was significantly smaller than his was, and so her spare helmet stood no chance of fitting him. To make due, he had bought a fairly nice, if baseline, helmet on his own a few months after she bought her first motorcycle. When she bought Big Blue, he had sold that one and bought yet another helmet, this one with all manner of fancy technology. Most important among them was a wireless radio that connected his and Sam's helmets so they could talk easily.

"Don't forget the most important part," Ben said, approaching the motorcycle. He had, in one hand, a burlap sack that looked like it was stolen from the set of a comedy about redneck life. The only thing missing, Owen thought, was the word "TATERS" printed across the front. Of course, the six and a half foot tall, walnut-skinned man decked out in fencing gear and firearms would have been rather out of place anywhere that bag would have fit in.

Owen knew what was in the bag and took it gingerly. It stank already. Between the smell and knowing that it held the severed head of a Korovega, Owen fought to keep his breakfast in his stomach.

Ben went to slap him on the back, but remembered the road rash this time and turned the motion into a light shove against the side of Owen's head. Ben smiled, a wide flash of white against his gray-and-red fencing gear.

Owen tied the ropes at the mouth of the bag to the top of the luggage rack on the back of the bike. "Keep your phone on you."

Ben's grin widened. He patted his back pocket. "If it ain't here, it's gonna be no more'n a few feet away. You run into trouble, and we'll come pull your ass out the fire. You run across a Korovega, you call me first before you try to beat it to death with a stick again, hear?"

Whether his mood was genuine or just a mask, Owen failed to tell. Either way, though, it was infectious, and he found himself smiling as he slipped the motorcycle helmet over his face. Thankfully the same mesh that kept bugs out of his teeth dampened the smell of the severed head next to him, though not much.

Helmet in place, Owen nodded. "We'll be safe," he replied. His voice was muffled by the face guard, but it came across clear enough.

"Tank's topped up," Sam said, setting a gas can—not the metal one Ben had used to light Jessie's pyre—in the grass behind the bike's rear wheel. "We're ready to go."

Owen nodded as she slipped her own helmet on and clipped the straps under her chin. Sam climbed aboard the motorcycle with practiced ease and keyed the ignition. Owen slid in behind her. He kept a hand on his sword to ensure it stayed away from any moving parts and placed the other on Sam's side.

Sam revved the engine, flicked the kickstand with her foot, and the bike shot forward. In its wake, Ben waved away the cloud of exhaust and coughed.

"Godspeed," he muttered.

* * *

Ben stood still, with his hands clasped behind his back, watching as Sam whipped the sapphire blue motorcycle around the switchbacks below his house. The engine roared in the straight parts of the road as she gunned it. She leaned far into the curves, nearly bringing the bike parallel to the pavement. Ben suspected that she could have made the run even faster, in fact he was sure he had seen her do just that, if they had not been loaded down with gear and supplies for the day.

After she was out of sight, he turned and scanned the yard. Marcus and Will were standing next to the tools and materials for the next phase of work on the shop, talking away. In the mounting heat, neither of them wore a shirt. The only thing above the waist either of them had were their gorgets, though Will wore a broad-brimmed hat. Katrina, outfitted in various pieces of fencing gear, none of which fit quite right yet, waited under the deck in the training area. George was nowhere to be seen.

"Michael!" Ben barked.

As if summoned by a spell, he appeared at the railing of the deck moments later. "Yessir?"

Ben grinned. The man was falling into the mental model of a fighter quickly, which might just be a good thing. Ben made a mental note to stay on top of him and make sure he never drifted too far into being serious all the time. He had to learn to fight, true, but learning to fight at the expense of enjoying the things he was fighting for would be tragic.

"Would you care to step inside and request Mister Sinnon's presence. I've got block walls that need built."

Michael nodded. "On it," he replied, turning around and heading for the nearer of the two doors to the living room. Ben could, just barely, see the top of his head inside. A few moments later George slowly rose from the table and made his way to the door behind Michael.

Ben turned back to what would soon be their workshop. Marcus and Will were already unloading the tools. The materials, most of them anyway, had been stacked nearby when they unloaded the truck from Owen and Will's supply run the day before.

He stopped in his thoughts, muttering, "God. Was it all really only yesterday?"

He shook his head, grinned a rueful smile, and turned his attention back to the two men waiting for their third. George was finally coming down the outside steps, Ben saw. He went slowly, but he went without much outward protest. Of that, Ben was glad to see.

"Marcus," Ben said. "You're in charge until shift change, alright?"

Marcus sketched a salute that, while crisp, would never have passed the approval of a real superior officer. Ben, however, grinned at the gesture. Being in command suited him, he thought. It was not quite what he had had in mind when he suggested taking everything to his house, but he approved of the way people deferred to him, Sam, and Owen. It felt right.

It let him focus on things other than the contents of the blazing fire a few dozen yards away, too.

But, he reminded himself with a reproving inward glare, he had to stay on guard and not let the sentiment go to his head. If everyone wanted to defer to him, that was good. He might even encourage it now that he saw it for what it was, but he would never let himself forget that he was still the same as the people he ordered around. At the end of the day, he was no better than the dear friend he had lost.

He sauntered over to where Katrina waited in the underdeck training area. Short of the "this is how you shoot" lecture Will had given her the day before, when she spent all day on guard duty, Ben knew Katrina had exactly zero experience with fighting.

That was alright, he thought. It meant he could start from the most important part of any martial art: basics.

"Alright," he said, once he stepped under the edge of he deck. Mentally, the gears were done shifting. For the next three hours, he was not Ben Stuart the man. He would be Big Ben the fighter.

"Lesson one," he continued. His voice had changed, becoming more even. He was, as the saying went, in the zone. "Hit me."

Chapter 20

The drive to Clinton had gone quickly, and Oak Ridge waited just a few miles on the other side. They avoided the highway this time, preferring a shorter, more scenic route. Thanks to the apocalypse, it was free of the cars that usually backed up the narrow road. They saw one other person the entire trip: a shopkeeper in Andersonville, trying to keep his corner store operating despite everything.

A few people were left in Clinton city proper, but many of the people who would ordinarily be milling around the various shops, antique stores, and cafes in Clinton's small downtown district on a Friday morning were gone. Owen suspected some of them were still around, living in apartments above or below the street level shops. Enough buildings had been put up during or shortly after the Second World War that bunkers and reinforced basements were relatively common. Still, seeing absolutely no movement on the streets was jarring, even for a small town.

Hopefully, he thought as Sam raced down Main Street, everyone was gone because they were holed up somewhere safe. There were mountains and retreats much closer than Ben's house, and he assumed many people had gone there. People also might have gone to Oak Ridge where the laboratory facilities and nuclear power plants would attract the more focused attention of the National Guard.

Fortunately, the Clinton police had better things to do than pay attention to one lone blue motorcycle racing through town at nearly twice the pedestrian-friendly speed limit. They made good time, much better than he had with Will had the day before, anyway. It seemed like the mass exodus was over, leaving the roads wide open.

Convenient though it was, it felt wrong. The emptiness felt like a prelude to something worse, foreshadowing what was to come when the Korovega made it there in numbers. Clinton was not exactly large, but there still should have been small crowds going about their business along the sides of the street.

Well, Owen thought to himself, that would be why we are doing this, right? To make sure that never happens.

Sam came to a semblance of a stop at the traffic light where Main Street crossed the highway. Speeding on an empty road, she felt, was something the cops could let slide in the face of everything else happening. However, should there be any around to see it, some part of her brain told her that they would still look unfavorably on her screeching into the intersection, past the red light overhead, without looking first to see if the highway was as empty as Main Street had been.

As it turned out, it was, or nearly so. Across the intersection was a bridge leading to the road to Knoxville. A car crossed the bridge, followed by a large truck loaded down with furniture. Beyond that, there was nothing. The stop had only taken a few seconds out of their trip and Sam turned right into what should have been heavy Friday traffic.

Instead, they were a lone speck of blue against an empty roadway.

"How are you doing?" Sam asked over the intercom in their helmets.

"I'll survive," Owen replied. In truth, he actually felt fine. His back itched and the salve in the bandages on his arm numbed things there. He was stiff, but not in enough actual pain to make a big deal of it. Sam had taken the curvy roads between Ben's house and what he referred to as "actual civilization" fast and hard, but everything quickly faded into a dull ache.

The fight that morning, despite his memory of it seeming to occupy hours, had taken less than two minutes—not long enough to make any of his muscles sore. All of the activity had torn open the scabs from his fight the day before, however. He felt a wet trickle against the small of his back, but had no way to tell if it was blood from reopened wounds or sweat from hours already spent in the hot summer sun. He decided not to check. It was easier assuming it was sweat; that made the dull pain easier to ignore.

"Owen."

"Sam."

She sighed. The sound was just barely audible over the intercom.

"What?" he asked.

"Normally, this is where I tell you to be careful. You know, after Ben's knocked you around, or vice versa, at fencing practice. But I don't think that's going to do much good, truthfully."

He shook his head. The gesture was lost on her, and he followed up a second later with, "probably not."

They passed a grocery store on the right side of the road. Surprisingly, upwards of a dozen cars sat in the parking lot. Of course, that lot had been designed to hold several hundred cars and so the overall impression was still similar to seeing Main Street deserted. Even the store itself looked mostly abandoned. Through the large windows, they could see that only about half of the lights inside were lit.

"Thank god we got most of our food already," he muttered.

"For the moment," Sam replied.

"What we have will last for a while."

Sam nodded. "But can we keep enough on hand to get us through the winter and to next summer when we can harvest things?"

"Eight of us? Probably not."

"Damn."

"It's not as bad as it sounds, though."

"Do tell."

"I've been talking to George and he's actually got a schedule written out for planting vegetables and fruit. There's apparently a lot we can plant in the fall. It won't help much now, but we can be ready for a decent harvest in the early Spring if we plant soon. Hell," he laughed, "there are even some greens that we could plant now and harvest in a month or two."

Sam sat a little straighter in her seat. "Really?"

"That's what he told me, anyway. I mean, greens aren't exactly the best food, but..."

"But they'll supplement what we've got."

"Right."

She sighed. This time it was a sigh of relief, the signs of which Owen could see in her shoulders. "Alright, I admit it."

Owen chuckled, already assuming he knew what she was about to say. "What's that?"

"He's actually useful to have around."

"Yeah. You just have to, you know, get around the fact that he's an asshole."

"Aren't you supposed to say, 'until you get to know him?'"

Owen laughed. "No. He stays an asshole, whether you know him well or not. He's hard to deal with, but when he opens his mouth, he knows what he's talking about."

"He just can't deal with people," Sam grunted.

"He can't understand anything that doesn't work on a set schedule or with set instructions. Machines? Sure. Calendars? Definitely. People?"

Sam interrupted. "Not a chance."

"Pretty much."

"Still," she said, "if his plans are half as useful as he claims they are, it's going to be," she paused, searching. "Good" was the wrong word, as was "pleasant." She finally settled on saying, "nice having him around after all."

"That was the plan."

* * *

They rode on in silence for another fifteen minutes as the number of buildings on either side of the road dropped off. There were the legal borders, but there was no clearly defined edge between Clinton and Oak Ridge. The road ran next to the river as buildings thinned out, then the river pulled away to be replaced with more buildings on either side. After a few more miles, which were covered in minutes at the speed Sam was pushing the motorcycle, the road ran up against the river again and the buildings dispersed once more.

Semantic arguments aside, they rapidly drew near the legal limit of the city itself. Past a small side road and a plant nursery, the city limits were just on the other side of a train bridge.

"Get your badge ready," Sam said, speaking through the intercom in their helmets.

Owen reached into his pants pocket, searching for the little piece of plastic, and failed to find it. He told Sam.

"Shit," Sam cursed, bringing the bike to a stop in a spray of dirt on the side of the road.

"Let me check again," Owen offered, dismounting.

He took both heavy gloves off and searched a second time, again finding nothing. Cursing, he pawed through his backpack, nearly unpacking it in the process. He set aside food, ammunition, the first aid kit—everything else was there, but the badge was nowhere that he could find.

He sank back onto his heels and started to stuff things back into his backpack. "Damnit."

Sam stood next to him, keeping watch on the empty road. After a minute, Owen stood up and slung the backpack onto his shoulders again. He clipped the waist belt and then put the sling for his shotgun back across his chest.

"So what now?" he asked.

Sam thought for a moment. "I'm technically still a resident of the city, but..."

"That might be enough," Owen replied before she could finish her thought. "Let's get closer and see how things look?"

Sam nodded and remounted the large, blue motorcycle. Owen followed, and, once she was sure he was secure, she accelerated again.

A short distance ahead, they could see the edge of the checkpoint. The sun was behind them, and no fog hung in the air to reflect or obscure the lights on top of the police cruisers parked ahead. All things considered, they had a much clearer picture of the blockade than they might have wanted.

The checkpoint sat in the same place as the one that had stopped Owen and Will the day before, but this one was vastly larger. Yesterday, the city police had stationed six officers, three cars, and a SWAT van which may or may not have had more people inside it, at the intersection. The police presence ahead of them looked easily twice that large. Where the officer checking IDs yesterday had looked bored, the three heavily armed police standing in the lane ahead looked anything but. They flanked a barricade light enough for two people to pick up and move but heavy enough to trash a car's undercarriage. Three more police and an identical set of barricades waited on the other side of the road. Three police cruisers with flashing lights, one between the barricades and the other two on the corners, completed the image.

Sam pulled into a cut-through in the median of the road and stopped the bike. From there, she scanned the blockade. Staring down the checkpoint, she realized that her driver's license would not be enough to get them through that intersection. Having "Oak Ridge" printed on it would only do so much if they had been tasked to keep anyone who might be trouble out.

A bright blue motorcycle speeding out of the midmorning sun was the last thing they had expected—or, perhaps, judging by their defensive posture, it was exactly what they had been expecting—and she and the police eyed one another with unease. Sitting there, Sam assumed they had already reported her presence, at least to whoever was in charge of the checkpoint. If not, they likely would if she made any more sudden moves toward them.

"Was it this bad yesterday?" Sam asked.

Owen shook his head. "Not hardly."

"Ideas? They're not going to let us through, that's for sure."

"But you're a resident."

"We have two people decked out in bits of leather and steel carrying enough weaponry to outfit a small squad."

Owen laughed, despite the situation. "And we have a head in a bag."

"Yes, there's that. I don't think that will help our cause any."

"Unless they're stupid," Owen said. He added a grim chuckle and went on, "we can assume they've seen us."

"Right, but what do we do about it?"

Owen shrugged. His mind raced. Walking up to the police during an invasion, declaring you were one of the good guys and there to help fight, and having them immediately accept you was the sort of thing that happened in video games and poorly written movies. No, he thought, if they rode up to a half-dozen armed Police officers with weapons and armor displayed for everyone to see, "welcome to Oak Ridge," would not be the likely reaction.

Watching the Police, Sam had the same idea. Honestly, she thought to herself, she would be surprised if the police even gave them a chance to say hello unless they drove up the rest of the way very slowly and with their hands in plain view.

Aloud, she said, "we come at that at any speed, and they're likely to shoot us."

"They're likely to anyway," Owen replied, patting the shotgun slung over his shoulder. "We don't exactly look like the sort of harmless civilian they're trained not to shoot."

Sam nodded. "Someone with a Q-clearance walks up to the gate and flashes his badge, they'd probably let him in no matter how many weapons he was carrying, but..."

Owen growled to himself. "But without it, we're out of luck. I'm going to pin that damn thing to my jacket when we get back."

"Do you think they'll follow if we turn around?" she asked.

Owen turned back to the blockade. No one there had moved, but he was unable to shake the feeling of six pairs of eyes watching him.

"I," he said slowly, "don't think so. I think if they were interested in detaining us right now, they would already have said something. The cops in the center of each line have megaphones, see."

Sam nodded. She had missed that detail, but looked again and saw that he was correct. More important, the megaphones hung unused from their gear harnesses. That meant they had no intention of talking, for good or ill.

Sam took the motorcycle through a low-speed turn away from the blockade, cursing quietly. They drove in silence for several minutes.

"Alright," she said, once they were a ways down the road, "where to?"

Owen thought for a second then, "take Sixty-One."

"Where's that?"

"Turn at the gas station!" he replied, reaching past her shoulder to point at a squat building.

"Oh," Sam replied. Owen could practically hear the eye-roll in her voice. "Oliver Springs Highway. You should have said that."

"I did."

She grunted and took the intersection at high speed, lowering the bike close to the pavement. When it was upright again, she asked over the intercom, "where to now?"

"Stay on here until you hit Key Springs."

Sam grinned. That much was abundantly clear from the tone shift in her voice. "Suddenly, I don't hate that blockade as much."

"Just don't get us killed before we get there," Owen warned.

"No promises," Sam replied. "Just hold on back there, alright?"

"What do you think I've been doing the last hour?"

"Hold on harder, then. This is about to get interesting."

* * *

Michael paced the house's upstairs deck. He spent most of his time on the opposite side from where the workshop was being built. He hold himself that it was because anyone coming to the house would most likely be coming up the road. The others would see anyone coming from the water and the odds of anyone coming down the tree-choked hillside were nearly zero. The Korovega's eagles circled overhead, but Michael's every attempt to shot one had failed, and he quickly gave up trying.

Practicality had not been his only consideration, though. Jessie's pyre still burned in the yard and every time he caught sight of it, his heart sank. Ben built the pyre with branches and leaves of various pleasant-smelling trees. Juniper, pine, and cedar mingled together with the earthy smell of woodsmoke. In truth, it was a nice smell, one that reminded him of long evenings and even longer nights around bonfires with his friends in college years before.

Unfortunately, that did little to assuage his feelings when he thought about it for too long. A scant few hours before, he and Jessie had been laughing and joking together as they finished out their watch. They were going to make breakfast for everyone, an act that was quickly becoming expected of the morning watch.

The day, Michael thought for the hundredth time, was supposed to be just like any other. Well, he corrected himself, not quite like any other. He supposed most days had nothing to do with ancient armies, or demons, or whatever everyone was calling the Korovega right then. Having the early watch theoretically meant they had it easy for the first few hours after breakfast.

But not today.

He leaned against the deck, conscious of the cutlass on his belt and the shotgun slung over his back. He had been sweating ever since putting on the protective gear Ben and Owen had given him, but he was not about to take any of it off. An empty water jug sat nearby, reminding him to fill it up again and stay hydrated. He ignored it for the moment; he had finished it off less than ten minutes before and could wait a few more minutes before getting a fresh drink.

Michael fingered the gorget at his throat, cursing silently. If only Jessie had been wearing one, she might still be alive. It felt like such a waste; why had no one thought of this sooner?

He had never seen so much blood. Much of it still stained the deck. Pressure treated wood or not, that much blood would be impossible to completely erase from the timbers under his feet. The brownish stain would be there as long as the deck stood, reminding everyone who crossed it just how fragile everything really was. He thought of the stain left by Ken's blood on the table inside. That made two of them gone. He cursed again.

He adjusted the gorget, settling it against his neck again. He had been constantly fiddling with it, especially when he remembered the sight of Jessie's neck laying open and pouring blood everywhere. His skin itched with the memory as he fought to focus on the here and now rather than the horror of the early morning.

With a long-held breath, he turned in place and marched to the next corner of the deck. The upper driveway was to his right and the door to the master bedroom's bathroom to his back. Right there, out of sight of everything else, he could pretend for a moment that everything that had happened was a dream.

The view from that spot was not as nice as it was over the water, but it was pleasant enough. The trees were vibrant shades of green, dotted here and there with flowers. The road wound its way along the hillside, peeking through the canopy in flashes of silver and black.

He had had those dreams before. Everyone had, Michael supposed. The sort of idyllic dream that turns into a nightmare one drop of terror at a time. When the news had originally broken, he thought it was some sort of hoax. It might have been a publicity stunt by a special effects company or even a movie trailer, but then it had gone on and on without ceasing. He kept waiting to hear an announcer say, "coming next Summer," or to start listing off the names of actors tapped for the parts, but none of that ever came.

He supposed he had George to thank for saving his life. The Korovega's attack on Knoxville probably would have killed him the other day if he had still been there. His apartment was well away from the burning of downtown, but he had no way of knowing what the fallout elsewhere was like. The news was doing its best not to report much of the rioting—not yet, anyway.

But George had led him to Owen's apartment, and now they were here. People he knew, even in passing, were dead, but he was still alive. Whatever guilt he might feel for his powerlessness at the time was buried deep by his relief at still being alive and his determination to make sure no one else died.

He adjusted the gorget again, turned in place, and retraced his steps.

* * *

"Again!" Ben barked. Katrina had been pushing hard during the last two hours of her training session. She displayed more determination than Ben would have expected, and also proved to be a fast learner. They had taken very few breaks, and it had been Katrina herself who set the rapid pace of their lesson.

Katrina darted forward and threw a wild punch. Ben reacted, moving as expected for the pseudo-drill they were working on, by throwing a strong block. Against a real attack, especially given their size difference, her punch would thud harmlessly against his forearm. The sudden, unexpected stop in her attack would have meant a loss of balance, which Ben would have taken advantage of with a haymaker from the other hand.

Katrina, though, had been working on feints ever since Ben realized how light on her feet she was. It had been easy enough to get her to attack—though the process of building up her toughness to being struck was still in its infancy—but she presently lacked the martial-mindedness to win a wrestling match against someone like Ben. What she had, though, was fast reaction times and Ben was cultivating those first.

Katrina's rear foot came down a fraction of a second earlier than Ben expected. It landed near her leading foot, allowing for an instantaneous change of balance. She darted that same foot out to the side, the formerly rear foot now leading her action, and crouched low.

She withdrew her initial punch, turning the motion from a seemingly uncontrolled attack into a snakelike defense. In one motion, she was inside rather than outside Ben's guard, pressing against the inside of his forearm with the back of her wrist.

With his guard opened, he started to step back, but she had calculated her followup strike properly this time. Her other hand hooked in, smacking against Ben's cheekbone. While her physical strength was not terribly impressive, she used her shoulder the way Ben had taught her and delivered a rather powerful blow. The thick pad on the back of her fingerless sparring gloves took most of the shock out of the blow, but it still knocked Ben's head back.

"I did it!" Katrina exclaimed, bouncing in place with excitement. Other than early on, when Ben was working on her confidence and he had her hit him in the chest several times, that was the first time she had hit him on purpose. For a moment, the ache in her muscles and the sweat soaking every inch of her skin was forgotten.

Ben grinned, but his own look of approval was short lived. He took a quick step forward and slipped one foot behind her feet. In one motion, he grabbed her rear shoulder and, using his hips as a fulcrum, tossed her onto the springy puzzle-piece floor.

Her look of excitement changed to confusion and then to frustration within the span of a few moments.

"What was that for?" she demanded.

Ben straightened up and extended a hand to help her to her feet. "Reminding you not to let yourself get distracted."

"Can't you let me celebrate just for a moment?"

"I did."

She rolled her eyes. "You know what I mean."

Ben shrugged. "Yeah, but what happens if someone's trying to kill you, or worse, and your brain stops you in the middle of the fight so you can celebrate landing the first hit?"

"That won't happen?"

"How you practice is how you fight," he replied. His voice softened for a moment and he added, "normally, it would be fine. Normally, we'd just be fighting for fun, so there's not much harm in a little celebration. But now? Now you celebrate too soon and you die."

She seemed to deflate."Point taken."

"Don't let it get to you." He clapped her on the shoulder in a gesture of camaraderie. "You're making progress, trust me. I wouldn't be so hard on you if you wasn't."

She nodded and dusted herself off. "Thanks, I think."

"Need a break?"

She shook her head. "Let's go one more time, then we can stop for some water."

He nodded. "Ready?"

Katrina nodded, or started to. She lowered her head in what seemed for half a second to be a nod and then sprang forward again, fists raised.

Ben, legitimately caught by surprise, brought one hand up to protect his face and threw the other forward in a counter attack. The conscious part of his brain was impressed with her speed and determination, but the unconscious part pulled the blow to one side because he was still in "training mode" and wanted her to learn to fight, not learn to be knocked backwards by a gloved hand to the face.

Katrina brushed the attack aside, a relatively easy task given that Ben had, whether he intended to or not, aimed wide. Her other hand came forward in a spiral to deflect anything coming from his other side as she aimed a kick at his left flank.

Her kick never connected, because Ben slipped backward with both feet and moved out of range. His brain was still thinking in terms of training, but now he mentally increased the level of his reactions. Rather than throw committed attacks to the wrong targets, he would throw committed attacks to the right targets, but at half strength.

Ben grabbed her ankle as it went by, lunged forward on one foot, and threw his hands upward. Katrina went off balance and her other leg collapsed as her center of gravity was thrown wildly backward.

She flailed for a moment before accepting fate as gravity pulled her to the Earth.

"If you're falling," Ben instructed, "let yourself fall. Better to go down and back up than be helpless because you can't get your feet under you."

She rolled over and came to her hands and knees. Ben stepped forward and telegraphed a kick to her ribs. She froze, but the toe of his boot merely poked gently at her side. She barely felt it though Owen's spare padded jacket, but the impact was more mental than physical.

"Let me guess," she said. "Don't do that?"

"Not unless you're far away. You want to learn how to get back up, you got to put me on the ground first."

She stood, ignoring the light coating of dust she picked up.

Ben stepped back with one foot, then brought it forward again in a snap kick. Katrina darted to one side, but with the wrong leg. Rather than lunging with her front leg, she moved the rear one on instinct, which should have put her at a brief disadvantage. Having her legs crossed like that was an easy way to be, once again, thrown on the ground.

Ben pivoted as his foot came back down and threw a long punch at the side of her head. In her rush to get her feet back under her, Katrina accidentally dropped to one side into the sort of sideways-leaning half crouch that Ben had seen rapier fighters use to avoid attacks to the head.

"Don't stop," she mumbled to herself, echoing the second lesson Ben had taught her an hour before.

She reached up for Ben's arm, but he was already recovering. Unfortunately for her balance, Katrina clamped a hand on his wrist and he jerked her forward. He raised his knee and caught her just hard enough in the stomach to convey that her plan had been a bad one. He stepped away.

By this point, Katrina was breathing heavily yet again. Ben seemed to be as well, but even she could tell he was not nearly as winded as she was. A sheen of sweat stood out on his forehead, but she felt like she was positively dripping.

She eyed Ben, panting and trying to find something in what he had told her that would give her enough of an advantage that she could throw him down at least once. That was all she wanted right then. The thought of actually winning a sparring match was distant, something that could be contemplated another day. At that exact moment, she had only one goal.

Her mind raced. Ben had told her early on that strength was not everything. He told her about leverage, pressure points, and a dozen other esoteric things that she could use to her advantage no matter how much stronger her opponent was. Several times, though, she had fallen into the same trap of trying to box him and she had always lost. Ben was bigger than she was and, more important, boxing was a sport. What she was doing was learning, or trying to lean, was how to disable someone to save her own life. No number of blows to the head from her fists would stop someone Ben's size before he could kill her if that was his intent.

Katrina stood there for a moment, ignoring the words he had said and instead focusing on the ideas. She watched Ben's body language. His guard appeared to be down, but her attacks had failed enough times to tell her that it was an illusion. Her eyes darted from his hands to his feet and finally to his eyes, trying to find some tell that would help her understand what she was doing wrong.

She looked at Ben's eyes and for a moment was shocked to realize he was not looking back at her. A moment passed while she tried to figure out exactly what he was looking at, but then it came to her: he was not looking at anything.

At that moment, Katrina started to understand. He was not watching her, at least not directly. Rather, Ben watched for any movement and let his reflexes do the rest.

How, she wondered, was she supposed to beat that? As the seconds ticked by, she remembered the way Sam had treated her the other day. She remembered the feeling when she realized that Sam trusted her not to be perfect, but to simply do.

And so she did.

Katrina leaned forward, shifting her weight onto her front foot. At the moment when she would have fallen, she sprang off of that foot and threw her other foot forward. Ben had called the move a fleche, something out of sport fencing, but it served her well enough right then. One foot hit the ground, then the second, eating up distance in moments. In three steps, less than a second and a half, she had closed the distance between them.

Ben threw a punch and shifted to the side at the last moment. Any committed attack would, if he timed it correctly, miss him while he himself landed a hit of his own. To his surprise, Katrina never threw an attack, and so there was nothing to dodge.

She threw a hand up to block Ben's punch but missed. The blow struck her in the shoulder like a hammer. In a heartbeat, the entire area was on fire despite the pads, but she finished the movement she had planned anyway. In a way, Ben moving to the side actually helped her. Her torso shot forward as her knees bent and she slammed her left shoulder into Ben's stomach.

He gasped involuntarily as the blow knocked the wind out of his lungs. He had been hit harder and with much more effect, but causing pain was not her goal.

Katrina reached under his thigh with her left hand. With her right, she grabbed at Ben's shoulder above her head. In one movement, she lifted with her left hand and pushed with her right, and Ben went over onto the ground. He had shown her the technique earlier, using it to nearly comedic effect on her in the process. It had almost gone forgotten in her stubborn insistence at trying to beat him at a strength game.

He hit the ground with an audible thud and she stood over him for a moment before pointing a finger at his chest and saying, "bang."

Ben laughed. The sound was mixed with gasps for air as his breathing slowed. "Well done," he said. Then repeated, "well done."

She nodded. "So?"

He grinned and laughed again. "Right, right."

Ben shifted on the ground, pivoting like the needle on a compass. In a single movement, Katrina went from standing beside him to standing between his feet. He raised one foot slightly and then spun in place. The higher of his feet hit her in the knees while the lower one raked her own feet out from under her. Ben then pushed upward sharply with his hands, brought his feet under his hips, and sprang upward. He almost made it to his feet before she hit the puzzle-pieces underfoot.

"That is how you get on your feet again." He extended a hand. "Now let's get some water, hmm? You're making me work awful hard."

Katrina took his hand and hauled herself to her feet. "Thanks."

Ben opened the basement door. The newest of their refrigerators had been installed just inside and stocked with nothing other than water, sports drinks, juices, and iced tea. He opened the door, reached in, and produced a pair of bottles.

He tossed one to Katrina, who completely missed catching it. It hit her square in the chest and thumped to the mat and she grinned sheepishly as she realized how much she had been flailing her hands, trying to catch it.

"I meant to do that."

Ben only grinned.

Katrina downed half of her water in one go, then replaced the plastic cap. "Just tell me you didn't let me do that."

Ben shook his head. He squatted on his haunches and leaned against the outside wall of the house. "Wouldn't dream of it. I'll give you an opening, yeah, but I ain't about to let you get away with bad technique. Y'did good."

She smiled. "Thanks."

"Any time," he said. "Really. I'd have taught you all this anyway, if you'd asked. It don't take the end of the world for me to enjoy teaching somebody something."

"I'm serious. I knew Will for a few years when I lived in Arizona, but that's about it. We 'sort-of' dated for a few weeks. It didn't work out, but we stayed friends, and right now I'm really glad of it. I had just moved to New Mexico a month or so ago and didn't really know anyone there, so when the news about the Korovega came on TV, I didn't know what to do."

Ben nodded, listening. He suspected that sort of thing was happening all across the country, if not all across the world. That was the worst part of the tragedy as far as he was concerned. People like him and the others who had come to his house would survive or they would die fighting because they had each other. People with no one, tourists or those newly-moved to an area would be in dire straights.

He shuddered to think of the sort of despair that people with no one to turn to would be facing. Assuming, that is, that they survived long enough against the Korovega's march to experience anything other than fear or confusion. Not for the first time, he wondered how many people had died in the first few minutes of their attack on Washington.

What made the feeling hit harder was knowing that, if not for people like Jessie and Owen, he would be one of the ones with nowhere to go.

Katrina went on, saying, "so until Will called, I was running in circles, trying to figure out where I could go. I never even thought about calling him first. I mean, we talked online, but I was in another state and..."

She stopped, took a deep breath and let it out slowly. Between the fading adrenaline rush from fighting Ben and the general timbre of her emotions right then, maintaining her composure was a challenge all its own. Her curly blond hair was tied up in a tight braid behind her head, but the sweat and exertion of their training had broken a few wisps loose here and there. Now that she had stopped moving, they tickled her face and ears and she swatted at them for a moment before stopping and, with forced calm, tucking them back.

Another deep breath, and she said, "anyway, he calls me and asks if I'd seen the news. 'Who hasn't?' I said, and he asked if I had anywhere to go. And, like I said, I didn't. I barely knew what I was going to do that night, let alone until the Korovega came for me. I mean, my first instinct was to hide under my desk. That tells you how prepared I was. I worked in an office, for God's sake. I can't fight. Or I couldn't fight before. I can now, I suppose.

"Anyway, he tells me he's on his way already and should be there that night and to pack everything I absolutely needed."

Katrina took another deep breath and continued. She spoke much calmer but no less quick, and went on, "and then we drove here nonstop. We'd all trade off drivers so that we could make it with as few stops as we had absolutely had to make. Will packed food where we could get to it, so we ate on the road and only stopped for bathroom breaks.

"I never want to do something like that again.

"But, yeah, now I'm here, and I just wanted to say thanks for taking me in."

Ben smiled. He thought of a dozen things to say, but none of them seemed quite right. One was too cliché, another too much like an empty platitude, and a third would have made it sound like she owed him when she did no such thing. Instead, he settled on a simple, "you're welcome."

Another few minutes passed as they finished their water and Katrina said, "come on, we don't have all day, right?"

Ben laughed and jerked a thumb over his shoulder at where Marcus, Will, and George were working. "Don't forget that you've got a shift building the wall coming up after we're done here, and guard duty after that."

She grinned in return and rolled her shoulders like she had seen Ben do. It worked, loosening up some of the muscles in there, especially the ones screaming in protest at having never been used that way before. Aloud, she said, "I've seen the schedule. You've got a shift too."

"Yeah, but I..." Ben started to say.

"You what?"

"I was gonna say that I was stronger than you were, but that don't matter all that much, really. It's determination that'll get you through today."

"What about tomorrow?"

"More determination."

"And the next day?"

"Same. You're still alive and you keep fighting."

Katrina smiled. For such a simple explanation of things, it was surprisingly comforting. She had been afraid before. Before getting into Will's car, she had been scared that the people he was taking her to stay with would reject her because she had no real survival skills. Knowing how much the others were pushing themselves to train her made her feel welcome, and it awakened something fierce inside her.

"Alright," Ben said. His voice had once again hardened into the tone he used when teaching, "you made a few mistakes last time..."

Chapter 21

To say that Key Springs was a "twisty-turny road" was to dramatically understate exactly how many sharp curves it possessed. The road itself was about twice as long as the distance between its two endpoints. In better times, it was a popular destination for drivers with fast cars who wanted a quick thrill on a road where they, probably, would not be pulled over and ticketed. As an actual connecting road, it left much to be desired. The very curves that made it popular for racers meant no end of headaches for people who lived in the area and actually had to use it to get around.

That morning, like so many other roads, the tight curves of Key Springs were devoid of other traffic. The road itself was so twisted because it carved a path through the convoluted valleys and hills that formed Oak Ridge's natural border. Sam suspected that the odds of people still being here were high, but they saw no one. Between the poor road connections and the hills themselves, they would have a better chance than most of hiding out and surviving.

In short order, the two of them made it to Oak Ridge. They were traveling too fast and the motorcycle was too loud for it to be considered sneaking. Nevertheless, the feeling remained because of how few people they had seen.

More importantly, they had seen no more police since the checkpoint. Sam made the turn onto the road that, a century before when Oak Ridge had still been the so-called the "Secret City" formed the original perimeter, and slowed down to something approximating the speed limit.

Owen spoke over their helmet intercom. "No cops."

Sam nodded. "Yeah. They're here somewhere though, they have to be."

"Unless everyone's on blockade duty."

She shook her head. "Doubt it. They probably don't have much more than a hundred officers on these blockades, assuming they've stopped up every major road into town."

"But not Key Springs," Owen observed.

Sam nodded agreement. "Yeah. No one's going to bring an army down Key Springs."

"Point. When the Guard gets here, that's going to free up a lot of manpower, too."

"The Guard's already here."

"It is?" he asked, surprise in his voice.

"Didn't you catch the news this morning?"

"No. I was a little preoccupied."

"Yeah." Sam was quiet for a moment, then, "I had it on when I was ordering supplies. After that Korovega showed up at Bull Run yesterday, they sped things up a little. Not that you'd notice," she added. Her sarcastic smirk came through clear in her voice. "Since you were so far away, and all."

"I'm not surprised. But then why were the guards by Elza still cops? You'd think the Guard would take over being, you know, guards."

Sam laughed. Not at him, per se, she simply found the way he phrased his comment funny. If Oak Ridge was truly on lockdown, then that was precisely what the National Guard was going to be doing. They had the firepower and the local Police knew the area; between the two groups, they could easily patrol the entire city with enough force to quell any rioting that might rear its head.

Without knowing how to fight them, though, Sam had her doubts as to how effective even the National Guard would be against the Korovega here. Privately, she even doubted how much they would listen to what she had Owen had come to tell them. They had killed one, true, but they were also "merely" civilians. She hoped the soldiers and police would take any help they could get, but she had rather low expectations of that actually happening without some sort of extenuating circumstances.

That was why they were doing things the way they were doing them. If they got the civilian population of the city behind them, preferably without having to demonstrate their claims against an actual live Korovega, then the Guard and the police would be that much more likely to listen.

Sam slowed to a stop. The roads were deserted, but a few cars still sat in driveways here and there. Even though no one was outside, the houses around them still felt inhabited. Sam could not put her finger on it, but the atmosphere felt different than it had in Clinton or Rocky Top. No one had been watching them there, but here in Oak Ridge, the air was charged with tension.

"Don't stop," Owen muttered into the intercom. He sounded as nervous as she felt. They were beginning to see heads and silhouettes in windows around them.

Sam nodded and stayed in low gear, cruising just fast enough to avoid falling over. Owen reached for his sword, but against scared human beings, it was a poor weapon from the back of a motorcycle. Instead, he kept one hand on his shotgun, not quite on the grip and trigger but close enough that he could raise it to threaten or defend. In front of him, he noticed Sam had done the same thing.

They proceeded like that for several minutes, watching for the nebulous spot that they could call "a good place to start."

A few turns later, the atmosphere changed. If there were people still watching them, something in the air told Owen that they were less scared. Perhaps this was a more heavily patrolled area, he thought, and so the people felt more secure. Or, his thoughts continued as he watched the buildings pass by on either side, perhaps this area was patrolled less and the ones who lived here were reminded less frequently of their dire circumstances. Either way, it seemed like a better place to begin their mission.

Sam had the same idea. Before he could give voice to it, she said, "we need to do this soon."

Owen nodded. "I agree. I'm turning off my mic so I don't yell in your ear."

"Thanks," Sam replied.

Owen could hear the amusement in her voice. At least one of us is enjoying themselves, he thought with a wry smile.

He twisted in his seat and retrieved the burlap sack from where it had been tied to the luggage rack.

"Now for the part that will either get us labeled heroes or psychopaths," Owen muttered, picking at the knot in the bag's strings with his gloved fingers. He failed, cursed, took one glove off, and returned to the task. "Who the hell tied this?" he muttered.

"Ben," Sam replied.

"Figures. This is some kind of freaky sailor's knot."

"Hand it here and I'll do it."

"No," he said, "I've almost. Got. There!"

Sam laughed. "Yes," she said to herself more than to Owen, "hand me the bag with the severed head in it; that's a great thing to mess with while you're driving, Sam."

She heard the amused grin in his voice as he replied, "that thought crossed my mind, too."

Owen set the bag between his knees, a process that was only tolerable because he was more fixated on getting his glove back on his hand than he was in the contents of the sack just then. It had long since stopped bleeding, before being stuffed into the bag to begin with in fact, but a severed Korovega head was still not high on his list of things he wanted in his lap. Only by ignoring what it actually was could he tolerate being in such close proximity to it.

Finally, with the bag untied and his gloves firmly back on his hands, Owen reached into the bag and withdrew the head, holding it by the hair.

"Strange" was the first word that came to Owen's mind to describe the head held in his hands. It was not quite ugly, but neither was it anything that a normal human would call attractive, or even particularly pleasant to look at. It was decidedly inhuman, and no amount of cognitive detachment could make him believe that the thing in his hands was anything other than a monster.

Up close, its ash gray skin was mottled with small scars and imperfections, most notably the half-healed gouge he had left in its cheek when he fought it outside Bull Run. Extensive bruising covered the face where Ben had beaten it to death, or at least to defenselessness, before removing its head. The nose, once a small and pointed feature, was swollen and had been caved in along with the bone around its left eye. Owen supposed it was even paler than usual, given how little blood there had to be left in the head, but the way the veins stood out against the nearly-translucent skin was unnerving.

Aside from the white topknot, the Korovega's entire head was covered with a fine fuzz of nearly transparent hair. There was nothing that could be called a beard or a mustache, or even eyebrows. Rather the hair was a uniform length everywhere. Owen searched his brain for what he knew about aquatic animals and their hair and supposed it made sense for something that seemed to spend a lot of time underwater.

Its eyelids were closed, but he remembered the eyes underneath all too well from that morning. He remembered burning yellow eyes, more snake than cat, staring back at him. Its eyes had pupils with vertical slits, further reinforcing the image of a crocodile or other sort of reptile. They were too wide and sat too close together in a face whose top half was too narrow and flat to be human. Alive, those eyes had held a fierce intelligence, perhaps even a philosophical mind. Even now that the creature was dead, Owen felt a strange majesty in its features.

The Korovega's jaw was long, narrow like the rest of its head, and lined with pointed teeth. Strong muscles anchored it to the monster's cheekbones, but now it hung slack.

Owen shuddered. He wanted to throw the thing away. He would have been happy to never look at it again. Despite his reservations, he knew that he would be looking at those faces many more times. Better to look a little longer at this dead face, he thought, than be unprepared for the horror when confronted with another living one.

And the people had to know.

Owen reached up to the side of his helmet and flicked the switch that controlled the intercom to the "off" position, unlatched the lower half of the helmet's face guard, and removed it. He lifted the visor as well. Neither gesture was necessary for his voice to carry, but it would be clearer without the face shield in place.

He raised the Korovega's skull high over his own head, careful to keep it slightly to one side just in case it was not done bleeding after all, and scanned the houses around him. The feeling of eyes watching him was intense, like looking out onto a packed theater where the audience was hidden by the glare of lights overhead.

He and Sam had discussed what to say on the drive there, but now that the time came, he found his mouth dry and throat tight. This was not where he imagined himself the week before. Never in his strangest dreams had he been sitting on the back of Sam's motorcycle with the severed head of one of the creatures that seeded mankind's nightmares hanging by the scalp.

He opened his mouth.

"My name is Owen Gene Madoc!" he shouted, brandishing the head like a trophy. He spoke clearly, enunciating every word by itself. "I. Killed. This Korovega!"

He fell silent for a moment, letting that sink in. He knew it was a lie, or at least a stretched truth, and so did Sam. She had insisted on telling it that way for the impact it would have on anyone listening. She argued that crediting Ben as well, because he was not present, would weaken the impact of his testimony.

His mind was still too busy. Owen closed his eyes and pushed all of the distractions, contingencies, and justifications out of the way. He was already committed to doing things this way and letting himself dwell on anything that was not right in front of his face would slow them down.

"You can fight them, but your guns will not work!" he continued, growing louder. It was another stretched truth, because the bullets themselves would still maim and kill just as easily as if they had hit a human. The hard part was getting the bullet to the Korovega in the first place. It was easier, they decided, to just tell them things this way.

Owen scanned the street around him. There were clear faces at some of the windows now, and a few doors had been cracked slightly to let sound in better. That was a good start, he thought. The news would spread on its own now.

He continued his address. There was more they had to know. "You have to fight them up close. They cannot use their energy weapons at point blank range! Take up machetes and knives, hammers and axes, poles and clubs and fight them!"

With his free hand, Owen drew his sword and held it above his head. Beside the dull lump of the Korovega's skull, the sword gleamed bright in the sun. He tried to avoid shining the reflection in anyone's window or door.

Rather than address the sword directly, he shouted, "take up arms and fight back!"

He slid the sword back into its scabbard, dropped the head back into the burlap sack, and held it by his side. Knotting it would have been safer, but would ruin the image. Ben and Will had impressed upon him enough the importance of perception that he was acutely aware of how his presentation would come across at every step.

If it worked as well as everyone thought it would, Owen reflected, he could deal with a few exaggerations and grandiose gestures here and there. He hated it, personally. It felt like showing off, but Sam disagreed. He hoped she was right.

He flicked the intercom switch on his helmet back on. He left the face cover off; there was no sense in attaching and unattaching it every few minutes as they rode around. He did, however, lower the visor.

"Alright, let's go."

Sam nodded. They had never actually stopped, only slowed down enough for people to easily hear him. He wished for a megaphone, but no one at the house had had one and, more to the point, using a megaphone would attract more attention at any given time than they were ready to deal with. He had not, at the time, realized that part of that "extra attention" might not even be human, but the thought crossed his mind now and he was suddenly thankful they were doing all of this without volume enhancements.

* * *

The two of them repeated the exercise over and over again as the sun climbed higher into the sky. After a few hours, they stopped for lunch under a shade tree far back from the main roads. Sandwiches, fruit, juice, and coffee did not exactly add up to a gourmet meal, but they made do. After riding all morning, it was nice just to get off of the motorcycle for half an hour, stretch, and relax.

Having eaten, they resumed their mission. Traveling and speaking on a full stomach proved to be much easier; the food balanced out their nerves. As they went, more and more people seemed interested in Owen's short speech. He suspected people were calling friends and relatives, telling them about the strange sight he and Sam must have made. Except for once when they encountered an elderly man sitting on his front porch, no one ever left their house when the motorcycle passed by. Despite that, they saw more and more faces in windows and at doors at the day wore on.

"You think they'll do it?" he asked through the intercom. They had finished speaking at yet another street and ridden on in silence for several blocks before his mind started to wander and the gears began to turn. If no one proved willing to fight the Korovega, their effort would not exactly be wasted, but a population unwilling to defend itself would be easy prey when the gray devils came for them.

Sam was silent for almost a minute more. Owen, thinking something was wrong with the bike or the road, was about to speak up again when she finally replied. Sam took a deep breath, but, "maybe," was all she said.

"You going to elaborate on that?" he asked, wishing he could see her face. Trying to discern her thoughts from the back side of her helmet was not terribly easy.

"How many people, between Ben, you, and me did we call Monday?"

Surprised by the question, Owen took a moment to reply. When he did, he said, "I don't know. A hundred? More?"

Sam nodded. "And how many showed up at your apartment?"

Owen sighed. "Three."

Her helmet bobbed up and down again. "So call it a percent and a half. And that's the people we knew—friends, coworkers, even a few relatives. And out of all those people, three showed up. Advertisers would kill for that kind of return. These people," she waved an arm at some of the houses as they drove, "don't know us. They've got no reason to believe us."

"But we've got the proof right here!" he protested, holding up the bag. He realized she could not see it, but he still felt compelled to brandish the thing as though it were the important part of his point.

"Proof, yes. But how often has that sort of thing actually swayed people?"

He hesitated. "Often?"

Sam shook her head. "I wish. No, we'll be lucky if we get a tenth of a percent of the city to fight, at least at first."

"When it starts working, though," Owen said, "the numbers will go up."

"Possibly," Sam agreed. "Or when people start dying, even if they're killing Korovega, others may give up. Throw down their weapons. Maybe even hesitate before picking one up in the first place."

"You're not telling me anything I don't already know."

"Then why ask?"

Coming from anyone else, that question in the tone she delivered it might have been an insult. Her words were certainly clipped and sharp like an insult. Owen had known her for most of his life, though, and knew exactly what that tone of voice meant.

She was challenging him, not insulting him. Clearly, she thought there was something, some crucial part of the plan or even of human nature itself that he was missing.

They turned a corner onto another street and slowed down. Unlike the others, people were actually out in the yards and on the porches here. They seemed wary, but not exactly tense. Perhaps they had heard about the two of them from others they had passed, or perhaps there was simply something different about this street versus the others.

Sam also saw weapons with these people. They had mostly shotguns with a few hunting rifles here and there and a scattering of pistols. The hair stood up on the back of her neck for a moment as she wondered if she had taken a wrong turn somewhere and ended up in a part of town she should not have.

Within the space of a few seconds, her hand had tightened on the throttle again. She was half a motion from rocketing away. She could shoot down the short street faster than any of the locals could aim at her and be on her way before any real danger could find them.

Before she did that, she scanned the street again. Her eyes picked out dozens of people with weapons, but then a single realization calmed her nerves. None of the people were actually holding those weapons. Rifles and shotguns were leaned casually against chairs and porch railings. They sat within easy grasp, but no one reached for them. They were ready for a fight, she realized, but not looking for one.

"Here?" she asked.

"What?" Owen replied, roused from his thoughts by her question. He had been trying to come up with a way to improve the odds of people actually taking up arms and fighting against the Korovega. Everything short of conscription, after he took into account how terrifying the Korovega were, resulted in abysmal numbers. Even with conscription, the numbers were poor, because he expected deserters.

"Do the speech here?" she asked. "This lot looks like they're more ready to fight than the others."

Owen raised his visor and looked around. He pointed past Sam's shoulder to a spot three houses further along the road. "We'll start there."

She nodded and applied a barely noticeable amount of force to the throttle. The bike sped forward slightly, covering the distance to Owen's spot in a few seconds.

He looked around, scanning the faces of the people watching them. They looked wary, he thought, then, "they're scared."

"Yeah."

That was what she had been getting at before they turned onto this street. The average human being would be terrified of what was happening to the world. Doubtless, they had all seen the news from Sunday, and so they had seen the Korovega destroying hundreds of well armed soldiers en masse. Not only that, but Knoxville was burning only twenty or so miles down the road and, just the day before, a Korovega had killed two police and dozens of others outside Bull Run. To add to the constant reminders, great, black-winged birds patrolled the skies.

They were scared because no one had any proof that anyone survived a violent encounter with a Korovega. Dozens of conflicting versions of the story about the fight at the Steam Plant circulated around. In their shoes, Sam knew that she would likely be just as scared. She had her friends, and together—all of them together—they would survive. Did these people, she asked herself silently, have that kind of moral support?

But now, the man who stood up to the Korovega was in their neighborhood. He was here to tell them how they could fight back. She wanted to believe that would be enough.

Tension grew around them as Owen withdrew the contents of the burlap sack and held the foul-smelling head high. The houses on either side erupted into a dozen conversations that melded into an unintelligible murmur. A few people even went for their weapons. Sam fervently hoped that no one would panic and do anything stupid before Owen could explain exactly why he was holding a severed head.

"I am Owen Gene Madoc," he said, "and I killed a Korovega!"

The neighborhood felt silent as he talked.

Unlike previous streets that day, no one seemed afraid to listen or even to talk back as Owen spoke. General confusion and a few cries of, "the hell they don't! Let me at 'em!" when he mentioned guns not working against the Korovega answered him, but even those died out quickly.

Like before, Sam let the motorcycle roll forward just fast enough to stay upright. By the time Owen was nearing the end of his spiel, they had passed four houses with their small, postage-stamp yards.

Owen ended his speech the same way he had done all morning, but this time the people listening cheered when he finished. He sat for a moment, watching their reaction and providing the ever-important image of him holding the Korovega's head aloft for everyone to fix in their brains. He lowered the head as Sam applied a little more pressure to the throttle and began accelerating.

That was when people began to leave their porches and yards. One by one, they came forward, toward the bike. At first, Sam was content to let them come. They were far away, relatively speaking, and she could twist the throttle wide open at any moment.

As more of them approached, especially coming into the street from the houses ahead of them, she grew nervous. People to the side, she could avoid. It would be much harder to thread between the crowd ahead of them without hurting anyone, and they continued to come closer to one another. She saw, too, that none of them were armed. The weapons that had been scattered around porches and chairs were still there, but that was little consolation.

The emotions of the crowd seemed primarily to be a mix of relief and celebration, but an undercurrent of desperation and a definite feeling of high energy stress ran through the air. Relief and desperation would explain why they were trying to surround the motorcycle; they wanted—no, they needed—to see up close that Owen had been telling the truth. But the tension in the air felt wrong, like something was waiting to snap.

The crowd was still cheering and hooting in a dozen different ways, but no one was rushing Big Blue. They came on steadily, but even a mob of tense and frustrated people knew better than to run towards a heavily armed man and woman atop a running motorcycle.

"Owen," she said warily, hoping he had switched the intercom back on in his helmet. At low speeds like they were at, they could normally converse without it. To be heard over the engine and the noise of the crowd, however, their voices would carry farther than she wanted. So she spoke too quietly to be heard without it.

"I'm watching them," he replied. His voice was, if possible, even quieter.

"So am I. And I don't like what I see."

"What do you want to do?"

"Do we gun it and go?"

Owen scanned the crowd. The mix of emotions on their faces was strange. Some came toward them wide-eyed and eager, and others came warily. He locked eyes with one man who seemed more suspicious of them than anything. He hung toward the back of the crowd, inching forward only as much as he had to to avoid being left out by himself. Across the span of people, he saw what he assumed to be a family huddling close to one another. They were all wide-eyed, but with terror, not excitement.

He understood how Sam felt. Too many conflicting emotions surging around them to be safe at close range. Suddenly, he knew why even beloved leaders often stood on balconies. Even if the crowd approaching them wanted to congratulate them or thank them or any of a hundred other good things, it was still composed of an easy hundred people with emotions running high.

The crowd was not dangerous as it was, he thought. But there were a lot of people around them now and the escape route was growing progressively smaller by the moment. It was a powder keg, certainly, and he had no idea what might set it off.

"Be ready," he muttered into the microphone. Sam nodded and he switched the intercom back off. Much louder, he shouted, "that's close enough!"

The crowd stopped, sort of. Most of them had not even made it out of their yards, though a few further ahead had sprinted out into the street before approaching more slowly. The general press of people ceased moving toward them as a whole, but only about half of them actually stopped moving. The others slowed by varying degrees and eventually stayed in place.

Big Blue continued to roll slowly.

"How'd you do it?" someone in the crowd shouted.

Owen's adrenaline spiked for a moment, as he watched the people around him coming even closer. Rather than watching the road ahead—he trusted Sam more than enough to leave the driving to her—he scanned the crowd over and over again. His eyes never landed on any one person for more than a heartbeat, just long enough to make a snap judgment about whether they were a threat or not. So far, no one was.

"I had help," Owen admitted. He had never put the Korovega's sword away, and now held it over his head. From a distance, there was nothing to show that it was inhuman to the average eye. Sam had his saber, but she was in no position to draw it. Another white lie would not hurt things, thought, adding, "and I had this!"

"Is that a fuckin' sword?" demanded someone in the crowd as, almost instinctually, the mass of people surged forward another few feet to get a better look.

Owen resisted, barely, the urge to roll his eyes and sigh in exasperation. There were not very many things that a three-and-change foot long, thin, piece of shiny metal that ended with a point at one end and a cage of wires and bars at the other could be. On that list, for all practical purposes, were "sword" and "really long dagger." Still, it was a question Owen had grown used to after years of practicing in public parks.

Hearing it in the middle of the apocalypse, however, was almost cause for laughter.

He wanted to yell something sarcastic back, perhaps along the lines of, "no, it's a car antenna, you bloody nitwit," but he resisted that urge as well. Instead, he simply sought out the person in the crowd who had asked the question and made brief eye contact with her.

After a moment, he said, "yes, it's a sword. In fact," he raised the Korovega head again, "up until I took it, this sword used to belong to this Korovega!"

"Took it from his cold dead hands!" yelled another anonymous voice in the crowd. The voice had an accent that sounded vaguely Irish, but Owen never found who it belonged to. "Hells yeah! Woo!"

"Goddamn right!" yelled another.

Shouts and cheers answered the two exclamations, but the crowd stayed where it was. The tension began to ebb as well, at least as far as Owen was concerned. He could still feel the restless energy in the air, but now it was directed at something other than him.

Someone stepped out into the street in front of the motorcycle. "Don't you think you're being a little irresponsible?"

The person, a man approaching thirty or so, wore a red t-shirt and cargo shorts. Owen recognized him as the man he pegged a few minutes before as being suspicious of them. What set him apart now was that he was directly blocking Sam's line of travel and stood only a few dozen yards ahead of them.

She cursed and eased off the throttle slightly. The bike remained upright, but the ride instantly grew less smooth as the big machine started to wobble slightly from left to right. She turned the handlebars back and forth, taking the motorcycle through a zig-zag pattern that kept it upright at the lower speed.

"Pardon?" Sam asked.

Owen lowered the sword and the Korovega head, but kept a firm hold on both. He leaned slightly to one side, but re-centered himself when Sam had to jerk the bike roughly to the other side to maintain balance. He settled for tilting his head slightly and watching over her shoulder, which was easy enough given their height differences.

"Riling all these people up," the stranger said. "Don't you think that's wrong?"

"I fail to see how," Sam replied. Her voice was flat, betraying none of the concentration required to keep the motorcycle upright.

The stranger laughed. "Really? Really? All you're doing is getting these people killed! Your little speech, your demonstration here, what's it going to do, hmm?"

The crowd murmured, unsettled.

"I..." Sam began, but the man continued.

"Everyone's going to go out and get killed by the Korovega!" he shouted, then turned in a circle, addressing the crowd. "All of you!"

A wave of unease passed through the crowd at that, as though they had not yet considered that option. They began to move in chaotic patterns.

"So you'd rather sit at home and wait than fight?" Sam asked, trying to keep her mounting anger out of her voice.

The man laughed. The sound was thin and tight. "Of course! At home, I have a couch and a TV and a microwave and a bed! At home, I can sleep on something comfortable and eat my own food and when the end comes, I'll still be comfortable!"

"Do the rest of you feel this way?" Owen shouted. He suspected most of the crowd was too far away to hear the other man's voice clearly, but his jerky movements and wide-eyed stare conveyed more that words could at a distance.

A murmur of, "no," and other, similar responses circulated around him. He heard a few answers of, "yes," but not many.

"If you fight, will you die?" Owen asked. Before anyone could answer the rhetorical question, he went on, saying, "possibly. I watched a good friend die this morning, killed by the Korovega!

"But if you don't fight, if you give up, will you die? Yes! They will find you and they will kill you just like they've killed thousands, maybe millions of your fellow men and women already."

A voice in the crowd, from somewhere behind and to his right shouted, "if we fight them, where will you be?"

Owen thought for a second. That was a question he and Sam had not prepared for on their ride into Oak Ridge. He knew staying in Oak Ridge was going to be impossible, least of all because his home was now at Ben's house. He and Sam had left the area for a reason and it would take an even more pressing reason to bring them back for good.

On the other hand, he thought, the man in the red shirt was right. Abandoning everyone after riling up their fighting spirits was cruel. He was no leader; he was a fighter, but someone needed to show these people how to do that. So he answered the best he could, trying his best to neither lie to them nor give them false hope.

"I'll be fighting them, too," he said.

"Alone?" The voice that asked was a new one, to his left.

Owen shook his head. His initial response was about to be something about fighting with his friends and relying on them, but just like he could not stay to oversee everyone here in Oak Ridge, neither could anyone else leave Ben's house permanently.

Plus, he thought with an inward chuckle, appealing to the power of friendship only works in the movies.

"Not if people like you," he replied, making a sweeping motion with his sword across most of the crowd, "are fighting them too."

Silence fell across the crowd while the stranger continued to bar their way. Sam examined him through her tinted faceplate. His posture looked scared, like everyone else's, but he seemed to be ready to fight. Whether or not he was going to be fighting her, Owen, or the Korovega remained to be seen. Despite his talk of hiding at home and being unwilling to fight, he stood there tense, ready to lash out. Whatever his ultimate intentions, he made no move to get out of the way of her motorcycle as it crept forward. Finally, she had to stop and put her foot down on the pavement.

"If you don't want to fight," Sam said, quiet enough so that her voice would not carry anywhere beyond the few feet between her and the stranger in front of them, "that's fine. Not everyone needs to, or even should, pick up a weapon. But we're all in this together. What were you doing last week?"

The question seemed to surprise him, and the stranger took a few moments to reply. Finally, he said, "stocking grocery store shelves. But before that, I worked in a machine shop."

"So don't fight." Once again, the man looked surprised. Sam continued, "build things instead. People are going to need machines, generators, even simple tools. Can you do that?"

He swallowed hard and nodded. His voice was shaky when he said, "yeah. Yeah, I can do that. I'll just, yeah, I'll do what I can."

Owen touched Sam's shoulder. "Good job," he muttered.

"Thanks," she said, then, "that better not be the head-holding hand."

He laughed. "I put it back in the bag."

"That's not much better," she replied, but he could hear the smile in her voice. "Anyway, good job to you, too. Looks like this may pay off after all."

Owen nodded. "If this errand of ours can save, well," he sighed, "if it can save a quarter of the people living here, we'll be better off than we would otherwise."

"If we make a difference for even one person, it was worth it."

"On to the next neighborhood?" he asked.

Sam sped up until the motorcycle was stable again. "Yeah, let's go."

"One thing first," he said. Louder, he shouted, "tell everyone you know that there's hope to beat them!"

The motorcycle's big engine only drowned out the roar of the crowd when they rounded the corner at the end of the street.

"Now where?" Sam asked once they had passed a few streets and things had quieted back down. Now that they were traveling at speed, they used the intercom again.

"Keep heading west as far as I'm concerned," Owen replied. Without the faceplate in place, his voice was muffled by the wind beating against the microphone inside the helmet, but still clear enough.

"You don't have a master plan?" she teased.

Owen laughed, loud. "Hardly. I'm making this up as we go. Can't you tell?"

Sam laughed. "I suspected as much. Why west?"

"That's where the labs and the reactors are. There are going to be more people with weapons on that end of town."

"You think so?"

"I assume so."

"I'd say we don't have all day, but," she grinned inside her helmet, and gunned the engine around a corner, "today, we do."

Owen gave his talk once more before they neared the highway to Oliver Springs. In the distance, the flashing blue lights of another Police blockade were clear.

Sam slowed at the end of the side street they were on. The police were set up in an intersection, using the same formation they had on the other end of town.

"Well, that kills that plan," she said with frustration. "I don't really want to navigate around that mess."

"Sam..." Owen said. There was wariness in his voice. He taped her on the shoulder and pointed.

She looked where he indicated. The blockade was a bustle of activity. Officers were moving back and forth, passing around what looked like a clipboard or tablet. An entire conversation passed between them, conveyed in a few moments of eye contact.

"Owen Gene Madoc," boomed a distorted voice from a megaphone, "please approach the line with your hands in the air."

Sam hesitated. "Do we run for it?"

Owen shook his head. "That would only end up with them chasing us, see?" he pointed to the cars on either side of the intersection. They had closed their doors and the officers inside were moving around, securing things in case they had to take off.

On the far side of the intersection, at the edge of his vision, something moved.

"You are not under arrest," the megaphone continued. Its volume brought his full attention back on the checkpoint. As strident as it sounded, the words themselves were of little comfort. "We only wish to talk to you."

Owen muttered into the intercom. "That doesn't sound all that ba—"

He never finished that thought, because all hell broke loose on the far side of the blockade. First one car disappeared in a blue-white flash, then a second vaporized in a sudden burst of actinic light.

As one, the police turned, Owen and Sam completely forgotten as reality sunk in.

Sam started to turn the bike away.

"No."

"What?" she demanded.

"We go down there."

There was no arguing with him, she realized. She knew instantly that if she turned away, that Owen would jump off of the motorcycle and run on foot to help. She also knew that if she ran, and if he survived, he would never forgive her.

With a snarled curse, she twisted the throttle hard and whipped the motorcycle around, leading it into hellfire itself.

Chapter 22

The world ahead of them burned. Ornamental trees on the left side of the road had been flash ignited by the Korovega's energy beam as it tore through the parked police cruisers. The car on the opposite side sat in the middle of a flat concrete pad flanked by turn lanes, or it had up until moments before. It and the two policemen inside it no longer existed. The only thing marking their presence was a shallow trench where the Korovega's beam disintegrated the concrete. The trench gradually deepened until the path of the beam disappeared under the crumbling pavement of the hillside.

The man who had addressed Owen over the megaphone seconds before had turned his back on the advancing motorcycle. He raised his rifle as his heart leaped into rapid-fire beating and fear-adrenaline raced like ice through his veins. To his left and right, his comrades in the service were raising their weapons as well.

Their job had been to guard the road to Oliver Springs, not one of the main roads. They were told to be there "just in case" something happened or some trouble came down from the mountains. The National Guard, the ones with the real weapons, were guarding the main ways in and out of the city by now. In fact, there were three different Guard blockades in straight lines from their position.

The horror in front of his eyes should not have happened, he thought. No one rationally expected this post to even run into any humans, let alone any Korovega.

Already, the other surviving police on the far side of the large intersection were shooting. The Korovega stood off to one side. Now under fire, they held their position behind glowing shields. No matter how many bullets went their way, the only thing that answered was a repetitive, buzzing zap as their shields spat sparks.

"My God," Owen muttered through the intercom. "There's four of them."

Sam nearly dumped the motorcycle as she saw them. Owen was right. Four Korovega, each with a shield out and swords sheathed at their waists, stood at the edge of the road. Behind them was a small green sward and then a creek. To either side of the intersection, the road was almost perfectly straight. Even the road on the far side, away from them, was relatively straight for a short distance. Two of the intersection's four corners butted against empty parking lots, the third held a few burning trees and then another empty lot.

The Korovega had come from the only direction without a decent line of sight. The creek was too small for them to swim in it, but it still would have provided reasonable concealment as they closed in on the intersection.

The buzz of bullets hitting the Korovega's shields was louder than the motorcycle's engines. Sam gritted her teeth against the whine. It was insane, she thought, to be racing toward the Korovega, but they had a duty. They knew how to kill the damnable things, and she could never life with herself, if she survived at all, if she ran.

"Owen do you thi..." she started to ask if they could cross the intersection fast enough to engage the Korovega with their swords, but Owen cut her off mid-word.

"Down!" he yelled. She felt his arms clamp tight around her waist. His scream would have carried over the engine, the wind, and the hiss of bullets against the Korovega. Through the intercom, his voice rang in her ears.

The animal part of her brain responded to his tone. Before her conscious mind had even registered what his word meant, long microseconds before she could even begin to think about why he might have said what he said, her reflexes acted. She shifted forward, as close to the body of the motorcycle as possible and wrenched the handlebars to the left. Her mind, the person that was Samantha Bennett, could only watch in horror as things happened around her faster than she could process.

The bike jerked to the side and threatened to tip forward, but she threw all of her weight the other direction, uphill and back the way they had come. Owen held onto her so tight that he shifted in the seat as well and the bike dropped dangerously close to the pavement.

Certain the bike was going to flip and roll in protest of the insane maneuver she had just forced it to make, she shut her eyes. A bright flash dazzled her vision through her tightly-clamped eyelids and tinted visor, and she opened them again.

Big Blue had turned nearly one hundred eighty degrees in its spin. Foul smelling smoke from the tires filled her nostrils, but underneath that she caught the scent of ozone. Up the road, no more than a few feet away, a deep hole had been burned in the hillside.

Her heart sped up, faster even that it had that morning, as she brought the bike upright again. She took immediate, instinctual stock of the bike. Everything seemed fine. Somehow, her maneuver had failed to trip the crash sensor in the fuel tank. Thankfully, it still ran.

As she shifted her right foot, however, it became immediately clear how close to oblivion they had actually come. The motorcycle had small wind deflectors near her feet, but the right one was now several inches shorter.

She cursed viciously, but silently. Behind them, what had moments before been in front of them, the sound of bullets on the Korovega shields had lessened. It had also, she thought, grown closer.

"Hold on!" Sam snapped.

The bike jumped forward. Long practice and Sam's familiarity with the bike kept both wheels on the ground, but only barely. They went twice the length of the motorcycle, looping around the smoldering hole in the ground that was almost their unmarked grave. In two seconds, the bike was up to speed, then she slammed it through another tight turn to reorient them toward what remained of the police blockade.

In seconds, it had been transformed from a normal, if militaristic-looking, checkpoint to a nightmare. All three cars on the far side of the intersection were burning. The third must have been destroyed when they nearly spun out avoiding their own deaths. A diagonal gash across the intersection smoldered in front of the center cruiser. The ground sloped upward just enough to keep that car safe from the blast that took out its opposite number. The edge of the hole was just under the side door of the cruiser—it, like Sam's motorcycle, seemed to have barely escaped, or at least slightly delayed, destruction by a matter of inches.

Next to the hole stood a policeman. He sagged to the ground on shaky knees. Sam tried to remember if there had been another officer standing with him, but her brain either could not or would not call that memory to mind. That, she decided, was probably for the best.

The center of the intersection collapsed. Between the two holes bored into the ground by low-aimed energy beams, the asphalt had no support under it anymore. The SWAT van, the one that presumably held all of their gear and electronics, nearly disappeared into the hole. Only the top of the roof and a plethora of antennas remained above ground level.

Big Blue roared closer as time slowed to a crawl. Five cruisers and fourteen policemen still stood in the intersection. Sam assumed each of the cars had a driver inside at all times bringing the total number of survivors up to fifteen.

A searing, bright light flashed across her vision in a line from the far corner and engulfed the police car sitting between the lanes of the Turnpike to the left of the intersection. The car disappeared in a concussive thump, as did the officer next to it.

Sam cursed again.

"Slow down!" Owen shouted. Over the intercom, his voice was loud and full of adrenaline and panic.

"What?" Sam snapped.

"Slow. Down!" Owen repeated.

Sam shot a glance at the Korovega on the far side of the street. For the moment, the gunfire had stopped and the monsters were simply standing behind their shields.

As far away as they were, Sam had no way of knowing if they were looking at her or not. She felt like they were.

She looked over her shoulder, saw the determination on Owen's face, and let off the throttle. The motorcycle continued to coast, but was slowing appreciably.

"There!" Owen said, pointing past her shoulder at the nearest of the police.

Sam shot him an inquisitive glance. Without having to give voice to any words, her face said, "are you sure about that?"

He nodded.

Sam turned back to the road, sighed, and guided the bike to a stop next to the policeman. He turned, a look of surprise and fear on his blanched face.

"Follow us!" Owen shouted.

"What?" Sam and the cop said in near unison.

"Those things are going to kill you. Get in your cars and follow us. Sam, go now!"

She nodded, turned the handlebars to the right, and twisted the throttle hard. The motorcycle's rear tire spun for half a second, throwing gravel and small pieces of debris behind them and attracting the attention of the Korovega. The one on the end of the quartet raised an arm and let lose with an energy beam, but in the smoke and chaos, it missed. Owen found himself unwilling, just then, to look back and see if the man he had just spoken to was now nothing but a smoldering crater.

"Shit," Owen cursed. What they were doing felt like running away. He and Sam and God only knew how many surviving police officers had turned tail and ran, leaving a quartet of Korovega alone to butcher until they got bored and just started setting things on fire.

"There was nothing we could do." Sam kept her voice calm, much calmer than he felt anyway.

"So now what?" he demanded, shutting his visor against the wind-borne whip of Sam's fire-red braid. Rather than defeated, he felt angry. Intellectually, he knew she was right. That fact mattered to him right then about as much as his own reminder that it was not a retreat but a regroup. Still, he wanted to stop the bike, turn around, and personally slaughter all four of them.

Light danced at the edges of his vision. By now he knew that blue-white glow far better than he would have liked. His heart sank as he wondered how many more people had just died in that moment.

Visions of the fight that morning danced in his mind. He saw Jessie fall, Ben go berserk, and he remembered how he had cut the thing's hand from its wrist before it could take Ben with it into death. That Korovega had remembered him and hunted him, and he could not shake the thought that these were after the same thing.

Sirens wailed behind them. A lifetime's conditioning tried to tell him that hearing a police siren start behind him was a bad thing, let alone more than one at the same time. Like most people, he had been pulled over a few times in his life for various minor things, and the immediate feeling of having done something wrong never quite went away.

He reminded himself that this time he wanted the police following him. After a minute, he dared to sneak a glance at the road behind.

Four police cars formed a ragged line behind the motorcycle. All four had their lights on, flashing the same pattern they had been while parked. The second and fourth ones had their sirens on as well. Owen wondered if the cars did that automatically or if the drivers had, in a fit of instinctive normalcy, flicked on their sirens when they shifted into gear.

He relayed the news to Sam. "Half of the cruisers are gone." His voice was carefully neutral. Right then, he had a job to do—that job was to survive and to make sure as many of the people following him survived as well. Letting himself be distracted by the warring emotions in his head would serve only to make that job harder, if not impossible.

Sam's voice was tense when she asked, "how many people?"

"I can't see from here. Their windshields are tinted."

"Let's hope those cars are full of cops, then," she replied. He heard her laugh over the intercom. "I'll have to add that to the list of things I never thought I'd say."

Owen watched for several more seconds. A few police had survived the initial explosions and the follow-up energy beams only to be unable to make it to an escaping patrol car. As he watched, they leveled their weapons and fired on the Korovega. They were far enough away that the sound of the shields failed to reach them even though the gunshots did.

He looked at the cars following them, and realized that those men and women back at the attack site had not been abandoned. One by one, six even more heavily armed officers—it was hard not to call them soldiers in all of their gear—climbed out of the hole into which the SWAT van had fallen. They faced the Korovega for a moment before advancing on them. Owen thought he saw riot batons in their hands.

The blue-white glow flickered for a second and the sky lit up with a flash. One trooper was gone from the knees up, while the one next to him lurched to one side, missing an arm.

Owen turned away, promising to remember what those men and women had done for him. He looked up for a moment, catching sight of a single black shape in the sky overhead.

After a short distance, the trees on the left side of the road thickened up into a dense forest. Plenty of driveways and side streets dotted the landscape as they rode. The Korovega had also come from that direction. Short of sighting even more of the creatures to the right of the road, Sam had to intention of turning left.

In contrast, the right side of the road had flattened out. Years before, it had been an active industrial area and it still bore some of the scars of the heavy machines that were once a common sight there. It was flat and relatively open, but the streets twisted around themselves in knots. The disorienting paths were once intended to confuse spies when Oak Ridge had been top-secret and worked on the nation's early nuclear weapons. Now, those same twisting streets would allow them to escape in a dozen directions if the Korovega caught them.

Or, truthfully, she thought, when the Korovega caught them. There was no "if" in that sentiment.

"Hold on," Sam said into the intercom. After the maneuver they pulled less than two minutes before, Owen was sure he never actually stopped holding on, but he tightened his grip on her waist, to to be safe.

She held her right arm straight out to her right side, signaling a right turn. A second later, the bike swerved hard to the right, cutting across the road and onto a side street.

"Can we not get the place with the good milkshakes nuked by the Korovega?" Owen asked.

Sam laughed, but the sound shook with fear. "I'll do what I can."

They pulled into a parking lot and waited for the police to catch up with them. In the short time they were on the road, they had traveled a mile and a half, roughly. The Korovega were on foot, and even if they ran at Olympic speeds the entire way, that still left them five minutes to regroup. More likely, the Korovega would finish killing the poor souls who had stayed behind to serve as a distraction and then come after them at a purposeful saunter.

Owen figured they would have close to fifteen minutes to themselves before they had to do something, regardless of what that something was. It would be smarter to play it safer, and he lowered that estimate to ten minutes. At that point, no matter what they had decided, they would either be preparing to fight the Korovega or moving further down the road.

Sam dropped the kickstand on the motorcycle and leaned it to the side, but left the engine running. It had plenty of gas left and letting it idle would make any further movements easier.

She slid off of the leather seat for the first time in hours and stretched. Her knees were tight and her muscles sore from holding the same position for so long. Flexing them was agony, but she was happy just to be on her feet and have her legs straight again.

Owen followed, landing somewhat harder. His back burned where the road rash from the day before was healing, but that had long since receded to a dull ache at the edges of his senses. He was aware of the pain, but it did not hurt, exactly. For most of the day, it had settled for minor discomfort.

Unfortunately for him, the muscles in his back had to be stretched just like those in his legs. He could avoid the pain now and not stretch, but that would only mean worse pain later. Steeling himself, he grit his teeth and stretched.

The police cruisers came screeching into the parking lot a few seconds later. They did not concern themselves with such niceties of civilization as "parking spaces" or "braking gently to keep the tires from sliding." More or less in unison, ten uniformed and armed police spilled out of the four cars that survived the Korovega's surprise attack.

One of the officers wore sergeant's stripes on the sleeve of her gear. Armored from head to toe like a twenty-first century knight, she cut an intimidating figure as she approached the motorcycle. Owen was glad to see that her face shield was raised and her hands, though they looked like they could draw any one of the half-dozen weapons she carried instantaneously, were not actively resting on anything threatening.

She stopped a yard and a half away and sized the two of them up, paying a few seconds' extra attention to their swords and unusual gear. Owen wondered if they intimidated her as much as she intimidated them and decided that the answer was most likely a solid "no." They probably confused the police, which given the tense atmosphere right then, meant everything he said would have to be carefully moderated.

"Sergeant Heather Allen, Oak Ridge Police Department," she said briskly. Her voice wavered somewhere between anger, sadness, and simple confusion. "I just left a dozen people to die back there. You'd better have some good news."

Owen nodded and raised his visor. Inside, he felt vast relief that she had not commented on his weapons. That, along with the fact that technically what they were doing by telling people to fight the Korovega could have been legally considered "inciting to riot" was one of the biggest fears they discussed on the drive into town. Now, she simply took in the fact that the two heavily armed strangers who had been displaying the head of a dead Korovega around town were standing right in front of her with a curt nod of her head. Her eyes lingered on the edge of the vivid bruise on the side of Owen's face where it peeked out from the side of his helmet, but said nothing about it.

"We do," Owen replied. "At least I hope so. We killed one this morning."

Sergeant Allen nodded. "So everyone says. I want to see it."

"We don't really have time."

"I want to see it," she repeated, firmer.

Owen nodded and took a step back toward the motorcycle. He retrieved the burlap sack from where he had tied it to the luggage rack after their previous stop, a lifetime ago. Out of the corner of his eye, he saw Sergeant Allen tense, probably an automatic reaction to seeing a potentially dangerous stranger reaching into a bag with unknown contents.

Owen withdrew the head and the sergeant took a step back. From one of the other officers came a muffled, "Jesus Christ." Owen held it out by the hair, displaying the gruesome thing like a trophy.

"It's real," he said.

Sergeant Allen, her face a shade lighter than before, nodded. "So I see. Good to know your talk was more than just talk." At Owen's somewhat confused expression, she added, "you kept telling everyone to tell their friends and family, yeah? I've got friends and family and they passed word to me. We aren't supposed to take personal calls on duty, but this week is a little different."

Owen turned and dropped the Korovega head back in the sack. He knotted the strings at the mouth of the bag and then tied it to the luggage rack once more. Over his shoulder, he said, "I'd say so."

"What do you know about them?" she asked.

Owen shrugged. "Not much, honestly. The one that we killed this morning remembered me from yesterday afternoon, and..."

"Wait a minute," Sergeant Allen interrupted, "yesterday. That wasn't you at the steam plant, was it?"

Owen nodded slowly. "We were on our way back from buying material to build a workshop. We got stuck in traffic and when I realized what had stopped things..."

"He did something stupid," Sam supplied. "And heroic, but mostly stupid."

"And you are?" Sergeant Allen asked.

"Sam," she replied. She had raised her visor, but left the helmet and face guard in place. The little slit of her face that was visible was a shock of white against the black of the rest of her outfit. Then she said, "Samantha Jean Bennett."

"She's the reason I'm still alive," Owen said. "In all seriousness, the pleasantries can wait. Sergeant Allen..."

"Heather," she said. "It's faster than 'Sergeant Allen,' and you're right. We need all the speed we can muster right now."

"Heather," Owen echoed, "we need a plan."

She seemed surprised. Eyes wide, she demanded, "don't you already have one?"

"Sort of," Owen answered reluctantly.

"Sort of?"

He nodded. "We had a plan for encountering one of them at a time, maybe we could kill two. We never thought we would run into four."

"How do you kill them?"

"They die just like anything else if you can get around their shields," Owen said.

"Problem is," Sam added, "they're fast. And they're incredibly observant. The first one we encountered stood up to a hail of bullets because it could anticipate where the next shot was coming from. Finally, we flanked it and managed to wound it, but it took a hundred bullets easy just to make one leg shot."

"That won't do." Heather frowned. "Anything else? My sister said you had a sword. That one?"

Owen nodded, suddenly more serious than he had been before. "It used to belong to that." He gestured with his thumb over his shoulder at the bag hanging from the motorcycle's rack. "As far as we can tell, their shields have three modes. I'd guess you'd call them that anyway. First one is that dome they were using back there. Alone, it can slow down handgun bullets and turn rifle rounds into nonlethal cuts. In DC, it looked like their shields stacked, so let's assume four of them with dome shields can stop bullets cold. You can still force your way through one, though.

"They've also got a shield mode," he went on. "It's stronger, but only about two feet across, maybe a bit more. It stops handgun and shotgun rounds, and just about stops rifles as well. That's what the one last night used most of the time.

"The last is a little buckler, and that's impervious. Period. Bullets, blades, whatever. Nothing that we were able to throw at it got through. But the buckler is smaller, more maneuverable. Both kinds of small shield free up their other hand to use their sword. And that," he patted his own sword, "is where this comes into play."

"And the beams?" Heather asked. From outside, it seemed like she was either bewildered or was soaking up the information without pause. Owen hoped for the latter.

"They use the same hand for both," he replied. "At least the one this morning and the one yesterday did. So if you can get in close enough that they have to keep their shield up, then you can fight them without worrying, much, about those beams."

"But if you step away," Sam added. "They're fast. You cannot stop attacking once you're in range, otherwise they'll open the distance and fry you."

Heather nodded. "I don't suppose you have any extra swords with you?"

Sam shook her head. "No. We weren't counting on outfitting anyone."

"Hell, we weren't counting on fighting at all, honestly. We just wanted everyone to know that they could be killed," he said, then, "that the Korovega could be killed."

"I knew what you meant."

He apologized, then laughed. "Running for my life seems to scatter my thoughts."

"That happen a lot?"

"Not usually. Like you said, though, this week's different."

"That's the truth."

"The men and women we left back there had melee weapons. Do you think they stopped those Korovega?"

"Honestly, it's possible."

"You sound skeptical."

He sighed. He really did not want to insult the capability of trained, professional policemen but, "they weren't trained to beat sword fighters," he said, carefully choosing his words.

"And we don't know how well the Korovega can coordinate their beams and shields," Sam added. "I don't want to kill the mood worse than it already is, but they may not have even gotten close enough to fight them hand to hand."

Heather glared for a moment, but then her expression softened. Her face said she knew Sam was right, but she was under no compulsion to like that fact.

"So." Her voice had changed. There was less wariness in it now, and slightly less abject fear. The anger was still there, but determination had replaced fear. "I repeat, what's the plan?"

Owen opened with, "unless we can surprise them..."

Heather interrupted him. "Let's assume we can't."

Before Owen could regroup his thoughts, Sam spoke up. "Explosives," she said. "Do you have any bombs, grenades, or anything like that in your cars?"

For a brief moment, Heather looked at Sam like she was crazy. Even Owen, for a moment, shared that feeling. The police were well armed, especially in their riot gear, but he highly doubted they carried high explosives around with them.

Heather confirmed his suspicions. "No, we don't. Unless you count gas."

Sam cursed under her breath, then laughed softly. With a shake of her head, she said, "I don't even know if that would work anyway."

"No idea's a bad idea right now," Owen said.

Sam nodded. "How do you propose we separate them?"

"That depends." Owen spoke quickly, thinking as he went. "Heather. We've only got a minute or two more before we've got to move. I don't know if the Korovega are chasing us, but we have to assume they are. Their eagles are, anyway. Before we break, we need to take stock of what we have. Weapons, skills, anything that might be useful."

"There's only ten of us left, plus you two," she replied bitterly.

"Any only four Korovega," Owen reminded her. "Two of us killed one this morning, and now that I know how they fight, I could take one myself."

He was not entirely sure if that statement was true, but he felt like it was more than bravado. He had, in truth, picked up on how the Korovega that morning fought, but he had no way of knowing if they all fought that way or not. Regardless, his apparent confidence seemed to buoy Heather's confidence, so he was not about to let her in on his doubts.

"If you could get close enough," Heather said.

Owen nodded. "That's the catch, yeah."

Heather gestured to herself and the other armored police. "We've all got guns and batons. One of the cars might still have a shield in the trunk, but we were supposed to offload all that to the armory in the van. If you can conjure some bombs, we'd be good to go on that front. Otherwise, we've got what you see. Guns, batons, tasers, gas, and a whole lot of desire to kick some Korovega ass."

"That's more than we had five minutes ago," Owen replied. After the words were out of his mouth, he realized how insensitive they sounded. The meager list she had was probably half if not a third or less of the force they had been given to blockade that intersection and protect that section of town, and it had been decimated in less than five minutes.

If she was offended, Sergeant Heather Allen seemed not to draw attention to it. In fact, she still had that same calculating expression on her face that she had worn the entire time.

"What do you have?" she asked.

"Same," Owen replied. "What you see here. Two shotguns, two pistols, a pair of swords, a monster skull in a bag, and a whole lot of hate."

"Alright," she said. "How far down the road do we go?"

"You're letting me decide?" he asked, surprised. The police sergeant handing off decision-making was not something he expected to happen.

"Make it quick," she said. Her expression was set. Whatever her reasons, she had made her decision. Asking about it would only take time they did not have, so Owen went with it.

"Let's go another mile down the turnpike."

"Two," Sam countered.

"Two," Owen echoed. He assumed Sam had a plan, or the beginnings of one, and was not about to second guess her.

"And then?" Heather asked.

"Now that we know what we have to fight them with, we do this again." Owen replied

Heather nodded. "Two miles down the road, you lead."

Sam sketched a salute. "Aye." She threw a leg across her bike and pushed it off of the kickstand.

"One more thing," Heather said. "You've got radios on those helmets, right?"

Sam nodded. "Yeah."

"Tune them to the same frequency as ours." She recited the numbers from memory.

In the console of the motorcycle was a touchscreen hidden behind a panel. Sam opened the panel and programmed the new frequency into their helmets.

"Can you hear me?" she asked. She heard the question echoed from the radio strapped to Heather's chest.

"Clear here," Owen replied.

Sam rolled her eyes at Owen's tone, but could not resist a grin. "Let's move, then. We have monsters to kill."

Chapter 23

The unlikely caravan pulled off of the main road a mile and a half from where they had stopped before. On the opposite side of the road was a park that, the week before, had been a rather pleasant place complete with soccer and baseball fields, and a small play area for dogs. Now, it looked like heavy machinery had been at work moving massive amounts of dirt around, though no signs of any purpose made themselves evident.

"This area's hilly," Owen said, sweeping his hand across the rolling ground and trees behind them. "We can use that to our advantage if we can lure the Korovega close."

Heather wished she had a map. She was only marginally familiar with the area they had chosen for their ambush. Sergeant or not, she spent most of her time on the other end of town. Either Owen knew the area intimately, she thought, or he was gifted when it came to thinking on his feet. Everything he said since they met made sense, logically speaking anyway, but with Korovega wandering around killing and destroying indiscriminately, logic had a strange new definition.

Yet he was, for lack of a better term, their expert in the subject at hand. He had killed a Korovega. She knew from the way they had slaughtered through her checkpoint that conventional tactics would not work against them. So she had no choice but to trust the one person in the city who knew how to make them die.

"Any additional gear in the trunks?" he asked, turning his attention back to her alone. He had his visor raised and she watched what little she could see of his face carefully. His gray-green eyes darted around, taking in everything around him. With the mouthguard still in place, she could see little else, but both he and his redheaded friend moved and spoke with authority.

"Just the one shield and a few rifles if you want to use them," she replied. "Or if you think we can use them."

"I'd rather use this." Sam tapped on the barrel of her shotgun with one finger. "I know I can hit with it and I'd rather not learn to operate an entirely new rifle in," she made a dramatic watch-checking motion, despite there being nothing on her wrist but the cuff of her leather jacket, "ten minutes."

"Same here," Owen agreed, trying to make it sound like he knew as much as Sam did about the gun slung over his shoulder. In truth, he would probably drop it once the Korovega got into engagement rage. Using it with one hand so that he could use his sword in the other seemed silly, and not using it at all gave anything he would be fighting an easy handle to grab him with.

Owen briefly considered forgoing a gun completely and taking the riot shield for his other hand. It would certainly come in handy for defense when they came down to sword blows, but one of the police would invariably need it more. The shield would be handy, but he could survive without it, while for the police officer who took it, it might mean the difference between life and death.

He was unsure when he had undertaken the task of saving their lives, rather than simply warning them, but the situation was what it was—to change it would require a time machine and the ability to predict where else the Korovega might attack from.

"Who's the best at close quarters combat?" Sam asked. She stepped in among the police, sizing them up based on outward physical appearance and trying her best to estimate their capabilities based on how the carried themselves. Out of the corner of her eye, she watched as Owen took a few steps away from the group and scanned their surroundings.

"Him," Heather replied, pointing to a tall, lanky man. He was no Ben; he lacked half a foot of height and probably a hundred of Ben's pounds, but he seemed to move with a flowing grace that Sam took for sort sort of martial arts training. "C'mere, Ash."

The officer in question approached and sketched a salute. Underneath the riot armor was a thin face that might have looked frail on someone not wearing police-grade armor. As it was, he looked like a coiled whip ready to move and strike.

He extended a hand to Sam. "Ian Ashford. Everyone calls me 'Ash.'"

Sam nodded approval, taking his hand. His grip was strong, but lacked the deliberate hand-crushing-machismo that she often encountered. "You take the shield," she instructed. "And if you've got anything more substantial than a riot baton, take that too. Once you're ready, go talk to Owen and he'll tell you where to stand."

Ash nodded and sauntered toward the nearest parked cruiser. He removed a clear plastic shield with "POLICE" emblazoned across the front from the trunk.

"Good kid," Heather said.

"Don't say it," Sam warned.

"What?"

Sam sighed. "Don't say, 'don't get him killed.' That's a promise I can't make."

Heather looked down at the dirt for a moment, seeing again the flashes of light and explosions that had ended the lives of people she had called friends for years. Finally, she looked back up and said, "yeah. I know."

Sam managed a weak smile. "We'll do our best, though."

"That's all any of us can ask for."

Between Owen and Sam, they worked out two plans to arrange the nine surviving police officers, Sergeant Allen, and themselves.

The first plan would be the ideal one, but it centered on the Korovega coming after they were set up and ready for them and on them approaching from the road. To goad the Korovega into the entrance they wanted the quartet to use, Heather had agreed to let one of their cruisers serve as bait and parked it at the entrance of the side street where they were set up.

The second plan, and the plan that both Owen and Sam not-so-secretly suspected they would end up using, covered two possibilities. First, it allowed for the Korovega coming at them from somewhere that was not the road. More important, it was the plan they would use if the Korovega approached before they had their ambush set up.

Five minutes after parking, the Korovega had not arrived, but they were ready. Without any firm idea of where the Korovega were or how fast they were moving, they wasted no time. Owen did his best to stay on top of everyone and made dozens of little adjustments to people's placements.

Five of the officers had been armed with rifles and hidden far away from what was to be the battleground. They had stripped off some of their armor as well, handing it over to the ones, including Owen and Sam, who would be doing the actual melee fighting.

Four of those five had volunteered to climb some of the uphill trees to get a better vantage point. The fifth had been against it, but acquiesced when his fellow officers explained their reasoning to him. Heather argued against it as well, saying they would have no way to escape if things got bad.

"A better sight line isn't worth being stuck in one spot if the Korovega get past the rest of us," she explained.

"Sarge," one of the cops said. His face was set in hard lines. "We won't be escaping from here if things go bad. Not all of us, anyway."

"He's right," Sam added quietly. "As soon as we engage the Korovega, the only way any of us are going to walk away from this safely is if all four of those things are dead."

"And the escape plan?" she asked, gesturing to her officers who were even now climbing trees. "Does it include them?"

Sam watched the police climb for a moment, struck by the absurdity of the image. "It does, but I can't..."

"You can't make promises, I know," Heather interrupted. She nodded grimly. "Alright then," she said, then turned to Sam directly. "Are the two of you ready?"

"As ready as we can be," Sam replied.

Sam took two pieces of gear from one of the soon-to-be-treed officers: a pair of—thankfully—one-size-fits-all thigh plates and a set of shoulder armor. The legs were not exactly the most comfortable things around, but Owen and Ben both had hit her there several times during their last sparring session and she had no intention of letting a murderous demon carve her quad open just because her low parries needed work.

She also left her shotgun slung from Big Blue's handlebars, preferring her pistol so that she could easily use Owen's saber in her other hand. That served two purposes. First, like Owen, she was not going to give the Korovega anything to grab onto while they fought. Second, part of their emergency plan, the one that was still only half-formed, centered around the motorcycle, and her using the shotgun to cover their exit.

The two of them also had to stay within a few dozen yards of the bike, because it acted at the base unit for their helmet intercoms. Straying too far from it meant no way to talk to their new police allies during the fight. Owen left his backpack with the bike as well, wrapping the straps around the luggage rack.

Ash and Heather stood off to one side, talking to one another. The other two police tasked with fighting the Korovega at baton range were doing their best to cover themselves with leaf litter and other debris. Without ghillie suits, there was a limit to what they could do, but their job was not to hide for hours. All they had to do was avoid being noticed long enough for the riflemen to occupy the Korovega's attention, then attack.

Heather completely swapped suits with one of the other policemen. To Sam's surprise, it had taken them less than two minutes to do so, during which time Owen was placing the others in their positions. The armor Heather had been wearing, she explained, was designed to be lightweight and reduce fatigue. She traded it wholesale to one of the riflemen, and was now wearing his suit of hard plates. It weighed much more, but it was also much stronger. Ash had already been wearing armor like that, and now looked even more intimidating carrying the riot shield and baton.

Owen wished they had another sword to give him, but like Sam refusing to switch guns with one of the arguably more effective police rifles, Ash knew how to use the baton. Changing weapons on him now would only diminish his ability to fight.

The sky thundered overhead. Moments later, it began to rain. There was no gentle leadup to the shower or gradual moving-in of the front. Rather, one moment the sky was cloudy but dry and the next, rain beat down on everyone's heads. The ground under the trees was still moist, too. If the rain kept up for more than a few minutes, the dirt they were standing on would quickly become a soupy mess of mud.

"And now it's raining," Owen muttered. "Great."

Sam laughed. "Welcome to East Tennessee."

"You sound like you feel better," Owen observed.

She shrugged. "A bit, I suppose. Between you and me, I'm looking forward to this."

"Revenge?"

"Maybe," she admitted. "But mostly I'm feeling the tension that's been hounding us all day disappearing. We could die in the next few minutes, but now at least we know when the Korovega are going to come. We know which direction. Hell," she laughed with nervous energy, "we even know how many of them there are."

Owen put a hand on the Korovega sword slung from his belt. "And I've got one thing they don't have."

"That?" Sam asked, nodding her head toward the sword.

Owen met her eyes and laughed. "No, I think they've got four of these things. No," he said and placed a gloved-and-gauntleted hand on Sam's armored shoulder. "I've got you watching my back."

Sam smiled with her eyes. The rest of her face was covered by the mouth guard of her helmet. In those eye swam a mix of confidence and determination, backed by anger. Owen could see, just barely, the undercurrent of fear at the very back of her mind and wondered how much of his own registered on his face like that.

"So long as you watch mine, yeah?" she asked. She slammed her helmet visor down and latched it.

"Yeah. Gorget on?"

She nodded once, slowly. Reflexively, she touched her neck, feeling both the leather and metal of the gorget and also the spot where the Korovega sword had ended Jessie's life that morning.

When she responded, her voice was weaker than she would have liked. "Yeah," she said. Then, with more strength, she asked, "yours?"

Owen nodded, but said nothing.

"Let's do this." The strength in her voice had fully returned. "For Jessie."

"For Jessie," Owen echoed.

* * *

"We got incoming," their lookout announced through their radios. She had been "voluntold" by Sergeant Allen to be the lookout when she made a comment about being an excellent tree climber. Now she waited nearly twenty-five feet in the air, watching the road for the Korovega's approach.

Sam's adrenaline spiked, but she kept her movements cool and controlled. She had seen what happened to people who let their movements get ahead of them, and the result was never good. She double-checked the latches on her faceplate, ran a finger over the buckle of her gorget again, and stepped toward her position.

"Positions!" Owen shouted, and realized that everyone was already on their way there. He slapped his visor down on his face and darted backward, away from the immediate line of sight from the road.

"...bile. Gray, local plates."

"Say again," Heather ordered over the radio. Her friendly demeanor was gone, replaced with the faceless black mask of riot armor and the stentorian tones that Owen would have expected from someone wearing that sort of suit. She made no comment about him accidentally shouting over their lookout's announcement.

"Incoming is an automobile, gray paint, local plates. Coming from across the street."

"From the park?" Owen asked.

Heather bit back an urge to tell him to shut up and let her command, but she had in fact given him the authority to make decisions and ask questions about what was going on. She wondered if this was how the cops tasked with working with the National Guard units felt when two people were trying to give orders.

"Affirmative."

"Any sign of the Korovega?" Owen asked.

"Negative. Car has slowed. Looks like it's going to pull in next to the cruiser."

A moment passed in silence as the mystery car's engine shut off. They heard a door open, then shut before Heather spoke up again.

"Lena," Heather whispered into her radio. "Any sign of the Korovega?"

"Still negative, Sergeant."

"And the driver?"

"Male," came the reply, "late forties, early fifties. He's armed, but no body armor and he's not acting threatening."

"Let him come past the trees, then. Speak up if you see anything on the road."

"Alright."

"Ash, Sam, Owen," Heather said in rapid-fire syllables, "be ready. Fire team at the ready."

A series of short, fast responses came across the radio, one, "ready!" after the other. Silence fell. Owen half expected to hear a series of dramatic clicks as the riflemen in the trees readied their guns, and was glad when his Hollywood-inspired expectations proved false.

A middle aged man strode onto the road they were encamped around. He was whistling and his hands were well away from the holstered pistol at his belt. Aside from what must have been a rather impressive physique before age and beer took its toll on his middle, he looked as though he was making every effort to be as nonthreatening as possible.

"Anybody home? I saw y'all head down this'a way and then y'all parked right outside. This got anything to do with stuff exploding up the road?"

"Keep your hands where I can see them," Heather ordered. She left the radio on, and her words were loud in everyone's ear.

The man looked around nervously. Her voice was quite clear, but he seemed as though he had no idea which direction it was coming from.

Heather stepped out of the copse of trees where she had been waiting. Owen, Sam, and Ash were positioned in other spots where they could see what was going on but, theoretically, could not be easily seen themselves. Other than her boots crunching the twigs and other bits of underbrush, there was no sound for a moment.

"Th' hell kind of Terminator-looking," he started, then closed his mouth with an audible click of his teeth and a sharp intake of air.

Heather stood there, armored, and with her black faceplate lowered. The word "POLICE" on her chest, and the afternoon sunlight glinting off of the various hard plastic pieces of her armor were the only things to break up the silhouette. She had hidden her rifle under a pile of leaves in case, like Sam leaving her shotgun with the motorcycle, they had to change plans and quickly retreat away from the Korovega. Her pistol and various other tools and weapons still hung from her belt, along with the riot baton in her hand.

Heather—Sergeant Allen—introduced herself with authority. "Who are you?"

"Carl," he replied. "Ah, Carl Blanchard. I saw the car there and thought..."

Heather cut him short. "I heard you the first time. This is a dangerous area. There are Korovega on their way here right now. I need you to get back in your car and drive away."

"Listen, I, uh, I wanted to help."

Heather said nothing, but her statuesque posture combined with the faceless intimidation of her suit, prompted the rest of his story a moment later.

"I got, well I had," he said quickly, stumbling over his words. Then, "shit. Look. A buddy of mine went to check on his brother a couple days ago. His brother lives, lived, hell maybe still lives in Knoxville. He had one of those little studio apartments above a coffee shop. Pretty nice place for a three room apartment. But, see, I haven't heard from either of them since..."

"Since Wednesday," Heather offered, when Carl never finished that last sentence.

He nodded and looked around the area. For half a moment, Owen caught his eyes, though it seemed clear that Carl had not seen him. He saw the same mixture of fear and anger that he had seen on a hundred faces that day. More telling than that, to Owen, was the fact that Carl wore the same determined expression that he had forced onto his own face every morning for the last four or five days.

"Ask him if he can fight," Owen muttered. The intercom in his helmet was still on, and the sound transmitted across the channel they all shared into Heather's earpiece.

She echoed the question, though with more authority than Owen felt like he would have had.

Carl shook his head, then shrugged. "Maybe? I've got a gun, but word's going around town that somebody killed one and he said guns don't do no good against those things."

Heather nodded once. In all black, the expression was barely visible save for the changing patterns reflected in her faceplate. "I've heard the same thing. But if you don't have a way of fighting them, then I'm afraid I'm going to have to ask you to get back in your car and leave the area immediately."

"I, um, uh, that is," he sputtered, trying to come up with the right words to say whatever it was he was trying to get across. Heather folded her arms and waited, head cocked to one side in a gesture of exasperated patience. "I've got, in the trunk, some, ah, you know. Things."

"Things?" Heather asked. Disbelief colored her tone.

"Yeah, you know." Carl made a blooming gesture with his hands. "Things."

"Uh huh. Go on. What kind of things?"

"Look, you're cops, and..."

Heather sighed. "We don't have much time," she snapped. "Either spit it out or leave, because if you stay here you're only going to get in my way."

"Please don't arrest me; I've got some pipe bombs in my trunk," he said, speeding through the words as though getting them out before she could react would save him.

"Pipe. Bombs." Heather carefully rolled each word over in her mouth. Owen noticed her fists tightening slightly. He imagined he could hear the creak of leather. "Uh huh. Care to elaborate on that, Mister Blanchard?"

Suddenly, he looked very nervous. She had not moved, but Owen detected a definite aura of tension radiating out from the black-clad riot cop.

"They're not hard to make, and I just thought that in case the Korovega came here, maybe I could, you know, boom."

"Boom," she said, once again echoing his words as though unable to believe what she was hearing.

"Please don't arrest me."

"Mister Blanchard," Heather said, stressing every syllable and turning each word into a carefully level tone. "On any other day, in any other situation, and perhaps in front of any other police officer, you would be thrown in jail. But today is, as they say, your lucky day. There are four Korovega headed this way, and if you've got functional bombs with you, bombs that we can use to kill them, then I might just award you a medal."

He brightened. "Really?"

"No medal," she said. "Bring them here, and hurry!"

He nodded, turned, and strode back to his car. After two steps, he seemed to feel her eyes boring holes into his back and he sped up to a run.

"Suddenly," Heather muttered, low enough so that only the radios picked it up, "things got just a little better."

"If they don't blow up in our faces," one of the other police said.

"Don't jinx it," replied another.

"Quiet," Heather ordered. "He's coming back."

Carl returned, carrying three small metal cylinders and a length of wire. From the outside, they looked relatively harmless, or at least no worse than the average chunk of inert metal pipe. The careful way Carl carried them, though, conveyed exactly how dangerous they were. He held them against himself, using his chest to brace the bombs and make absolutely sure none of them fell. Every movement he made was a dozen times more careful than anything else he had done since entering their area.

"You want to see one?" he asked.

Heather nodded once, slowly, and extended a hand.

"Could you, you know, my balance isn't that great and..."

She sighed and stepped closer. Their proximity only served to make him more nervous, but she ignored that. With a gloved hand, Heather picked up the topmost of the three bombs. Examining it would have been easier with her faceplate raised, but she left it down. Maintaining the image, she decided, was more important than a little extra visual clarity. Besides, she could see well enough to know what she was looking at.

"These are too complex for you to have made them in the last day or so," she observed, turning the bomb over with her hand. Owen noticed the riot baton still rested in her other hand down at her side. It remained collapsed, but her grip on it was every bit as tight as her other hand was relaxed.

As if continuing a trend, Carl grew even more fidgety. Sweat sprang out at his hairline and he struggled to look anywhere but at the black-clad titan in front of him. "Uh, yeah. I, you see, that is, kind of..." he stopped, fidgeted a moment more, and said, "already had them."

"Uh huh," Heather said, nodding once. The featureless mask she wore lent the noise an air of both interest and of threat.

"You know," Carl said. He rubbed nervously at the back of his head. "For the terrorists."

"Terrorists."

He seemed hopeful. "Yeah?"

Heather sighed and placed the bomb back on the stack in Carl's hands. "You help us today," she said, "and I'm going to pretend I never saw you. Alright?"

"Yes!" he said, excited. "I mean, yeah. That's probably for the best, right? Look, I've got tripwire here and..."

Heather's radio popped in her ear. "Movement on the horizon, Sergeant."

Carl, oblivious, continued talking, "...bury them in the ground and set up the wire and when the Korovega show up here, we c..."

Heather held up her hand. The gesture stopped Carl in the middle of a word. "We don't have time for anything fancy," she said. She channeled the urgency in her voice into authority rather than panic. "ETA?"

"They're close," the lookout replied. "Running. Maybe five minutes."

Heather cursed. The Korovega were coming down the road, and five minutes was not enough time to break through the street surface to plant a trio of pipe bombs.

"How big are they?" Heather demanded.

"Big?" Carl asked, confused.

"Big," she repeated. "How much powder? How big an explosion?"

"I, ah, don't really know? It was a while ago and I used black powder I made at home and they're really not that heavy, so maybe not all that large? Less, in the rain, I suppose. Look, I don't really know and..."

He trailed off and Heather stopped listening as she processed this new information. Where in the hell are the Guard and their engineers when she actually wanted them? A pair of claymores, or even some hastily rigged grenades would be a hundred, a thousand times better that trusting some homemade pipe bomb.

Heather cursed again, wondering if she was just wasting time. If there was nowhere to plant the bombs where she and the others would be safe from the blast, there was no point in using them. Unless they planted the bombs and completely relocated or pulled well back, but then if—or, she thought, when—the Korovega survived the bombs, they would be too far away to fight them.

Heather scanned the area, looking around.

"If I may?" Sam whispered into her helmet's radio. Her voice barely carried over the link, but she spoke clearly enough with a stage whisper.

"Go ahead," Heather replied, eliciting a confused look from Carl, which she ignored.

"From here, it's hard to judge, but those don't look like they are that powerful. If we move a little, we can shelter behind some of the larger trees here. There's still danger from the pressure wave, but that should keep us safe from the explosion itself, and any debris."

Heather contemplated a moment, then, "good. Do it. Everyone on the ground, move. Follow Sam's instructions."

Carl jumped and nearly dropped his collection of pipe bombs when the six people, including Sam and Owen, emerged from their hiding places. His bombs looked well made, and Heather doubted a short drop would set them off, even onto asphalt. However, she tensed slightly, ready to dive and catch them if one or more did leave his hands.

He regained control of all three of them, and she relaxed slightly.

"They're close, Sergeant," their lookout announced. She whispered, quieter than before. The urgency in her tone, combined with the lack of volume, kicked Heather's adrenal glands into high gear.

"You have triggers?" she demanded.

"Yeah, but..."

She interrupted. "Good. Set them up in the middle of the road, there," she pointed, "with the trip wire so that all three go off at the same time. Got it?"

"But won't they see th—"

She interrupted again. "Let me worry about that. Owen, Sam," she said into her radio. "I need you two. Gather up as many leaves and as much debris as you can without making it look like there are big piles missing from beside the road. We're going to cover this area with leaves and hope to God the Korovega don't look down."

Rather than reply verbally, both Owen and Sam sprang into action, collecting armloads of leaves and twigs and cut grass. The two of them coordinated wordlessly, efficiently. Out of the corner of her eye, Heather watched them work together. The sight reminded her less of two people cooperating and more of two hands, both attached to the same body, working toward the same goal. They needed a lot of debris to cover enough of the pavement to make it look convincing, but the pair did it in under a minute.

"They're almost here. I see three Korovega."

"Cover, now," Heather ordered. The fact that one Korovega was missing from the group that attacked them before never registered. Then, "Carl. Hide or run, but do it now. Be fast."

In response, he ran a few yards away from the road and dove messily behind a bush. He hit the ground with an audible thud. Owen expected he would stay down the entire time the fighting was going on, not that he could be blamed for wanting to sit things out.

For two full minutes, there was no sound other than the ran beating down on everyone's heads. The rain muffled minor sounds, a fact about which Owen was pleased. He had no idea what sort of stealth training the police around him had, but he certainly had none to speak of. As the rain increased in intensity, it became almost impossible to hear the creaks and twig-snaps as he shifted his feet in preparation for attacking.

The downside to the rain's concealing noise was that he had no idea how far away the Korovega were. His pulse raced as he mistook every shift in the light filtering through the trees for their approach.

As long last, less than three minutes after resuming his hiding spot and a good thirty seconds after the voice in the back of his head had convinced him that maybe the Korovega would fail to take the bait, or simply move on, he saw them.

Two Korovega stepped past the treeline and Owen's heart skipped a beat. He looked around, moving his head as quickly as he dared to. He saw no sign of the third creature their lookout spotted. Worse, he still saw no sign of the fourth one. His mind raced as he wondered from which direction the missing monsters might come.

Watching the Korovega advance, hoping to every god he could think of that they would hit the trip wire, Owen's pulse raced. The riflemen in the trees waited, and presumably were equally as tense as he felt. He sank back further into the shadows, then placed his back against the tree that should protect him from the blast.

Three more steps, then two, then one last step separated the lead Korovega from the tripwire. It showed no sign of having seen the half-buried cord and it lifted up its foot one last time and shifted its weight.

Owen could hear the noises of their boots on the leaves and twigs, but hidden behind his hopefully bomb-proof tree, he could see nothing. Suddenly, though, he knew something had gone wrong. Their footsteps stopped and he heard a guttural hiss.

Mentally, he swore. "Son of a..." The world exploded before his brain finished the thought.

The crack was deafening. Half a heartbeat later, his chest and every part of his body not covered with rigid protection felt like it had been hit with a ten pound sledgehammer wrapped in foam. The pressure wave was over in moments, replaced by a blast of heat.

The tree rattled behind his back, and Owen was suddenly even more glad to have something sturdy between him and whatever shrapnel was in those bombs.

He heard something in his ear, then the telltale cracking of rifle fire. Owen realized his ears were ringing and fumbled for the volume control on the outside of his helmet. His hands shook with adrenaline and he had a hard time finding the control surface, let alone manipulating the volume rocker.

"...eam, go!" came Sergeant Allen's voice as the volume in his ears quickly increased to a level he could hear above the ringing. He assumed, since the riflemen were already firing, that that had been the order for the rest of them to close to short range.

Owen rose to his feet and rounded the tree. Nails, iron balls, caseless bullets, and bits of other debris were embedded in the side opposite his hiding place.

As he turned, he drew his sword. The weapon he had taken from the Korovega that killed his friend felt heavy in his hand. He took a step forward and stopped— only one of the Korovega still stood. It bled from a few shallow wounds in its legs and one shoulder, but otherwise looked unharmed. Murderous rage glinted in its eyes.

The one on the ground lay in pieces, blown apart. One entire leg lay a few yards to one side, while parts of the other leg had been thrown much farther away. One arm and its head was still attached to the torso, but the other arm was nowhere to be seen until it dropped from an overhanging tree limb like a wet sack.

Something was different about the surviving Korovega. To Owen's eyes, it seemed larger, taller. It might even have been stronger, but the dust and smoke from the pipe bombs obscured such trivial details. He could see that it wore ornate jewelry and its clothes were of brighter colors than the two he had seen thus far. The hair was different too, more elaborately arraigned despite the rain of debris. Under its brilliant emerald-green shirt shimmered some sort of armor as well.

There was no time to examine its bearing, but it seemed more aggressive than the other one had been. Where the others he had seen so far had fled at the first sign of effective resistance, preferring to sow fear and then disappear, the Korovega ahead of him seemed ready to fight and bleed if it meant killing the humans in its way.

He locked eyes with the thing, and a spark of recognition flashed through the Korovega's eyes. It grinned, displaying twin rows of needle-like teeth.

Did it somehow know, Owen asked as he put one foot before the other, that he had been displaying the head of one of its fallen comrades all day? Or did it simply recognize the sword in his hand and make the logical connection?

"The hrel spoke true, khat-manus!" the Korovega pronounced, staring him down.

Gunfire pocked the surviving Korovega's shield, buzzing and zapping against the dome-shaped projection. The bullets made it through, but most clattered to the ground harmlessly.

All the riflemen had to do, he reminded himself, was to cover him for another few feet. In a fair fight, he could close the distance and engage the lone Korovega, kill it, and then they could worry about the other two, wherever they were. This fight, however, was anything but fair.

Sam came up to his right side and Heather to his left. Two more police joined them a second later from other directions. The Korovega grunted and, with a hand gesture, replaced the thin dome with the larger of its shields. Three heartbeats passed and Ash stepped out from his hiding place behind the Korovega and charged.

Owen swung first. The Korovega parried with its sword, pivoted, stopped Ash's blow with its shield, finished its turn, and struck out at Heather's face with its sword. She jerked backward out of the way, and the beast turned its attack to the policeman to her left. Its sword skidded off of the side of his helmet, then buried itself in the man's neck in a spray of arterial blood.

Heather struck out in anger, but the Korovega pivoted out of the way. It aimed a cut at Sam's head. She parried, riposted, but was unable to land a hit of her own. Owen was about to attack again when the air lit up and the reek of ozone filled his nostrils.

"Jesus Christ!" came a panicked shout over the radios. "Fire! Shoot that goddamn thing! Shoot it!"

Gunfire erupted behind them, but Owen only heard three distinct rapports. Two of the shooters were missing. He pivoted through a cut, trying both to reach around the Korovega's shield and to see the trees behind him.

Ice filled his stomach as his brain registered what his eyes saw. One of the three trees their team of riflemen had been using no longer stood complete. A large swath had been burned out of one section, a clean hole that smoldered at the edges but left nothing inside.

"Ash! Jack! Go! Lena, down here!" Heather snapped. Owen thought he detected a waiver in her voice, but could not be sure. She struck out with her baton, but the Korovega parried with its sword, relaxed its wrist and snaked its sword hand around the forearm of Heather's baton-hand. The sword actually struck her hard on the side of the head, but did little more than produce a long gouge in her helmet.

Owen readied a cut, but the Korovega moved first. It turned, throwing Heather off balance and into Owen's side. She slammed into the guard of his sword, but he managed to get the blade itself out of the way. Even through her hard armor, he was afraid the impact my have broken a rib.

"You are going nowhere, perz-manus!" The Korovega snapped.

Ash hesitated for a moment, glanced at Heather and Owen and Sam, and then turned away and ran toward where the other flash came from. The man Heather addressed as Jack lingered two steps behind him. The Korovega lunged, spitting him through the back with its sword. He fell backward as the demon jerked its blade free of his chest.

Gunfire erupted again from the trees, covering Ash's movements.

The Korovega engaged with Owen, Sam, and Heather wrenched its sword away from the dead cop, turned, and aimed a blow at Sam's head with its shield. She slipped to one side and parried with her guard, deflecting the blow at the last second. Her wrist screamed, but she was still alive.

Heather's legs tangled under Owen's and they both fell. Sam moved to cut at the Korovega's exposed arm, and realized only at the last moment why it was exposed.

Its shield was gone and something evil glowed in its palm. The thing's hand was aimed at Ash's retreating back. All of the gunfire was directed the other direction.

Sam swung, the Korovega moved away, clenched its fist to recover its shield in buckler mode and aimed a thrust at her ribs.

Heather had freed herself and was halfway to her feet. She yelled, turned her rise into a dash, and tackled the Korovega in the gut. They both went over, but not without it bludgeoning one of her shoulders with its shield and the other with the pommel of its sword.

The Korovega fell backward, but as Owen rose, he realized its movements were still under control. The beast hit the ground hard, but it rolled and threw Heather into the air and onto her back.

The fall, Owen saw with a sick feeling, also took it several yards away from his and Sam's positions, and its shield was gone again.

It raised its hand.

Owen cursed vehemently in his head. He moved, both terrified and furious, toward the Korovega, knowing that somehow he had to stop it before it could kill again. He lunged once, twice, then hit the pavement as a tackle from behind threw him roughly to the ground.

Blue-white light streaked past his head. He looked back; Sam had a tight grip on his knees and the trees behind them were less several burning branches.

Gunfire cracked overhead. One shot even struck the nearby Korovega in the shoulder before it realized it, too, was being shot at again and expanded its shield completely.

Owen looked further back. Only one of their three rifleman trees still stood. The second tree was gone, obliterated at the trunk by the blast from his Korovega. The two men in the tree might have survived its collapse, but a cross-wise blast from the other, still unseen Korovega vaporized the entire section where the two riflemen had been perched.

The cop Heather had assigned to be their lookout stood at the base of her tree, rifle raised. She fired another burst into the Korovega's dome-shield

"We have to fall back!" Owen shouted, not knowing or caring if the radio in his helmet picked up the sound or not. He closed with the Korovega, trying his best to occupy it until they could get away.

Heather swayed unsteadily. "How many..."

"Doesn't matter," Sam said. "Time for Plan B."

Heather's voice instantly crystallized into authority, all fuzziness gone. "Everyone to the cars, get away now!"

Chapter 24

The ground once again screamed underneath the motorcycle. Behind them, a single police cruiser ran full out, lights and sirens flashing. From the outside, they must have looked every bit the law enforcement officer and the fleeing criminal. The truth could not have been more different.

Owen had no idea how many of the police escaped. Their retreat plan, such that it was, left no time for him to look backward until they were on the road. He clung so tightly to Sam's waist that her braid filled his vision like a whip of fire. He knew only one car out of the four that entered their ambush area made it out intact. A second one had started, but one of the Korovega destroyed it before it could move, taking at least one life with it. The car behind them could hold as many as four people with their gear, assuming there were even that many left alive.

In front of him, Sam hunched over the handlebars of the motorcycle. She had made the first part of their escape using only one hand to control the heavy bike, firing shots in the Korovega's direction, over Owen's shoulder, with her shotgun in her other hand. The twelve-gauge threatened to bruise her wrist with every wild, single-handed shot, but she fired until it was clear that they were so far away that her shots would never hit.

That part of the trip had not exactly been pleasant for either of them, even ignoring the emotional pain. With every shot, the bike would tip to one side or the other as she over- or under-corrected for the recoil.

Somehow, though, it had worked and the two of them made it out of sight of the Korovega. Smoke from their bombs and from the destroyed trees climbed high into the sky behind them, a black pillar reminding them of everything they had lost in a matter of minutes.

Now, Sam had both hands on the handlebars. The shotgun hung at her side, bouncing along with every twist and bump in the road. Owen's own gun still hung from the luggage rack—he had not had the presence of mind to grab it until long after it was too late to use. It had taken him long enough to remember to put his sword away, and even longer to manage to insert the razor-edged steel into its scabbard without slicing open his other hand. Motorcycles, clearly, were not designed with swordsmen in mind.

They rode in silence as Owen finally relaxed his tight hold on Sam's waist. She took twisting back roads and streets in an ever-expanding loop that kept their ambush site near the center. No matter how they twisted and turned, a black shape followed them overhead, mirroring their every move.

When Sam, finally spoke, her voice was ice and steel, perfectly level and full of control. Owen wondered how she did it. "Call Ben," was all she said.

"Are you sure?" Owen was acutely aware that his own voice had very little of the authority he perceived in hers.

"Yes."

"Will they get here in time?"

"It doesn't matter," Sam said, grating out every word individually. "He'll get here and we'll stop this stupid circling and kill those demon bastards, even if it takes two hours."

"Who's Ben?" Heather asked. Her voice sounded hollow, but not defeated or broken in any way. If anything, she sounded just as determined as Sam did, only different somehow.

Owen jumped. He had forgotten, in their rush to escape, that their helmet intercoms were still synced to the same channel the police were using for their radios. It was a relief to hear her voice.

"He's my best friend," he replied.

"Another guy with a sword?" she asked, skepticism tinting her voice.

"Yeah. He's probably better than I am." Owen paused, wondering whether or not to come clean. The truth, ultimately would not affect their current situation. But, he asked himself, would knowing that he had been telling an incomplete truth before hurt Heather's trust in him, and in Ben by extension? He inhaled sharply, aware that the sound would carry through the radio, and continued with, "he's the one who actually killed the Korovega this morning."

Heather exploded over the radio. "You didn't kill it? I've just lost another eight people, including Ash, for your information, and now you tell me you didn't actually kill the damn thing you told me you killed? What the hell kind of con..."

"Heather," he said. He realized his hands were tightened into fists and he forced them to relax. He continued, "Sergeant Allen. Please. Let me explain."

"Make it good," she growled.

"Ben and I fought it together. It killed one of our friends before we could stop it. Ben was the one who actually landed the blows that killed it. One in the stomach and one to the neck."

"And just what did you do?"

"Protected him, fought beside him, and," he said and, growing either confident or reckless, added, "cut the Korovega's hand off and saved his damn life. I think I know a little about what I'm saying, alright?"

"I'm," she paused, "sorry. Look, it's just me and Lena in here. I think everyone else is dead and I never saw Ash after he went to fight that other Korovega. There's," she sighed, "there's just two of us left now. I don't know where Carl Blanchard went. I think he ran as soon as the Korovega showed up. I hope he ran."

"Look," she continued. The tenor of her voice changed, sliding back to where it had been when she was giving orders before their failed ambush. "I don't know what to think about your sword-thing. It didn't work back there, but maybe that was because of the second one."

"It was." Owen tried to put as much absolute confidence into his voice as he could manage.

"But you fought well before they got ahead of us. I think you're right. I think we could have killed that one if not for the second one.

"Go ahead and call Ben," she continued. "Any help we can get right now will be useful."

"Can you call in any other police?" Sam asked.

"I," Heather replied, "don't know. Until we kill these things, anyone approaching without knowing, I mean really knowing, how they fight will get themselves killed. I don't like it, but I think any backup I call will just be walking into a trap."

"He's about thirty miles north of here. On an average day, it's close to an hour's drive. Can we keep this up for that long?"

"What road?" she asked.

"What do you m—"

"What road will Ben be driving down?" she demanded in clipped tones.

Owen sputtered over his words, trying to articulate street names and federal road numbers at the same time.

Sam spoke up instead. "He's going to come in 61 to 95," she said, "through Clinton."

"What's he driving?" she asked.

"Either a gray, surplus Police Charger or a black '77 Firebird," Owen replied. Those were the two fastest cars at the house. He would undoubtedly bring one of them. The trucks simply did not have the top speed he would need and Ken's motorcycle would only hold one.

"We won't need to keep it up for that long," Heather said. All of her previous authority had returned to her voice. "I'll handle that part of things. You just call him and be ready when he gets here. Tell him to hurry."

The controls for the motorcycle's communication system were on the outside of the helmets. In addition to volume controls, it also had a switch to toggle between different modes. The default mode, of course, was the intercom they had been using. Another setting could be used to listen to music, while the third patched into their phones.

Just before Owen hit the switch, he heard Heather's voice again. Just to make sure he would miss nothing important, he listened for a moment. She was quiet, and he realized what he was hearing was her voice picked up by the microphone in Lena's helmet.

"...argeant Allen, 62-95 checkpoint. Elza Gate Checkpoint? Be on the lookout for a gray Dodge Charger, police surplus, or a black 1977 Pontiac Firebird. We have had an emergency here and the driver of that vehicle will he assisting us.

"Additional units?" she asked a curious tone in her voice. She paused, probably listening, then, "another Korovega group toward Knoxville? Mobbed by a crowd? Jesus, how many... no, don't tell me.

"ETA," she said after another pause, "as soon as he can get here."

* * *

Ben's phone rang, playing the simple little song he had assigned for when Owen called.

"Hold up," he said. He stopped moving suddenly, trusting in Will's sense of self control to do the same. He panted, but resisted the urge to lean forward and rest his hands on his knees. His breathing came hard and fast, not that his heavy gambeson and the hot afternoon air made things any easier. The only solace was in the shade of the deck, but the light rain had driven the humidity levels through the roof, so every drop of sweat on his skin stayed there rather than evaporating. Between the two of them, they had consumed a full gallon of water in the last hour alone.

Will froze in place and Ben laughed. He made a rather amusing sight right then. He, like Ben, was soaked with sweat. His hair was plastered to his scalp and his mouth was slack, letting in as much air as possible without gaping like a fish. One gloved fist was raised, ready to punch. He had been trained not to heave his shoulders when breathing deep like he was, and his sides bulged in and out rapidly as he stood upright.

The bruises from where the Korovega that killed Jessie slammed him with its shield stretched in garish red-and-purple blotches across his torso. One covered the outside of his right bicep and the other spread across the right side of his chest. Both spots had been steadily bruising worse as the day had gone on. He refused to admit they hurt, but Ben had noticed him favoring that side of his body when they sparred.

Before sparring with Ben, Will had been working on the shop's walls. He wore the tshirt and pants he had had on since that morning and a gorget around his neck, but no other protective gear. Ben, on the other hand, was still swathed in his thick, gray gambeson despite the heat of the afternoon sun. He sweated profusely, but he insisted on wearing it as often as possible to, "get used to the heat."

"Everything alright?" Will asked, relaxing. The rush of adrenaline and exertion had done wonders to calm his nerves, he thought, and wondered how much of that was obvious to the others.

Ben shook his head slowly, picking his phone up from the railing beside their training area. "Probably not. Owen wasn't supposed to call unless he ran into a problem they couldn't deal with on their own."

"Maybe they're out of gas?" Will offered, hopeful.

Ben chuckled. "Could be, but I know Sam, and she'd have tossed an extra gas can into a saddlebag before she left."He held up a hand for silence. "Yeah?"

"Ben, we're in trouble," Owen said. His voice was muffled by the wind beating against the outside of his helmet.

Ben chuckled. "I could'a told you that."

"Seriously," Owen said. His tone made Ben stand a little straighter as his attention snapped to the phone and only the phone. Beside him, Will felt the change in his level of tension and drew himself up straighter as well.

"Spill," Ben ordered.

"Korovega. Four."

Ben's blood ran cold. "Holy shit."

"Sam's alright."

"I know she's alright," Ben said. That much he could hear in Owen's voice. "Are you alright, dumbass?"

"Yeah," he replied. His voice was quiet. "Listen, we're near the west end of Oak Ridge. The cops will let you pass straight through; don't even stop."

"I'll be there as soon as th' laws of God an' man let me."

"Call me when..." Owen started to say, but Ben had already lowered the phone from his ear and hit the, "end call," button.

"Owen?" Will asked.

Ben held up a finger in the universal "one moment" gesture, and turned to address those working in the yard. "Alright!" He kept an iron rein on his voice. "Everyone gather 'round. We got a few changes to the plan."

Will pivoted on his heels and faced Ben. He stayed quiet, waiting for news, orders, or both. He had a particular way of furrowing his eyebrows without actually narrowing his eyes when he was concerned or stressed. Right then, he looked both concerned and stressed at the same time. Tension that had finally started to unwind as he sparred returned, and worry lines creased the skin around his eyes.

George and Michael, with the latter in the lead, were already on their way as well. They both had stopped working at Ben's first outburst and now left their half-finished wall behind. Michael hurried, apparently eager to get out of the sun, though with his soaking-wet shirt, the shade would offer little comfort. George, behind him, hurried as well, but more slowly, with reservation in his steps.

Marcus, on the other hand, had continued working until Ben called everyone over. Like Michael and George, he was soaking wet from the rain showers that had passed through earlier, but he mitigated most of the discomfort by never putting a shirt back on after his first shift. He adjusted the cinderblock he had just stacked on the wall, nodded, and slapped a blob of cement on it. He spread it around, then picked up the one sitting at his feet and stacked it on top of the previous block. Satisfied, he walked away from the work site and toward where everyone else was gathering.

Ben looked around at the assemblage of faces. "Katrina?" he called.

"Up here," she replied from the deck. She leaned out over the railing. The black fencing mask gave her the appearance of a high-tech security robot. The thick, blond braid sticking out from under the mask's leather shell ruined the image, though.

Ben repeated the gist of what Owen told him, then, "and, I'm going out there to save his ass. Anyone who wants to come's got five minutes to be in the car."

"I'll go," Katrina offered. "I'm already geared up."

Ben nodded. "Alright, that's one."

"I volunteer," Will announced.

Ben shook his head. "No dice."

"Why not?" Will demanded. "You know I can fight!"

Ben nodded in agreement. "That's why you and Marcus are staying here. I want at least two people I can count on to hold their own here."

"I'll go too," Michael said. He wore a gorget and no other protective gear. He had been working on the workshop in the sun, and then in the rain, and shed everything but the steel collar that reminded him, in a twisted way, of Jessie.

"Are you crazy?" George asked. His eyes went wide. "We go out there and we could get killed."

Michael closed his eyes, and when he opened them again, something different lurked behind them. Something stronger had taken the place of the mild-mannered peacemaker who had first shown up at Owen's apartment, blindly following his friend.

"What the hell is that supposed to mean?" he growled. "Of course we could die if we go out there! We could die here, too. The Korovega could come kill us all tonight and if we don't stand up and fight, then it's not going to mean a god damned thing when we die.

"Besides," he went on, softening slightly, "they'd do the same thing for me."

George flushed bright, angry red. He clenched his fists at his sides, then released a long breath of pent-up air.

Following Ben into what was sure to be a hellhole was the last thing he wanted to do, especially considering that he knew for a fact that they would be heading toward the Korovega, but Michael was going. He drug Michael into this mess in the first place, he thought, and he was not about to give anyone the idea that he would abandon his friend. Certainly, he could not let Michael go off on his own with someone with no sense of self-preservation, like Ben.

After mulling it over for all of three seconds, he nodded once and said, "fine. But if you're going, I'm going too. Someone has to watch your back."

Michael smiled. "Glad to hear it."

George did not look similarly glad, but he was not backing away from his statement.

"Alright," Ben said, "grab your weapons and get in the Charger. MOVE!"

Katrina sprinted to the stairwell and dashed down it, heedless of the rain-slick steps. She slipped on one near the bottom, but caught herself on the hand rail and continued her descent.

"Katrina!" Ben called.

"Yeah?"

"You know where my keys are?"

She nodded. "The rack behind the bar in the basement?"

"Right. Grab them, start the car while I get weapons for these two," he pointed to Michael and George. The latter still had a Bowie knife hanging from his belt, but no other weapons.

She nodded, then sketched a salute. Between Michael's idealistic use of the gesture, and Will and Marcus's former-Military habits, the act had spread fairly rapidly among their small group. Katrina herself picked it up, near as Ben could tell, that morning from Marcus.

Ben saluted in return, then turned to the others.

"Michael," he said with a nod, then with somewhat more reluctance, added, "George. Upstairs, grab weapons."

Michael saluted. "Will do. Does it matter which..."

Ben shook his head. "No. Take what you want, but be fast about it."

Michael nodded, then turned to George. "Come on. You'll need something heavier than that knife..."

They disappeared inside, leaving Ben alone with Will and Marcus.

"Hand me that, will you?" Ben asked, pointing to where his sword belt leaned against the exterior wall of the house. Marcus, standing nearest it, picked it up and handed the heavy weapon over.

"What do you need us to do?" he asked.

"Watch the house," Ben replied, fighting with the buckle on the sword belt. In gloves, it was not the easiest thing to manage, and so he stripped them off and dropped them on the ground while he tightened and fastened the belt. "You two have more combat training than the rest of us combined, so I ain't worried about leaving you here alone."

"Not that it did us much good this morning," Will replied, massaging his bruised arm.

"We did all that we could be expected to do," Marcus said. Carefully, keeping Ben in the corner of his vision to measure his facial expressions, he went on, "mistakes happen in combat. You and I should know that more than anyone here. It's more important that you fought and fought well."

"He's right," Ben grunted. "I saw you 'fore you got your ass handed to you, and you probably kept Jessie alive longer'n she would have been otherwise." He looked away, refusing to meet either of their gazes for a moment. "Thanks to you, I got to see her alive 'fore that thing," he sighed, "before it killed her. So thanks."

Will smiled. He had not thought of it that way and wondered how Ben could remain to optimistic after losing such a close friend. "You're welcome, I..."

"Don't worry about it," Ben said. "Just don't forget, alright?"

Will nodded. "I won't."

"Good."

"Alright, so who's in charge?" Will asked. His demeanor changed, becoming more regimental.

Ben shrugged his broad shoulders. "Don't matter to me, t'tell th'truth. You two figure it out between y'ownselves. I need to go inside and make sure those two didn't break nothing upstairs. Probably won't see you again until we get back, so you two be safe, hear?"

Will grinned. "Shouldn't we be saying that to you?"

Ben shrugged again. "I ain't the one staying here by my lonesome."

"But you're going toward danger."

Ben's mouth twisted in a toothy smile, but the light in his eyes was anything buy joyful. Will thought he had seen the same look in the eyes of a lion once, right before it brought down its prey and tore it to pieces. "That just means that I know where the danger's at."

"Come on," Marcus motioned for Will to follow him up that stairs to the deck. He paused. "Ben," he said, "bring everyone home."

Ben nodded once. "I will. Don't you worry none."

* * *

Ben came up the stairs from the basement into an argument. "The hell are you two going on about?" he demanded.

Michael started first, "he doesn't..."

George interrupted. "Nothing."

Ben crossed his arms. "Listen." His tone indicated that he would accept no arguments of any sort. "You two have exactly two minutes from right now to get in the car before we're leaving. What's the problem?"

"Michael's trying to make me carry one of your damn swords."

"And he's saying he doesn't want to."

"I don't!"

"I don't know how much that really matters."

"It matters to me!"

"Hold it!" Ben snapped. "Ninety seconds left. Michael, there any issue with your gear?"

He shook his head. "No, sir."

"Good. If you're going, get your ass in the car. Katrina probably claimed the front seat, so pile in the back."

"But, what about..."

"Move!" Ben roared. He jerked a thumb in George's direction. "I'll take care of him."

Michael gathered up his shotgun and slung the short-barreled weapon across his torso. He stopped halfway to the door to check the chamber and safety, then exited. Ben hid a sigh—some things, he thought, could only be taught through repetition, but Ben was confident that Michael would get it eventually.

He wheeled on George. "Now, you," he growled. "We ain't always seen eye to eye, but I ain't got time for that right now. If you're coming with us, you're coming armed. You got a problem with that?"

George folded his arms across his chest, doing his best to look like Ben's size and proximity was not intimidating him. He glared defiance. "No, but Michael was trying to make me carry that machete-thing he had this morning. I kept trying to tell him that I didn't want the damn thing, but he wouldn't listen. Kept telling me my Bowie wasn't enough. I don't know how to use a sword yet, and..."

Ben raised a hand, palm toward George. "Hold up. The only problem was that he didn't like your weapon?"

George nodded, smiling and pleased that Ben seemed to be siding with him.

Ben sighed. "Get in the car. There's no time to argue, and if that knife's what you're comfortable with, then that knife's what you got.

"Now," he continued, "if you're coming, come on."

George took a step, then stopped. Thoughts surged through his mind, each one fighting for dominance. "One second. I need to get something."

Ben stopped and turned. "Unless it's a weapon, forget it. We're leaving as soon as I get the car in gear, so hurry it up."

Ben turned away and made for the door. He went outside without looking back; either George would come with him or not, but he was not about to take up any more time waiting or coaxing.

George took another step as his head swam in ideas and plans. He looked at the door Ben had gone though, spared a look back through the picture windows, and dashed for the bedroom. His backpack and a heavy leather jacket were waiting just inside the door. In a moment, he had it slung over one shoulder and was on his way.

He grumbled and adjusted his jacket under the backpack's heavy straps. There had been a spare fencing jacket, but he had packed a leather jacket in his luggage before coming to answer Owen's original phone call. Like his knife, a weapon that was his and not some hand-me-down borrowed on pity from someone else, the jacket was his and his alone. He had worn it for years, but frequently in colder weather, and the heat and humidity of a post-rain Summer afternoon pushed well past his comfort zone, but he was going to need it.

When he got down to the ground, Ben had just shut the driver's door of the Charger. The massive engine roared even at idle, sending vibrations through the air and into his gritted teeth.

The front passenger-side door opened and Katrina leaned out. She waved him forward. "Come on!" she yelled. "Hurry!"

At her insistent tone—and he wondered if he would have done the same thing if Ben was the one shouting for him—George broke into a sprint. The back door opened, Michael pushed it out from the other side of the car, and he slid into it.

"'Bout damn time," Ben grunted. "Buckle up, boys and girls, because it's going to be a rough ride."

George raised an eyebrow. "How rough?"

"It's thirty-odd miles from here to there," Ben replied with a grin. "Most of it's twisty little roads through the hills. If you follow the actual speed limit, it'll take an hour to make the drive to Oak Ridge from here."

"Do we even have that kind of time?" Katrina asked.

Ben shook his head and turned back to the car's dash. "No," he said, quiet. "We don't. That's why we're going to do it in twenty minutes."

"What?" George exclaimed.

"How, exactly?" Katrina asked.

"Left that part out of the news before," Ben replied. "Owen promised me his cop buddies in Oak Ridge aren't going to stop us or get in our way."

Katrina nodded as though that made perfect sense. She understood the implications, the sort of emergency that would be required to give them that sort of leeway with the laws of the road, but she never allowed that concern to show on her face. She was unsure if she trusted Ben far more than she thought she did, or if, after the past few days, she was simply unable to feel fear about anything anymore.

George instinctively grabbed the seatbelt with both hands, holding on to the cross-body strap as though it were a lifeline. Michael seemed to not be bothered by the thought of rocketing through tiny streets at insane speeds.

The car eased onto the concrete of the driveway and off the grass. For a moment, it seemed to his passengers that Ben had been joking or perhaps exaggerating things. That sensation lasted all of ten seconds and Ben shifted again and accelerated hard. He held just enough back from the gas pedal that the tires never skipped or smoked in the driveway, but their trip down the switchbacks below the house went by much faster than it ever would have under any rational circumstances.

Ben mumbled under his breath. "Hang on, Owen. Don't you die on me. Sam, you too. You both stay alive, you hear me? You two stay alive or so help me, I'm going with you."

Chapter 25

The Charger roared down the turnpike, going at least twice the legal speed limit. True to Owen's promise, no one had stopped them on their breakneck journey. They had seen several police cars, even been followed for a short time before the car veered away, but none had attempted to pull them over. Even the blockade at the edge of town let them through without incident, though Ben thought he detected a definite hint of nervousness in the air as he blew past what should have been a traffic stop and checkpoint. At his admittedly reckless speed, they made the trip in less than half the time it should have taken.

He gave Owen's number to Katrina, too preoccupied with keeping the car on the road to do it himself. She called, gave Ben the general area they were heading to, and hung up. Ben was quietly impressed with how she sounded on the phone. Gone was the nervous rambling of that morning, replaced by an energetic confidence.

"I'd kinda like to know what street they're on," he grumbled.

"He couldn't tell me," Katrina replied. "He said they were still moving around, but we should be able to find them when we get there."

Ben nodded, but said nothing.

"There's a fire," Katrina offered, "from where they fought the Korovega. Maybe two. See the smoke?" She pointed at a faint pillar of gray-white haze smeared across the sky from the other side of town.

"You think that's them?" he asked.

"I don't know," she replied, hesitant. "I'm not from here, remember? I don't know the street names of anything in this city, but..."

"Slow down."

She took a deep breath. "Owen said the Korovega had started fire in some trees, and he said they were still on the West End and we're heading west, so I think this is the right direction."

"Good. That's what I'm feeling, too."

She offered a smile. "Needed a second opinion?"

"Something like that," he said. He returned a perfunctory smile, but seemed no happier than he had moments before.

At the speeds they were going, it only took another few minutes to drive across town. Police watched them, tension evident in their postures, as they went. Some idle part of Ben's mind wondered how hard it was for them to fight their training and sit there as a car driving not only far in excess of the legal speed, but rather in excess of safe speed as well, roared down the road.

In any event, he was glad they let him pass, because he would not have stopped had they tried to impede him and dragging a dozen or so more police to their death at the hands of the Korovega currently setting the west end of town on fire would not have been a pleasant way to spend his afternoon.

The intersection where the Korovega attacked was just past the high school. Katrina wondered how much that affected their choice of starting points. If the school had been in session—it had mercifully been canceled when the Korovega attacked Knoxville, though she suspected people were already using the sturdy buildings as shelter even now—the death toll would have been sickening.

Up ahead, smoke rose into the air and the stench of burning rubber and plastics assailed their noses. Ben reflexively jammed the "recirc" button on the car's air conditioning control, sealing the inside of the vehicle off from most of the smell. It did little for what had already gotten to them, though.

"Jesus!" Ben swore as the gentle slope of the road gave way to the gaping hole that had once been an intersection.

Burned-out wrecks of police cars had been scattered around, most of them missing large sections where the Korovega's energy beams had carved them into bits. The SWAT van, still half-buried in the hole, had been smashed, but not by energy beams. From the brief half-second it was clearly visible as Ben swerved, still cursing, around the wreckage, it looked as though the van had been the victim of an angry gang with hammers—or indestructible energy shields.

Bodies in various states lay around the area, too. A cluster were piled near one corner of the intersection, away from any of the burning wreckage. The further away from that pile they went, the less mangled the bodies became. The furthest ones had simply been blown apart by the Korovega's beams, while the ones closer showed conventional burns and shrapnel damage, especially around the cars.

The sight made Katrina sick, but she refused to look away. It was something she had to see, she told herself, something that she not only could never but should never forget. This was what she was going to be fighting for.

Her enemies, the things that had killed Jessie Santiago, had done this.

The car slid sideways, tires screeching in protest as Ben whipped it around the sunken pit in the center of the intersection, then between two burning cars. The ground was uneven everywhere and the asphalt crumbled beneath the big car's wheels. Ben silently prayed that the street directly in his path was still intact underground. He hoped there was not a larger collapse just waiting to happen. They would avoid this route on the way back.

A glint of light amid the matte blackness of the pile of dead policemen caught Katrina's eye. It was little more than a glittering streak of silver-gray amid the black gear and blood. The sight was visible for less than a second, barely more than a single thump of her rapidly-hammering heart.

"What the..."

"You see something? I need to stop?" Ben demanded in rapid-fire syllables.

She shook her head emphatically. "No, no. Don't stop for anything. I just thought I saw something shiny under all those bodies."

"Probably just wreckage," George offered from the back seat, speaking up for the first time in fifteen minutes.

"Probably," Katrina agreed. "It almost looked like an arm, though." She looked back to the horizon. A dense black cloud, low and billowing in a stiff wind, hung over the area a few miles down the road. It was low enough that it had been hidden by the treetops until they crested the small hill where the two highways intersected. "There!" she called out.

"I see it," Ben said. Louder, "keep an eye out, all three of you. If you see anything moving, I want you to speak up. Be loud!"

"Got it," Katrina said.

"Yes, sir," Michael added.

George refused to say anything. His face was white as a sheet, but he kept a dutiful eye out his window. Trees and streets and other things unidentifiable at their speed rushed past. How, George thought, they would spot a tiny blue motorcycle without slowing down below eighty was beyond him. But the sooner they found Owen and Sam, the sooner he could be out of Ben's screaming metal deathtrap and on his own feet again.

To George's surprise, he was the first one to notice the glint of blue a few streets over. Katrina had taken her eyes off of that particular spot to watch the road ahead, but George had the good luck to be looking in exactly the right place at the right time as the brightly colored bike passed between two buildings.

"There!" he shouted, pointing.

"Keep an eye on 'em!" Ben yelled, spinning the wheel hard to the right. The back end of the car skidded around, whipping the Charger into a tight turn that ended with them driving sideways across the road. He added that to the list of things that, on a normal day, would have gotten them arrested in the last hour hour alone.

"Kat, you see 'em, too?" Ben asked.

"No," she replied. She wondered where the nickname came from, but had the good sense not to ask about it right then. "Wait, yes! There!"

"Right here!" George called.

Ben jerked the wheel to the right.

"No, next one!" Katrina barked.

"Too late," Ben grunted. "Everything connects here, anyway. Keep watching."

After the turn, it became clear that Katrina had been right, but there was nothing they could do about it. Sam's motorcycle was two streets over now, to the left of the car. He looked back and forth between the road and her motorcycle, trying to determine whether or not Sam had seen them yet.

"Call Owen again," Ben said. "Tell him we're here. Tell him to find a safe spot to park so we can get this done and go home."

Katrina nodded and pulled her phone from the thigh pocket of her pants. "Owen," she said. "It's Katrina again. You do? Great. Tell Sam to find a place to park. Good. Tschuß."

"We good?" Ben asked.

She nodded. "Yeah. Just follow them."

Ben whipped the car around another tight turn, this time to the left. They went down a block of residential streets, then turned sharply to the right. They were going much slower now, but the car was still close to doubling the posted speed limit.

As the car straightened out onto the new road, they fell in behind another, slightly newer Charger painted in the colors of an Oak Ridge Police interceptor. On the far side of the car, which itself was driving far faster than the speed limit, was a bright blue motorcycle.

"Found 'em!" Ben yelled. "Woo!"

"Alright!" Michael added.

Ben eased his death grip on the steering wheel. "Now we can relax."

"The hell we can," George growled.

"Oh, come on," Michael said. "We found Owen and Sam before anything happened to them. We can celebrate for a minute or two at least."

"Take the time you got," Ben said with a small shrug.

"Have it your way," George grunted. "Yay. We found them and now we get to fight the Korovega again."

Ben glared into the rear view mirror. "You didn't have to come, you know."

"Yes, I did." George refused to meet Ben's eyes. There was something more than defensiveness in his tone, but Ben could not spare the attention to decipher it.

"Have it your way."

"Guys," Katrina said, "they're turning."

Ben followed as first Sam's motorcycle and then the police car turned into an otherwise empty parking lot. Sam dropped the kickstand on her motorcycle. Owen slid off the side, and Ben was pleased to see that he was moving relatively well, if a little stiff. He had been worried, given how Owen had been tossed around by two fight after fight in the last few days.

Stubborn bastard, Ben thought with a grin.

Sam slid off of the other side, moving with more fluid grace in her muscles, but what looked like twice as much fatigue. She carefully kept her gaze directed at Owen or across the parking lot, deliberately not looking over her shoulder at the police car pulling into the lot behind them.

Not wanting to crowd the armed and probably jumpy police officers, Ben guided the car into a gentle stop behind them as the front two doors opened. He waited for the rear doors to open, and when they remained closed, he realized exactly why Sam was avoiding looking at the police just then. Riot cops never operated in teams of two.

He imagined seeing what happened to Jessie multiplied a dozen times over and it frankly terrified him. He had no desire to empathize with what those two police officers had been though.

"Masks and weapons ready," he ordered, setting the parking brake and taking the car out of gear.

* * *

Ben was the first one out of the car. Michael followed him, then George, who took a moment longer to retrieve his backpack. Katrina was last because she had to disentangle Ben's sword belt and mask from her own gear. Everyone except Ben, because he was driving and needed his feet free, had their gear in the floor underfoot. Katrina, because Ben's had no other place to be, had his as well.

Ben buckled his sword belt and looked back up in time to see Owen and Sam approaching. They skirted around the two police officers, but the pair of cops followed a few steps behind. Owen raised his visor, revealing a face with deep bags of fatigue under eyes that were red with either dust or emotion. His smile showed despite the fatigue.

"You made it!" he said, as though Ben was arriving early for a party, rather than coming to his aid on what might as well be a battlefield. He threw his arms into the air and hugged Ben. "I'm surprised to see you three here."

"Thanks," George growled.

"She volunteered," Ben said, gesturing toward Katrina, then to Michael. "Same with this guy."

"I assumed you'd bring Marcus and Will."

"Thanks for the vote of confidence," George said. Owen could see the a mix of anger and fear on his face. He looked the same as he had that morning, and Owen wondered what had prompted him to accompany Ben.

Ben shrugged. "Needed to have them guard the house."

"Makes sense. In any case, I'm glad to see all four of you," Owen replied.

"You seem chipper for someone who just escaped death," George observed dryly.

"That was then," he said, stepping back and looking from person to person. "Now that you all are here, things are going to be alright."

George shrugged and turned to Michael. "Come here for a sec. I've got a question."

Michael nodded and followed George a few feet away from the others.

"Are you sure?" the taller of the two riot-suited police behind Owen asked. Ben was surprised at the softness of the voice coming from that black-clad monolith. He expected to hear a gravelly, serious voice that was more suited to barking orders than discussing things rationally. Instead, he heard a voice that sounded like she was addressing him like a friend.

Ben buckled his sword belt and adjusted his sword on his hip so that the sword hung right where he wanted it. Mask under one arm, he held out a gloved hand, smiled, and said, "Ben Stuart."

The riot cop held out her own hand and took his in a firm grip. "Sergeant Heather Allen," she replied. He could not see anything behind her black face mask, but her voice sounded relieved. "You're the one Owen told us about?"

Ben nodded. "I assume so," he replied with a grin. He took his hand back, slipped his mask over his head, and adjusted the straps inside and outside of the thick leather cover. Now clad in armor as intimidating as the cops in front of him, if designed for a different century, he asked, "where are the Korovega?"

Heather nodded and pointed. "That way. About a mile and a half."

"Running?"

She nodded again.

"Figure we got fifteen minutes, then," Ben said.

"Less," Katrina offered, stepping into the circle with her mask on as well. "If they're running full out, which I assume they are?" She gestured at Heather, who nodded in reply to the question. "Then we've got less than ten minutes."

Sam said she agreed.

Ben took half a step forward to physically interpose himself in the middle of the circle of people. "Point is, we ain't got much time. What's the plan?"

"Can we sneak up on them?" Michael asked. "I mean, it's not night time, but you're all in black. Maybe we can sneak up on them?"

Heather shook her head. "We don't have anything to ambush them with anymore. There's eight of us and two of those things, though, and if we can get in close, we'll have it made."

"I've got an idea," Katrina said, "if that's alright?"

Heather nodded. "I'll entertain any serious suggestion right now."

"Well," Katrina said, then explained her thoughts, outlining an ambush plan based on what she had seen of the area they drove through to get there.

"I agree," Sam announced, once she was finished.

"It's sound," Heather said. "Objections?"

There were none.

Sam added, "we still need to be careful, though. Stick to the shadows and overhangs where their eagles can't see us."

"You boys good shots?" Heather asked, turning slightly to address Michael and George.

"What?" Michael asked. He had been focused on George's gesticulating and missed the question.

She repeated herself.

Michael started to answer. "Not rea—"

George overrode him. "We're decent, why?" he asked. He felt like he knew what she was going to say, but went with it anyway, so that it would not seem like it was his idea.

"You're not wearing as much gear as the rest of us," she said.

"We didn't have enough," Ben interjected.

"Talk to me after we kill these things. The least I can do is pay you guys with some surplus armor."

Ben nodded. Inside his mask, he smiled.

"Anyway," Heather went on. "You two don't have as much armor as we do, so if we can get you two, and maybe Lena, to cover us with rifles while we close..."

"I can do that," Michael said.

"You've got a shotgun," George argued.

"I think Sergeant Allen was implying that we could borrow one of hers."

"You've shot one of those things?"

Michael nodded, then with reluctance, admitted, "at a range."

"It'll do," Heather said. "Just stop shooting when we get within twenty feet. What about you," she asked, turning her attention to George. "Mister...?"

"George," he replied, then, "Sinon. I'm a good shot, good enough, anyway."

"Alright," Heather said, "Gather 'round. Owen, Ben, you two have fought these things before, so say something if you've got any better ideas, but..."

She outlined her plan of attack based on the ideas Katrina had given a few minutes earlier. Owen insisted that the five of them going in with melee weapons operate in a group of three—Ben, himself, and Sam—and a group of two containing Katrina and Heather. Katrina spoke up against that plan, arguing that her limited experience was based around working with Ben, a point that Ben himself backed up. At Ben's insistence, the teams ended up being himself, Katrina, and Heather in one team; and Owen and Sam in the other. That left Lena in charge of Michael and George.

With everyone in agreement, they split up. Lena, Heather, and Owen were designated as "team leaders" since they, along with Sam, had access to the radios. In minutes, the three teams were out of visual range of one another as they moved through the heavily industrialized area. Each group had a rough route to take based on where they assumed the Korovega to be, but each person with a radio was instructed to alert the others when they came into sight of the pair of surviving Korovega.

By default, the radios were all left on, but they had agreed to stay silent until someone made contact.

* * *

Sam and Owen crept among large storage crates and pre-fab sheet metal buildings, trying to get a better idea of where both they and the Korovega were. She tried to hold her breath, or at least to keep it quiet. Hearing everyone else's magnified in her ears for the past hour had made her self-conscious of how loud simple breathing could be.

Somewhere outside of her vision were the other teams. Lena, Michael, and George were supposedly sneaking on separate paths through the buildings, each searching for the Korovega. Ben, Heather, and Katrina moved in a large arc around the area, sweeping wide around Owen and Sam's search area.

As it happened, she was the first person to sight the Korovega. A little more than five minutes after the large group broke up, she caught a flash of sunlight on the monster's armor. One of the many things she packed was a small mirror, which she fished out of a jacket pocket and used to spot the Korovega directly.

Two Korovega stood on the far side of a small, open area. Where they stood would have been the perfect killing around if only bullets could penetrate their energy shields.

She took a moment to actually look at the Korovega. Their initial assessment still seemed to be correct. Something was different about these two. The one they killed that morning had not been armored like these, but it went beyond that. These two were definitely taller, she thought, possibly larger as well. The Korovega that attacked the house was only a hair taller than Owen, but these were closer to Ben's height. Where the others had crept around, sneaking in dark clothing, these swaggered.

They moved like soldiers, she realized. They had been right in calling the other ones scouts, because these were clearly part of the main fighting force of the Korovega army. That explained why these were so much tougher, at any rate.

One of the Korovega gestured angrily at the sky, then at the area around them. She caught a few words, including "perz-manus." She recognized that as the term the Korovega used to refer to humans, or so it seemed from the few brief words they had said amid trying to kill her.

At last, she saw a street sign. "We see them," she whispered into her helmet mic, and read off the two street names on the intersection. "About five hundred feet away from the road. They're searching the area, but I don't think they know we're here yet."

"You're a block from our position," Heather replied, equally quiet. "Hold there and don't break silence unless they see you. Where are you Lena?"

"We're close. I see the stop sign Sam described. Awaiting orders," she replied. She spoke quick and crisp. It reminded her of how Marcus and Will had spoken when fighting the Korovega. Sam wondered if she had previous military experience.

"Keep moving until you make visual contact, then report in."

"Roger," Lena answered. She relayed her orders to Michael and George, giving each a direction to travel so that they could spread out their fire. Sam dimly heard two voices acknowledge her orders. Then, "don't fire until I do."

"Owen," Sam hissed. He realized she had, for the moment, turned her radio off. He did likewise, ensuring whatever they said would not be picked up. "What?"

"We both have radios," she said, then stopped to make sure he was following. "Yes?"

"Split up. Come at the Korovega from two directions."

She waited as he considered their possible tactics. Emotionally, she disliked the idea of letting him out of her sight. They needed to watch each other's back and the idea of spending the next few minutes not knowing where Owen was made her uneasy. Intellectually, she knew she was right. The more targets the Korovega had to deal with, the more confused they would inevitably be.

Owen thought for no more than half a second before nodding once. She wordlessly adjusted her path to put distance between the two of them. Her thoughts lingered on him for a moment longer before she focused her entire attention on the task at hand. They could not afford any distractions.

* * *

"Targets in sight," Heather whispered. "We're at the north perimeter."

"Targets in sight," Lena echoed.

"Fire in ten," Heather ordered.

"Roger."

Mentally, Owen counted backward from ten. When he reached three, he heard the crack of a rifle shot, followed by several more. In and among the metal buildings, sheds, and containers, the rapports echoed off of a hundred surfaces, making their origin impossible for him to pin down. There were so many echoes that it was also impossible to tell how many shooters there were, which helped their ambush.

The first shot took one of the Korovega in the arm. Subsequent shots bounced harmlessly against a pair of iridescent blue shields. As the shooting grew more intense, stray shots hit the metal buildings around the Korovega as well.

Owen took a deep breath, forcing himself to relax. Nothing he could do now would improve their chances. The plans had been made and they had been executed with a precision he had been afraid to expect.

He tightened his grip on his sword, then forced his hand to relax. Too tight a grip and his blows would be sloppy, and his arm would tire too quickly. Time seemed to slow to a crawl as he, according to plan, counted backward from five.

Four. The sound of gunfire and the crackle of Korovega shields combined and echoed, building to a deafening crescendo. He turned the volume on his radio down. No one would be whispering anymore.

Three. He caught movement out of the corner of his eye. One of the Korovega moved toward him, sidestepping away from the hail of bullets.

Two. The Korovega had not seem him. His pulse thundered in his ears and he wondered if, like Edgar Allan Poe's unnamed narrator, his heart would betray him and beat so loud the Korovega would hear it.

One. He took a deep breath.

Zero.

He whirled out from his hiding place, sword at the ready. The Korovega spat something in its guttural language and actually flinched in surprise. Owen caught the words "khat-manus," but nothing else sounded familiar. He gloried in the brief flash of fear he saw in the thing's eyes. That shock was over in a moment, before his second footstep hit the ground, and the Korovega's sword was ready.

It raised its shield to block Owen's cut just in time to save itself. It swung its own sword and Owen parried, then parried the follow up blow. The Korovega punched with its shield, but the blow was clumsy; its feet were not yet completely in sync with its attacks, and Owen dodged easily enough.

The Korovega cut again. It was even faster than the one he and Ben killed that morning. No matter; he was ready for it now. Moreover, he owed it payback for the massacre half an hour before. Owen parried, and pushed forward, pivoting his sword against the Korovega's and turning his parry into a thrust. It would have hit the thing straight in the face had it not jerked out of the way at the last minute.

It threw its shield hand at Owen to counter-balance the dodge. The blow was low, aimed at his ribs, and would have hit him had Sam not interrupted.

She made a cut to its arm, forcing the Korovega to throw its momentum into yet another wild evasion. It worked, and the creature ducked low to avoid Owen's next cut, sweeping Sam's legs out from under her as it went.

Owen cursed. The alley where they now stood was too narrow for him to easily step around her. He spared one look down, mouthed, "sorry," and leaped over her temporarily prone body. He barely avoided landing on her arm.

Jumping in combat might have been stupid, but he had no other choice. To stay away from it was to give the Korovega the second it needed to drop its shield and use a beam. So, he jumped at the creature. It held its sword out like a spit, but Owen knocked it aside with his own sword. He was unable to do anything with its shield, though, and crashed into it.

He was prepared for that, and hit the shield with his shoulder. The impact still sent an agonizing shock through his wounded back, but the adrenaline pumping through his veins turned a scream-worthy pain into a minor annoyance that was quickly forgotten in the wake of a flurry of attacks and parries.

Sam got to her feet then and joined Owen in attacking. The Korovega, now fully invested in the fight, moved around like a snake. Its sword lashed out here and there, just often enough to prevent Sam and Owen from pressing their numerical advantage.

It came around a corner, using the pivoting motion of rounding the edge of the shed to backhand an oil drum with its shield. The drum rang like a bell and thudded to its side, shuddering like a half-full water bottle.

Owen put a hand on the side of the oil drum and vaulted over it. Sam was a step behind him, and cleared the obstacle even easier than he had. To his surprise, the Korovega never dropped its shield to use its beam on them. Instead, it stared him down as he closed, and he felt a strange sense that it was somehow personal to the gray monster.

That was just fine as far as Owen was concerned.

Out of the corner of his eye, he saw the other Korovega. Three black-suited figures were pushing it backward as well. They seemed to be doing better than Owen and Sam were, but they also had more people involved in the fight. A riot baton, a saber, and a schiavona traded blows with the Korovega's sword and shield, and Owen spared a moment's thought to express respect for the Korovega's skill. He could only hope that he would be able to fight that well as things went on and they needed to use their swords more and more.

Owen also caught sight of another figure dressed in black armor. He assumed that was Lena. She had her rifle leveled and swept it constantly between the two Korovega.

The Korovega were only a few dozen feet apart when Sam realized just what they were doing.

"Keep them apart!" she yelled.

Both groups fanned out, trying to come between the two Korovega. Despite their best efforts and their numerical superiority, none of them were able to flank either soldier. The two creatures moved too quickly, too assuredly, for any of the humans to come between them. Each step they took put them exactly where they wanted to be, cutting off each effort to come between them before anyone could get more than a few steps in any direction.

Suddenly, the Korovega were nearly back to back. They moved in a tight circle around each other, blocking cuts and thrusts and strikes coming in from five different directions as through their two swords could each be in three places at a time.

Heather swung her baton, and one of the two Korovega—no one could tell which was which anymore—parried it. Its sword slid down the riot stick and slammed into her forearm. The blade sank deep into her armor, but no blood answered the cut.

Next to her, Owen cut at that Korovega. It dodged, and its foot struck out and hooked behind Heather's leg. She fell to one knee as it wrenched its sword free of the hard plastic sheathing her arm. As it came back upright, it flicked out its own sword, aiming for Owen's head.

Owen blocked and make a clean riposte. The Korovega caught it on its shield as it turned its sword and slammed the edge into Heather's head. She went over sideways, nearly collapsing against Ben as she toppled, but Owen still saw no blood.

"I'm alright!" she shouted into the radio.

Owen moved to fill the gap she had left, deflecting another cut from the Korovega that had knocked her down. He cut, the Korovega blocked it and cut against him. Owen caught that attack on the bars of his sword's guard. Before he could aim a riposte, the heavy blade of Ben's schiavona swept across his vision. "His" Korovega's sword was tangled in a bind against it and he managed to hit, and gain control of, the other Korovega's sword as well.

The Korovega Owen had been fighting barked something and the other one ducked. Owen's Korovega turned its wrist, escaped the bind, and lashed out with an overhead thrust. It aimed over its partner's head, directing the point at Ben's chest.

Ben stepped backward, pulling his sword free to defend himself as he did so. Sam and Katrina both aimed at the crouching Korovega. It parried Katrina's thrust with its sword, but Sam's blade came in around its shield and left a long red gash on the inside of its bicep.

Owen aimed a cut for the exposed back of the Korovega he had been fighting. Remembering at the last second that they wore armor on their torsos, he bent his wrist backward against the sword's momentum and slammed the pommel against the thing's back. Its breastplate rang with the impact and it stumbled, nearly falling over its partner.

It lashed out, off balance, but its first attack went so wild no one had to parry at all. The second attack was on target for Sam's head when another low cut forced its partner to parry as it rose. They collided, tangling into each other's arms for a split second.

The two Korovega were on their feet properly a moment later, but they had been off-balance just long enough for Katrina to jam her saber up under one breastplate. A spray of bright red blood erupted from the wounded Korovega's torso and it roared in pain and fury. It slammed its shield down on her arm and twisted. The two motions wrenched the blade out of her hand, and forced her to one knee.

The Korovega swung at her head and she jerked away from it, trying to come to her feet at the same time. The tip of its sword raked across her mask and she screamed. She, barely, resisted the urge to turn away, instead retreat as quickly as possible before it could make another attack. Her uninjured hand cradled the other arm as she felt for broken bones.

The Korovega's wound was surely fatal, but unless the head or neck is wounded, assuming Korovega were the same inside as humans, it would be some time before it bled out and died. It ripped Katrina's bloody sword from its guts and threw it aside, in no hurry to give up the fight.

If anything, it attacked harder now, knowing it was going to die. It parried a cut from Sam's saber, bound it, and slammed its shield into her face. The cracking of plexiglass, at least Owen hoped that sound was her visor, echoed over the radio as she hit the ground.

Owen landed a cut on its shoulder, just past the metal armor, as it made the attack that hit Sam, but if the Korovega noticed, it never hesitated. Now, Owen landed another blow on its arm. The stolen Korovega sword in his hand bit deep into the creature's arm and Owen, enraged, shoved forward. The long slice nearly severed the thing's arm and it took a moment to move its sword to its other hand as it stepped toward Owen.

With a scream, it slammed its nearly-severed arm into Owen's side like a flail. The impact knocked him off his feet. It raised its sword and aimed the point at Owen's chest. It descended before he could react, but a blur of motion from the corner of his vision intercepted the coup de grace, and slammed into the Korovega like a freight train.

When his vision settled on the figure, Owen realized it was Michael. His rifle was lost somewhere between his firing spot and where he now stood, hammering the Korovega's face and breastplate with blows from his cutlass. Out of the corner of his eye, he saw Lena and George sweeping the fight with their rifles, keeping them covered in case the Korovega somehow broke free from hand-to-hand range.

The Korovega screamed again, saying something that would likely have been incoherent even if Owen understood its language. It stepped forward as Michael embedded his sword in the thing's thigh. It stumbled, but that only meant its thrust took Michael in the gut instead of the throat where his gorget might have saved his life.

It withdrew its sword and kicked Michael aside. He was wide-eyed, staring at the blood on his hands when Owen lost sight of him on the other side of the Korovega. The creature streamed blood from a dozen fatal wounds, but still it came on. It stumbled and Owen thrust his sword through its face and out the back of its neck.

It made a gurgling sound that might have been a roar if not for the sword tearing its face apart and the blood spilling out of its mouth. It fell to the ground. Owen kicked it in the breastplate, pushing it away while recovering his sword.

He turned. Heather was back on her feet, fighting again. The baton, he noticed, was in her other hand now. The arm she had been using hung limp at her side. Katrina held a long knife, Ben's knife if Owen's memory served, and circled the remaining Korovega. Her knife was much too short to be of use against its sword, but Ben and Heather were taking care of that part of things. Katrina, he saw, seemed to be watching for openings in the Korovega's defense. She lunged here and there, but none of her blows connected. She succeeded, however, in dividing its attention.

Owen started to kneel by Sam's side, but she shoved him roughly away. Less than thirty seconds had passed since she had been knocked down.

"Help them!" she screamed. He saw blood underneath her helmet, but she seemed to be moving well enough as she came to her feet. Her visor was shattered and a network of spiderweb cracks spread across what little plexiglass remained.

The last Korovega turned its head and saw Owen approaching. It also saw its fallen comrade and hissed something sibilant. It dropped to one knee and slammed its shield fist into the ground. A shockwave knocked everyone away for a moment as its shield abruptly converted from buckler to the dome version. It was easy enough to penetrate that shield at close range, but conjuring it gave the Korovega enough space to quickly step out of the circle of attackers around it as the blast wave knocked them all to the ground.

Heather was closest. It plunged its sword into her chest with only a moment's warning. Gone was the mocking posture the other had displayed before trying the same on Owen. This Korovega attacked with no flourish, only brute utility. Its sword cracked through the hard plastic armor she wore with ease.

Lena screamed, too frozen to fire.

The Korovega turned and aimed its sword at Ben.

Sam and Owen were the farthest away, unaffected by the shockwave. She had barely gotten to her feet at that point, but she turned her rise into a lunge. Owen, ahead by two steps, lunged. Even Katrina scrambled to her feet and tried to lunge, but they all knew the same thing: they were all going to be too late. They would reach the Korovega before it could withdraw its sword and fight them off, but its death would mean nothing if Ben died, too.

Ben was having none of it. He lurched to one side and the Korovega's sword buried itself in the ground where his heart had been moments before.

Ben rose to his feet. The Korovega left its sword where it was and slammed into him like a wrestler. Unfortunately for the Korovega, Ben was a wrestler too and much larger than it was. Even with only one hand, he threw the creature to one side.

It rolled, came up to one knee with a hideous grin, and raised a hand. In its palm glowed an orb of blue-white energy.

Ben took a step. By now, Owen was even with him and Sam was only a half-step behind. Katrina lagged behind her.

The Korovega grinned and Ben wondered how close he would get before the thing sent them all to hell.

And then its head exploded.

Chapter 26

The Korovega, or what was left of it, slumped to the ground. Ben swept the horizon like a cornered animal. The others did so as well, with varying degrees of success. Ben's nerves shook more from what happened in the last few moments than everything that had happened the hour before put together. He had been absolutely certain that he was about to die, but then something had happened. Someone he could not yet identify had saved his life and he either wanted to thank who or whatever it was, or berate them for taking a shot that could have killed him.

He looked to his right. Nothing but buildings that way, and the road on the other side. Any shot coming from that direction would have been close. Lena, or possibly Michael or George, would have been shooting from that direction. Something from that close would have been easy for the Korovega to block.

The bullet could not have come from behind, either. It, or fragments of it, would have continued on to hit Ben as well. That only left one direction. He looked to his left. A man stood on the roof of one of the lower buildings nearly a hundred yards away, aiming from a vantage point where he would have a clear shot across the entire industrial compound. His platform was barely more than a corrugated metal awning, but it held his weight. He peered through the scope of his rifle, sweeping it back and forth across the area.

Ben had almost settled on thanking the policeman when his brain ground to a sudden halt. A feeling like electricity went through his nerves and he spun in place. The shooter was momentarily forgotten. The cop killed the Korovega; neither merited further attention just then.

He spun in place, ripping his mask off and letting it fall forgotten to the ground. Likely, he would have dropped his sword as well, but the schiavona had a pair of bars inside the hilt that his fingers wrapped around. Even with his hand relaxed and the big sword nearly forgotten, it stayed in his hand. That, he would decide later, was a good thing. He would have berated anyone else for dropping a weapon, even after the fight was over, possibly especially then.

"Michael!" he yelled. Michael had fallen only a few yards behind him. That was distance that he could cover in seconds. Ben fell heavily to his knees; his armor made a dull clunk as he dropped to the asphalt.

Owen and Sam were by his side moments later. Sam removed her helmet with practiced deftness, while Owen fumbled at the catch for two angry seconds and then gave up. Instead, he smacked the visor upward.

"Get his shirt off!" Sam shouted, setting her saber on the ground next to her knees. She produced a pocket knife and used it to slice the front of Michael's shirt open.

Ben grimaced. He had seen enough blood in his time as a cage fighter, but sword wounds were a whole other level of gruesome. Sam blanched and Owen turned a putrid shade of green. The sword had slid in cleanly enough, but in their mutual frenzy, the Korovega's blade had dragged to one side, opening the wound wide. Another tear showed where the sword had been ripped free of his stomach.

Sam swallowed hard and probed the wound, looking for organs and arteries.

Michael's eyes flew open and he screamed. Sam withdrew her hand with a jerk as Michael's scream turned into a gurgle. Pink, frothy blood spilled from one corner of his mouth and Sam cursed. That sort of unusual color only meant one thing: a punctured lung.

"Get me a tourniquet!" Sam yelled, already doubting the efficacy of having one. She cursed silently, damning the decision to leave her backpack, with its first-aid kit, with the motorcycle. What she really needed was something to pack the wound with.

Ben picked up Michael's discarded shirt. It was sweaty, and already bloody, but it was all they had. It would staunch the bleeding some, but it was dirty and the wound would have to be washed thoroughly when they got home. It was still better than nothing.

Ben sliced the shirt in half with his sword and handed one half to Sam. He balled his half tightly and pressed it against the wound. With Owen's assistance, he raised Michael's torso up off the pavement slightly. Sam used the other half to fashion a makeshift bandage. The shirt had been black, but he was bleeding so severely that it left an impossibly dark stain.

"Michael?" she asked.

He nodded weakly. "Hurts worse than band camp." The comment elicited a laugh from Ben, and a smile from Sam and Owen. "How bad is it?"

"It's not bad, really," she replied, making her face smile.

Ben stepped away, watching the area around them. One Korovega remained unaccounted for.

Michael's expression, despite the lines of pain turning his face into a twisted caricature, was clearly disbelieving. He had felt the sword enter his guts, after all, and could still feel the blood leaving his body. That part felt strange, like standing under a warm shower from whence only the tiniest trickle of water came.

He tried to turn his head to look at Owen, but found his muscles already refusing to cooperate. He had heard that the dying felt cold, but he merely felt warm. As the pain in his stomach died away, it was replaced with a pleasant comfort. He felt, for just a moment, like he did after drinking a hot mug of apple cider.

And then he coughed and the searing white-hot pain in his stomach drug him back to the harshness of reality.

"Captain?" he asked. His head still refused to turn, but he locked eyes on Owen with a feverish intensity.

"Yeah," Owen replied. He made a second attempt to remove the mouthguard of the helmet, and was successful this time. He did his best to smile.

"Doc won't tell me," he said. One arm twitched like he was going to point at Sam, but no real motion happened. He coughed again and dribbled more pink froth. He took a moment to force down a breath, then asked, "how bad is it, really?"

Owen sighed. Michael wanted the truth and, in his dying moments, he supposed he owed him nothing less.

"It's bad," he admitted after a moment. "I'm not going to lie to you."

"Fatal?" Michael asked.

Owen looked at Sam for a moment, but she was the one who answered. "Yeah. Maybe if we had a field surgeon on hand, but..." She stopped and looked away.

"I understand."

Ben stepped into his view again.

"Hey, Big Guy. I messed up."

A fleeting smile touched half of Ben's mouth, but morphed into a grimace. He squatted next to Michael and put his hand on the smaller man's shoulder. He looked down at the ground, sighed, then made eye contact with Michael.

"Y'didn't," he said. Ben's voice was gravel, the sound of the earth itself expressing an opinion. "You did everything right. Shit just happens sometimes."

Michael's mouth twitched. He struggled for a second or two, then managed a smile. "Thanks, man," he said, then coughed again. His breathing had become rough. Every breath gurgled in his throat amid the steady stream of blood and foam coming out of the corner of his mouth. "Hey. Cap..."

Owen leaned closer. Michael's eyes were unfocused, and Owen moved in front of his face, trying to catch Michael's dim eyes with his own. He failed, and took Michael's hand instead. "I'm here."

Michael smiled again, but his eyes never saw Owen.

"I'm here," Owen repeated.

Michael's eyes closed, but he continued breathing. He opened them again a few seconds later. For a brief moment, his eyes held Owen's own. "Front pocket of my pants," he grated. "Left side. Take..."

"Michael?" Owen asked, then repeated it. He shook his shoulder gently, then slapped at one cheek. "Michael!"

Sam put a hand on Owen's shoulder and he looked up. He met Ben's eyes. The latter's dark face shook slowly left and then right.

Owen blinked back tears, but followed Michael's last request. In his front pocket, Owen found Michael's wallet. He looked at it, confused for a moment. Of course, they had all agreed that even after death everyone's money was to be shared, but surely there was more to his request than that.

"Look inside?" Sam offered.

He did. The interior was bloody, but the leather and fabric were not yet saturated. He looked at the cards one by one, wiping the blood off on his pants as he did so. Finally, he came to the cash pocket. It was empty except for a single card.

Hidden in the cash pocket was Jessie's driver's license.

"I think he wanted us to have this." Owen held up the little card.

Ben took it and looked it over. He slipped it into the back pocket of his pants. "Make sure to take his ID, too. We'll put them in the box where George put Ken's."

Sam spent the next few moments oblivious to what anyone around her said or did. She was dimly aware of Ben moving around and voices talking, but that was it. She touched the side of Michael's face gently with one hand and with the other undid the bandage holding the bloody t-shirt to Michael's stomach. Maroon blood ran like water onto the ground. She had no idea if he was still alive just then or not, but there was no chance of him surviving much longer. If he was alive, he had passed out or fallen into a coma.

It was better that he die peacefully than wake up to the horrendous pain of his wound again, she thought. She turned away from the others and allowed herself to cry for a brief moment, then forced it all back down inside once again.

* * *

"Where the devil..."

"What?" Owen asked, rising.

"George!" Ben called. He stood and looked around the area. After a moment, he spotted George standing near the edge of their battleground. A blank look was on his face and his eyes were fixed on Michael. "There you are. You alright?"

"George?" Sam called. He did not move. The borrowed police rifle hung from its sling by his side where it had fallen from his slack hands. Sam took a step toward him. "Are you..."

A thousand emotions and expressions flashed across his face in a moment as George shook himself back to reality. Fear, anger, and rage won out, or at least they did in the brief moment where Sam could see his face.

Sam took a third step and George turned and ran.

"George!" Sam shouted.

Ben turned and laughed. Rather, he made a noise that was like laughter but was devoid of everything except hatred so all consuming that, for that moment, he felt nothing else.

"You son of a bitch!" Ben yelled, leaping into a run. "Get back here!"

George ran, cradling the rifle against his chest like a stuffed animal. Despite his figure, he was fairly light on his feet and darted through the buildings and around machinery with ease that Ben had a hard time matching.

"You let him die!" George called back.

"God damn it, George Sinon!" Ben shouted. "The Korovega..."

"The Korovega will kill us all!"

"The Korovega..."

"You'll get us all killed, you fucking psychopath!"

"If anyone let Michael die, it was you!" Ben accused.

Silence answered him and Ben stopped running. He had lost sight of George. Even so, he unslung the rifle from his back and fired two shots into the air. Ben roarer. "He trusted you! You hear me Sinon? You hear me! Your friend is dead because of you! Coward! Bastard! Worthless piece of shit! I will find you, George Sinon, and I will tear you to pieces with my own two fucking hands. Do you hear me?"

He went on like that for another minute, yelling, screaming damnation on George's soul. He invented new curses and laid them at George's absent feet.

"Ben," Sam said. She approached warily, from the front where he would not be surprised by her sudden presence. She had never seen him so mad. "Ben," she repeated, placing one gloved hand on Ben's armored forearm. "He's gone. Let it go. He'll get his in due time, I promise you that, but right now we have more important things to take care of."

"What's it matter?" Ben growled, but he made no move to shake lose of her grip.

"It matters." Her voice was firm, commanding. "We can't let ourselves be controlled by anger."

"Don't you go all Jedi on me, woman," Ben growled, but his expression softened a bit. It was not yet a smile, but it was something more pleasant than a scowl. He sighed. "We need to check on the cops."

Sam nodded and followed him to where Lena bent over Heather's body. The mystery cop from the hill stood a few feet away, watching. He held his rifle and scanned the horizon around them, still on guard for anything that might come their way. After Ben's tirade, he eyed Ben with suspicion as well.

Owen followed, silent. He felt exactly like Ben did, but Sam was right. There would be a time for yelling, and that time was after they found George again.

Hell, he thought, he might even kill him himself.

* * *

Katrina, finally able to even look at his body, sat beside where Michael had fallen. She watched the blood pool spreading on the ground underneath him without saying a word, and wondered how close she had come to sharing his fate. For that matter, she wondered how she had managed to stay alive at all. She had done practically everything wrong, from losing her sword to failing to protect Michael and Sergeant Allen.

She rocked back and forth, and scooted away from the blood where it was flowing down a slight incline and toward her. She kept her mask on, the only one other than the mysterious policeman to do so. The metal mesh and leather comforted her, serving as a barrier between her and the violence outside.

Across the small open area that had been their battlefield, Sam approached the three remaining police. "Is she...?"

Lena looked up. "Yeah," she sighed. She wiped blood off of her mouth, transferred from Heather during her attempts at resuscitation. "I've tried CPR for the past five minutes and nothing. Her skin's cold and then there's the blood."

"Michael, too," Ben rumbled.

Lena sat back on her rear, falling limply to the ground beside the body of her sergeant. Everything about her seemed contradictory as she dropped her face into her hands. She wore hard riot armor, yet she sat slumped into her own hands and ignoring the world for a moment. Her clothes projected an image of being a tough cop, but her red face and defeated posture said the opposite.

"I suppose I should thank you." Ben addressed the policeman who killed the second Korovega.

"I was just doing my duty," he protested.

Sam recognized the voice instantly. "Ash?"

He nodded.

"You're alive! How?"

"You know him?" Ben asked.

"He was with us the first time we fought the Korovega," Sam said. "Ash, I thought you'd been killed!"

"Those reports were exaggerated," he said, trying to make his voice sound light. He raised his faceplate. The entire left side of his face was black and blue and several red gashes streaked across his cheek and jaw. "The Korovega knocked me for a loop. I guess they thought I was dead when I went down."

"They didn't, ah, check?" Ben asked, making a downward stabbing motion with his free hand. He chuckled with dark, bleak humor.

"Apparently not," Ash said. He tried to grin, but only half of his face moved. He rubbed at his helmeted head. "I don't really remember a lot of the fight. We stopped to make plans, and I caught some flashes of fighting, but that's it."

Ben held out his hand. "However you did it, I owe you one."

Ash took his hand and shook it, but said, "you don't. Without you, we'd probably all be dead."

Ben grinned. "I insist."

Ash released his hand and returned the smile. "I can't argue with that. We need to get back to the station and make our report, though. Heather, and everyone else, is going to need a proper funeral as well."

Ben nodded. "Us, too. I want to get away from this spot as soon as possible."

Ash held out a hand. "Lena?"

She looked up, then to his hand, and took it. He helped her to her feet.

"Give us a minute," Owen said, "and we'll walk back with you."

Lena shook her head. "We're staying here."

Owen's eyes went wide. "You are?"

She nodded. "At least for a few minutes. I'm going to call for a van to move the bodies."

"I understand," Ben said. He clapped Ash on the shoulder. "Thanks again."

Ben turned to walk away, but Ash stopped him. "Hey. I've got one more thing to offer."

Ben turned back. "What's that?"

"You know the checkpoints around town?" he asked. All three of them nodded emphatically. "I can put in a word to let you guys through. Maybe even get you a permanent pass so you don't have to deal with the blockades at all."

"You do that and that'll be two I owe you for."

Ash nodded toward the fallen Korovega. Katrina, who had finally taken her mask off, was kneeling over one of them. She wore a thoughtful, curious expression.

"You've done a lot for us already," the policeman said.

"Not enough," Ben said. "And that's that. You need us, you call me, ok?"

"You've got my number," Owen volunteered.

Ash nodded. After he called Ben, Heather had insisted they all trade cell numbers in case the radios gave out. Of course, the more damage the Korovega did, the less likely the cell towers were to continue working. As long as they did, though, Owen wanted to maximize their usefulness. Although the irony of the police calling him for help, rather than the other way around, was not lost on him after the day they had had.

* * *

"Guys?" Katrina called. "You might want to look at this."

Owen turned and practically sprinted over to her. Ben followed, his long legs eating up the distance with easy strides now that his adrenaline was settling down. Sam brought up the rear, motioning for Ash and Lena to join them. They declined and Lena took the base unit of her radio out of its pocket and adjusted the frequency.

Katrina held up a single glove. It was made of red leather, or whatever sort of animal hide the Korovega used for clothing and armor. Thin metal bars the color of polished bronze were attached to the back. They looked like the bones of the hand, and were perhaps meant to sit in the same places when it was worn. The bars seemed too thin to be armor, though they did flare out into small, articulated cups that covered the joints. A wide band of ornate metal filigree covered the knuckles and connected the finger bars to another set of five bars running to a segmented brass cuff around the wrist.

It looked very ostentatious, Owen thought. Made of the right material, he supposed it could be decent armor for the hand against light strikes, but nothing in the way Katrina was holding it said "armor." In fact, she seemed to avoid touching the metal pieces.

"It's a glove," Ben observed.

"It shocked me when I touched the metal," Katrina replied.

"Really?" Sam asked. She reached out in the instinctive human reaction to touch the one thing they were just told not to. It shocked her too.

Katrina nodded. "Not bad. It was like a static zap, like when someone shuffles around on the carpet and pokes you."

"Probably best not to mess with it," Ben said. "Some freaky Korovega glove is hardly worth getting shocked over."

"I was going to put it on," Katrina said.

"That's probably not the best idea, Katrina, no, wait," Sam protested, but Katrina already had the glove on her hand. Owen reached for it, and it rewarded him with an uncomfortable, but not painful, shock.

"Do you feel anything?" he asked.

Katrina shook her head. "Not really."

She flexed the fingers one by one. The glove seemed to have near perfect mobility, which was good. Owen supposed if she wanted to keep the glove for herself as a sort of souvenir, he had no reason to stop her. He had one of their swords, after all.

Katrina shrugged. "Maybe it doesn't do anything," she said. Just then, she made a fist and a scintillating blue disk flashed into existence in front of her hand. It floated half an inch in front of her knuckles. She yelped in surprise, opened her hand, and the disk vanished.

"Holy..." Ben muttered.

"That was one of their shields!" Owen said. Suddenly, his fatigue was gone, replaced with excitement on a near child-like level. "Do it again!"

Katrina took a deep breath to slow her raging heartbeat and slowly closed her fist again. Once more the shield appeared—perhaps a foot in diameter and shot through with veins of energy like frozen lightning.

"You know what this means?" Owen asked.

"We can use their weapons against them." Katrina's face brightened as the realization washed over her.

"Guys!" Owen called. "Ash! Lena!"

They looked as Owen leaned to one side to reveal Katrina's glowing shield. They stared, mouths agape.

"Take the other one," Ben offered, "Call it a gesture of good faith. Hell, I said I owed you one anyway. Take one of their swords, too, while you're at it."

Ash nodded and moved toward the Korovega as Ben turned back to the others. He impulsively hugged Katrina, enveloping her in his big arms. When he let go, he was grinning from ear to ear.

"You did good to notice that," he said.

She flushed. "Thanks. Think the one at the house has one?"

"It's worth looking at," Owen said. "Come on, let's go back to the cars and head home. I've had enough of Oak Ridge for a little while."

"We need to come back for Michael," Ben said. The elation of discovering that they could use the Korovega's shields for themselves overshadowed his grief and anger at Michael's death, but not completely. "Let's bring the Charger back here. We'll take him back in that and give him a proper funeral at the house."

Owen nodded. "We'll get the bike and wait for you."

Despite everything, their spirits were much higher as they make their way through the half-mile of industrial streets between their battleground and where they had left the cars. They were, of course, exactly as they had been left. Big Blue was in front, with Heather's—temporarily belonging to Ash or Lena, Sam supposed—police car behind it and the Charger behind that. The cruiser's blue lights were still on, but everything else had been shut off. No one seemed to to around for miles.

Ben fished the keys to the charger out of his pocket and unlocked the doors. With a weary sigh, he unbuckled his sword belt, tossed it unceremoniously in the back, and slumped into the driver's seat. It was going to be a long drive home.

* * *

The sun was low in the sky when the two-vehicle caravan pulled into the driveway. Marcus and Will stood like statues on the deck, watching for anything coming. Will, with his extra-long rifle and bayonet at the ready, stood at one corner. Marcus, AK47 in hand and one of Ben's machetes strapped to his waist, watched from the next corner.

Sam reached the house first. She left first and had been in the lead for most of the journey home. Their trip back home had taken much longer than either trip to Oak Ridge—vastly longer than Ben's, especially—because they stayed close to the speed limit. She doubted the police would have stopped them since they had not stopped her on the first leg of her trip, but she wanted to take no chances. True to his word, Ash arranged for them to enter and leave Oak Ridge through the checkpoints with no hassle, but she felt like anything more would be pushing their luck.

"You're back," Marcus said, coming down the stairs. His grip on the rifle had relaxed slightly. The black bayonet drooped toward the ground. "Are you alright?"

Sam opened her mouth, then closed it. Nodding was wrong, because she had just watched nine good men and women die, including Michael. But the survivors were all in one piece, if a little worse for wear and they learned something important, so an abject "no" would also have been the wrong answer.

She opened her mouth again, licked her lips where they had grown dry, and chewed on her bottom lip for a moment as she thought. Finally, she shook her head. "We're alive," she answered slowly. Her voice was muffled and thick, presumably from the smear of dried blood covering it and her upper lip. "Most of us."

"Most?" Marcus asked.

She nodded. "Yeah. I'll tell you more inside," she whispered, easing the motorcycle forward.

"When we get inside," Sam said, sotto voce. She spoke only once they were out of Marcus's hearing. The radio in their helmets picked it up well enough and transmitted it to Owen. "I'm going upstairs and getting into the bathtub. I'll come down after a while."

"Alright," Owen said. "How's your nose?"

"Not broken." She waited for Owen to get off, then killed the engine and slid off herself. As she guided it to its resting place next to the basement wall of the house, she said, "so that's a good thing, at least."

Owen nodded. "Yeah."

"And you?"

He sighed. "I hurt. Back. Arms. Legs. Neck. Everything feels like I've been dragged into the yard and beaten with a broomstick for an hour."

"Ok, so you get the bath first."

Owen flicked off his intercom and raised his visor. "Sam," he said. He placed a hand on her arm. "I'll be fine for an hour or so. I had my time off last night. You've earned the chance to relax, alright?"

She nodded reluctantly. She hated to be relaxing when she knew everyone else was working. The idea made her feel like she was goofing off, or taking advantage of the others, even though she knew nothing could be further from the truth. Just thinking about it made her tense, but she supposed that was Owen's point.

And, Sam admitted, the thought of a hot bath was appealing.

Behind them, she heard Marcus's shout of, "hey!"

Sam turned to see Ben's car driving past Marcus without stopping. The dark gray car came up the driveway, then drove into the yard to return to its parking spot behind the trucks.

Marcus trotted up to the car, rifle bouncing against his back, as Ben opened the door. "The hell's the matter with..." he started, then stopped when he noticed the grim expression on Ben's face.

"Bring me a cup of coffee and we'll talk about it," he said. His expression was set like granite in a scowl and his eyes never quite focused on Marcus. Marcus hesitated, and Ben punctuated his request with a snapped, "now!" then a much quieter, "please."

Marcus nodded and turned back to the house. He passed Owen, who fell in behind him. Sam heard the murmur of hushed conversation start as soon as the two of them were out of Ben's hearing.

Sam crossed the short distance between her parking spot and Ben's. She removed her helmet completely for only the second time since setting out that morning. Her hair and face were plastered with sweat and she tried in vain to tuck the stray locks behind her ears and out of her face. Her nose and upper lip were covered in dried blood. Eventually, she gave up on her hair and held the helmet under her arm.

"Is everything alright?" she asked.

"What do you think?" Ben growled.

Sam nodded once with closed eyes. "I meant," she said in firm tones, "did anything happen on the drive home?"

Ben shook his head. "No," he replied. "Nothing else."

"We actually had a rather nice talk," Katrina said, climbing out of the passenger seat. "It wasn't what you'd call pleasant. I don't think any of us, not right now anyway, could manage anything like small talk or even polite conversation, anyway. Not... not right now. We did talk a lot, though, about what's happened."

Ben nodded and leaned against the roof of the car, resting his elbows on the sun-warmed metal. He looked out into the yard, across the water, and away from where Sam stood.

"Damnit," he muttered. His voice was weary. "Why'd it have to be him?"

"What do you mean?"

"It could have been any of us. Should have been me."

"The hell it should have," Sam retorted.

"You, me, Owen, hell, even that cop lady were all fighters. We knew what we were getting into. Him..."

"You think he would have volunteered if he didn't know?" Katrina asked. "He's a good man. He understood..."

"He knew alright," Ben grunted. "But it still ain't right. Odin's supposed to take the ones who fight well, not the kids who only picked up a sword last night."

A long moment passed before Sam asked, "can I get you anything?" Just then, that was the only thing she could think of to say. It felt hollow, but silence would have been worse. She hoped the abrupt change in subject would help take his mind off things.

Ben sighed and buried his face in his gloved hands. The polished leather gleamed in the gathering darkness. "I want a drink," he confessed.

"No."

He sighed, but that turned into a laugh. "I know, I know. I ain't coming within a dozen miles of a bottle, but that don't mean I don't want one right now," he said, then turned serious. "Damn it, Sam, this ain't fair."

"Hey," Katrina said. Her voice was quiet, but it echoed in Ben's sudden silence. She laid a hand on Ben's arm. "Life may not be fair, but you do what you can while you're alive, right? Determination will get you through today. Somebody told me that and I think it's important right now."

"Don't placate me with m' own platitudes, Kat," Ben said, but he smiled.

She looked crosswise at him for a moment.

"Sorry," he said, grinning wider still. He turned to Sam. "Anyway. To answer your question, no. Not right now, anyway. Marcus is bringing me coffee; that's enough for the next few minutes. Let's get through them first, yeah?"

"By the way," Sam said, "thanks."

Ben nodded. He plastered a smile on his face. "Couldn't let you two die out there, you know? I kinda like you, after all."

Sam laughed. "Well, thanks," she said. Nothing else seemed appropriate.

"Besides," Ben continued as they stepped, one by one, though the basement door. "If you got yourself killed by a Korovega, who'd make my coffee?"

Sam, despite everything, smiled. "You don't like it the way I make it."

"It's coffee, woman. I'd drink it with a little kittycat drawn on top if it tasted good."

Sam and Katrina both laughed. The sound was nearly free of the sort of hollow despair that had clouded over them since that morning.

Marcus met them at the bottom of the stairs, carrying a small plate with three mugs on it. He left his rifle somewhere on the upper floor. His face had fallen. Fatigue showed through his expression, no matter how he tried to hide it. He, like the others, looked tired.

"Christ, man," he said. "I'm sorry. I didn't know."

"It's alright," Ben replied. "You didn't know."

Marcus held the plate out. "One black and two with cream and sugar. That one," he pointed to the mug with the lightest liquid in it, has extra cream."

The three of them took their coffees one by one.

"Is the body of that Korovega scout still in the yard?" Ben asked. He and Katrina, on the drive back, had compared the Korovega they had fought in Oak

Ridge with the one that killed Jessie. They came to the same conclusions Sam had, that a scout had come to their house, while the ones from Oak Ridge were some sort of actual soldier.

Marcus nodded. The non sequitur was a surprise, but he went with it. "Yeah. We didn't want to burn it until Jessie's, ah," he swallowed hard, "until her pyre had burned down. Didn't want to mix the ashes, and all."

"Good," Ben said. His face visibly brightened. "Because I think we might just have a use for that thing after all."

Marcus raised his eyebrows. "Oh?" he snapped his fingers as a thought came to him. "Yeah, Owen said to ask you about that, Katrina."

She held out her coffee. "Mind holding this for a moment?"

Marcus nodded and took the mug.

Katrina stepped away from the others. She still wore the glove she had taken from the Korovega in Oak Ridge. In fact, she had spent half of the car ride back to the house summoning and then dismissing the buckler, trying to learn exactly how it worked. That had continued until Ben asked her to stop because it was distracting.

She held up her hand and flexed the skeleton-like bronze bars on the back of the glove. Then, without warning, she made a fist and a glowing blue-white shield sprang into being. In the dim basement, it gave off a faint glow, illuminating her face and some of the surrounding furniture with Cherenkov blue.

Katrina opened her hand and the shield was gone as abruptly as it appeared.

"That is awesome!" Marcus exclaimed, smiling wide. "How does it work?"

"No idea," Katrina replied. "Other than how I move my hand determines what it does. I have no idea how the glove does it, though."

"But we've got two of their weapons now," Ben proclaimed.

"Two?" Marcus asked. "Ah. That's why you needed the one in the yard. It had a shield as well."

"Right on the money. But there's two things more important first."

"What's that?"

"First," Ben said. "We need to get Michael's body ready to bury or burn."

"If we bury him," Sam interjected, "it needs to be tomorrow. It's too dark now."

Ben nodded. "I agree."

"What's the second?" Marcus asked.

He looked at him for a moment, then laughed. The sound was empty, hollow, expressing incredulity at the situation rather than actual amusement. "I'm hungry."

Chapter 27

Dinner went quietly. No one who had made the trip to Oak Ridge had the energy left to cook, and so Marcus prepared things himself. Most of it had already been started in the slow cooker sometime that afternoon and only required a little bit of tweaking to nudge things along into a finished dish.

Contrary to her promise, Sam did not immediately go to the bathtub. Because dinner was nearly ready when they arrived, she consented to wait until after eating to bathe. More to the point, as soon as she heard Ben mention being hungry, she realized that she was practically starving as well. She took the time to clean up, though. Eating dinner with her face covered in dried blood was not exactly the dictionary definition of civilized behavior.

Everyone needed a few minutes to change clothes, anyway, and she was not the only one who had been bloodied in their desperate fight. Owen's arm bled from the wounds the Korovega inflicted that morning. The wounds themselves were fairly shallow and probably would have closed up reasonably well inside the bandages by the end of the day had he not spent most of the evening fighting. Short of dental floss and a lot of alcohol, they had no real way to stitch it up, either, so and he cleaned and re-bandaged it under Sam's watchful eye.

And so those of them that remained gathered around the dinner table. They should have, according to "the rules" had one person on watch while they ate, but no one wanted to push it. After the disastrous trip to Oak Ridge, everyone wanted to be together. There were fewer of them now, and the survivors had lost a lot. Each of them wanted to preserve that feeling of camaraderie as much as possible.

Ben sat at one end, with Owen and then Sam to his right. Katrina sat directly to his left, where Michael, and then George, sat that morning. Now, Will took the next seat and Marcus sat beside him. The chair at the end of the long table, the table that the previous day had nine people clustered around its eight place settings, stood empty. Between fatigue and pain, they all moved slowly. Bruises and cuts abounded on the faces and arms around the table.

That the food was good was the general consensus. No one, though, could remember exactly what it was afterward. It was hot, flavorful, and filling, and that was enough. On any other day, it would have been a feast worth enjoying and telling stories over. Instead, as the six of them ate, they picked and prodded at the food as though it were underheated leftovers from two days prior.

Conversation drifted around, touching on various subjects. Ben, Owen, and Sam told various parts of the day's events for the benefit of the two who had not accompanied them. All of it, though, was colored by Michael's, any by extension Jessie's, death. The day had not been "good." Rather it had been "good, until."

Ben refused to discuss what happened with George. Owen told that part of the day's events, glossing over as much of Ben's reactions as he could. He was unsure how much to really blame George for, but refused to discuss it any further.

"He'll get his," was the only comment Ben would make on the subject.

Talk drifted to the Korovega themselves. Apparently the evening news had been discussing them while the rescue team was away. People had killed one an hour to the south of them, in Maryville near the college there, through sheer luck. A dozen people rushed out and beat it to death with their fists and feet, but it killed four of them before dying. There had been scattered sightings in some of the less populated areas of the state, but no reports of any deaths there, assuming that sort of thing would even make the news.

"Dean gave another address," Will said.

"Dean?" Ben asked.

"That Republican Senator," Will replied, "or former Senator, anyway."

Ben nodded. "Right, right. Th' last congressman alive or somethin' like that. What'd he have to say?"

"He talked a lot about hope, survival, that sort of thing. He said they'd deployed the military and called for people to enlist, but that's about it. He didn't talk like he had a plan beyond throwing people at the Korovega until we human wave them to death."

Ben quirked an eyebrow. "He said that on TV?"

Will shrugged, but his eyes darted around the room, watching everyone's reactions. "Not in so many words, no, but that was what I got out of it."

Ben eyed Marcus, who said, "what he said was, 'I encourage every able bodied American to enlist in the military. We will fight to defend our country and our planet until the last man or woman.' He emphasized that there was no central command anymore, and that most units would be under local control."

Ben nodded. That seemed a little more official. Even if Will and Marcus had ultimately said the same thing, there were ways of phrasing bad news that made it seem like it was slightly less bad.

"Did they news say anything about their technology?" Sam asked.

Will shook his head. "Not that I heard, no. We weren't inside much, to tell the truth. I only caught bits and pieces. We turned up the volume so we could hear outside, but that's about it."

"That's the sort of thing you'd think they would talk about over and over if they discovered it," Marcus observed.

Will shrugged. "Unless they're keeping it for themselves."

"Maybe they're researching it?" Katrina offered. "That's what I would do if I was in their position."

"Could be," Sam said, "but unless they're running a con to deceive the Korovega, I don't think they have the facilities to do anything like that."

"So you're keeping it after all?" Will asked, deliberately ignoring the implications of Sam's statement. He nodded his head toward where Katrina left her sword leaning against the counter behind them. The Korovega glove was draped over the pommel.

Katrina nodded, realizing he was asking her. "I'd like to," she replied, "if that's all right with everyone else. I'm not exactly the best fencer here, and I don't want to take it away from..."

Ben held up his hand. "You found it," he said, "you keep it."

"Besides," Owen added a moment later. "We'll get more."

Marcus raised his glass in toast. "Hooah!"

"Hooah!" echoed Will. He looked around the table expectantly. After a moment, everyone else joined in with variations on the shout.

"Now," Sam said. "About tomorrow."

She was answered with a chorus of groans and other, less articulate noises of pain. She ignored them. Rather, she paid them only enough attention to grin with amusement. She met their various eye-rolls and grunts of frustration with a smirk and a glitter in her eyes. The protests did not last long under her amused stare.

There was pain under her own grin, true enough. The mock pain that answered her, played up for laughs, did little to cover the true pain they all felt. They had lost too much in one day and they all hurt in various ways. Many of them bore the cuts and bruises of physical pain, but that would fade soon enough. That was not the sort of pain that worried her.

"I'm serious," she said. She sighed. For just a moment, as she said her next few words, she deliberately allowed her mask to slip. The corners of her mouth drooped and her eyes lost their sheen. The transformation only lasted a few moments, but it was long enough.

"We've been though a lot. I don't think anyone will argue with that. I don't ever want a repeat of today. There's a lot of work still to do out there," she gestured to the yard where the half-finished workshop loomed in the house's floodlights. "And we have to keep improving our skills if we want to survive the next fight."

She allowed silence to fall around the table while she regained her composure. "We need a day off."

"I don't think that," Ben said, then what she actually said filtered through his brain. "What?"

Sam nodded. "For five days we've been running, fighting, and building, and we just barely made it through today. We're all tired."

She met Ben's eyes for a moment. In his face, written at a subconscious level where no one still alive other than her and Owen could ever see, she saw the same sort of soul-fatigue she felt. In his face, though, the pain was ten thousand times worse. He lost a friend of nine years and a new friend he had just taken under his wing.

In that moment, too, she understood why she could never blame herself for what happened. If anyone in the room had a right to feel responsible for the deaths today, it was Ben. Jessie had been his friend and sparring partner, and he had been in charge of training Michael as well. Her losses, painful as they were, could never compare to what he was suffering right then.

"Some of us," she started, then stopped. She met Ben's eyes again and he nodded once, almost imperceptibly. "Some of us," she repeated, "did not make it through today at all. Jessica Santiago, Michael Campbell, Heather Allen, and dozens of policemen and women whose names we were not privileged enough to know all lost their lives today.

"There is a lot of work left to do," she repeated, "but we can take a day off. We have to rest at some point. We have to clean our wounds and we have to recuperate. Even more important than that, we have to take time to mourn our dead."

"Taking it easy doesn't mean we can slack off," Ben said. "We'll still run guards tomorrow. One person at a time in two hour shifts. Anyone object?"

No one did. Will even said, "that sounds good to me. I don't see that we have much of a choice."

Ben nodded. "Then it's settled. Tomorrow, we don't do a damn thing, and..."

Owen's phone rang. He took it from his pocket and checked the name on the screen. "Hold on," he said, sliding his chair back away from the table. "I'll be back in a minute. Sarah? Yeah, I'm ok. How..."

The others watched for a moment as Owen headed to the upstairs loft, then turned back to one another.

"When Owen comes back downstairs, let him know I want to talk to him," Ben said. He turned to Sam, and added, "go ahead and write out tomorrow's schedule." He too pushed away from the table, but he headed toward the basement stairs.

"Ben," Sam called. "Is everything alright?"

He paused. The pain was still there, but he nodded after a moment. "Yeah," he said, then disappeared down the steps.

Will pointed over his shoulder with a thumb. "What was that about?"

Sam watched the stairs for a moment before answering. "I'm sure it's nothing bad. Ben just likes his privacy at times. I suspect, no, I'm not going to guess. If he wants to let the rest of us in on it, he will. Otherwise, whatever they discuss is going to be between the two of them.

"Anyway," she said, turning back to the others. "tomorrow we're all going to rest and try to recover some. Sunday, we hit it again. We need to rearrange some furniture, George put his desk in the bedroom for some damn reason, and I'm sure there's a better way to set up the living room. After that, we get to finding people."

"How do you mean?" Will asked.

"We look through our contacts again," Sam replied, "hell, try the yellow pages if that doesn't work. We're going to need doctors, pharmacists, and engineers."

"A blacksmith would be good," Will added.

Sam nodded. "Agreed."

"Fair enough," Marcus said. He was silent for a moment, then looked at Katrina, who was fiddling with the last of her food. She poked at it with a fork, putting small bites here and there into her mouth, but not really seeming to actually eat anything. "You alright?"

"I," she replied, "guess?"

Marcus nodded. That was the fewest words he had heard her say at once since they met the other day. That alone made him worry, and he wondered once again how bad things actually had been in Oak Ridge. The version of the story the other told had left out, or glossed over, a lot of the gory details, but he had seen enough combat between human beings to guess at the sort of things she saw.

"If you need to talk, you know where to find us."

Katrina replied with a wan smile. After a moment, she also waved lazily at the house around them. "I don't think any of us are really going much of anywhere anyway. I don't think we really have anywhere to go, come to think of it."

Sam sighed. She thought of her apartment. If it had not been burned down already, it was probably home to squatters making use of the furniture she left behind. "Not anymore."

Will, to her surprise, laughed. "The three of us," he said, pointing to himself, Marcus, and Katrina, "haven't had anywhere to go since we got here. Kind of why we're here in the first place."

"I, for one, am glad you came," Sam said. "A lot of what's happened the last few days would have been impossible without you three."

"Aw, shucks," Will said, with feigned humility. "We didn't do that much."

Sam took a drink from her glass of juice and smiled at him over the rim. "Well that's true. I mean, all you really did was shoot that Korovega in the leg and watch the house so that Ben and Katrina," her voice choked for a moment, but she continued, "and Michael could come save Owen's butt."

"Not yours?" Will asked, grinning.

Sam shrugged and made a lazy grin. "I had it under control."

"Had the apocalypse right where you want it?"

Sam nodded. "Completely."

Marcus laughed, making a sound the was halfway between humor and pain. "Me? I could have done without the apocalypse."

Sam sighed. "Yeah," she replied, then, "but I met you guys because of it. You're good people and I'm glad to have met you."

"Thank you." Marcus's smile was broad and bright.

"But," she continued. She ticked the names off on her fingers as she said them. It felt like a practiced list, though each loss hurt for different reasons. "I also met George, and Michael, and Ken, and Jessie, and Heather, Lena, and the others."

Katrina turned to Sam and smiled, but a lot of sadness still shaded the gesture. "Are you sure you should thank me?"

Sam froze for a moment as her comment hit home. She turned, slowly, and regarded Katrina with a very careful expression. The other woman looked at her with expectant eyes, waiting not to be condemned, but simply for an answer. There was no self pity, at least none that Sam could see, in that expression.

"What do you mean?" she asked, carefully keeping all emotion out of her voice.

"I wasn't much help in that fight," Katrina replied. "Ben said I had a lot of potential, but when things got bad, I blew it. I lost my sword and then I couldn't really do anything else to help you guys. He would have been better off taking one of these guys," Katrina pointed to either side of her, at Marcus and Will. "Nothing happened here. I could have stayed and watched the house and let one of the guys who can actually fight go out there."

Sam listened with a neutral expression. Carefully, she considered exactly what Katrina was saying, because, though her justifications were different, her thoughts were the same ones Sam had had that morning. Katrina's feelings were not illogical, insofar as feelings could be logical at all, but in a way that only made things worse.

Objectively, as things played out, the day might have gone differently if they had Marcus or Will along. Yet, as she continued that train of thought, she wondered if Marcus or Will might have been a liability. Katrina was comparatively unskilled when it came to combat, but all of her training had been aimed at fighting something that fought like a Korovega. Marcus and Will, except for a short session with Ben, had not had that sort of training.

It definitely would have gone differently if they had left George and Michael at home and taken the two former Military men. Yet there was no way they could have known that nothing would happen at the house. They could have just as easily been killed at home as they were in Oak Ridge, not that that sentiment did much to assuage her feelings.

"Tell me something," Sam said after a long pause. She hoped she had not let Katrina fidget too long while she mulled things over in her mind. "Was what happened with George your doing?"

Katrina shook her head slowly. "No?"

Sam went on. "Michael died," she said. Her voice was level, but she allowed the pain to show through in her eyes, "because he saved Owen's life and my life. He didn't die because you lost your sword."

"But I..."

"Let me see your arm," Sam ordered, talking over her.

Katrina held up her arm, as requested. After they came home, she had washed her face and changed clothes. She now wore a long-sleeved shirt that seemed, from where Sam was sitting, to be too warm for the hot summer evening outside.

Sam made a gesture, rolling one hand over in a circle as if to say, "continue."

Katrina took a deep breath and rolled up her sleeve. She winced as she bumped the back of her hand against her arm. A moment later, her sleeve was out of the way, revealing an ugly, swollen, red-purple bruise on her forearm. The bright red center of it was about an inch wide and stretched across the top of her arm, but a bloom of color stretched out for several inches on either side.

"Holy..." Marcus exclaimed.

"You never mentioned that part," Will said, at more or less the same time.

Katrina explained, in more detail, what had happened in the fight. The bruise, she explained, came from the edge of the Korovega's shield. Sam credited the armor she wore for preventing her bones from being broken and keeping the injury as comparatively—compared to being killed, at any rate—mild.

"I was afraid it was broken," she admitted, "but in the battle, I just kept going. I suppose if it had actually been broken, then I wouldn't have been able to use it at all, right?"

Will shrugged. "Maybe. Being hopped up on adrenaline can do some weird things to you."

"But I'd know, right?" she asked. "If it was broken, I mean."

"Probably, yeah. At this point you definitely would. You'd find your arm bending in strange new directions."

"Not to mention the mind-numbing pain," Marcus added, straight-faced. Katrina was not sure if he was joking or not.

"There's that, too," Will added. He grinned.

Katrina shrugged. "I don't know, really. I saw an opening, and I took it. I think, maybe, what I did actually killed it, but it didn't do it fast enough, it still had time to fight."

"Hold on," Sam said. She of course had been there, but phrased the next question as though she only knew what Katrina had told her. "So you, not knowing whether or not you'd live or die, stabbed one of the Korovega hard enough to kill it?"

Katrina nodded. "Yeah. But then I lost my sword, and..."

"But you killed one, right?"

"I think so?"

"And it came a mask's thickness from hitting you, in the face, with a sword, and you kept fighting?" Sam continued.

"I," Katrina began, then, "yes."

"It sounds to me like you didn't do poorly at all," Sam said. She shrugged, but her voice made her next statement sound more like fact than opinion, "it sounds to me like you did really well."

"But Michael..."

Sam interrupted with a sigh. It had been an instinctive reaction, and partly had come from her own feelings surrounding Michael's death. The noise was not meant to stop Katrina in the middle of her sentence, but it did, and Sam took advantage.

"It wasn't your fault." Sam stopped a moment, thinking. This was not going quite like she planned it in her head. "I know it's hard to accept that, but you've got to know, up here," she tapped her forehead, "that nothing you could have done would have saved him."

"That's horrible," Katrina protested.

"It's true," Will replied. He was quiet, but his voice carried a lot of weight. Something in it suggested to everyone hearing it that he knew, in this case, what he was talking about more than he might let on. "Sometimes," he spread his hands before him, "things happen. I don't want to sound like I don't care, because he was my friend too, but when it comes down to life or death, there's no such thing as safety."

"No matter how good you are," Marcus said. "There's always luck. You can't bribe luck and you can't seduce luck. It just," he shrugged and spread his hands in a similar gesture to the one Will had just made, "is."

"I don't think I like that idea," Katrina said.

Will turned slightly in his seat to face her. "Think of it like this. Warriors throughout history have gone into battle saying that 'today is a good day to die.' Do you know why that is? It's not because they're suicidal and wanted to die."

"Because," Katrina said, then stopped as she thought through what she wanted to say, "they knew they might die and wanted to make sure they weren't afraid?"

"Bingo," Will replied.

Sam spoke slowly. "Every time I pick up a weapon, there's a chance I'll die. Someone could attack us, a Korovega could kill me, or I could die any of a hundred other ways."

"So why do it?"

"Because the alternative is giving up," she replied, conviction in her voice. "It's knowing that everyone else may die if I don't fight."

Marcus and Will nodded in turn. That was a mindset they were all too familiar with, but unfortunately, Sam was right.

"While you're alive," Will added, echoing the phrase he had heard Owen and Ben using, "you fight."

"I'll understand if you want to stop fighting," Sam continued. "There are plenty of other things that need to be done. Machines we need to build, food to grow and prepare. There are plenty of ways to help out without lifting a sword."

"I don't think I want to do any of that," she said. Her grip on the fork in her hand tightened for a moment of white-knuckled determination. "I wouldn't like that. I've never really been good at much, but this is something I can do."

"Are you still willing to fight with us?" Sam asked. "Even if it might mean dying in battle or, worse, seeing more friends die?"

Katrina met her eyes for a moment, staring right through her facade and deep down into Sam's soul. The feeling was unnerving, and Sam wondered if this was how other people felt when she did the same thing to them.

"I'm willing to take that chance."

Sam nodded, then smiled. "Thank you," she said, then pushed her chair away from the table and her empty plate. "I'm going to go upstairs and check on Owen, then get into the tub. If anyone needs me, I plan to not move for a good hour or two."

* * *

When she came to the top of the stairs, Owen had just hung up the phone. He was also smiling rather more broadly than he had since they all got home.

"Everything alright?" Sam asked. She paused on the way to the bathroom long enough to hear his response.

"Better than alright," he replied. He reflexively glanced out the large windows on the opposite side of the house, as though he were warding off some sort evil spirit that his mention of good fortune might have summoned. Nothing but the inside of the house, reflected in the two-story glass panes, was visible through the windows. In the darkness Michael's sheet-wrapped body waited its turn for either burial or cremation. He shuddered, then turned back to where Sam stood, already half undressed.

"You remember on Monday when we called all those people?" he asked.

She nodded, threw her shirt on the bed in a lazy arc, then stopped. Her eyed widened and she smiled. "You mean some more people finally called you back?"

He nodded. "Not just one or two, but six more people!"

"Six?" Sam asked, struggling to comprehend the logistics of fitting six more people in their house. At last she gave up and said, "where are we going to put them?"

Owen's smile grew. "That's the great part. You remember Sarah Pickett?"

"Vaguely?" she replied. "Brunette, tall, fenced with a rapier?"

Owen nodded.

"Hounded you for months?" Sam added with a smirk.

Owen laughed. "That's the one. Turns out her brother has an RV and they've spent the last three days driving around, avoiding the Korovega and stocking up on food and things. They picked up a few other people, too."

Sam folded her arms over her chest, thinking. "And they're coming here?"

Owen nodded. "With the RV."

She laughed. "Good luck getting it up the road."

"They'll manage, I think. Anyway, she said they were going to be here tomorrow morning. The RV is packed full of food and can sleep five comfortably, and seven or eight if they really pack in tight and some people sleep on the floor. It's got a kitchen, extra bathroom and shower, and everything."

Sam put the pieces together in her mind. "So we have the sketches that Ge..." she paused and pursed her lips as though the very mention of his name put a bad taste in her mouth, "that Mister Sinon left us for extra power, water, and so on. Can we hook everything together? The house to the RV?"

Owen nodded. "Yeah. I think so, anyway."

Sam thought for a moment. They could, conceivably, fit more than a dozen people in Ben's house if everyone was willing to sleep on couches and chairs. More than that if, as Owen said, they really packed in and people slept on the floor. Walking space itself would be tight with that many, but if they were adding another bedroom with two or three more beds and its own kitchen, then things were not quite as bad as she initially thought.

She smiled. "That's wonderful news, Owen."

"I thought so," he replied. "I'm assuming, since you're kind of naked now, that you were on the way to the bathtub?"

She nodded. "That was the idea." She gestured toward the bathroom, as if to ask, "is there anything else, or are you done?"

"Yell if you need anything," he said.

"I will," Sam replied. She turned to the bathroom, but stopped in the doorway. She turned her head and called over her shoulder. "Oh. Ben wanted me to tell you to head to the basement. He wants to talk."

"Thanks."

"Hey, Owen," Sam called from inside the bathroom.

"Yes?"

"Thanks for watching my back out there."

"Same to you." He waited a moment in case Sam had anything else to add, and trotted down the stairs. He moved, despite the fatigue and pain in his muscles, with more of a spring in his step than he had in days.

* * *

"Ben wants to see you," Will said, leaning back from the table on two chair legs. He pointed to the basement stairs. "He went that way."

Owen waved. "Sam told me. Thanks, though. He seem alright?"

"Eh," Will replied with a shrug.

Owen laughed, and headed down the second flight of stairs to the basement. At the bottom, he called, "Ben?"

"In here," a voice rumbled from the bedroom that was tucked in the basement's back corner.

The door was actually behind the counter that had once been a bar. When Ben's parents owned the house, the basement bedroom had been a guest room. It was the smallest of the three bedrooms, and consequently the last one usually filled when the place saw guests staying there. Since Ben became the sole occupant, he claimed that room for himself, preferring the cozy little space to the larger rooms upstairs.

Owen opened the door onto a darkened room. The overhead light was off, leaving only a small bedside lamp to illuminate the space. The lamp worked well enough—the room was barely larger than the few pieces of furniture in it—but the dim light made the room seem less than inviting.

Ben sat on the bed, cross legged from all Owen could tell. The lamp was to his back, leaving Ben little more than a dark silhouette. Owen could just barely make out the cover of a paperback sci-fi novel laying open and face down on the sheets.

"What's with the film noir lighting?" Owen asked, immediately upon entering.

"Th' light was hurtin' my eyes. Have a seat." Ben waved a long arm lazily at the small chair tucked in the corner beside the dresser. When Owen had settled into the well worn seat, Ben said, "before you ask, I'm alright. Ain't no drink in this house, and I'd sooner join her than fall of that wagon."

Owen did not have to ask who "her" was.

"What did you need?" Owen asked. A lamp sat on the dresser next to his seat that could turn the chair into a comfortable reading nook, but he left it alone. Between his height and the thick mattress and tall bed, Ben towered over Owen in the low chair.

"I was thinking," he drawled. "'Bout what happened today."

"Michael and Jessie?"

The silhouette on the bed shook its head. "George."

"Ah."

"Yeah."

"What about him?"

"I kept puttin' two and two together and getting six," he admitted. "A couple of things weren't making no sense. I mean, I hated the sumbitch, and I'm sure he returned that particular feeling, but I couldn't ever see why he'd up and run off on us like that."

Owen nodded. "I know what you mean. I couldn't figure it out either. Sam had an idea, though. She told me how George kept trying to impress everyone. He'd always shove into the center of things."

"Yeah," Ben said. "I noticed that. Afterward, you know. Thing I finally figured out, though, is that he planned it from the start."

"How do you figure?"

"I stole a look at those notes of his when we got home, what he didn't make off with, anyway. He'd had everything cataloged by the amount of time it'd take to finish, and he had stuff we never even talked about. House plans, that sort of stuff."

"I think he was scared. He became," Owen paused, thinking of the right word. He finally settled on, "skittish after Jessie's... death." He quickly added, "not that it excuses what he did, but it may help explain it."

Ben rumbled agreement.

Owen shifted in his seat, leaning on one arm of the chair. He rested his chin on one hand and regarded Ben carefully. If he was honest, he could see the chain of logic Ben was following, but he had never put the pieces together and so was having trouble justifying it to himself. He wanted to avoid jumping to conclusions supported only by "he's a jerk."

Finally, he said, "I could see, I think, that he was never happy here, and..."

Ben interrupted. "Creepy bastard."

Owen chuckled, humorless. "Yeah." Then, he added, "anyway, I don't think he planned it from the start."

Ben scoffed. "You don't? Get this. That backpack he had? Th' big, overstuffed thing he lugged around Oak Ridge? Guess what was in it?"

"His work?"

"Bingo."

"I don't think..."

Ben overrode him. "Not just that, but I heard him talking to Michael in the car on the way over. Kat an' I had the radio cranked up, so I guess he thought I couldn't hear him. Anyway, a quiet part of a song hits and I hear him telling Michael how much better off they'd be if they got the hell away."

"I saw him take Michael aside and talk to him back in Oak Ridge. Maybe that wasn't the plan. Maybe he just saw an opportunity and took it, but I maybe you're right. Maybe he planned to take Michael with him and leave."

"Whole fuckin' lotta 'maybe' goin' around today." Ben grunted. "And when Michael..." He refused to finish that sentence. Instead, he said, "I'm surprised he never cut my throat in my sleep."

"I don't know if a little slit throat would slow you down much."

Ben laughed. "Probably not, yeah. At least not if 'throttling George Sinon' is my reward for not dying."

Owen's laugh was more quiet than Ben's, but no less amused. After the two of them calmed down, Owen went on in a quiet voice, "I don't think a mutual rant about how much George played us today was why you called me down here, though."

"Oh?"

"That's the sort of thing you'd want everyone in on."

"Probably."

Owen sighed. Something was eating at Ben, but he was being too obstinate to let any of it out. They had played this game before, though. Owen would either prod and prod until he missed the target bad enough for Ben to open up anyway, or he would poke at things until he grew frustrated and neither of them would have a productive conversation. The other option was to just go right for what he assumed was bothering him.

"It's Jessie, isn't it?" Owen asked.

Silence for a long, tense moment answered him. Finally, the great shoulders attached to the silhouette on the bed moved. It was still too dark for Owen to see what was happening, but the sound of rustling fabric accompanied the sight.

Finally, Ben slid forward and perched on the end of the bed. It had no foot board, and Ben's long legs reached the floor despite the tall mattress. With their difference in height exaggerated by the furniture, Ben looked more like a golem than a man in the dim light. He certainly moved like one, and Owen wondered just how much of that was physical pain from the fight and how much was psychological.

Ben folded his hands in his lap. The meek posture ruined his intimidating silhouette as his shoulders relaxed. "I ain't going to go on about how I messed up, or you messed up, or how anything any of us did got anyone killed."

Owen found himself smiling weakly, but stayed quiet and let Ben talk.

"But we did mess up," he continued. "That's not an argument. Jessie stuck her arm in the wrong place. Michael didn't protect himself either. Me," he laughed, "I got fucking cocky after I killed that Korovega this morning and it almost got me killed to. That cop, Ash, saved my life and damned if I don't remember every second leading up to that moment."

Owen nodded. He had been replaying moments like that over and over in his head since getting onto the back of Sam's bike for the trip back home. A hundred things had gone wrong in that fight, but a hundred and one had gone right and so they, most of them anyway, walked away at the end of it all.

"We've got a lot to learn."

"Yeah," Ben replied, "but that ain't why I sent for you."

Owen took a gamble on Ben having talked around the issue long enough to tell him the real reason at last. "So spill."

"You were right, before. I was thinking about Jessie. I miss her, Owen. Already. We didn't talk for a long time, you know, but having her around reminded me of the old days when we used to take on whole schools ourselves.

"We'd walk right in the door, talk some smack, and knock every one of the other guys on the floor." Ben laughed. "You know, maybe it was for the best."

Owen's eye went wide. "How?" he asked, doing his best to keep the surprise out of his voice. The last thing he wanted was to come across demanding or condemning, when it was merely a desire to understand how Ben had come to that conclusion.

"Jessie and I never did live together well," he replied. "We'd butt heads a lot, but I don't think I could have ridden into hell itself today without seeing her again, even if it was only for a few days."

"Michael, too," Owen said. "The way he charged that Korovega today might have been suicidal, but it was pretty darn impressive, too. Just a little more training..."

"Yeah," Ben said, softly. "What if."

"That's not what I meant."

Ben cocked his head to one side. "Ain't it?"

"Not really."

In the shadows, Ben made a motion for him to continue.

"Just that we need to be aware of what happened to him. He's dead, and I see his dying moments in my mind every time I close my eyes. His and Jessie's and Heather's last breaths bleed into one scene in my head. We need to make sure they didn't die in vain."

Ben nodded. "Grief won't bring them back, but grief ain't all we got, neither. We're smart folks, least I am." He grinned, teeth shining in the darkness. "And we can learn from what happened to them."

They sat in silence for a moment, never quite making eye contact with one another. The air was not quite tense, but it was something less than relaxed. The closest thing to "pleasant" that could be said about those few minutes was "companionable." Merely by sitting together—comrades in arms with shared experiences, shared triumphs, and shared grief—they comforted one another.

Finally, Ben said, "that's all, really. I guess I just needed someone to vent to, after all. Me and Jessie, since she'd been here too, we had these talks at night. You ain't half as good looking as she was, but it's nice to have people you can trust."

Owen stood. He and Ben regarded one another for a long moment before he said, "we've known each other a long time, man. If you need anything..."

Ben grinned and slid off the edge of the bed. He put a hand on Owen's shoulder and drew him into a crushing embrace. When they stepped apart, he said, "thanks. Now go upstairs. The others are probably afraid we're down here trying to kill each other or something."

Owen laughed. "You never know with that bunch."

"Owen," Ben said, stopping the other man halfway through the door. "Do me a favor. Do me two favors, actually."

"Done and done," Owen replied. "What are they?"

"First, I call dibs on the glove the Korovega that killed Jessie had. It's," he paused, "right that you have its sword and I've got its shield. Katrina took the sword from the one she killed, too. It all fits together, proper-like."

Owen nodded. "And the second?"

Ben's eyes narrowed. "You never run across George Sinon again, you let me kill that bastard, understand?"

"Deal."

"Good."

Owen turned back to the door, took another step, and then stopped again. He turned around once more. "I almost forgot," he said, then told Ben what he learned from the phone call earlier.

Ben whistled. "Six people, and they're bringing food, beds, and fuel? I think that's the second best news I've heard all day."

"What was the first?"

"That you and Sam were still alive when I got to Oak Ridge." His voice, for a moment, held even more emotion that it had when he had spoken about Jessie minutes prior.

Owen smiled and turned his back on the small bedroom for the third time. Neither of them had any more last minute thoughts, and so he left the room with a simple, "goodnight, Ben."

* * *

When Owen returned upstairs, Marcus and Will had moved to the couches. Sam was still upstairs in the bath. Katrina, too, was missing from the ensemble.

"Everything alright down there?" Marcus asked, nodding his head sideways in the general direction of the stairs.

"Yeah."

"Anything you want to share with the class?" Will asked.

Owen shrugged. "Nothing important. Ben just wanted my input on some things about what happened today. Nothing major, trust me. We won't keep that sort of stuff from you. I can promise you that."

"Aye, aye," Marcus said, with a sardonic grin.

"Where's Katrina?" Owen asked.

"Same place Sam is," Will replied absently. Then, as if realizing how that statement could have been interpreted, added, "not like that. She's in the bathroom over there," he thumbed his hand toward the master bedroom. I'm about to hit the other one."

Marcus grinned. "You cheated."

"You can't cheat at rock-paper-scissors," Will replied. He laughed, and Owen was pleased to see their spirits so high.

He went upstairs and knocked on the bathroom door. "Sam?"

"Yeah?" she replied. "You need anything?"

"No," Owen said. "I just wanted to check on you and see if you did."

Her voice sounded much brighter, even through the fancy wooden door, when she said, "thanks, but I'm alright."

Slowly, and with far more pain than he would have liked, Owen peeled his shirt off. The bandages kept most of the blood off of the fabric, but the motion of removing it still hurt.

He sighed, then laughed at the absurdity of it. He had survived not just one, but four encounters with the Korovega, had killed or helped kill several of them himself, and watched people he had grown in a few short days to consider friends die. Between bruises, scrapes, and cuts, he hurt everywhere. His mind and soul ached with what he had seen, and yet he still managed to keep going.

Owen settled onto the bed and, for the first time since that first dreadful afternoon when the news first came across his TV set, felt relaxed.

Epilogue

A dream of a field stretched out before Owen. He marched at the head of an army, clad in black. In his left hand was the sword he had taken from the Korovega, and on his right was one of their gloves. Ben stood to his left, carrying the sword he called "The Beast" and sporting a Korovega's glove of his own. Sam, to his right, carried the saber that was once his before he claimed his new sword. She too had a Korovega's glove on her empty other hand. They all wore their fencing gear—the gear they had fought, and nearly died, in during their mission to Oak Ridge.

Far in the distance to his left and right, lost in the haze of miles of intervening air and fog, mountains loomed. Titanic monoliths of rock, impossibly far away, rose up to tear at the heavens. Their tops were lost in the sky, hidden behind a veil even denser than distance.

The sky was a sickening gray-green color. It moved and twisted in ways no safe sky ever should. Clouds rolled over one another, churning in powerful winds high above their heads. He had never seen the sky like that, but stories of people stuck on the ground as hurricanes rolled in had described similar sights.

For a moment, the air hung still. The very blades of grass under his feet stood motionless as an electric charge filled the air. Through his mask and jacket and under his gorget, Owen felt the hair on the back of his neck rise. He felt more than personal tension in the air, like the very planet itself was tensed like a spring. Something was ready to give way, only he had no idea what that something was.

A curtain of darkness spread across the horizon. It began at one mountain range in the infinite distance and crept its way across the sky to the other. Over such a great distance, it seemed to move at a crawl, but it made the trip in seconds. Directly above him, the sky remained the green of rotting things, but in front of him, the sky had turned black.

The trees dotting the landscape ahead of him swayed and rippled. They moved under an unseen hand, gently at first. For a few moments, the air around the trio remained still while the trees ahead bent and swayed.

One tree bent in half. The crack could be heard where they stood an infinite stretch of miles from the broken tree. Another followed it, then another as the wind sped up. It reached them moments later, whipping at their faces through the fencing masks.

The wind roared, building in intensity without any apparent plans to stop. The force of it nearly swept Owen from his feet, but he, like Sam and Ben to either side of him, bent lower and leaned into the fury bearing down on them. A tree, ripped in half by the hurricane, tumbled past them. It spun like a giant, two-ended pinwheel, making low thumping noises that echoed through their feet every time it struck the ground.

The curtain of blackness approached. Inside it, shapes moved. An army of silhouettes, blacker than darkness against the curtain of the storm, writhed and surged like the clouds over his head.

In a moment, the clouds were no more. Blackness enveloped the three of them as suddenly as an eyeblink. The sound of rain thundered around them, beating down on Owen's head like drums. The wind whistled, rising and falling in pitch in response to some mysterious cues. The sound of rain beat down harder, but nothing touched him. He never felt the impact of the raindrops that his ears told him were barraging him, and he never got wet.

Streaks passed his eyes that looked like rain, but the ground stayed dry. The air smelled like ozone and strange spices and it felt wet on his skin, but it was the damp of dense fog, not the pouring wetness of a storm.

The noise never ceased. Neither did the wind.

Around him surged a mass of formless shapes. Here and there arms or heads would emerge from the mass, brandishing swords or glowing shields. Eyes glittered in the darkness, shifting and moving fluidly from point to point.

A gleaming spike shot out at him from the darkness, but he swatted it aside with his sword.

Owen tried to call for Ben and Sam. His mouth opened and he yelled, but no sound came out that could be heard over the din of the wind, the rain noise, and the gibbering horde. He looked around, suddenly frightened, but they were still with him.

The leather-clad oval of metal mesh that covered Ben's face nodded once. He turned to Sam. Her mask, especially in the darkness, concealed her face just as well as Ben's had. Still, he knew they they made eye contact through the darkness somehow.

He raised the hand that held no sword and made a tight fist. A disk of light appeared in front of his knuckles. A moment later, similar shields came alive in Sam's and then Ben's hands.

The three glowing lights were answered by ten thousand thousand lights from the horde around them. Collectively, their shields and those of the horde banished the darkness.

The rain noise stopped and the wind died. The air grew still and dry in a moment. Overhead, the sky itself seemed frozen. The clouds, boiling with chthonic rage only moments before, had stopped their dance. They hung where they were, black and green and menacing, but motionless. Even the lightning was frozen in time.

Around them, Korovega circled. They all wore the splendor of the soldiers they encountered in Oak Ridge. Silk of every color flashed through the mob, covering glittering pieces of armor. The three of them had been cut off from their army, and all around them moved nothing but Korovega as far as they could see.

The horde, as one maddened voice, roared. They fought for what must have been hours, killing Korovega methodically. First a few became many, then many became dozens. After a personal eternity, Owen wondered if dozens had yet become hundreds. Ben and Sam carved similar paths through the Korovega horde, but nothing seemed to stem the tide of their numbers. No matter how many they killed, another always took its place.

The Korovega drove them, sweating and panting for breath, together again. Back to back to back, each of them surveyed the scene around them. Korovega lay dead, littering the ground with their bodies. The ground itself had turned red and the grass was long since dead from blight and crushed to dust, but the bloody color was the only change. It was still as dry as it had been before the fighting started.

They had been fighting toward one of the mountain ranges. It seemed somehow closer now, if such a thing was possible. It felt closer to the three comparatively tiny human beings regarding its infinite height. Something about it called to them, but Owen could not say what that feeling was, only that there was a rightness and a feeling of home to those mountains in the impossible distance.

"How many more do you think there are?" Ben gasped.

"A lot," Owen replied. Despite the fatigue dragging his limbs to the dirt, he laughed. "But that just means a higher score, right?"

Ben laughed. "Good point. I don't think I can keep this up much longer, though."

Sam said, "I think maybe we won't have to."

She raised her hand and pointed with the shield itself. The other two turned around. Behind them, a single mountain had come to them. It towered above them, reaching to dizzying heights and disappearing into the frozen black sky above them.

In the shadow of the mountain, three more black-clad figured walked. The smallest carried a sword like Owen's, one taken from a Korovega. In her hand glittered one of their shields as well. To her right walked a man with a great rifle, turned into a spear by the long bayonet affixed to the end. The third figure carried a smaller rifle with a bayonet, but both of them wore the metal-backed shield gloves.

Though the new trio was an infinity away, though they were lifetimes closer than the mountains had been moments before. They met the edge of the Korovega horde seconds after Sam pointed them out.

Owen raised his sword over his head, then pointed it in their direction. Wordlessly, he rushed into the horde again, followed by the black shapes of his companions.

Acknowledgments

First off, I want to thank Jason McTeer and Joseph Beaubien, who helped me turn a draft into the finished product you, I hope, just enjoyed. Without their help, this book wouldn't be what it is now. Thanks also to "Lord" Pruitt and Matthew Souders, who helped in their own ways with factual details. Thanks, again, to my wife Stephanie, who put up with me while I buried myself in this project. Finally, thanks to my parents; it's their fault I started reading (and then writing) Science Fiction in the first place.

Made in the USA
Middletown, DE
30 May 2016